Praise for Megan Ha...

"Ms. Hart is a master . . . I am absolutely in love with [her] writing and she remains on my auto-buy list. Take my advice and add her to yours!"
　　　　　　　　　　　　　　　　　　　　　　—Ecataromance

"Megan Hart is one of my favorite authors . . . The sex is hot and steamy, the emotions are real, and the characters easy to identify with. I highly recommend all of Megan Hart's books!"
　　　　　　　　　　　　　　　　　　　　　　—The Best Reviews

"Terrific erotic romance."　　　　　　　　*—Midwest Book Review*

"Unique . . . Fantastic."　　　　　　　　　*—Sensual Romance*

"Megan Hart is easily one of the more mature, talented voices I've encountered in the recent erotica boom. Deep, thought provoking, and heart wrenching."　　　　　　　　*—The Romance Reader*

"Probably the most realistic erotic romance I've ever read . . . I wasn't ready for the story to end."　　　　*—A Romance Review*

"Sexy, romantic."　　　　　　　　　　　*—Road to Romance*

"Megan Hart completely wowed me! I never read an erotic book that, aside from the explicit sex, is [also] an emotionally powerful story."　　　　　　　　　　*—Romance Reader at Heart*

Berkley Sensation Titles by Megan Hart

PLEASURE AND PURPOSE
NO GREATER PLEASURE

THE BERKLEY PUBLISHING GROUP
Published by the Penguin Group
Penguin Group (USA) Inc.
375 Hudson Street, New York, New York 10014, USA
Penguin Group (Canada), 90 Eglinton Avenue East, Suite 700, Toronto, Ontario M4P 2Y3, Canada
(a division of Pearson Penguin Canada Inc.)
Penguin Books Ltd., 80 Strand, London WC2R 0RL, England
Penguin Group Ireland, 25 St. Stephen's Green, Dublin 2, Ireland (a division of Penguin Books Ltd.)
Penguin Group (Australia), 250 Camberwell Road, Camberwell, Victoria 3124, Australia
(a division of Pearson Australia Group Pty. Ltd.)
Penguin Books India Pvt. Ltd., 11 Community Centre, Panchsheel Park, New Delhi—110 017, India
Penguin Group (NZ), 67 Apollo Drive, Rosedale, North Shore 0632, New Zealand
(a division of Pearson New Zealand Ltd.)
Penguin Books (South Africa) (Pty.) Ltd., 24 Sturdee Avenue, Rosebank, Johannesburg 2196,
South Africa

Penguin Books Ltd., Registered Offices: 80 Strand, London WC2R 0RL, England

This book is an original publication of The Berkley Publishing Group.

This is a work of fiction. Names, characters, places, and incidents either are the product of the author's imagination or are used fictitiously, and any resemblance to actual persons, living or dead, business establishments, events, or locales is entirely coincidental. The publisher does not have any control over and does not assume any responsibility for author or third-party websites or their content.

PRINTING HISTORY
Berkley Sensation trade paperback edition / October 2009

Library of Congress Cataloging-in-Publication Data

Hart, Megan.
    No greater pleasure / Megan Hart.—Berkley Sensation trade paperback ed.
        p.   cm.
    ISBN 978-0-425-22981-1
    I. Title.
    PS3608.A7865N6   2009
    813'.6—dc22   2009025920

PRINTED IN THE UNITED STATES OF AMERICA

10   9   8   7   6   5   4   3   2   1

No
Greater
Pleasure

MEGAN HART

B

BERKLEY SENSATION, NEW YORK

Five Principles of the Order of Solace

1. There is no greater pleasure than providing absolute solace.

2. True patience is its own reward.

3. A flower is made more beautiful by its thorns.

4. Selfish is the heart that thinks first of itself.

5. Women we begin and women we shall end.

Chapter 1

A flower is made more beautiful by its thorns.

Glad Tidings was a house with a great many thorns seeking to hide its beauty. If ever a house had been more ill-named, Tranquilla Caden had never seen it. She lifted the heavy brass knocker and let it fall against the door three times before stepping back to look up again at the manse.

The stone façade had weathered to gray without even ivy or moss providing a hint of green. The shutters, black. The gabled roof, black. Even the door, black, the brass knocker weather-dulled. The twin towers on each end of the house gave it an interesting roofline, but they were more buttress than fae-story spirals. It lacked not for glass windows, but even those looked purely practical and not for ornament.

Glad Tidings looked well and fashionably maintained, a grand manor house. It looked like raised eyebrows and pursed lips, like mutton for supper and a clean-your-plate demeanor. Then again, those who lived in whitewashed cottages with flower-filled gardens rarely seemed to have need for a Handmaiden.

"Sure you doona want me to wait, mistress?"

Quilla turned to give the coach driver a smile. "No, thank you, Steven. They're expecting me."

The man who'd been her traveling companion for the past seven days looked doubtful. "Are you sure'n? For I'd not like to leave you here, alone."

Before she could reply, the door creaked open. Quilla turned to see a rolling blue eye peering at her. "Hello?"

"You the Handmaiden?"

The lack of welcome didn't disturb Quilla, who put on her best smile. "I'm Tranquilla Caden. I'm here—"

"I know what you're here for."

A snort and a grumble preceded the door opening to reveal a stout, broad-faced figure in a flour-dusty dress worn over a pair of ankle-high breeches. A head of untidy gray curls and a streak of soot on one cheek completed this unusual ensemble.

"You," said the woman—but was it a woman? The mustache and manner made it difficult to be sure. She pointed at the coach driver. "You've been paid, hent ya?"

He nodded. "Aye, but I've come to deliver—"

"And deliver you've done! Get gone!"

Steven made a rude gesture, but lifted down Quilla's sturdy case and handed it to her. "Pleasure making your company, mistress. May the Invisible Mother keep you."

"Today and all your others," replied Quilla. The case stayed next to her feet as she watched Steven get back in the coach and start the horses on their way again. She looked back at the person standing in the doorway with arms folded, brows beetled, and a frown so fierce it would have frightened a boogen. Quilla took in the flour and soot, and more importantly, the haughty manner. "You must be the chatelaine."

"I'm Florentine. You might as well come in."

The name gave no more clue to the person's gender, but the ac-

ceptance of the title did. A man would never have been named
chatelaine. Florentine stepped aside to let Quilla enter the grand
entrance hall. The interior of Glad Tidings was no less impressive
and no more joyful than the outside had been.

Quilla looked around with interest. The grand staircase curved
upward to a landing above. To her left and right arched doorways
led to well-lit rooms furnished with exquisite taste. Most interesting to Quilla were the woven tapestries she glimpsed on the walls.
Even from this distance it was clear they were the finest she'd seen.

"If you've finished gawking," Florentine said over her shoulder
with a sniff, "might as well follow me."

Quilla hefted her case to get a better grip and followed Florentine down the hall tucked beneath the front stairs. More doors
opened off this hall, but Florentine ignored them all. At last she
turned through another archway and then down a short flight of
steps to the kitchen. A fire crackled in the large stone fireplace, and
the smells of baking bread and roasting meat filled the air. Quilla
took a deep sniff, her stomach rumbling.

Florentine quirked a bushy eyebrow at her. "Dint eat afore you
came?"

"I had a long journey. My last meal was yestereve, almost a full
day past."

Florentine huffed. "Sit down."

Quilla did with a grateful sigh. It might not be her place to
complain, but the journey had exhausted her. Her nose wrinkled.
She was famished and dusty and certain she smelled unpleasant, if
not downright horrid.

Florentine plunked a bowl of something steaming and hot in
front of her, along with a hunk of fresh brown bread and a crock of
sweet butter. At the smell of it, the simple but sufficient quantity of
it, Quilla's mouth watered. Florentine set a mug of creamy milk on
the table, with a pitcher full of the same, and Quilla murmured a

blessing of thanksgiving and drank the cup within moments, then filled it again.

"Don't make yourself sick," cautioned Florentine, watching with her arms crossed over her chest. "There's plenty more where that come from. Our master Delessan ain't generous with much, but he don't stinge us on the eats."

Quilla wiped her lips. "Don't worry, Florentine. I won't make myself sick. I'm just hungry."

Florentine's huff seemed to be a common reaction. She moved toward the massive fireplace to poke and prod the large joint turning on the spit. Quilla dunked her bread into the stew, soaking up the rich broth, then savoring the flavors. Her last patron had been an elderly gentleman who could chew naught but the softest foods and stomach only the blandest. When her tongue detected the hints of garlic, onion, springbulb, and others, Quilla moaned at the pleasure of good food.

Florentine shot her a narrow-eyed look, mustached mouth pursing. "Wotcher?"

Quilla swallowed the mouthful of food and drank some more milk to wash it down. "It's so delicious. I haven't had anything like it in a long time. Thank you."

"Don't look like you've been missing many meals, I'll say that."

Quilla paused in raising another bite of bread to her mouth to answer without rancor. "I am as I was made. No more, no less."

"He don't like fat girls. He's not going to be happy when he sees you. He likes 'em skinny, the master does. Starved, like."

Quilla swallowed and wiped her mouth again. "The Order sent me based upon what Lord Delessan requested. If I don't please him, he can send me away."

She looked down at the plain, deep plum-colored gown she wore for traveling. It buttoned from throat to hem, and the cut of it emphasized her ample breasts and hips, covered the soft curve of her belly, clung to her strong, rounded thighs. "Woman I began and woman I shall end. I can only be what I am, Florentine."

The cook huffed and added a sniff, perhaps of disgust or disdain, Quilla couldn't be sure. "Spare me your philosophies, if you please."

Quilla bent back to her meal. "I meant not to offend."

Florentine squatted to poke at the fire, making it blaze up to char the joint. She stood and turned, putting her hands on her wide hips. "He'll take one look at you and howl like you'd got three heads, you mark my words. 'Tis not his nature to be satisfied with anything. Or at least, not to admit he's satisfied with it."

Quilla had long experience with those who were not easily satisfied. "Has he complained about his previous Handmaidens?"

"Never had one, so far as I know, and I been with him since I used to be a boy. Which I don't need to tell you was a long time ago," Florentine said. "And in another place."

Quilla smiled. "If he's sent for a Handmaiden, he must feel he has need of one."

The chatelaine rolled her eyes. "He's got a wife who sufficed him for a goodly long time in that manner. Whatfor he needs a new wick to wax, I'm not privy to say."

"Ah." Quilla ate a bite, chewed, and swallowed, then looked back to Florentine, who was still watching. "I'm not a whore, you know. None of us are."

That seemed to get a different reaction out of the chatelaine, who stared, mouth agape. She shut it with a snap and frowned, brow furrowing as she shook her finger at Quilla.

"Don't you tell me what you izzerarnt! I know what you're here to do!"

Quilla looked at the other woman for a long moment in calm silence. If there were going to be problems, best to confront them now. Saying nothing was the best response. She sipped more milk.

Florentine scowled. "'Tis not my place to say what my lord Delessan does, you understand. He deems he needs a Handmaiden, so I sends away for one. What he does with you is of no concern to me."

"Exactly," said Quilla gently. "I am here to serve him and no other in any way he pleases. That is my role, one I have trained to do and would miss sorely should I leave it. It does not make me a whore, who is paid to provide her body, only."

The other woman rolled her eyes. "I don't believe in that rot you of the Order make your faith. Filling Sinder's Quiver. Waiting for the Holy Family. The Holy Family is long gone from this plane and won't be back no matter how many of us you try to soothe. I don't believe it, not a word."

"Then how fortunate for you that I do." Quilla buttered another slice of bread. Defending herself and her faith had long ago ceased to make her angry. "And for whatever his reasons, it would seem our mutual master does."

This made Florentine grin, exposing startlingly white teeth. "We'll see. I warrant he won't like you at all."

"I might not please him, though I'll do my best to try. It will be his choice to send me back if I fail."

"I don't see as how you can't," replied Florentine. "He's hard as stone, Gabriel Delessan. No pleasing him. Believe me, I've tried. There's not a meal what comes out of this kitchen he don't bitch about, not a mote of dust he don't notice. He can't keep house staff long enough to keep up with the cleaning. We're down to just three maids and two houseboys, which has made my life and Vernon the butler's quite a pain in the arse, don't you know it. He can't keep assistants, as he tends to scream them into apoplexy. Our lord Delessan is a cantankerous, discontented, disillusioned, and aggravating son of a bastard."

Not a flattering portrayal. "Why do you stay, then?"

Florentine looked at Quilla as though she were stupid. "He took me in when I had no place to go. He didn't care about where I came from, what I'd done, or what I'd been. He gave me a place in his house when I'd probably have starved otherwise."

"You make him sound like a hero, when just moments ago you were denouncing him as a curmudgeon."

Florentine rolled her eyes. "Sinder's Arrow, girl. Are you daft? Don't you know he can be both?"

"I do know that." Quilla smiled. "And as I said, if I fail to please him, he can return me to the Order."

Florentine regarded Quilla with a squinted glance. "I wouldn't bother unpacking much, then, if I were you."

"Fortunately I haven't much to unpack."

"Does naught disturb you?" Florentine threw up her hands.

Quilla shrugged. "Why are you so determined to frighten me away? Are you so afraid I'll what . . . replace you? Or does your innate tenderness cause you to worry his rejection is going to hurt me? Because I can assure you, Florentine, that won't be the case."

"I'm not worried he's going to hurt you." Florentine glowered. "But the moment I laid eyes on you, I knew you'd hurt him."

Quilla had been unable to convince Florentine to expound upon her surprising statement. As if realizing she'd revealed too much, the plump chatelaine had clamped her lips together and refused to say anything more. She'd rung for one of the house lads, Bertram, to take Quilla to her quarters.

"Florentine wasn't kidding when she said he wasn't overgenerous."

Quilla looked round the small, sparsely furnished room. A narrow bed, covered with an unadorned comforter and a single flat pillow. A fireplace. A small settee with a sprung seat and a tear in

one arm through which a tuft of stuffing peeked. A wardrobe that
did, at least, have a mirror on the door. A window with no curtain
but a cushioned window seat. A small washroom with a basin on
a stand, a wastechair, and a plain but sufficient tub for bathing,
heated by a small brazier beneath.

Far from the finest quarters she'd ever been granted, but clean
and sufficient. No evidence of rats or spiders, two creatures she ab-
horred.

"You've got a grand view from up here. Better than mine." Bertram peeked out the window. He turned with a grin, a fine-looking
lad with a shock of red hair and dusty freckles sprinkled across his
nose.

Quilla returned the grin. "This will be lovely, I'm sure."

Bertram nodded. "If you need anything, let me know. You can
find me belowstairs, most days, though I'm to run errands and do
handy chores if needed, too."

"Thank you, Bertram. I'll remember that."

He hesitated, as though wanting to ask her something but afraid
to. She'd also encountered this before. Quilla smiled warmly at the
lad, who was probably a good eight years younger than she.

Bertram's cheeks flushed the color of brick while the tips of his
ears went more crimson. "Florentine says you're going to be sent
away right off."

"I might be. Do you think I will?"

"I don't see how anyone could want to send you away."

Quilla smiled. "Thank you."

"Well, if you need anything . . ."

"I know where to find you."

He nodded, still blushing, and beat a hasty exit. Quilla watched
him go, amused. She always elicited the same reactions. Fumbling
embarrassment or veiled disdain. Shaking her head, weary from the
journey and the effort of arriving in a new household, she sank

onto her knees, hands folded in her lap, the back of her right hand inside the palm of the left.

The uncarpeted floor was cold and hard, but she didn't notice. Quilla was Waiting. Waiting was a clearing of the mind, of thought, of the physical. Waiting was the first practice any servant of the Order of Solace learned. Waiting created calm. Serenity. It allowed a Handmaiden to focus her attentions fully on her patron.

Invisible Mother, grant me serenity enough to share, for there is no greater pleasure than providing absolute solace.

In the absence of her patron, Quilla Waited for herself. Every new assignment was difficult at first, no matter how well her training allowed her to hide it. Smiling when she wanted to weep, murmuring when she wanted to scream, saying yes when she wished to say no. It always passed once she settled in.

Invisible Mother, grant me patience enough to share, for true patience is its own reward.

In a way, Quilla preferred the homes in which she never settled, never became a part of the family. It was hard to love a place and its people, only to be sent away, in the end. Yes, that was her life, her role, what she did, but it didn't make it any easier to accept when it came time to pack her bags and leave a place she'd come to consider home.

Invisible Mother, grant me beauty enough to share, for a flower is made more beautiful by its thorns, and I have many.

Glad Tidings did not seem to be destined for that sort of ending. Quilla rubbed her temples. Would her new patron be as awful as Florentine had said? And what had the chatelaine meant with her cryptic statement that Quilla might hurt him?

Invisible Mother, grant me generosity enough to share, for selfish is the heart that thinks first of itself.

"How can I possibly hurt him?" she murmured aloud. "'Tis my place to serve him."

Woman I began and woman I shall end.

She could do no more nor less than that. She sighed and got to her feet, wanting only to wash away the grime of her travel and prepare herself for her new patron. She opened the wardrobe to see what sort of uniform she'd be wearing. She'd been dressed in everything from tight-corseted formal gowns to loose shifts more appropriate for sleeping, but what she found hung inside and folded in the drawers made her smile.

She touched the fabrics, none of them expensive but all of them fine enough quality. No harsh or scratchy wools. Soft linen and flaxen gowns in muted shades of green and blue hung from the hangers, while plain but clearly new undergarments took a place in the drawers. Warm stockings, for winter was coming. A soft, black woolen cloak with a hood, a bow of red startling against the throat of it. Slippers and one pair of plain black lace-up shoes.

She took out a deep blue gown and held it up to herself in front of the mirror. Long sleeves would come to a point over the back of her hand. Plain satin ribbon banded the high neckline. Buttons ran from throat to hem as on the gown she wore, but of higher quality. More plain ribbon adorned the hem, which reached to her toes and looked to be full enough to swirl when she turned.

In short, he expected her to dress the part of the traditional Handmaiden. Dark colors and demure style. An insight into what he desired, or merely laziness on the part of whomever had ordered the clothes?

It didn't matter what she wore, if anything. She would be what he needed, no matter what that was. In dark blue or flaming red, covered from throat to toes or naked, Quilla's place was to serve.

A bath and good teeth brushing. Wash her hair. Perhaps a chance to sleep in the narrow bed. Those were her plans until the knock on her door made her turn. She opened it, though of course there was no lock and the person on the other side could simply have walked in. It said a lot about this household, though, that privacy was respected.

"Come in."

Florentine stuck her head around the half-open door. "He wants you."

Quilla looked at the gown in her hands and her own dusty dress. "I haven't even had a chance to bathe—"

"Now."

"All right."

Quilla hung the gown back in the wardrobe and brushed her skirt clean as best she could. The bath would wait, but she did take a gulp of water to rinse her mouth before following Florentine out of the room.

Quilla fixed her hair with swift fingers as she walked, tucking her curls into a tight braid that hung to the middle of her back. It was the best she could do on short notice, though she was certain she still looked journey-worn. She followed the chatelaine down the narrow garret stairs and a short, wide hallway to the carved wooden door at the end. When Florentine pushed it open, it revealed another set of narrow, steep steps. Quilla counted twelve. Not too many. Just enough to trip her up as she followed Florentine.

"He's in here?"

Without waiting for an answer, Quilla pushed past the fat chatelaine and opened the door. It swung open on creaking hinges that sounded like an old man's joints complaining, and she made a note to take care of that. It couldn't be pleasant, always hearing the door scream when it opened.

The room inside wasn't much more pleasant. The fragrance in the air was acrid and slightly burnt, though the fireplace looked to be in good enough repair. The floor of bare, unwaxed wood had made the acquaintance of a broom and mop some time ago, for small stains and speckles of grime played hide-and-seek amongst the tattered woven rugs. The tapestries on the wall were nondescript and out of fashion, though of fine workmanship and probably quite expensive.

Four tall windows provided ample light, but the numerous lamps upon the walls would provide illumination when the sun did not. A massive table dominated the room's far corner. On it, glass beakers and simmering cauldrons crouched over tiny gas-powered flames. The scorch marks on the wood and the wall behind it showed her the source of the burnt smell.

An untidy but well-made desk squatted along the other wall, its surface heaped high with books, papers, pots of ink, and all manner of detritus that looked as though it might simply tumble over at any moment. More interesting were the rows of small cages in which mice squeaked and fat rabbits squatted, complacently chewing.

Quilla took in all of this, including the high-backed chair in front of the fire, with such swift unobtrusiveness that none but another Handmaiden would have noticed her scrutiny. There were innumerable ways to make this room more pleasant, the first a thorough cleaning. Quilla noted the battered kettle hung over the fire, the tea chest with the splintered lid, the chipped cups with missing saucers. So he liked tea but did not seem to take much comfort from it.

"I was expecting someone older." The flat comment turned Quilla's head toward the man who'd stepped out of the doorway at the back of the room.

Without a word, Quilla sank gracefully onto her knees, folding them beneath her so she could rise in the same smooth motion as she'd dropped. She folded her hands in her lap, the back of the right tucked into the palm of the left. She Waited.

"My lord Delessan, this is—"

"I know who she is, Florentine." Gabriel Delessan stomped toward Quilla in great black boots in need of a polishing. "Didn't you hear what I said, Handmaiden?"

Quilla looked up at him. This was to be her new patron. A challenge.

"I am who the Order assigned, yes. If I do not please you, all you must do is send me back. My age is one of the few things I am unable to change for your pleasure."

That seemed to mollify him a bit, because he said, "Really? What are the others?"

"The color of my eyes, the size of my feet and hands, my height, the roundness of my breasts," Quilla told him matter-of-factly.

Most times, the answer stumped them, but not this man. He scowled, deep blue gray eyes made dark with the expression. "I didn't call for you because of the size of your breasts."

Quilla nodded again. "But if my age—"

"'Tis not." Delessan's scowl further creased his face. "Florentine, you can go."

The chatelaine nodded and glared at Quilla, then bustled out of the room. Quilla remained where she was. This man was going to be more than a challenge. He was going to be downright difficult.

Quilla had never left an assignment. It had been a point of pride for her that no matter how difficult or demanding a patron, she stayed until she provided them absolute solace, or they sent her away. In the Order of Solace, no shame came from failure to ultimately please. It was understood that some people refuse to be pleased no matter what they are offered. Shame came from giving up.

"How old are you?"

"Eight and twenty, my lord."

He snorted and put his hands behind his back. Gabriel Delessan was a tall man and broad-shouldered. He had the body of a laborer dressed in a gentleman's clothes, rather formal for the time of day and the work he did, she thought. Her eyes assessed him as she had the room. He could have been any age from thirty to forty, his dark hair without hint of silver. Black trousers. White shirt buttoned up high at the throat. Gray vest, four-buttoned, none undone. His black coat had been tailored to fit him exquisitely, the sleeves hitting him at the wrist instead of midhand, as was the current fashion, and in a flash Quilla understood that was not because his clothes were out of fashion, but that he'd had them tailored that way. He worked with his hands. Shorter sleeves were more practical. The jacket, on the other hand, came to midthigh instead of the currently popular waist length. The clothes made him look severe, forbidding, not a man who could be bothered wasting time with trivialities.

"Is it always the policy of your Order to teach its servants to stare?"

Quilla blinked, startled at being caught. She lowered her eyes. "No, my lord. I plead your mercy."

"For Sinder's sake," her patron said. "Get off your knees."

Quilla did as he'd asked, standing in one fluid motion gained from years of practice. She waited a moment, watching him. His gaze traveled over her with the same apparent attention to detail she'd given him. Quilla was used to being scrutinized. It wasn't unheard of for new patrons to ask her to strip down to skin the first time she met them. Particularly the mistresses, who often seemed to want to reassure themselves her body was no more seductive or luxurious than theirs; even if it was, they always managed to find some flaw to point out and feel better about.

But this man looked her over, fully clothed, and made her feel more naked than if he'd ordered her to strip. When at last his eyes settled on her face, she knew he could see the heatroses blooming on her cheeks, the brightness of her eyes.

"If I wanted a whore I could get one from the market for a tenth of the cost of having you," he said, his indifferent tone worse than if he'd sounded condescending.

She'd been well trained in keeping her emotions in check, but this bald, bored statement slapped her harder than if he'd sneered the words. She blinked, her mouth dropping open enough to allow a small hiss to escape her lips before she gathered her presence of mind and pressed them together.

"I am not a whore."

Delessan's face proved perfectly suited to amused sarcasm as one brow lifted and his mouth quirked into some sad semblance of a smile that had no humor behind it. "Then what makes you think I want you on your knees?"

For there is no greater pleasure than providing absolute solace. The words calmed her enough to reply without a dip or change of her voice.

"The position is called Waiting, Readiness. It shows I am ready to please you."

His smirk became a full-blown sneer. "And if it pleased me to have you strip out of that nasty, travel-worn rag?"

"I would do it."

"And if it pleased me to have you suck my cock?"

She flinched a bit at the harshness of his words. Did she imagine the flicker in his eyes? Pleasure at seeing her flinch? Disgust? Quilla discovered she could not read him, and she did not like that. Not at all.

"If it pleased you for me to do that, then I would."

"So how does that make you not a whore?"

She centered herself by letting her heart beat another four times. Taking another four breaths. Blinking a quartet of times more.

"The fact I am here at all tells me the Order approved your request," she said evenly. "Which means the Mothers-in-Service were satisfied you understood the purpose and place of a Handmaiden. It has never been my experience that they were wrong. So if they sent me to you, 'twas because they felt your petition was worthy of merit. That you had need of what I could provide. I trust the Mothers and I trust the Order. I am a Handmaiden. I am here to please you. To provide one small part of your life that is perfect solace. If that includes sucking your cock, then it is my pleasure to do so."

"It's not your pleasure," he corrected. "It's your job."

The vehemence that coated his last word raised her eyebrows. "My job, then, if you insist."

"Then don't claim you'd do it for the pleasure of it." Delessan gave her his back. "I abominate lies and I abhor pandering. I sent for a Handmaiden so I wouldn't have to deal with that. No simpering maids thinking a bedding will provide them extra favors. No kowtowing servants who bluster and flatter with the thought of bilking me out of an extra Festival bonus. No sly assistants filling my head with tales of my own brilliance while they steal my work out from under me."

He turned, eyes flashing. "I want someone to serve me in all ways because it is her job and her duty, and so I will know it's her place to do so without thought of reward. I want to trust that when I tell you to do something it will be done the way I want it done, when I want it done, and how. Immediately and without interpretation. Without hope of personal gain. I want a Handmaiden because it's your sole function to provide me with what I need, and I am not required to concern myself with the bloody awful task of actually trying to provide anything in return."

Quilla had been beaten by patrons who gained their pleasure from physical proof of their dominance. She could handle pain. She was trained in that. She'd been insulted. She'd been treated with coldness and impersonality, even with disdain.

She had never, until now, heard anyone distill the essence of her function into something so soiled, so awful, so utterly devoid of joy.

She blinked and heard her voice, faint and just a bit shaky. "I am here to please you, my lord."

His gaze traveled over her once again, from head to foot, his face twisting with slowly growing disgust. "It would please me to see you clean and dressed appropriately, and not looking like you'd just come off the rubbish heap. Get out and don't come back until you're clean."

She nodded, an unfamiliar pricking at the back of her eyes making her realize she was close to tears. "If it—"

"You're dismissed!" he barked. "No chatter! Get out!"

Without another word, Quilla did as he'd ordered. When the door had closed behind her, she leaned against the wall, one hand out to support herself on knees gone weak. She swallowed the lump in her throat and blinked away the unaccustomed sting of tears, straightened her back, and began to make her way back to her quarters.

He didn't even ask me my name.

He'll call for you when he's ready to, and not before. And don't go up there until he does."

Florentine's words of wisdom made Quilla roll her eyes. "It's been four days, Florentine. I wasn't sent here to idle my days away."

The chatelaine snorted. "I've plenty for you to do, don't you worry."

Quilla smiled as she hulled peas and put them in a large wooden bowl. "I'm sure you do. But nevertheless, it's not my job to peel potatoes and stir soup."

Florentine put a finger to the tip of her sharp nose and pushed it upward, offering Quilla an unappetizing view up her nostrils. "Well, hoity-toity do, excuse me."

"You know it as well as I do," said Quilla. "If he wanted another kitchen maid, he'd have hired one."

"I don't pretend to know what the master wants. I only take care of the kitchen. And oversee the others."

"And run this household," added Quilla, who couldn't help a fondness for the large, brusque woman. "'Tis no simple task to be chatelaine and cook, as well."

Florentine bent over the pot of stew simmering on the fire. "Used to be another, but he up and married the twit eight years hence, and the house has been up to me ever since. He never ought to have hired the girl, and I told him so at the time, for she was little more than a pair of bright green eyes and a mop of golden hair. She came highly recommended, of course, from that finishing school what likes to turn out pretty young things looking to wed a successful man. She did well enough. She knew what she wanted, at least. Knew how to run a house to please herself—and her man."

Quilla paused, thinking. "There's been no sign of her. Is she ill?"

Florentine stood up with a groan, rubbing her lower back. "Ill? The twit's gone mad. Before the boy was born—"

"Boy?" This stopped Quilla's hands again in surprise. "He has a son?"

"Aye, young Dane. Off someplace with his uncle Jericho right now." Florentine gathered a bundle of dried herbs and began grinding them with her mortar and pestle. "Forgive me for trying to tell you the story, my fine miss. I suppose 'tis my lack of social grace that makes it all right to keep interrupting me."

Quilla bit the inside of her cheek to keep from smiling. "I plead your mercy, madame. Please, go on."

"Like I was saying," continued Florentine with an exaggerated sniff. "Before the boy was born, Mistress Saradin found the responsibilities of marriage somewhat more trying than she'd imagined. Also, the master's work keeps him secluded and distracted. Not the way you'd like to be when you have a pretty young wife who's used to your attention. Oh, he doted on her, sure enough, no question. But his work, you see. 'Tis all about his work."

Quilla could imagine the end to this tale. "She had an affair."

"Oh, not just one, my know-it-all miss. Many. Seems the Mistress Saradin wasn't happy without a slew of beaux dancing attendance upon her, especially when she could nary seem to keep her husband's focus. He gave her whatever she wanted, but not enough of it. Naught was ever enough for her."

"She sounds perfectly lovely," said Quilla wryly.

"Lovely she was in face and form, but she was also young. Too young for the master, who's been old since he was born, I believe." Florentine dropped a handful of herbs and spices into the stew, tasted it, then smacked her lips. "So it came to pass that the master discovered his wife in the arms of another man. His assistant, as a matter of fact, a young bloke by the name of Ravine. Turns out Ravine had been working for another alchemist before he come to apprentice himself to the master, and was intending to take away what he learned here back to his old master. I'm not sure which hurt the master more greatly, the betrayal of his wife or of his 'prentice. At any rate, he threatened to turn them both out, and when it came to be told that Ravine had no money of his own to provide the mistress a place in keeping with her standards, she left off with him and tried to woo herself back into the master's good graces by telling him she was going to have his child."

"Sweet Invisible Mother," Quilla murmured. "No wonder he's such a curmudgeon."

Florentine snorted. "He was always like that. Dark, like. Kind beneath it, but dark all the same. Of course, after she poisoned herself he lost much of the kindness."

"Poisoned!"

Florentine gave Quilla a shrewd look. "Oh, aye. Found out the master had been slipping it to the housemaid assigned to clean his rooms, and her belly was sprouting, too. When Mistress Saradin found out, she wrecked his studio and took a draught of sommat meant to kill herself. Well, she didn't do her studying, because what she took didn't kill her, only sent her mad, like. Didn't hurt the boy, thank Sinder, though she might have killed him. Came out fine, the spitting image of his mother, fair-haired but blue-eyed. Not a speck of his father in him, that one, aside from his smarts. Dane's smart as Sinder, he is."

"Why does he not make a dissolution?"

Florentine looked at her as though Quilla were an idiot. "Because of the boy, of course. He sends the mother away, he must needs send away the lad, too. No man has the right to keep his own child iffen he sends away the mother. Not here in Gahun, at least, and I don't think 'tis any righter than making it go the other way, mind, but 'tis the way it is."

"But surely, if she's mad—"

"Mad when she wants it," said Florentine dismissively. "Mad when 'tis convenient. Mad when 'twill get her sympathy."

The entire story had left Quilla almost breathless. "And the housemaid?"

"Took the money the master give her, conveniently 'lost' the child, and disappeared."

"You don't believe she was pregnant."

Florentine rolled her eyes. "Not my place to say who or what the master does, my uppity miss, but seems far likelier to me he couldn't be bothered with the girl and she took advantage of his situation to push her luck. But he never denied her claim, not to anyone I know of, and he took care of her. So did he, or didn't he? 'Tis not my place to judge."

"That's possibly the most horrible story I've ever heard."

"'Ware it don't make you all gooey with compassion for him," Florentine muttered, adding more vegetables to the stew. "There've been those who've tried that route afore, and failed mightily."

"I'm not here to fall in love with him, Florentine. I'm here to be his Handmaiden. Nothing more. And it seems I'm not even to do that, unless he calls me, which is beginning to seem unlikely from the stubborn, spiteful git."

Florentine's face had been red from her exertion, but now her cheeks flushed deeper and her eyes widened. A smirk stretched her lips, her gaze went over Quilla's shoulder, and Quilla's stomach sank.

She turned, knowing before she did what she was going to see.

"The stubborn, spiteful git requires your presence in the studio." Delessan's face was impassive, his voice cold. "Immediately."

He turned on his heel and left the kitchen, and Quilla got up to follow him.

"Good mazel," called Florentine after her. "You'll need it."

Quilla didn't bother to answer. She knew Florentine was right.

The door still squealed on its hinges, and again, Quilla made a note to fix it. It was easier to focus on that than what lay ahead of her. Delessan slammed through the door ahead of her, not even pausing to be certain she'd followed. Quilla made sure to close the door behind them.

He stood at the mantel, his hand upon it not as though for balance, but as though by clinging to it he might prevent himself from making a fist. Quilla watched him carefully, using all of her training to try and judge him. He didn't move. Didn't speak for so long she did the only thing she knew to do.

She Waited, this time not in Readiness but in Remorse, her

palms not folded in her lap but flat on the floor in front of her, and her head bowed. The subtle shift in position was as much mental as physical, an outward representation of her inner regret at having displeased him.

After some long moments, he looked down at her. The firelight cast his face in shadows tinged with red and gold, and lit his dark eyes with dancing flames.

"It's not your purpose and place to discuss me."

"I plead your mercy. I was wrong to talk about you. I wanted to learn more about you, the better to serve you. I should have waited to speak to you in person."

"Florentine is an abominable old gossip."

Quilla kept her expression neutral and her voice calm. "I plead your mercy."

"You want to know why I waited four days before calling you."

"If it pleases you to tell me, yes." She lifted her head and returned to Waiting, Readiness.

He cast her a suspicious gaze. "I was seriously considering whether or not to keep you or send you back to the Order for someone more suitable."

His admission stung her more than she'd have suspected. Pride, one of Quilla's thorns, lifted her chin. "You haven't even given me a chance."

Delessan frowned, looking into the fire. "Florentine doesn't know as much as she thinks."

Quilla rose gracefully and stood in front of him, pausing until he'd looked at her face before speaking. "It will be easier for both of us if you start by telling me what you'd like from me."

"I told you what I wanted."

Quilla suppressed a sigh, then glanced around the room before looking back at his face. "More specifically."

Delessan frowned. "I want you to come here, every day, while

I'm working. If I need refreshment, or something fetched, or if I need—"

"Solace?"

"I don't need solace," he retorted.

"Everyone needs solace."

"What I need is someone who will fetch and carry and provide me with the things I need without my having to ask. Isn't that what you're trained for?"

She nodded. "Yes. Part of it."

He looked at her for a long moment. "Good."

Quilla smiled. "Tell me what time you rise and I will be here, Waiting."

"Sunrise."

If he thought to surprise or discontent her, he'd failed. "I will be here when you arrive."

"See that you are."

"And what, exactly, would you like me to do when I arrive, my lord?"

"I don't have the housemaids come in here to clean. They disturb things. Everything must be kept exactly where it is. Everything. I presume it's not beyond your ken to manage that?"

Quilla nodded. "Do you prefer to work in discord and grime?"

Delessan paused, looking around, his mouth pursed. "Of course not. But I'm a very busy man, and can't be bothered to run a dust mop around the place, can I? And since the maids can't be trusted, I do what I do."

Quilla nodded again, adding to the list she'd begun. "It would not be above me to clean your studio."

He scowled. "Don't touch my table. Or my desk. The rest of it, do what you like, but leave that alone."

She bit back a smile, sensing he wouldn't take kindly to it. "If it pleases you."

"Is that all you bloody ever say?"

True patience, Quilla thought before answering. "If you'd rather I say something different, I could."

Delessan narrowed his eyes. "I don't care to be mocked, Handmaiden."

"No, my lord."

"You'll be here before me tomorrow morning."

"I will be here until you give me leave to go."

That seemed to set him back. He nodded, his frown becoming a bit perplexed. "I work long hours. Often I don't break for meals. I forget myself. Lose myself in the tasks until the day has passed without my knowing."

"Then I will be here to make certain you do not faint over your cauldron from lack of food."

In his eyes Quilla thought she might have glimpsed a hint of humor, but it fled so fast she might have imagined it.

"And I'm quite uncontrollably rude and demanding. I don't have time to be anything else."

"Really?" Quilla replied calmly, keeping her eyes on his and allowing the faintest of tilts to turn her lips upward. "I'd never have guessed that about you."

Another flash, this time brighter, of something that almost managed to be amusement before his eyes darkened again. "Take care with your tongue, Handmaiden, else it put you into trouble."

She knew better than to push. Quilla ducked her head. "Your mercy, my lord." But with her eyes fixed upon his unpolished boots, she had to struggle to keep from grinning.

"My personal chambers are through that door." He pointed as she looked up. "I will not require you to serve me there. I didn't bring you here to warm my bed."

"I am here to please you. If you don't wish me in your bed, I won't go into it."

Delessan made a low, disgruntled noise. "Do you never take offense to anything?"

At that, she did return her gaze to his. "I assure you, my lord, 'tis possible to offend me. Perhaps you need to work harder at it."

"Perhaps I shall."

And then he turned and left her to her work.

Chapter 2

Her tasks had been laid out before her, easy to perform. Quilla oiled the door so it no longer squeaked. She polished the battered teakettle until it looked a bit more presentable and threw away all but the least chipped cups. Just a few things, here and there, that would make his space seem a bit less . . . unbearable.

By the time the sun tinged the sky pink through the large windows, she'd done all she could. There was no purpose to re-creating the room all at once, aside from the fact she didn't have the means to do it. She'd run out of time to do any sort of cleaning, really, so when she heard stirring in the master's bedchamber, she smoothed back her hair and Waited.

When he came out of the bedroom, she knew better than to expect a sleepy-eyed, tousled, and yawning man. Gabriel Delessan, despite the early morning hour, was impeccably groomed, perfectly dressed, and looked as though he'd been awake for hours. He entered the room without looking at her and puttered with some bubbling beakers before turning to face the fireplace where she knelt.

When he turned, Quilla got to her feet and poured the just-boiled water into the teapot to steep. She set the teacup on the tray, added sugar and the steaming liquid. She had it held out to him before he even made it to the fireplace.

"Less sugar," was all he said after sipping.

"I brought you some breakfast." Quilla indicated the round table next to the chair. She'd set it with a white cloth. "I'm sure you're hungry."

"I never eat in the morning."

True patience is its own reward.

She had to repeat the principle three times in her head, even as she smiled and replied, "I'll have it taken away, then."

He gave an aggrieved sigh. "Never mind. I'll eat it. It would be wrong to waste it."

He sat and lifted the lid from the covered plate. "Scrambled? I prefer poached."

"I'll remember that for tomorrow, my lord."

He gave her a suspicious glance. "I already told you—"

"You don't eat in the mornings. I know." Quilla tilted her head to smile at him. "But you might change your mind tomorrow morning, as well, and as it is my place to make sure all your needs are met, I will be sure to have food here should you require it. It's easy enough to send back if you don't eat it."

He stared at her for a long moment, then turned in his seat to face the table. "I don't know what they teach you in the Order of Solace, Handmaiden, or in the other houses to which you've been assigned. But here in Glad Tidings, we don't waste food. Alchemy is not so profitable as to allow that."

Quilla paused in the refilling of his tea, which he'd drunk despite his protest about the sweetness. "My lord, the food would not be wasted. It could feed the stable staff or someone in the kitchen."

He scowled. "I suppose you pride yourself in thinking of a retort to my every comment?"

This was going to be harder even than she'd first imagined. "It's my place to know what you desire and to provide it without you having to ask. That is why you brought me here, isn't it?"

He looked her over without expression. "Yes."

"If you truly don't wish me to bring food in the morning—"

He waved a dismissive hand. "No. It's fine."

She nodded and took a step back. "If it pleases you."

Gabriel said nothing else for a while, during which time, Quilla Waited. She used the time to meditate on the Five Principles. *True patience is its own reward.* Of the Five, she thought she would need this one most of all. She felt his gaze upon her, and she looked up with a smile.

Gabriel was not smiling. "Do you do everything only if it pleases me?"

She nodded. "Of course. That's my function here."

"But what of what pleases you?"

"I am your Handmaiden, my lord. I am your comfort. I am here to give you what you want before you want it. I'm here to give you what you need before you even know you need it. I am here so you will not have to think about anything else other than your own comfort and your own pleasure. If what you ask of me is within my ability to grant, I will do it. I will do whatever it is that you want, whether it be serving you on my knees or taking a whip to my back, if it pleases you, I will do it."

Quilla paused to contemplate him. "You do understand, don't you, what I offer? That this is my pleasure and my purpose? To provide you with absolute solace, beyond dusting your books and making you tea?"

"Why do you do this?"

"You mean, beyond because you sent for someone, and they assigned me?"

He nodded, watching her.

She'd never had a patron who had not had at least the minimal instruction in the Order's history and reason. She had seen no signs Delessan practiced any faith, but she assumed that even if he were not one of the anointed he'd have at least a basic grasp of the canon.

"I do this," Quilla told him, "because for every patron to whom I bring absolute solace another arrow returns to Sinder's Quiver."

"And when his Quiver is filled, the Holy Family shall return to this plane and peace shall be restored."

His answer pleased her. "You do know."

He shrugged. "Foolishness."

Quilla lifted her chin. "You need not believe in my reasons for providing service, my lord. You need only be served."

"And 'tis all the same? You clean for me and help me around the workshop, you cater to my every whim, and in the end you'll have done your part in bringing back the Holy Family."

"I do so believe, yes."

"And do you think this will happen in your lifetime? Is that why you work so hard at pleasing me?"

Quilla shook her head. "I do not do it with hope that Sinder's Quiver will be filled in my lifetime. That would be a selfish reason. Selfish is the heart that thinks first of itself."

Delessan stared at her, one hand to his chin. "This is what your Order teaches you?"

"It's one of our Five Principles. Yes."

He didn't ask her what the others were. "There is no such thing as an unselfish heart."

"No," she agreed. "But 'tis not impossible to rise above selfishness and find selflessness in its place."

She thought he meant to speak, but then without another word, he turned and stalked to his worktable and proceeded to ignore her. Quilla stared after him, bemused. What had Florentine said about him? *Dark, like.* Kind beneath, but dark on the surface.

Truth be told, she'd rather have it that way than the other. On the grounds of the Order there was a vast lake, so deep the bottom had never been plumbed. Sometimes the water in Loch Eltourna was gray, other times, black with depth. Sometimes it grew choppy when there was no wind, and sometimes, some rare times, the water tasted of salt. People boated on the lake, and fished in it. They bathed and swam and washed their clothes in it. They drank from it, too. But only the foolish did not respect and somewhat fear it, because even on the days when the sun shone brightly and dappled sparkling ripples on the lake's surface, nothing changed the dark depths beneath.

Quilla had known people like that lake. Sparkling and pretty on the surface, black and dangerous beneath. She preferred it the other way around, definitely.

His faint muttering caught her ear and she tilted her head to better catch his words. He was not asking for her. He was reciting some sort of list, perhaps of ingredients or a formula. She went back to what she was doing, unobtrusive, silent, allowing him to forget she was even there at all.

Quilla kept to the far side of the room, away from his workspace. Every so often the sharp, acrid smell of something burning made her pause to see what he was doing, but she did not go closer to see.

She'd oiled the hinges of his door, and now she used a cloth soaked in flax oil she'd taken from the kitchen to polish the carved wood until the dust had vanished and gleaming wood remained. She used the same oil on the picture frames, the mantel, the bookcase, the chair, until the wood in the room no longer shrouded itself with dust. She ran a finger over the back of the chair. While the cloth covering the seat might be faded and patched, the wooden frame was of very high quality. Either the master had fallen into harder times than he was used to, or else he simply did not care. Likely the latter, she thought, stealing another peek at him.

The white coat he'd put on over his clothes bore several stains. He'd donned a pair of heavy gloves reaching all the way to his biceps. A startling contraption of leather straps, eyepieces, and different-sized lenses covered his face, making one eye look twice the size of the other. As he turned, still muttering, she caught sight of the color of his eyes, magnified behind the lenses.

Gabriel Delessan had eyes the color of Loch Eltourna, like sun-dappled water, gray and green and blue . . . and with a hint of darkness beneath.

" 'Twas my understanding I would not need to provide you with a list of tasks to keep your attention, Handmaiden."

Heatroses again bloomed in Quilla's cheeks, but she kept her voice and expression neutral when she replied.

"Nay, my lord. You do not. I was merely pausing to be certain you had no additional need of me. The way you turned made me think you were going to speak to me."

"If I had something to say to you, I'd say it, and likely without bothering to turn 'round to capture your attention." Delessan looked around the room and took off the contraption over his eyes. His gaze flickered as he looked at the polished wood. "A subtle change, Handmaiden. One would almost not notice you'd done anything at all."

Quilla pressed her lips together so as not to seem impertinent by smiling. She inclined her head by way of response, instead. "It's often the most gradual of changes that affect us most, my lord Delessan."

"Indeed." He seemed about to say more, then put his lenses back on and started back to work.

Still smiling, Quilla returned to her own tasks. Any heavy cleaning she would save for a time when he was not in the room, so as not to disturb him. Although, she thought, watching him bend over a series of beakers, it seemed unlikely she'd even be noticed.

His concentration was admirable, but then she supposed it would have to be. Alchemy was not an easy discipline to practice. The work was complicated and sometimes dangerous, from what she understood, and though the rewards could be great, there could also be much disappointment.

Much like serving the Order, she thought as she ran her cloth over the rickety side table and arranged a lace cloth over the top to hide the splintered wood. Vast potential for personal reward and also much disappointment.

She judged the time by the growling of her stomach and assumed his would be as empty as hers. She slipped out of the room to head for the kitchen, where she found Florentine hunched over a pot of bubbling stew, her gray curls askew beneath her floppy cap and her broad, coarse face red with exertion.

"Florentine, I need to make the master a tray."

"What?" Florentine stood up so fast her cap flew onto the floor.

Quilla bent quickly to pick it up and handed it back. "A tray? For his midday meal."

Florentine snatched the cap from Quilla's hand and slapped it back on her head. She snorted. "Master don't usually eat midday."

"And he's far too thin because of it," replied Quilla. "I'm going to make certain he eats today. He can't work all day long without food."

Florentine gave her a squinty-eyed glare. "No? He's done it plenty o' times afore."

Quilla put her hands on her hips. "Florentine, what, exactly, is your problem with allowing me to do my job?"

The fat chatelaine sniffed, nose in the air. "I ain't got a problem, Miss Fancy Breeches. None 'tall."

"Fine, then. A tray? I'll be happy to fix it myself if you show me—"

"You might be going to have your fingers in all of the master's spaces, Mistress Fancy, but this kitchen is my place! I'll fix Master Gabriel his tray, I will!"

Quilla knew when to step back. "Very well."

She watched Florentine pull out a tray with carved wooden handles and set it on the thick butcher-block table in front of the fire. The cook ladled a generous helping of stew into a bowl, added a loaf of thick-sliced bread and a small crock of butter. Utensils. A flagon of ale. A small saltcellar, a luxury Quilla noticed but did not remark upon. The household couldn't be in very dire straits if the cook had enough salt to send an entire cellar along on the tray without needing it in the kitchen.

"Napkin," Quilla prompted.

Florentine raised a bushy eyebrow. "What?"

"A napkin. Surely you have them?"

"For fancy dinner parties, sure and I do."

"He'll need one to wipe his mouth on from the gravy." *True patience, Quilla.* "Surely you don't expect him to use his sleeve?"

"Nah, but I thought he might use your'n," Florentine said slyly. "Or mayhaps you'd lick his mouth clean—"

Quilla had been rearranging the items on the tray to balance the weight. At Florentine's words, she slammed her hand down on the table hard enough to make the dishes jump.

"You will not speak to me that way!" Her voice echoed around the room. She stepped closer to Florentine. The much larger woman took a step back. "You will accord me the respect I deserve, Florentine. I am a Handmaiden, and in the employ of your master. Beyond that, I have never done aught to give you reason to disparage me. Think you not because I am mild-tongued and calm of manner that I am some addlepated twit you can shove about to serve your own purposes, or insult without retribution. I have served in lowly houses and fine palaces. I have been Handmaiden to shepherds and to kings. And while you may not approve of my function, and you may not understand it, let not your own jealousy make a mockery of what I am and what I do. I accord you the respect your position demands. I ask you do the same to me."

"Or what?" Florentine's sneer seemed halfhearted, the threat in her tone forced. "You'll tell the master on me?"

"Do you really think I'd have to?" Quilla regarded the other woman carefully. "Master Delessan impresses me as the sort of man who'd find out all on his own. Think you he'd be pleased to discover his cook berating his Handmaiden? Even if he holds no great affection for me, he is paying dearly for my services. He'd be no more likely to accept you treating me badly than he would if you abused a fine carriage horse or hunting hound."

"You liken yourself to a horse or a hound and yet you get affronted when I call you a whore?"

Quilla shrugged and went back to arranging the tray to make it easier to carry. "I'm no more that than you, Florentine. We're both paid to perform a service to the master. You to feed his body, I his soul."

Florentine huffed. "But you don't deny you'd warm his bed if he asked."

Quilla regarded Florentine with a raised eyebrow. "And you wouldn't?"

That seemed to stun the fat chatelaine into silence, jaw agape and eyes wide. Yet she didn't deny the assertion, and Quilla pushed past her to open the glass-fronted doors to the pantry cupboard.

"This will do." She plucked a white linen napkin from a pile of them and settled it onto the tray. "Thank you, Florentine."

"You don't . . . you don't . . ."

Quilla paused in lifting the tray to look at her. "You'd do it if he wanted it, because you love him and are grateful to him. But you would not do it because you desire him. So why is it so hard for you to understand my place? I would do the same."

Florentine seemed to recover a bit. "Our lord Delessan has been naught but kind to me. Always."

"And you'd do anything to repay him. I understand." Quilla cocked her head and hefted the tray, then carried it to the small cupboard lift set into the wall. She put the tray inside and closed the door before turning. "You know, Florentine, should you ever wish to talk—"

"To you?" The sneer became more pronounced. "As if I'd share my soul with the likes of you!"

"Sometimes it feels good to share it with someone." Quilla tugged the rope that operated the lift, and when the tray had made its way up, she left the kitchen.

He was still working when she returned to his lab. He didn't even turn when she opened the door, and she congratulated herself on the now silent hinges. Quilla busied herself with setting the small table next to the chair, arranging the food and utensils in a pleasing display that also allowed the maximum ease of access.

"Your mercy, my lord." She kept her voice pitched low, an interruption as nonjarring and subtle as the oiling of the hinges. "I've brought you some food."

He turned, gaze cloudy at first but clearing within moments. "I didn't ask for any."

"You did not need to ask, my lord. It's my purpose and my pl—" She paused, remembering how he'd taken offense at the rote Handmaiden answer. "It's my purpose to provide what you need before you need it."

He nodded. She expected a snide comment, perhaps even a frown, but Delessan instead took off his apron and ran a hand through his dark hair. A strand fell over his eyes and he pushed it back impatiently, striding to the chair and flopping into it without much seeming enthusiasm at the prospect of a meal.

He reached for the utensils, but Quilla had already lifted the napkin and shook it out, then placed it on his lap. He stopped, fork in hand, as though she'd burned him. Quilla watched him from lowered eyes, her outward appearance still calm as she poured his mug full of ale, continuing her work while pretending not to notice his sudden reaction.

She gestured to the bowl of warm water and the soft towel she'd added to the tray. "Surely you'd care to wash your hands before you eat? To rid them of the chemicals?"

Delessan put the fork down with a click against the table. "Of course."

Quilla lifted the pitcher of water and the small cake of soap. "Will you allow me to help you?"

She always had to ask, the first time, lest a patron did not wish assistance. She'd found phrasing the question as a request made them more comfortable.

Apparently, not Gabriel Delessan. His eyes widened for a moment before narrowing, his lips parting briefly before pressing into a thin, grim line.

"Think you I am incapable of washing my own hands?"

"Of course not." Quilla held out the pitcher and the soap. "If you don't wish me to help—"

"By help you mean doing it for me."

"If it pleases you."

Delessan made a noise low in his throat. "You would wash my hands for me as though I were a child."

"I would wash your hands for you if it pleased you to allow me to serve you in that way," Quilla replied. "And if it is your pleasure that I do that for you, then in the future, every time you eat when I am present, I shall provide the same service, so that you won't ever have to think of it for yourself."

"I rather like thinking for myself, Handmaiden. I've grown somewhat accustomed to it."

Nodding, she held out the pitcher and the soap. "You might allow yourself to grow accustomed to my service as well."

Silently, he held out his hands over the basin. Quilla poured a stream of water over them to wet them, then put the pitcher down and wet the soap, rubbing it between her hands to create a soft lather. Then she set it aside and took each of his hands, one after another, in hers and gently rubbed them clean. She laid them down in the basin and rinsed them both with more warm water, then used the soft towel to dry them.

Then she stepped back and Waited. She hadn't been looking at his face while she washed his hands, concentrating instead on making certain she removed all traces of residue from his skin. Now, the intensity of his gaze startled her.

He stared at her with burning eyes, two bright spots of color high on his pale cheeks. His hands stayed where she'd left them, on the table next to the bowl. Only now, his fingers had curled, gripping the table edge.

"My lord—"

"Don't do that again," he interrupted harshly. "I did not care for it. Not at all."

Then he bent his head to the food and did not speak to her again.

When dusk purpled the windows, he left off his work and vanished into his bedroom without another word to her. He had not, in fact, spoken to her since the midday meal. Quilla had spent the rest of the day on her hands and knees, scrubbing the wooden floor and sending out the faded rugs to be beaten. Now, her body ached with the pleasant aftereffects of a day well spent in physical labor, and she wanted little more than to go to her quarters and take a hot bath, put on a night rail, and slip into dreams.

She put away the cleaning supplies and smoothed the tangled tendrils of her hair off cheeks she was certain were smudged with grime. From inside his bedroom she heard the sound of shuffling. She tapped the door frame.

"My lord, if you have no more need of me today—"

"Go. You're free to go."

She nodded, though of course he could not see her. "Would you like me to bring you something to eat before I retire?"

"No." More shuffling. The door cracked open and he peered out with one wary, loch-colored eye. "I am to dine with my wife this evening."

"Then I'll go?"

"Yes, yes, go. I said go, didn't I?"

The door shut in her face, and she paused a moment, then let herself out of his rooms. Climbing the stairs to her room left her weary and winded by the sheer multitude and steepness of them, and the winding, narrow curves.

"An odd location to house a Handmaiden," she grumbled through gasps as she let herself into her room. "The farthest point away from him."

She didn't mind the garret room, which was plain but comfortable enough, and the luxury of her own bath chamber was something she truly appreciated. Still, the thought of climbing these stairs day and night did make her resolve to eat more and seek a restorative concoction from the local medicus, if only to make sure she didn't wear herself down.

"He needn't make it quite so difficult," she said to the empty room.

She knew there would always be those who would not be soothed and satisfied, no matter what was offered them. She was beginning to wonder if Gabriel Delessan was such a man.

"So many blessings," she murmured, folding the soiled gown and setting it aside to be cleaned. She tugged her shift off over her head and folded that, as well. "Yet so little joy."

True, a mad wife and a son possibly not his own would be cause to make any man frown. And yet, there was more to him than that. From what Florentine had said, Master Gabriel had never been joyous.

She refused to think the task might be too great for her. He had called for her, at least he'd done that, and while his motives might not have been as pure as she could have hoped, it showed he was at least interested in appeasement. On some level, anyway.

She recalled the way his eyes had blazed when he'd told her never to wash his hands again. It had made him angry, that simple act of caretaking that was as natural and unaffected to her as opening a door for someone whose hands were full of packages.

On the morrow she would see about replacing his battered kettle and ruined cups and creating some special teas. Something a bit spicy, to complement his temper and prevent him from becoming too complacent, tempered with a calming herb, like lady's lace, to soothe his easily provoked temper. The art of tea had been only one of many Quilla studied, and she took pride in brewing special mixes suited to the personality of her patrons. Something with a hint of sweetness to chase the bitterness from his tongue, but not so sweet as to make him sour in response.

A flower is made more beautiful by its thorns. Gabriel had many thorns and few blossoms. And yet, there was something, a glimpse, a hint, of something beneath the prickly exterior. She pondered it all the while she bathed, and while she slipped between clean sheets to fall asleep. What would make him soften?

She awoke to screaming. Quilla sat up in bed, heart pounding and eyes bulging wide against the darkness. She could see naught but the bright sparkles her fear had created in her vision.

She listened. The scream rose again, a thin wail that pierced her ears despite the distance from which it must have come. Then it cut off. Silence once more.

She lay back on her pillow and pulled the covers up around her neck. What on earth had that been? It could have been a beast outside, a great cat stalking its prey or the prey itself squealing. Yet it hadn't sounded like it came from outside.

So it had come from inside. A scream in the night was never good news. She waited, listening, but it didn't come again. It was a long time before she could fall back to sleep.

By the time Delessan entered the workshop in the morning, Quilla had already replaced the soiled rugs and rearranged the furniture in front of the fireplace. She'd added a footstool and covered the faded chair with a woven throw. She traded the battered kettle for one in better repair, along with a set of plain but unchipped teacups. In the pinkish light of dawn and the red gold light from the fire, the room had become almost pleasant. She'd done nothing to his worktable, but the rest of it well pleased her.

She could do little about the smell from the chemicals, but the scent of the brewing tea and the freshly baked simplebread at least covered it up somewhat. Today, he appeared dressed no less formally than the day before. Quilla paused, bent over the pan of simplebread, to look at him.

"Good morning, my lord."

He grunted and took two steps toward the worktable before pausing and turning back. "What do I smell?"

"Tea and simplebread, my lord."

"What kind of tea?"

"Something I brewed for you myself."

"The kitchen is the place for baking, not my studio." Yet he took another step forward, as though his nose were leading him despite the protests of his mind.

"It's only simplebread," Quilla explained, lifting the pan with the help of a thick towel. "Really no trouble at all."

Delessan's mouth turned down, but he sat in his chair, smoothing his fingers over the throw. "And what's this? And that?"

He pointed to the kettle and cup she'd filled with tea.

"I thought the blanket might look nice. The kettle and cups I found in the storage closet downstairs. The others were in disgraceful repair. I thought you deserved better, but these were the best to be had."

She'd been slicing the simplebread and arranging the thick, fragrant slices on a plate, not looking at him. When she looked up, she met his eyes. He was staring, lips parted. When her gaze met his, he closed his mouth, thinning the lips.

"Think you I cannot provide my own repairs to my chair? Replace my own kettle when it needs replacing?"

Quilla handed him the plate. "Think you can? Certainly. Think you would? Nay, else you'd have done so. 'Tis my duty to provide you with what you need, my lord, so you don't need to ask for it. I saw the kettle was imperfect, and thought to replace it, but if you prefer the old one, I will bring it back."

He held up the plate of simplebread, smelling it. "No. The new one is fine."

She waited, watching while he took a bite of the firm, fresh bread. Then she handed him a napkin. He wiped his lips free of crumbs. "I'm surprised you didn't offer to wipe my mouth for me."

"You didn't care for me washing your hands," she pointed out matter-of-factly. "I would not assume you'd care to have me wipe your mouth."

That look again, as though she'd grown an extra eye. Quilla kept her expression serene as she swept the hearth clean, aware of his scrutiny. When she looked up again, he was still staring.

"How might I serve you?"

He looked momentarily startled. "I will arrange for you to have access to a credit account of your own. You will use it to purchase anything you think this room needs. And anything you need beyond what I've already given you."

Quilla inclined her head in acknowledgment of his generosity. "Thank you."

"In the afternoons, when I wish not to be disturbed, you will have time to go to the market, if you wish. Otherwise, tell Florentine or Bertram what it is you wish to order and they will arrange for the craftsman to come."

"Thank you."

He nodded abruptly and set the plate aside with only crumbs left upon it, then got up from his chair. "I don't have all day to stand about chattering, Handmaiden."

He pushed past her and headed for his worktable. Behind him, as she tidied up the remains of his breakfast, Quilla smiled.

I heard screaming in the night. This has been the third time." Quilla watched Florentine roll out the thin dough, pat it with some flour, then cut it into strips and hang the finished noodles over the rack to dry.

Florentine looked up at her. "You didn't. You was dreaming."

"I wasn't dreaming, Florentine."

"You might as well have been, for all the gossip you'll pry from my lips."

Quilla smiled and handed the cook another ball of soft dough. "I wouldn't dream of forcing you into telling tales. I'm merely telling you what I heard."

Florentine pausing in the rolling to give Quilla a narrow glare. "I thought Handmaidens was supposed to be respectful. You've got sassiness in every bone, you have."

Quilla laughed. "Handmaidens are trained to provide subservience of manner and provision. We are not required to be cowering mice. You can respect someone and still tease them, and likewise, treat a person with the utmost outward appearance of solicitude while inside you mock them."

"Either way, you're sassy." Florentine gestured at the young woman who'd just entered the kitchen. "You! Watch where you're stepping, you'll drag flour all over the place!"

The young woman sniffed and lifted the hem of her skirts to show delicate ribboned slippers. "I merely came down to prepare the tea for my lady's afternoon respite."

She smoothed a blonde curl over one shoulder and looked over at Quilla, who smiled though she could already tell this young woman was going to cause her trouble. "I'm Allora Walles, companion to my lady Saradin. Mistress of this house. And you are Tranquilla Caden, the master's Handmaiden."

"You mean you came down to have me prepare the tea," cut in Florentine, grumbling as she left off the noodle preparation and moved toward the fire to hang the kettle over the flame. "And Quilla, I daresay, already knows who the mistress of the house is."

"Does she?" Allora pursed perfect pink lips and stared at Quilla without bothering to hide her disdain. "I suppose a . . . Handmaiden . . . would."

The contempt she put into the word made Quilla grit her teeth, but she kept her smile pleasant when she replied, "I have yet to have the pleasure of making Mistress Delessan's acquaintance."

"And 'tis quite unlikely that you will." Allora moved closer to Quilla, looking over her clothes with a raised brow. "Our master has been generous with you."

Quilla looked at her plum-colored gown. "I brought this with me. It's mine."

"Really? The fabric is exceptionally fine." Allora reached a hand to pinch the cloth of Quilla's sleeve. "The cut is rather elegant, too. Funny, I thought Handmaidens wore rather less than this."

Quilla pulled her sleeve from the other woman's grasp. "This dress suits my preferences. If our lord Delessan chooses to clothe me differently, then I shall acquiesce to his wishes."

"Of course." Allora's smirk made Quilla purse her lips briefly, but long enough for the lady's maid to see. The maid smiled, her blue eyes glinting. "You must tell me more about your work, Tranquilla. What a charming name, and so apt. It means calm, doesn't it? And that's what you do? Calm people?"

"Yes, that is part of my function. Yes. And Allora means 'devious beauty.'"

Allora tossed her hair over her shoulders. "I need to bring my lady her tea. Otherwise she gets . . . disturbed."

"More'n she already is?" Florentine scoffed, but pulled the whistling kettle off the fire and poured the hot water into the teapot. "Allora, take the mistress some of those cinnamon biscuits from the cupboard. They're in the tin with the hounds etched on top."

Allora heaved a sigh so great it lifted her shoulders, as though Florentine had asked her to walk a mile across broken glass, but she sauntered to the cupboard and pulled out the tin. "Extra sugar on the tray, Florentine. You know the mistress likes her tea sweet."

"I know you like it sweet, Allora Walles. The mistress could use a bit of sugar in her. You, on the other hand, could likely stand to cut back a bit."

Allora whirled, tin in hand, chin up, and eyes blazing. "A fine one to talk you are, you old fat cow!"

Florentine only chuckled. "Fat I may be, but this is hard-earned. A badge of honor to my profession, like. You, on the other hand,

my plumpy, should mayhaps concern yourself less with stuffing
your face and more with some brisk walking round the gardens."

Allora's mouth worked without sound while the spots of color
in her creamy cheeks grew increasingly hectic. "You! I! Never!"

"Never walk? That's right, I'm being unfair. You spend plenty of
time walking back and forth in front of the looking glass." Florentine arranged the tray and handed it to the gasping Allora. "And
beyond that, well, my little buttercup, my advice to you is that the
sort of activity you're accustomed to is well and good, but you'll
need to get off your back at some point and take a brisk jog, if you
want to rid yourself of that second chin I see starting."

Allora gasped louder. "You hag! You nasty old thing! You . . .
you . . ."

"I believe the word you're struggling so prettily to find in the
vast echoing chambers of your mind is *bitch*," Florentine said grandly.
"And believe me, love, I've earned the title."

"You're barely even a woman!" Allora cried and swept from the
room, tray in hand, so affronted she had forgotten to use the lift.

"Which makes it all the sweeter, doesn't it?" Florentine started
to laugh, moving back to her noodles.

"You plagued her on purpose." Quilla tried to sound reproving,
but couldn't.

Florentine looked up. "Ah, but it got her off your back, did it
not?"

"You didn't need to."

"It gives me great pleasure to needle that stuck-up bint, Quilla."

Quilla studied the cook. "Why?"

"Because she's convinced the purse between her legs entitles her
to treat people badly. Because she acts as though she shites gold
coins and pisses lemon sugar water, and it burns my biscuits. She
uses her tits and her pretty blonde hair to manipulate people who
ought to be smarter but ain't, Quilla."

"I see."

Florentine turned to look at her. "You don't see. I am Alyrian by birth. Do you know what that means?"

Quilla thought for a moment before answering. "Alyria was a closed country for many years. It had a revolution within the past twenty-year cycle. And I've heard the men of Alyria hold themselves in greater esteem than they do the women."

Florentine patted out another ball of dough, her strong hands thinning and stretching it to make it the right thickness. "'Tis far more than that. For a hundred years the women of Alyria were no more than chattel. Slaves. Made to cover themselves from head to foot so as not to affront any man with the sight of their faces. Women had no rights in that land but for the right to bear children and die."

Quilla got up to use some of the kettle's hot water to brew another pot of tea. She stood with her back to the fire, warming herself, while Florentine spoke.

"I was born to a merchant father who had vowed to kill the folly, my mother, if she bore him another daughter. That's what they called them. Follies. After Kedalya's Folly."

Quilla had heard the story. Though it featured the Invisible Mother, the tale was not one in the canon of her faith. "He would have killed your mother for having another girl child?"

"And been praised for it, no doubt." Florentine's tone wasn't bitter, just resigned as she sliced the dough with her sharp knife into thin strands. "But instead, she gave my father a son. Me. Florentine Allumay. And I lived as a boy until the revolution when the women threw off their veils and took back their lives."

Quilla had been trained to always know what to say, even when at a loss for the right words. "She risked much. Your mother."

Florentine gave her a shrewd, sideways look. "Aye. She did. She died before she ever got to take off her veil."

"I'm sorry."

Florentine hung the noodles on the rack and took the last of the dough from the bowl. "We were given the choice, us lads who were really lassies. Live as we'd done our whole lives, or take on new roles. I chose to leave. I went to Firth, where I met Master Delessan. I had no money. No belongings. I was slaving away in a tavern kitchen, paid with gruel and the occasional beating for good measure. He took me away. When he found out what I was, or rather what I was not, he encouraged me to leave behind the twig and berries I'd never really had betwixt my thighs. Become a woman." She gave Quilla a sly look. "As best as I could, anyway. But a dress is only clothing. It doesn't change who the person is, inside it."

"Of course it doesn't." Quilla watched Florentine's strong hands work the dough. "But you are a woman."

"I am." Florentine finished the last of the noodles. "Which is why that little cocktease Allora makes me so angry. She takes her twat for granted. Uses it to get things she wants. She's a disgrace to her cunt."

Quilla bit her lower lip. "You think the same of me, don't you."

"You"—Florentine pointed the knife at Quilla—"don't manipulate, so far as I can see. Do I think 'tis right you spread your legs for anyone who thinks a fuck will solve their problems? No. But do I think you do it out of true purpose rather than simply to scratch an itch or further your own needs? Yes, Quilla. I do believe so, and 'tis what makes the difference."

Quilla didn't much care for that assessment, but she supposed it was better than being a disgrace to her cunt. "I'm sorry, Florentine."

"Don't be sorry for me."

"I'm not sorry for you. I'm sorry you had to endure what you did."

Florentine finished the last noodles and pushed the rack closer to the fire. "If I hadn't had the life I did, I'd not have become the person I am. Crotchety, stubborn, and a right old bitch."

"You are a trifle difficult to endure," said Quilla.

Florentine looked up with a broad grin. "Yet you keep coming round. I might start to think you fancy me."

Quilla laughed. "Let's just say you don't scare me as much as you might like."

Florentine straightened and put both hands to her back as she stretched it, twisting at the waist. "Whatever, you've taken the harsh side of my tongue with a smile. 'Tis more than many could do."

"I'm trained to do it."

"Trained to be pleasant to those who berate you? I'd not make a good Handmaiden, then."

"No. Perhaps not. But you're an excellent chatelaine."

Florentine fixed her with a serious look. "That I am, and don't think that just because I've gone all soft and emotional with you today that I don't run this house with an iron hand."

"I wouldn't dream of it."

Florentine nodded, seeming pleased. "And as for Allora, well, I like to snap her garters when I can. She's too hoity-toity for her own good."

"I don't think she likes me," Quilla said and fixed cups of tea for Florentine and herself.

"She rides so far up Mistress Saradin's arse she practically lives in her throat. Of course she won't like you. Mistress Saradin doesn't like you."

"Mistress Saradin has never met me."

"She doesn't need to meet you, Handmaiden. She knows what you're here to do."

"And what, exactly, does she think that is?" asked Quilla, refusing to be taunted into an angry response.

"She knows, as we all do, that you're here to heal the master's heart."

"And you all think his heart should remain unhealed?"

Florentine shrugged. "'Tis not for me to say."

"But you will and you do, Florentine."

The cook nodded slowly, looking at Quilla. "I would like to see the master smile again."

"But his lady wife would not?"

Florentine laughed. "Not unless 'tis her who brings it to his face. Don't you know anything about jealousy, Quilla?"

She knew too much about it. "I thought you said she was mad."

"Mad, not stupid. Insane, not incoherent."

Quilla sipped her tea. "I'm here for a reason. I'm sorry it won't please everyone else, but I answer to the Order of Solace and to Master Delessan. I'll be here until my work is done."

"And until you can add another arrow to Sinder's Quiver. I know."

"Yes."

Florentine pulled out another bowl and began sifting flour into it. "Mistress Saradin will never like you, noble purpose or no."

"She doesn't need to like me."

Florentine laughed. "No. She surely does not. But 'ware her, Quilla, for she'll try to make your life so miserable you'll think banishment to the Void a better ending."

Quilla shook her head. "Thanks for the warning."

"Oh, 'tis no warning," said Florentine. "'Tis a promise."

Chapter 3

So many books. From the sacred to the mundane, dozens of volumes graced the shelves. While all of them were bound in fine leather, with expensive paper, many were in disrepair. All of them were dusty. Today, Quilla had decided to begin the task of ordering them.

"Good morning, my lord," she said when he entered the room. She left the shelves and pulled the kettle from the fire just as it began to whistle, poured the hot water into the pot, and took the napkin off the basket of fresh-baked scones she'd brought with her from the kitchen.

"How do you do that?"

She paused in buttering the scone. "Your pardon?"

Delessan slid into his chair and waved at the teapot. "How do you know when to put the water on so it's ready the moment I walk out the door? 'Tis been two morns in a row."

"Shall we make a game of it? See how many times I can do it?" she said lightly, finishing with the scone and adding a dollop of tumbleberry jam to the top of it. She handed him the plate.

"How did you know I like tumbleberry jam?"

Quilla regarded him with a straight face. "Magic."

His lips thinned for a moment, the faintest hint of a smile quirking the corners. "You asked Florentine."

"Of course I did. I need to know all about you, if I'm to be your Handmaiden. What you like and what you don't."

He bit into the scone and then sipped some tea. "Perhaps I should make you a list."

Quilla smiled, then Waited. "If it pleases you."

It was his turn to regard her with a serious expression. "Do you wake every morn with such an abominably cheery manner? Or is it something you put on, like your gown?"

"I was blessed with an easily contented nature. No matter how I feel when I go to my bed at night, there are few mornings I do not wake with the knowledge that each day is mine own to control."

"So you're happy all the time?"

She shook her head. "Of course not, my lord. I am sad, or weary, or irritable as any other. I just make a rather greater effort at finding joy when it insists on hiding."

He snorted. "You speak as though joy were something anyone could find, like a slug beneath a rock."

"More like a flower in a garden of stone, my lord."

"Ah. You've been walking the grounds."

"Walking is good for the legs." She watched him. "Your garden, forgive my saying, could perhaps use a bit of color."

"We have the conservatory and greenhouse to provide flowers. The stone garden is not a place for frivolity, but for meditation."

"Of course. 'Tis your garden, and should be planned however you choose."

Delessan finished his scone and reached for the second she'd already prepared. "Don't you want anything to eat?"

"If it pleases you for me to eat with you, than I shall."

He frowned. "Are you hungry?"

"I am."

"And if you were not?"

"If I were not hungry but it pleased you to have me eat with you, I would do so." Quilla put some jam on an unbuttered scone and took a bite. It was delicious. Better than her simplebread.

She looked up to see Delessan looking at her with a mixture of appalled astonishment and speculation in his eyes. "Do you not have limits, Handmaiden?"

Quilla took a swallow of tea and wiped her mouth before answering. "I do, my lord."

"And what are they?"

"I don't know. I have never had them tested."

"Never had—" This seemed to set him aback. He stared down into his teacup, brow furrowed, mouth pursed. "Why not?"

"I have never been assigned to any patron who has pushed me farther than I am willing to go."

The answer was simple, but true. She'd been asked to do many things, and she'd always done her best to provide them. She hadn't always succeeded, of course. Eating food that turned her stomach had made her ill more than once. Her poetry had earned disdain. She'd fallen asleep when requested to stay awake. Overall, she did her best to provide what her patrons needed.

"Then how do you know you have limits?" His gray blue eyes burned into hers.

"Everyone has limits," she said, her voice huskier than normal, before she cleared her throat self-consciously. "I am not without morals."

"So you would not say, steal, for a patron?"

"I think not."

"Even if it made him happy?"

Quilla had heard stories of Handmaidens who'd committed

crimes in the names of their patrons. It didn't matter in the eyes of the courts, or the priests. They'd been held accountable for their actions.

"Theft rarely makes anyone happy, my lord. When happiness is measured by wealth or assets, then accumulating more, even by theft, rarely satisfies. If a patron wished me to steal in order to provide him or her happiness, I would likely decline, knowing no matter what I did, my efforts to provide that joy would be fruitless."

Delessan looked at her while he sipped his tea. "Likely would refuse. But you're uncertain."

"I have never been told to steal. I believe I would refuse. But I cannot say I would never acquiesce, for there are always situations which defy reason."

"Can you think of a situation in which you might agree?"

Quilla put down her cup and folded her hands, the back of her right in the palm of her left. "I have known of Handmaidens who became thieves for their patrons. All the cases I heard of, and we are all taught of them as cautionary tales, my lord, had one situation in common."

He sat back in his chair, one leg crossed over the other, teacup cradled in his long-fingered hands. "Which was what?"

"They all fancied themselves in love with their patrons, my lord."

"Ah." He sipped. "You say fancied themselves in love. Is it difficult for you to believe they actually were?"

Quilla shook her head. "It's not my place to judge their feelings, only that whether or not they had given their hearts in addition to their service, committing a crime is immoral and the intensity of emotion cannot make up for it."

"So you've never been asked to steal but you believe you would not do so, even if you were in love with your patron."

"I have never been in love with a patron, but no. I do not believe I would steal. Nor murder, if that is your next question, and yes, I have heard of Handmaidens who did that, as well."

"It would seem you are a most violent bunch, then. Thieves and murderers? I thought the Order of Solace would not condone such practices."

She bristled at his cool tone, but kept her voice calm. "We are all human. There are far more thieves and murderers who are not members of the Order than are."

This made him smile. "Agreed. And I see that though I try to make you angry, you refrain. Tell me something, Handmaiden, how much harder would I have to try?"

"Much harder, my lord, for I have heard every insult to my profession you can imagine and likely many more you have not. I have been called a whore, a demon, a temptress. I have been spit upon in the streets, set upon by jealous spouses; I have been slapped and kicked and bitten. I have been told I will freeze in the Void and there is no place in the Land Above for me. I've endured insult and degradation aplenty."

"Why, then, do you continue?" He seemed genuinely curious, so Quilla gave him an honest answer.

"Because 'tis my pleasure to bring comfort and solace. Because I find joy in bringing joy. Because I truly believe in the higher purpose and that by following this course I am doing my part to fill Sinder's Quiver. I believe there is a place for me in the Land Above, I do not believe I am a whore or immoral, and because I know the goodness of my heart and of my soul, I care little for those who denounce me out of their own insecurities. I don't go 'round forcing my services on anyone, my lord. I am assigned to people, such as yourself, who have a need for what I can provide."

Again, the intensity of his gaze rippled through her. She could admire his eyes, now showing flecks of gray and gold in them when the firelight caught them. Full black lashes fringed them, and thick but well-shaped black brows, a shade darker than the hair on his head, arched above.

He seemed to be scrutinizing her as much as she him, for his eyes traveled over her from head to her gown puddled around her on the floor.

"So, short of theft and murder, you have no limit to what you will do?"

"You make it sound rather ominous when put that way. But, the answer, I suppose, is yes."

"Would you crawl on your hands and knees for me?"

She lifted her chin slightly. "If it would please you to have me do so, yes."

"You would not find it degrading, to be treated so?"

"You cannot degrade me if I refuse to find humiliation in the task you set before me."

"Many women would refuse to crawl willingly."

"Many women are not Handmaidens," Quilla replied.

Delessan set down his cup and rubbed his hands together, the long fingers twining and twisting. "And your limits have never been tested? Not ever?"

She smiled. "No, my lord. But should you wish to try, I am certain I will be able to accommodate you."

This reply made him frown further. "I assure you, Handmaiden, I have no desire to force your limits. I brought you here for a purpose, and 'tis not to break you."

She nodded. "Of course it is not."

He scowled, running a hand through his hair and mussing the strands. "What of your family? What say they about this avocation?"

"My parents were less than pleased when I announced I meant to go into the Service."

"I can imagine. Tell me."

A smooth command. She obeyed. "I have three brothers older

than I. Three sisters younger. My father is an ointment merchant who provides oils to the temples. My mother is beautiful and languid, and would never have been able to care for seven children without the help of an army of staff to help her cook, clean, and dispense order."

This account made Delessan smile. He watched her. "Go on."

"I grew up wanting for nothing except, perhaps, for deprivation. In our house, material goods expressed affection as much as hugs and kisses did. My parents love each other greatly, their children as well. They raised us with as much privilege as they could provide, and in return, I spent the first ten and five years of my life indulged and complacent."

"And when you turned ten and six?"

"At ten and six," Quilla answered with a small grin, "Venice Bengley asked my father for my hand."

"Ahh." Delessan nodded. "And you did not wish to marry him."

"Venice Bengley was sixty years old and smelled of pickled cabbage."

His eyes flashed. "And yet, your parents thought him a good match?"

"He is wealthy. Kindhearted. He'd had three wives already, and a passel of children he wanted me to raise. Mind, some were already older than I." Quilla shook her head. "I could not marry Venice Bengley. No matter what my parents proposed, nor how they pleaded, and not even when they finally demanded it of me. Bengley, you see, in addition to marrying me, wished to join partners with my father. It would have been a good deal all around."

"Selfish child."

"I was, indeed, to disappoint my parents so. And it surprised them. I had, until this time, been most agreeable to all they'd wished for me to choose. Clothes, habits, lessons. I was the eldest daughter and had been perfect until then.

My mother gnashed her teeth and rent her sleeve. My father reacted more practically. 'You have ever had a nurturing nature, Eysha,' he said."

"Eysha?"

"My birth name. Eysha Caden."

Delessan sipped some of his tea. If her revelation had surprised him, he did not reveal it through expression or words. "So your father was more understanding?"

"To a point. He told me I could nurture my husband and children as well as, and better than, strangers."

"I understand your father's reasoning."

Quilla nodded. "As do I, my lord, but the fact remained, I did not wish to marry Bengley, not for any reason. So I told my parents I had no wish to shackle myself to one place or one person forever, and that I wished to travel. And I would join the Order of Solace. My mother fainted. My father growled. But in the end, they had no choice. I was of age. I could choose."

"And you did."

"Yes. I did. I was given the name Tranquilla, and considered it an honor to be so named."

"And the Order of Solace instead of any other? Why?"

Nobody had ever asked her that, not in all her years of Service. Quilla paused, thinking. "The Order of Solace is the only one that does not indenture its novitiates."

"Is that so?" Delessan lifted his teacup, and she got to her feet to fill it again before he even asked. He watched her kneel again. "And this appealed to you."

"Yes, my lord."

"Why?"

She did not need to hesitate to think on this one. "Because I choose how to live my life. I am free to leave any assignment, at any time. I am free to leave the Order at any time, and would be sent on my way with the blessing of the Mothers-in-Service, should I choose to no longer serve."

"This independent nature would seem to be at odds with what your Order provides."

She smiled. "My lord, the Order of Solace did not train me to accept the will of others over my own, but rather to re-create my own to match that of those whom I serve."

"And you don't feel this compromises your freedom?"

"No. It provides me with more of it. Serving in the Order allows me to travel. It allows me to contribute Arrows to Sinder's Quiver."

She thought he might show disdain at that, but he only nodded. "You really believe that?"

"I do."

He sighed heavily. "I suppose if you can believe that Sinder walked through the Void and created valleys with his footsteps and rivers with his piss and winds with his breath, and if you can believe he found Kedalya in the forest and begat a son from her, I suppose you can believe his Quiver, once filled, will bring about an age of peace and prosperity to all the faithful."

"Even if you don't believe those stories as truth," Quilla said, "is it such an awful thing to want to make people happy?"

His gaze locked upon her for so long and so hard she thought she had made him angry. He stood. "You've kept me from my work long enough. Less talking in the mornings, Handmaiden. Breakfast is an activity that should be undertaken as swiftly and efficiently as possible. I'm a very busy man."

"As you wish," Quilla responded, getting to her feet and beginning to clear away the dishes into the basket to take downstairs.

He huffed, then moved past her to head toward his worktable

again. She watched him from the corner of her eye, thinking much upon what he'd said.

She had limits, indeed, though they were far broader than those of a woman not in the Service of the Order. But she had them.

Delessan had been muttering for the past twenty minutes. Muttering and pacing. Quilla watched him from her place at the bookshelves, where she'd been taking down each book, cleaning it, and replacing it in alphabetical order. She'd been working as silently as possible, not taking all the books off at the same time in order to prevent making a mess. The work was slower that way, but she suspected if he turned round to see the floor piled high with texts he'd be rather more upset than if only one shelf was empty at a time.

Now he exploded into a string of colorful curses that made her bite the inside of her cheek to keep from smiling at the sheer absurdity of the phrases.

She put down the book and the dustcloth and moved closer to him. Not too close. He was still pacing, hands on his hips, scowling and muttering.

"Surely that would be an awkward and uncomfortable experience, my lord," she said in reference to the last string of curse words he'd spouted. "And it might possibly kill the duck."

He stopped and glared at her. "What are you babbling about?"

She repeated his phrase. "I can think of a better way to solve your problems than that."

Would he explode in anger or had she successfully diffused him? Quilla braced herself for a torrent of fury. For a moment, it appeared uncertain if Delessan himself knew how he was going to respond.

When he did, with a huge, utterly despondent sigh, she let out the breath she'd been holding. Her limits were broad, indeed, but that didn't mean she enjoyed being berated.

"'Tis this last set of calculations," he explained, waving his hand at his worktable. "I've done something similar hundreds of times before. The elements are all the same. And yet I cannot seem to re-create the results each time. In order for this formula to be valid, it must end up the same in every use. Else it's worthless."

He scowled again. "It's making me bloody mad!"

Quilla took another step closer and held out her hand to him. "Come here."

His wary look made her smile. "What?"

"I'm not going to bite you. Come here."

His eyes narrowed and his brow furrowed, but he allowed her to take his hand and followed her a few steps toward the chaise lounge. She unbuttoned the front of his white coat and helped him out of it despite his protests.

"I need that—"

"Shh," she said firmly, setting it aside and removing the vest beneath. "Sit."

"I thought Handmaidens were supposed to be subservient," he grumbled, but did. "You're unbearably bossy."

"So I've been told before, my lord. But perhaps 'tis not so unbearable, really. You seem to be surviving."

He huffed, less grouchily than before. "You are interrupting my work."

"Your work was at a standstill, unless you consider pacing and proposing illicit advances upon harmless waterfowl to be part of your work." Quilla stood behind him and put her hands on his shoulders. "Now hush and let me help you."

"Help me? What do you know about Alchemy?"

"Nothing," she replied, her fingers finding the tension in his neck and beginning to work it. "But I know much about men."

"I am not *men*," he grumbled.

Quilla said nothing, just kept rubbing. He groaned under his breath, which made her smile. She dug in a bit harder.

"Damn it! Are you trying to incapacitate me?"

She rubbed harder and the knots beneath her fingers began to loosen. He sighed, tilting his head down to allow her greater access to his neck and shoulders. She changed from kneading to smooth, flat strokes, from his shoulders and up his neck, running her hands through his hair and stroking his scalp. Then down again, starting at his shoulders and moving upward. Slow, steady movements.

His breathing slowed, and every so often a small moan crept from his throat when she passed over a particularly tense spot. She worked his shoulder blades and along his spine, using her knuckles to press along the knobs of bone.

The smooth linen of his shirt felt good beneath her fingers, and Quilla lost herself in the repetitive movements. She could not have pinpointed the moment he finally relaxed beneath her fingers, only that one moment he seemed all coiled wires, and the next, soft feather pillow.

Quilla pulled a small vial from her waistpurse and uncorked it, dabbing scented oil on her fingertips and replacing the vial. She put her fingertips to his temples and began rubbing them. The smell of gillyflowers filled the air.

"What is that?" he asked in a voice that sounded like he wanted to be harsh but couldn't quite manage. Instead, he sounded languorous, mouth full of syrup. Oozing, liquid.

"Gillyflower oil, my lord. 'Tis good for headaches."

"And you knew I had a headache the way you know when to put the kettle on."

She continued rubbing, smiling. "Yes, my lord."

He sounded drowsy. "Because 'tis your purpose and your place to know it."

"Yes."

"And your pleasure."

"That, too."

He put a hand over hers to stop her from continuing. "My headache is gone, Handmaiden. And I think I have figured out the flaw in my equation."

Quilla took her hands away and rubbed the oil into her skin until her hands were no longer greasy. "I'm glad."

Delessan stood a bit unsteadily, and she reached out a hand to grab his arm. He looked down at her hand, then straightened. "Thank you."

"You're welcome."

He seemed unable to look at her as he began to shrug into his jacket. Quilla helped him slide it over his arms, then stepped in front of him to button it with swift and efficient fingers. He was looking at her face when she glanced up. She smiled. He did not return it, instead gazing at her with a look so pensive it made her ask, "Is there something wrong?"

"No, Handmaiden. There is naught wrong."

She nodded. He was a puzzle, Gabriel Delessan. She thought she understood him, but then wasn't sure.

"Tomorrow is seventhday," he said abruptly. "You don't need to come to my laboratory."

"No?"

"No," Delessan repeated firmly. "I do not work on seventhday, and neither should you. You're free to do what you like."

She nodded. "You're very generous, my lord."

"'Tis part of your contract, Handmaiden."

She smiled. "My contract says I am to be given one half day of rest. You already provide me more than that by not requiring my service beyond the afternoon. To add a full day in which I am not required at all is beyond what is necessary."

"You'd wish me to take it away?" He turned, frowning.

"Of course not. I'll be glad to have it. 'Tis rare I have an assignment where I am allowed this measure of freedom. I'm grateful to you for it." She looked into his eyes. "I am expressing my pleasure at your generosity. Does that make you uncomfortable? Would you prefer I didn't?"

"'Tis not necessary," came the brusque reply. "I told you, I am fulfilling my contract. I fulfill my obligations."

"Would it please you better if I took what you offered for granted and did not thank you?"

Delessan put his hands on his hips and glared at her. "Of course it would not. You are being impertinent."

Quilla inclined her head in apology. "I plead your mercy, my lord. I did not mean to be."

"Why do I not believe you?"

"I'm certain I don't know."

He scowled and huffed, though seemingly without fire. "Is that what you're taught in the Order? To sass your patrons?"

"Only if I think 'twill please them," Quilla said and went back to the shelves of books.

She waited for him to comment, smiling, back turned to him so he could not see her face. He didn't, as she'd expected he would not. But he didn't mutter quite so loudly after that, and once she even thought she heard the faintest sound of a chuckle.

S eventhday had passed, for Quilla at least, in meditation. Glad Tidings had a small chapel that didn't look as though it got much use. She hadn't minded. A day to herself was luxury, indeed.

The next morning, Delessan surprised her with conversation. "My son will be arriving this afternoon. My brother is sending him ahead and will arrive later."

"How lovely for you." Quilla poured him another cup of tea, adding the sugar and lemon he preferred, and set it in front of him. "You must be looking forward to that."

Delessan frowned. "I shall have to put aside my work for the afternoon to greet him."

She slanted a glance at him as she sliced the simplebread she'd baked for his breakfast. "And this displeases you because you feel it will set you behind in your tasks."

He nodded, slowly, his eyes traveling over her face. "You know how to judge me, yet you seem to make no judgment."

"'Tis not my place to judge you, but to understand you."

"But surely you can't help having an opinion," Delessan said.

"My opinion is irrelevant, my lord." Quilla Waited at his feet on the rug before the fire.

"What if I told you it would please me for you to give it?"

She smiled. "Then I would provide it for your pleasure."

Delessan made a disgruntled noise. "Do most of your patrons find a mindless puppet pleasing?"

"Actually, yes, my lord. Many of my patrons find their greatest solace in having their own opinions and feelings reflected to them."

"So you lie to them."

"I do my best not to lie, but rather to adjust my thinking to theirs in order to provide them the best service."

He frowned again, watching her over the rim of his teacup. "I love my son, yet I find it difficult to interact with him."

She nodded. "He is how old?"

"Seven. No. Eight."

"And you feel you ought to be able to interact with him as you would . . ." She paused, allowing him to finish the sentence.

"As I would my son."

She Waited. He looked at her, frowning, brow furrowed and

mouth pursed. He gave a heavy, long-suffering sigh. "Or so I suppose. Why? How do you think I expect to interact with him?"

"Perhaps you find yourself impatient with him because you feel you should be able to interact with him on a higher intellectual level than he is capable of maintaining. Perhaps you are impatient with yourself because you don't have the patience to speak down to a child, or to wait for him to catch up to you."

He stared at her for so long she was certain he would not speak again, but when he did, she did not imagine the tone of respect in it. "How do you know this about me?"

"'Tis my purpose and my—"

"Yes, I know," he interrupted. "And your place, I know this. But how? How do you do this?"

Quilla sat back, thinking about it, really thinking about it for the first time in a long while. "It helps to know people collectively in order to know them individually. I have studied many people."

"I don't find I much care for being compared to many people."

She smiled. "Most people don't. They like to think of themselves as individuals."

That earned her a faint upward curve of his mouth. "You're doing it again. Using what you know of other men to think you know me."

"I have no other choice," she said, "until you allow me to know you, instead."

The fire lit his dark eyes as he watched her. Finally, he gestured. "Come here."

Obediently, she stood and went to him. He reached up to tug the cord holding her braid at the bottom. The weight of her hair sprang free, loose dark waves tumbling over her shoulders and back. He ran his fingers through it, catching them in the curls and pulling enough to make small, bright sparks of pain tingle along her scalp. Quilla said nothing, watching him, her eyes on his.

"It would please me to see you wear your hair down upon occasion," Delessan said.

"Then I shall."

He took his fingers out of her hair and looked toward the fire. "My son. How do you suggest I interact with him?"

"I would suggest, perhaps, that you play with him."

He gave her a slanted, assessing glance. "Play? I'm not sure I know how."

"I could teach you," she said gently. "But I do think it would be better if you learned from him."

Delessan rubbed his eyes and sighed heavily. "You suggest I play with him."

"Children seem to like that." She began tidying the tea things, putting the cup and saucer back on the tray, scraping the crumbs from the table.

"And you know about children as you know about men?"

"Not as much, no. But I was a child, once. And I remember something of what it was like." Quilla smiled at him, brushing her hair off her face. It was more inconvenient to wear it this way, loose and dangling, but she would do it if it pleased him. "Don't you?"

"I don't think I ever was a child."

"Did you spring full grown from an egg? Or perhaps from a trumpet's blare?" Quilla laughed, comparing him to the stories of myths.

Delessan looked at her and shook his head. "Sinder's Arrow, but you're impertinent."

"I plead your mercy."

"To answer your question, impertinent miss, no. I did not spring fully grown from an egg, nor from a trumpet's blare. I came into this world in the usual manner."

She settled the supplies on the tray and wiped her hands free of crumbs. She made to lift the tray and take it away, but his voice, continuing, stopped her. She settled the tray back down, turning her gaze to him.

"My father was, ostensibly, a fabric merchant, but though his business often took him away from home for long periods of time, 'twas really his brother, my uncle Larken, who ran the business while my father gallivanted around the world on buying trips."

"It must have been difficult for you as a young boy, not to have your father about."

He smiled very, very faintly, eyes still staring at the fire. "Again, you compare to me to what you know of men."

Quilla shook her head and Waited, this time kneeling close to his legs. Close enough for her to feel the heat of him against her. "Not only of men, my lord. But of you, also."

He nodded, never taking his gaze from the fire. "My mother's name was Violette, and she used to sit me on her lap and tell me stories about when the earth was young, and how we all grew out of the ground. Even as a boy I knew her stories weren't quite true, but my mother painted pretty pictures with words. I became interested in Alchemy because of her stories of turning lead to gold, and how it could be done."

Quilla leaned a bit closer as he talked, her arm brushing his leg. "And have you found a way to do that?"

He gave the barest shake of his head. "No. I have discovered a great many things, but not that."

"Your mother sounds lovely."

Shadows flitted across his face. "My mother was a liar with a mouth full of sweetness to cover up the fact that she was a betrayer."

She watched him but said nothing, sensing there was naught she could say. Delessan continued, voice bitter and expression stormy.

"My mother betrayed my father by fucking his brother, my uncle, and getting pregnant with his child. Jericho is Larken's son and my half brother, not my full."

That explained much. She wondered how much of his anger at his mother had been exacerbated by his own wife's infidelity. "And what did your father do when he found out?"

"He never did," said Gabriel bitterly. "He died while on a buying trip. They were married within days of his body being returned to the house. My bastard half brother was born three months later."

Quilla put her head on his thigh, her hand cupping his calf loosely. "I am sorry, my lord. I can hear how this distresses you. And yet you allow your brother to come and stay with you. That takes great strength of mind."

She felt rather than saw his gaze upon her, and felt the weight of his hand as it came to rest on her head. He stroked his fingers down through her hair, smoothing it a few times before lifting his hand away.

"'Tis not his fault he was born to a conniving brother and a faithless whore. And as he inherited our fathers' business, he spends much time on the road with little need for a house of his own."

"It gives you pleasure to offer him a place in yours?"

He shifted his legs and she turned her head to look up at him. "It does not please me, Handmaiden. 'Tis a necessary obligation for me to provide space in my home for my brother."

She settled her cheek more firmly against him. "Your brother is a man grown. You're not obligated to take care of him."

He looked down at her, eyes narrowed. "Don't argue with me about my obligations, which you can know nothing about."

She lifted her head from his leg and looked into his eyes, then nodded. "Your mercy."

"Do you see your parents?"

"Not as much as they'd like, I'm sure. But I write to them regularly. And when I have time between assignments I visit them, sometimes."

"*Assignments*. That's what you call them?"

She smiled. "What else would I call them?"

He shook his head, a little. "I don't know. How many assignments have you had?"

"You are number four and thirty."

"And how long have you been with the Order?"

"Twelve years. I began at six and ten years. I'll have been there thirteen years in the summer."

"More than one patron a year?"

"Yes, my lord. My first three assignments ended rather abruptly. My first patron died in a hunting accident. My second had a wife who did not approve, and when the ultimatum came, I was asked to leave. The third was so easily satisfied I needed only to stay for two months before she no longer needed me."

That earned a raised brow. "She? And how did you so easily satisfy her?"

Quilla laughed. "She fell in love and wanted to be married. The love of another gave her the solace she needed, and my presence was no longer necessary."

"I see." Delessan crossed an arm over his chest and put his hand to his chin to look at her. "And you are not sorry when you need to leave an . . . assignment?"

"I grow to have great fondness for all my patrons," Quilla replied. "But when the time comes for me to go, though I might feel sorrow because of that fondness, I can't regret it. 'Tis part of the duty. I believe you can well understand. Fondness is not the same as love."

"No. It is not."

Quilla studied his face, the blue gray eyes, the full mouth, the high cheeks, and hair tumbling over his forehead. "I am sorry when I must leave a patron unfulfilled, for whatever reason."

"And has that happened?"

She nodded. "Of course. I can only strive to be what each patron needs, but 'twould be unrealistic to expect that I can meet the needs of every person to whom I am assigned. Human nature simply does not allow for it."

"You try very hard, though, do you not? To be what your patrons need?"

"I try very hard to please, my lord. Yes. I do."

For a long, long moment his gaze locked with hers. He reached to tuck a loose curl behind her ear, then withdrew his hand and went back to looking at the fire.

"You've been doing a fine job, so far."

The compliment pleased her, and she smiled. "Thank you."

"Don't let it make you lazy," said Delessan grumpily, waving a hand at her. "Get off your knees and do some work. I didn't bring you here to sit at my feet and gaze at me adoringly."

Quilla unfolded herself, and on impulse leaned nearer to place her mouth close to his ear. "No. I daresay if you wanted that, you'd have been better off getting yourself a puppy."

She squeezed his shoulder, well aware of the way he'd startled slightly at the whisper of her breath on his cheek. Then, smiling, she moved back to the bookcase to continue her work.

Chapter 4

Dane Delessan looked so much like his mother and so little like his father, Quilla wouldn't have been surprised to find out the fae had left him without Gabriel's intervention at all. And of course, based upon the story she'd heard about the lad's birth, quite possibly at least part of that might have been true.

"Mama! Papa!" The lad tumbled out of the carriage as though he'd been catapulted.

Saradin Delessan, who had dressed as though she were going to an embassy ball rather than for an afternoon with her son, opened her arms wide. Dane flew into them. Gabriel stood next to his wife. Tall. Stern. Even from her viewpoint from the window, Quilla could see the tense line of his shoulders.

She watched the lad step up to his father and offer a hand. Gabriel shook it. Saradin pushed Gabriel to the side and swept the boy into her arms again.

"Oh, why does he not simply hug the boy?" she mused aloud.

"Mistress?"

Quilla turned, embarrassed at having been overheard. "I'm spying on our master and his son."

The girl who'd entered the parlor lifted her feather duster. "Us, too."

Rossi, this girl's name was, one of the three housemaids. Quilla gave a relieved smile. "'Tis great news the boy is home?"

"Oh, we all miss him when he's away. He brings a lot of laughter to the place, him."

"I can imagine." Quilla peered back out the window.

Saradin had taken Dane's hand and started toward the house. Gabriel followed them, watching. Quilla turned to Rossi. "'Tis good to see the mistress up and about."

Rossi's expression turned wary as she ran her duster along the table crowded with delicate porcelain bric-a-brac. "Oh, aye. Mistress is much better up and about than wailing in her bed."

So she hadn't imagined the nighttime screams. Quilla lifted the curtain again, but the family had vanished from view. Gabriel had dismissed her for the day so as to spend time with his wife and child. While Quilla appreciated the time to herself, inactivity bored her.

"Can I help you with that?" She indicated the dusting.

Rossi looked shocked, duster pausing. "With this? The cleaning?"

"I have no small amount of experience with it."

Rossi seemed taken aback by Quilla's statement. "Oh, but 'tis not your job, Mistress Tranquilla."

"I'm not needed to do my job, at the moment, and you look as though you could use some help."

"The master might be angry, him," Rossi replied.

Quilla realized something. "Rossi, are you frightened of me?"

Rossi's laugh was so false it made Quilla's head hurt. "Me? Afraid of you? No!"

The way she dusted furiously and wouldn't look at Quilla told a different story. "Rossi. Look at me."

The younger girl did, reluctantly. "Aye, mistress."

"You can call me Quilla. I'm not your superior, you know."

"You're the master's own Handmaiden. I'm only a cleaning girl, me."

Quilla couldn't deny the truth of that, so she sighed. "Are you afraid I'll tell the master you haven't been keeping up with your work?"

Rossi shook her head. A tall girl with skin the color of tea with cream, her dark ringlets piled high beneath her cap, she could easily have worn a ball gown instead of an apron. 'Twas her demeanor, not her features, that set her class.

Quilla sighed again. "Then what?"

"I don't want to dishonor you, me."

The words had been murmured so low Quilla had to strain to hear them. "Your pardon?"

"Lolly says Handmaidens is special, and should be treated special. Lolly says you're to bring about the return of the Holy Family, and we ought not dirty you with our base natures. Lolly says you're like unto an angel, Lolly says."

As Quilla had never even passed a word with Lolly, this seemed to be a broad assumption on her part, but Quilla nodded anyway. "Think you angels dare not dirty their hands with common chores?"

Rossi looked confused. "Nay, mistress."

"Think you the Invisible Mother didn't care for her family and house?"

This seemed to give the maid pause. "I supposed she had servants to do it for her. Like our lady Mistress Delessan does."

Quilla laughed. "No. Kedalya had no servants. She'd have picked up a dustcloth, too, if she'd had dusting to do. She was a woman before she bore Sinder's son, and a woman after, even though she had the love of a god."

"Ain't that always the way it goes?" Rossi smiled. "We's women first, no matter who loves us or what they gives us."

Truer words had never been spoken. "Women we begin and women we end."

"You ain't like we thought you'd be."

"I rarely am, Rossi."

Rossi held out the dustcloth. "If you really want to help—"

Quilla took it. "I'd rather have busy hands than idle ones."

Rossi laughed and got back to work with her feather duster. "No fear of idle hands around this place, Quilla Caden. Plenty of work to be done."

So they got to it, and Rossi talked while Quilla listened. Rossi spoke of her childhood, which had begun far away, and how she'd come here in the back of a gypsy wagon and was left behind when her family moved on and she decided life on the road was no longer for her.

"I liked the big house, me," she told Quilla with eyes gleaming at the memory. "I liked the hot water for baths, me. And the clean clothes. I liked the never-hungry bellies, me."

"I don't blame you for that. I also like hot baths and a full stomach."

Rossi lifted a large vase so Quilla could dust beneath it. "I had ten brothers. I'd never have been married off. Too many men thinking they knew best what to do for me."

Rossi had been at Glad Tidings for two years now, she said, and she didn't intend on ever leaving. "I loves it here, me."

From where the pang came, Quilla wasn't certain, only that it hit her right in the breastbone and made her put a hand there, startled at the emotion. What would it be like, to have a home? A place you loved so much you never wished to leave?

She had her parents' home, of course, to which she could always return and be welcomed with open arms. Yet on the occasions she did return, her childhood room and the narrow bed both seemed too small to contain the woman she'd become. Once upon a time she'd skipped without thought along the halls of her parents' home, but now she walked them carefully as a guest.

When she returned to the Order between assignments, she had a private room. A cell, bare and sparse, though comfortable enough. She had a place to keep her clothes and what personal possessions she might have, of which there were necessarily few. She walked those halls with more comfort than she did those at her childhood home, and felt less a guest, but even so, 'twas not home in the way Rossi thought of Glad Tidings.

Quilla nodded and smiled at all the right places in Rossi's conversation, but her thoughts spiraled around this sudden discontent. A home, a house, a place to call her own, with people in it who loved her, and not what she could do for them or what she meant to them. A place where she need not fear being cast out for not being what she was expected to be, because she was accepted as she was.

Disturbed, she paused in plumping the cushions on the floral-patterned settee. Rossi, despite her earlier reticence, continued chattering, not noticing Quilla's sudden silence.

In all her years of Service, Quilla had never minded moving on. She'd never regretted, nor looked back with anything but fondness on the patrons whose lives she'd touched, no matter how briefly. She'd done her job the best she could, satisfied with the knowledge she was doing her part in filling Sinder's Quiver.

Never had she thought beyond that. Not until today. Not until this place . . . and this patron.

"You keep squeezing it that way, it won't fit back on the settee."

"Your pardon?" Quilla looked up, realizing she still clutched the pillow. She looked down and softened her grip. "Oh. Mercy. I was distracted."

Rossi's merry laugh was like the burble of a spring-running creek. "Ah, I talk too much, me. Florentine does say so, all the time."

Quilla smiled and put the pillow back and smoothed the fabric. "No, your company is most pleasant. Don't let Florentine tell you otherwise."

Rossi tossed her hair and looked coy. "Oh, I know how to work that one, me."

What exactly she meant by that, Quilla had no time to speculate, for the pounding of feet in the hall outside made them both turn. In the next instant, the parlor door flew open, and a small figure with bright golden hair burst through it, mouth chattering.

"And there were monkis, on leashes," he was saying. "And Uncle said he would buy one for me if I was a good lad and did my studies, but I said no, I would rather have a dragon."

"Indeed," came a familiar, deep voice, and Gabriel followed his son into the room.

Quilla paused, but Rossi froze. The maid ducked her head and curtsyed, bobbing up and down with so stiff a posture Quilla was afraid the lass was going to hurt herself. Quilla straightened her back and smoothed her hair off her face.

Gabriel's eyes flickered over her, then to the maid, but he said nothing. The next figure through the door was the Mistress Saradin, who swept inside like a queen entering her court. Her attire had looked spectacular from a distance. This close, Quilla could see how fine it truly was. Not one part of Saradin's gown, not the buttons nor the thread, was of common material. She wore it with the same casual air she might wear a flaxen slop dress—but only, perhaps, because she saw no reason to flaunt it at the moment.

This was clearly because she did not notice she and her husband were not alone in the room with their son. Her eyes slid over Rossi and Quilla as though they were part of the furnishings. Rossi looked relieved. Quilla caught Gabriel's eye. Did the mistress not know he had a Handmaiden? Or did she not care?

"Dane, love, a dragon would take up far too much space, and can't be house-trained." Saradin's voice was like the chirping of a bird. Dainty and bright, like her hair and her dress. She settled into a chair by the window and patted her lap for the boy to sit, but he ignored the gesture and bounced up and down. "A monki would be a far better pet."

"Dragons are more fun because if you yank their tails, they fall off and grow another one!"

Saradin chuckled. "'Tis up to your father, then."

Dane wiggled around. "Papa! May I have a dragon, please?"

Gabriel tore his eyes from Quilla. "No, Dane."

This started a round of protests so violent Quilla winced. Saradin laughed and pouted toward her husband. Gabriel looked pained. Rossi had begun easing out of the room, her fingers on Quilla's sleeve encouraging her to follow, but Quilla wanted to see how her patron handled his son. She could not imagine he would suffer such impertinence.

"Oh, Gabriel. Tell the lad he can have a dragon."

And Quilla learned something new about her patron, something she would not have guessed had she not seen him struggle so mightily. No matter what his wife had done, and no matter how ill-behaved his son, Gabriel Delessan carried an enormous burden of guilt. Quilla saw it in his eyes when he looked at the pair of them, two golden heads so much alike, two sets of merry bright eyes. Guilt forced him into indulgence . . . and he hated it.

"Should Jericho be able to find him a dragon—"

Dane whooped and jumped up and down. Saradin clapped her hands. Gabriel scowled and let his gaze slide over Quilla's face as she at last let Rossi pull her from the room. The last she saw of him was his pained expression as Dane began running around him in circles.

H and me that—"
     She placed the vial in his hand before he could finish, and Gabriel nodded. They'd been mixing chemicals for hours, setting each to bubble over the small gas flames and moving to the next without pause. He worked in silence broken by little more than occasional muttered calculation or exclamation of annoyance. Quilla had thought Alchemy to be more mystical, akin to sorcery almost. She found the reality of the craft, the sheer laborious difficulty of measuring and mixing, astounding and dull. No wonder he was so often grouchy.

And then, the joy.

"Huzzah," Gabriel murmured.

She couldn't have been more shocked had he leaped into the air and done a jig. She looked up from the notebook in which he'd ordered her to write down everything "And by everything, Hand-maiden, I mean each and every one, not only the ones you feel are worthwhile."

"My lord?"

Using a pair of metal tongs, he lifted one of the vials from its place over the flame and held it up to the sunlight. The liquid within, which had begun as a cloudy, stinking concoction of dull gray, had turned into a clear, odorless substance shimmering with a faint rainbow of color.

"This is worth its weight in gold. More than its weight, as it weighs very little." Gabriel snapped his fingers for a funnel, which she gave him, and he poured the vial's contents into a bottle and stoppered it, then set the bottle in a rack.

"What is it?"

"A cure for lovepox."

Her impressed expression must have pleased him, for he gave her what, for him, was the equivalent of a broad grin, though it really only touched the corners of his mouth. "That will feed this household for the next year and keep it clothed, as well."

"That small bottle?"

He nodded and held out his hands for her to strip the gloves from. "The men with the money to buy a cure, fortunately, are also the ones most likely to contract the disease. One to three drops of it will suffice for all but the most advanced cases."

Quilla looked at the bottle, then back to him. "You must feel very satisfied."

He'd been looking over the notes she'd taken, but now he looked up at her. "Because my work will provide for my family and staff? Yes. Of course."

She shook her head. "I meant because your work will help people. 'Tis easy enough for a man to earn a wage at work that helps nobody but himself."

He straightened. "Men who contract the lovepox deserve to face the consequences of their lasciviousness."

Quilla hung his long gloves on the rack and brought the basin and cloth to him from their place on the small table near the chaise lounge. "Your judgment is harsh, my lord."

He dipped his hands in the water and washed them, then held them out to her for drying, an unconscious action that made her smile inside. He would be allowing her to wash his hands next, without knowing it.

"Lovepox is perhaps the most easily prevented disease you can get," Gabriel said, "when all you must do in order not to contract it is bother to bathe. Stick your cock in whatever you please, but by the Void, wash it after."

Quilla knew little of lovepox, as it was a man's disease and not a woman's. "Yet you make the serum anyway."

"Because no matter how simple a thing it is to wash your prick," Gabriel said, "there will always be men who can't be bothered to do it. And if their filthy habits can provide coin for my family's benefit, why should I not?"

There could be no disputing that logic. Quilla unbuttoned his white coat, and hung that on the rack as well. She smoothed his vest and reached for his black jacket, holding it while he slipped his arms into it. Her hands tightened his tie while she spoke.

"Surely there are other things you make that have a more noble purpose."

He pointed at the wall of cages full of skittering mice, which she had learned were experiments. Not pets. "I'm working on many things. Yes."

"So you see, your work is so satisfactory. Because you do help people with it."

"Why must you insist on turning what I do into some sort of noble crusade for the good of the world?"

"Why will you not allow me to admire your efforts?"

The retort stopped him as he'd been preparing to turn from her. He looked down to where her hands still rested on his tie. "'Tis hardly as wondrous an occupation as filling Sinder's Quiver."

The words were kind, but the mocking tone was not. Quilla took her hands away. "I plead your mercy, my lord. I meant not to overstep my bounds."

Something flickered in his eyes. "I do what I must, as we all do. If there is any great benefit to society because of it, 'tis of little consequence to me."

"Your work is difficult and tedious, and requires great presence of mind to complete," she told him, not because she wanted to make him angry but because she thought it was what he needed to hear. "'Tis a pity you take so little joy from it."

"Joy?" he snapped, and then did turn from her. "Do not speak to me of joy, Handmaiden."

He stalked away, and she murmured, "I would teach you of joy, if you would allow it."

He paused in the doorway, and spoke without turning. "I have no need to learn it, as I know it full well already. Joy is naught but a pretty word to describe an emotion that exists only to exacerbate despair."

She spoke no more of it, and when he'd gone she set about tidying the mess he'd left behind. But what to do, she wondered, of the mess someone else had left, not in Gabriel's workshop, but in the man himself.

Another seventhday had arrived. Another day of rest and meditation. Quilla visited the small chapel again, this time lighting a candle as she sent her words to the Invisible Mother. She did not kneel to pray; kneeling was for Waiting, which she did in Service. Speaking to the Invisible Mother was something she did for herself.

She knew rote scripture, prayers of supplication and of thanks. Ritual words designed to bring comfort when one did not have the presence of mind to think of them oneself. Today, Quilla avoided the structured prayers, which had been written by priests, who were all men. And what did men truly know of what lay in a woman's heart?

"Help me to help him. Help him to let me."

She'd been at Glad Tidings for more than four weeks. Time for her body's cycle to have made one full pass through, though she took daily the dose of powdered tea which kept her from fertility. Time for her to learn the names of all the staff, to be invited to play at their cards and to take meals with them when her day's service had finished. Time for the people who lived with her to learn about her, and she them.

But not time enough for Gabriel to accept her.

He allowed her to help him with his work, and to serve him meals, and to help him with his ablutions, to a certain extent. Sometimes he shouted at her with impatience, and never apologized. Sometimes he spoke to her of his work, and exactly why one chemical mixed with another created a third, but only when heated or cooled a certain way. Some days he treated her with cool indifference and others as though he could barely stand the sight of her.

She didn't expect adoration, in fact appreciated that he did not expect her to adore him in return. It wasn't that she minded, either, the brusqueness, for she'd quickly determined it was his nature and not any fault of hers when he barked. What bothered her most was that no matter what she tried, or what she offered, he would not allow her to serve him with grace. He balked at every turn. Everything she offered brought a fight. Sometimes, he outright refused her offers. She was not to polish his boots, nor mend his clothes, nor to tie back his hair. She was not to tempt his palate with special foods, though she did her best to ignore that injunction and noticed he grumbled but always ate what she brought, anyway.

In short, she was an apprentice and a housemaid and a cook and serving lass, but she was not what she'd been brought there to be. A Handmaiden.

She thought she knew why, well enough. He didn't trust her. And she knew why he didn't, as well. But without him trusting her, she would never be able to fulfill her function.

"Help him trust me, Invisible Mother. Help me be what he needs."

The sound of shouting made her pause, head tilted to listen.

Shouting on seventhday could not be a good thing. She went to the door to listen further, and heard again raised voices, Gabriel's among them.

She left the chapel and hurried toward the sound of the commotion, which seemed centered in the entrance hall.

"Do not shield him behind your skirts!" she heard Gabriel cry as she came to the edge of the doorway and could see him.

Saradin stood in front of the door, Dane hiding behind her. Tears had streaked his face. His clothes were stained. From her place in the front room arch, Quilla could see his hands were black, as though from soot, or ink.

"I will shield him as I wish!" Saradin cried.

"He has been warned to stay out of my workspace time and again, and he ignored it yet again! He has gone and made a ruin of it, not to mention how much he has set back my work!"

Quilla had thought she'd seen Gabriel angry, but no harsh words could compare to the fury on his face as he paced back and forth. If Gabriel had been a storm, he'd have had lightning sparking from his every step and thunder booming with his words.

Saradin sneered. "Your work. Oh, yes. Your precious work."

"My work that provides you with those pretty dresses you wear, and the food you eat."

His voice dipped low. Dangerous. Shouting would have been less ominous, but Saradin either did not notice or did not care.

Dane peeked around from behind his mother, though she tried to push him back. His bravery touched Quilla's heart, for facing his father's wrath had to be daunting.

"I wanted to see the animals," he said. "I'm sorry, Papa. I wanted to see the animals you keep in cages."

"And you needed to stop and mess with the soot bucket on the way?" Gabriel fixed his gaze on the little boy's. "I found ash strewn all over my floor. Black handprints on my walls and on my chair. I found ink spilled on my desk, Dane! My notes have been ruined!"

Dane's lower lip quivered. "I'm sorry, Papa."

"My workshop is not a playground."

Quilla watched Gabriel interacting with his son, and something else became clear to her. He meant to forgive the boy.

Saradin ruined it in the next moment. "You leave him alone, Gabriel. He's a lad!"

Gabriel looked at her. "He has done wrong and needs to be punished."

"No! You will not! I will not allow it!"

Dane seemed better able to accept his fate than his mother, for the lad stepped forward, only to be yanked back by her hand. "Mama—"

"No." Saradin tossed her head and fixed Gabriel with a glare of contempt. "He won't touch you."

The woman played a game. A power game. For what prize?

"Dane, come here."

Saradin kept her grip on him, tight. Quilla felt someone brush against her, and she turned to find Florentine watching also from the shadow of the arch. The chatelaine shook her head.

"Such drama."

"The boy made a mess in his father's workspace, so I gather."

"And the mother will not hear of him being taken to task for it." Florentine shook her head again.

"You have seen this played before?"

"Oh, and aye." Florentine shrugged. "Watch her."

"He will be punished, Saradin. Do not defy me on this."

"You won't touch him!"

"And here it comes," murmured Florentine.

Saradin put a hand over her heart and staggered, eyes fluttering. The performance smacked of exaggeration to Quilla, but Dane reacted as any small boy would at the sight of his mother seemingly in pain. He cried out and ran to put an arm around her waist.

"Now they ring for Allora Walles."

"I need Allora," gasped Mistress Delessan, sinking onto the bench along the wall.

Whatever else one might say about Allora, Quilla thought, she knew her mistress, for she appeared almost before the words had left Saradin's lips. The maid put her arm around Saradin's other side.

Gabriel watched the scene without expression, and Quilla watched Gabriel. Guilt made him indulgent, she had seen that already. Now she saw something else. Love made him tolerant. Guilt and love, all tied together so he likely knew not the difference between them any longer.

And she understood him a bit better.

He turned on his heel and went up the stairs, leaving his weeping son and prevaricating wife behind. Quilla followed, reaching his rooms mere seconds after he did. The sound of crashing and cursing reached her before she got through the door.

She found him standing in the middle of the room, fists clenched, staring at the destruction one small boy had made and which had been made just a bit worse by his father.

"'Tis not so terrible," Quilla said as she came up behind him. "Nothing a bucket and mop can't fix."

He didn't look at her. He kicked an overturned basket, sending it flying. He swept the rest of the glass from a table, and it shattered. "He has been warned, repeatedly, not to come in here!"

"And so he should listen," she said. "But small ears have a way of not hearing what they ought, and small minds not retaining."

"You would excuse him, too?" He turned on her, as though she had accused him of a crime. "You would think me overharsh to punish him?"

"No, my lord."

"No?" He calmed at last, running a hand through his hair and seeming to take forcible control of himself.

She shook her head. "The lad needs structure and boundaries. Needs to learn respect. Aside from that, your workspace is dangerous. He could have been hurt."

"And yet my lady wife—"

"Your lady wife loves her son as much as you do. She simply does not love him in the same manner. Your son does need chastisement, my lord. But might I suggest an alternative?"

He had seen Waiting, Readiness and Waiting, Remorse. Now she turned her back to him and went to her knees, not sinking back on her heels and resting her hands on her lap, but linking the fingers together behind her neck. This was called Waiting, Submission.

His boot heels thudded as he stepped back, and his voice rasped. "What are you doing?"

"My back is strong. If you should feel the need to beat someone—"

"Sinder's Arrow, no!"

He sounded so appalled she turned her head to look at him. His eyes had gone wide, his cheeks paled from their normal tawny glow to the color of white cheese. "My lord?"

His expression had turned so disgusted she put down her hands and got to her feet. "I plead your mercy, my lord."

He shook his head. "What do you think of me, that I would take a strap to your back because my wife refuses to allow me to punish my son?"

She had truly distressed him, and his caused her own. She went to him and took him by the sleeve, leading him toward his chair in front of the fire. A sign of his consternation was that he allowed her to lead him, and to push him gently into the seat, and to Wait at his feet with her head against his thigh. He was shaking.

"My lord, I plead your mercy. I did not know 'twould upset you so."

"Is that what you think of me? That I am a violent man? That I gain pleasure from hurting others? Have you had other patrons who took their enjoyment at the expense of your back?"

She put her arms around his calves and held him tight. "I have had some, yes, who have needed the release of giving pain."

"My father used to use a strap on me when I stepped out of line. My father seemed to think I often stepped out of line."

She looked up at him, but he was not looking at her. His eyes stayed locked on the fire, and the flames danced in the dark depths, creating the illusion of fire in his eyes.

"And you think beating your son with a strap is your duty as a father? Or do you believe a beating would hasten a change in his behavior?"

His head snapped around to glare at her. "And what if my answer is both? Will you judge me overharsh then?"

"Perhaps your father felt 'twas the only way to be a father."

"To create fear in one who has never done aught but love him?" Gabriel sneered. "I vowed I would never be like him. A stupid, blind fool. Blind to the fact his wife had made him a cuckold, blind to the fact that his son did not need the back of his fist to love him. I vowed I would never raise my hand to someone weaker than I, Handmaiden. I would never have to look into the face of someone and know they feared me."

"I plead your mercy, my lord. I did not know. I will not offer it again."

He looked down at her, and his hand hovered over her head as though he meant to stroke her hair, but he did not. His fingers curled into a fist, and he settled it on the arm of his chair, instead. "You claim to know what I need before I know I need it. What made you believe I needed that?"

It had been something in his eyes, but she did not want to tell him that when it was clearly an abomination to him. "I misjudged."

"Even Handmaidens are not omniscient?"

"No, my lord. We are not."

Then his hand did come down to rest briefly upon her hair, the heat of his fingers like five tiny stars against her head before he took them away. "I would like some tea."

So she made it for him, and he drank it, and they spoke no more of Dane that evening.

Chapter 5

Y ou act like you've never been to a marketplace before." This
came from Florentine, who thumped the roof of the carriage
to make the driver stop.

Quilla peered out through the carriage's window. "And I suppose knowledge of something should always lead to lack of joy in it?"

"Familiarity does breed ennui, or so the saying goes, and for good reason." Florentine jiggled the door handle and shouted out the window, "Billy! Get your arse down here and open up this door!"

Florentine had gone all out for market day. Fresh gown only a season or two out of fashion. Gray curls brushed and held off her face with a scarf. Even a hat tied securely beneath her wobbling chin with two long ribbons.

Quilla had made little concession for the market, donning the same dark plum gown she'd brought with her. The ones Delessan had provided were fine enough, but her own clothes fit better. She hoped to find some cloth in the market to make a new dress. New stockings, as well, warmer against the winter draughts. Perhaps a new pair of boots that would come to the knee and protect her legs against the snow she'd heard fell soft and deep in these parts.

Billy tugged open the door with a grumble. "Don't get your knickers in a twist, your ladyshipness. I'm coming."

Florentine sniffed and held out her hand for Billy to help her down. "Once a week, Billy, is all you're asked to do. Try to be a little less a pain in the arse about it."

Billy took Florentine's hand and kissed it, running his lips lasciviously over the back and waggling his brows when he looked up at her. "And once a week just ain't enough."

Florentine jerked her hand out of his grasp and slapped his face, but fondly. If a slap could be called fond, Quilla thought, watching them.

"Get out of my way, you great bloody fool, else I turn you on your arse in the street."

Billy grinned and held out his hand for her to take again. "Promises, promises."

Florentine sniffed but let him help her down. "Come on, Quilla. Don't let this bloke scare you off."

Quilla took the hand that Billy offered, not expecting to get the flirtatious treatment from him and not disappointed, either. Billy held her hand with respect bordering on reverence, or awe. He wouldn't even meet her eyes.

"Thank you, Billy," Quilla said as her feet hit the street.

He mumbled a response and received a rap on the skull from Florentine for his troubles. "Answer the lady when she speaks to you, imbecile!"

"Welcome," he mumbled, rubbing his head and scowling.

"No worries." Quilla rolled her eyes at Florentine. "Really, Florentine. You're going to give him a headache."

"Well deserved," Florentine said with another haughty sniff.

"Take the carriage round to the stable and meet us back here at the sixchime."

Billy nodded, gave Florentine a wink and Quilla a nod, then hopped back up to the driver's seat and clucked to the horses.

Florentine didn't bother watching him go, just hoisted her market basket over her shoulder and moved off into the throng. "This way."

Quilla had to step lively to keep up. "I think Billy likes you."

"Billy is an idiot."

"Because he likes you?"

Florentine turned to look at Quilla as she walked. "Among other things."

Quilla dodged a threesome of well-dressed, chattering ladies who didn't bother to watch where they were walking. "You don't like his attention?"

"Billy Felton is interested in sating the little man between his legs, naught else." Florentine shouldered her way past a group gathered round a man with a dancing monki on the end of a leash. "Believe me, it's no great flattering thing to get his attention."

Quilla lifted her skirts to keep the hem from dragging in a puddle of ale leaking from a cask in front of a booth. "He didn't lick my hand. He does discriminate."

Florentine stopped, turning her bulk and disregarding the way the basket on her shoulder smacked a tradesman in the head while she did. Giving him a quick "Bugger off," which made him grumble but sent him away, Florentine gave her attention to Quilla. "He'd be on you like a fly to shite if you weren't the master's. Mark my words."

"How flattering a comparison of my desirability." Quilla laughed. "And I'm not so sure. He seemed quite enamored of you."

Florentine made a sour face as she turned toward the booth behind her and slapped down two coins. She lifted two tins of fruit preserves and put them in her basket, haggling only a moment over the price. "I spent long enough living as a lad to know how they think, Quilla Caden. Billy is not interested in courting, only fucking."

"And you're not interested in that?"

Florentine looked over. "Not interested in either, Miss Hoity-Toity. Thought you understood. I don't take my pleasure that way."

"Ah." Quilla nodded, following Florentine on her journey through the market. "It's not my business, really."

"No, 'tisn't, Miss Nose-in-My-Basket."

Quilla smiled at Florentine. "I wonder, then, why you've dressed so tidily today, and taken such pains with your hair. If not to impress poor Billy, then who?"

Florentine stopped in front of another booth, this time to put some fruit in her basket, which she paid for without much further quibbling. She fixed Quilla with a steely glare. "Who says I has to have a reason to wear nice clothes?"

Quilla shrugged. "No reason. I just thought—"

"Not all of us is ruled by what's betwixt our legs."

"I know that." Quilla decided to stop teasing the other woman. "I just thought to be glad for you, that's all. If you had someone special."

Florentine let out a guffaw so loud it turned heads. She yanked Quilla into an alley, out of the flow of traffic. "I don't need you to be glad for me, Handmaiden. And would you only be glad for me if you knew I had a lover, is that it? Can I not have a good life without a fuck partner?"

"No, of course not," Quilla soothed. "I didn't mean that at all."

Florentine straightened her shirtwaist and smoothed her skirt, visibly regaining her temper. "If I have a lover, 'tis none of your concern."

"Of course not."

Florentine sniffed. "As it happens, I do have plans to meet a friend of mine."

"Not that 'tis any of my concern."

"That's right." Florentine sniffed again. "And as a matter of fact, Miss Full-of-Herself, we are also here today to retrieve the other lord Delessan. He's arrived and will be at the Foxglove Inn. It doesn't do to represent our master looking as though I came right from the kitchens, does it?"

Quilla shook her head. "I suppose not. Where shall we meet the infamous Jericho Delessan, then?"

"At the fivechime we'll go and pick him up, with plenty of time to do our marketing before then." Florentine hiked her basket higher on her shoulder "Now, I'm off, and don't think you can follow me round like a stray dog. I've got business of mine own to attend. You find your own amusements, hear me?"

"I hear you." Quilla gave a mock pout. "Though I am so disappointed I won't get to spend the day in your company, Florentine. 'Tis always so pleasant an acquaintance."

Florentine's grin seemed reluctant, but she gave one, anyway. "Get on with you, ya great prat."

Quilla laughed. "I've business of my own, as well. I've money jingling in my purse and an entire day in which to spend it."

"Don't let it go to your head. I don't need to tell you there's thieves in this market as well as honest merchants."

"I believe I can take care of myself."

Florentine shrugged. "Don't come crying to me when your purse is empty and your hands emptier." She looked Quilla up and down. "What are you planning to buy?"

Quilla smiled and winked. "Now who's being a Nose-in-the-Basket?" she called over her shoulder as she ducked out of the alleyway and back into the crowd.

Quilla walked for a while, looking at all there was to see. She stopped at many of the booths to look at the goods and chat with the merchants. Most of them were thrilled to talk about the quality and perfection of their wares, and she played them as she did her patrons, flattering and listening with all the right responses. Consequently, most of them smiled and talked with her without getting irritated when she didn't stop to buy.

There were a few who saw her Handmaiden's attire as a badge of shame, something to be commented upon. She nodded and smiled at their indiscreet insults and moved on. More people didn't notice, or didn't bother to comment.

She stopped to run her fingers along several bolts of fine linen, flaxen, and silk, all woven in vivid shades of red, purple, green, and gold. The material was expensive, exorbitantly so. She had enough money to purchase a piece the size of a head scarf, and even that would have taken all the cash in her purse.

"It's absolutely lovely," she told the wizened merchant as she held up a length of the silk to her sleeve to see the drape of it. *Exquisite.* "But far too expensive, I'm afraid."

"It's Alyrian," said the merchant, like that should make a difference. "Old Alyrian, not new. From before they broke the borders. This is rare, this is. You won't find cloth like this anyplace else in the market. Or the city, for that matter."

"I don't doubt it." She stroked it. "I've never seen finer."

The merchant rolled one blue eye at her; the other was blind white. "And I doubt you ever will. Go on, hold up the linen, too. You'll fall in love with it."

Quilla didn't want to waste the merchant's time, but a quick glance around showed her nobody waited to buy this particular cloth. The merchant knew that, too, and urged her to drape an additional length of the linen over her arm.

"Banded with this fringe of gold, I can see it on you. A lovely gown. For a party, or for a wedding, perhaps?" The merchant grinned, showing gapped teeth, surprisingly white.

"Even the flaxen is too dear for my pockets, I'm afraid." Quilla put the cloth down with regret. "Though 'tis truly gorgeous. I haven't any place to wear it, even if I could afford it."

The merchant's good eye flickered over her unadorned gown. "Maybe a patron would be pleased to see you in't?"

Quilla quirked a grin at him. "You are trying to play upon my sense of duty, sir. How utterly unfair."

The merchant spread his fingers with a shrug, but looked unapologetic despite the gesture. "Just speaking true."

"If 'twould please my patron to dress me in cloth this fine, then I shall leave it to him to buy it. He was most adequate with his coin, but not generous enough for me to buy this." She let her hand linger once more on the silk. Softer than any cloth she'd ever felt, superb in design and craftsmanship, the liquid, flowing colors almost made her want to weep at their beauty.

"'Twould look magnificent against your skin."

She turned at the sound of the voice, meaning to chastise the merchant for trying to tease her into the purchase again, but stopped herself. The man standing next to her was tall and fair-haired, with bright, laughing, blue-sky eyes and clothing of high quality. His vest, bright blue, made his eyes seem even bluer, and she got an immediate sense he'd chosen it for that exact reason. He looked back at the cloth.

"It suits you."

Quilla took her hands away. "It doesn't suit my purse, unfortunately."

The man nodded. "Alyrian fabric, especially Old Alyrian, is costly. Worth the price, but costly."

"See?" cried the merchant, clapping gnarled hands. "What did I tells you?"

"Nevertheless, I can't afford it." Quilla replaced the bolt firmly. "Thank you. I will take three lengths of the dark blue flaxen, however."

The merchant nodded and plucked up the bolt, taking it to the measuring table to cut the piece for her. Quilla looked at the other offerings at the fabric booth, aware the fair-haired man had not moved away.

"Wait," he called out to the merchant, who'd lifted his pair of silver shears to cut the fabric. "She doesn't really want that."

The merchant turned. "She don't?"

"I don't?" Quilla wasn't sure whether to laugh or frown at his presumptuousness. "How do you know?"

"Because you don't want another gown of dark color." The man shook his head, his eyes twinkling with good humor she felt compelled to return, even though his assumption annoyed her.

"No?"

"No."

She looked down at the dress she had on. "And why not? It's served me well enough before."

He shook his head again. "Perhaps in function, not necessarily in form. Dark colors are well enough if you want to be solely functional. But not if you want to bring beauty to that function."

Quilla pursed her mouth, taken aback. The merchant had begun to grumble, putting back the bolt of material she'd chosen.

"Let me know when yer ready," he said sourly, moving around the booth's edge to help another customer.

"And who are you to presume anything about me?" His unsubtle accusation that she was less than beautiful stung, not because she thought herself as such, but because she did not believe herself not to be.

"What woman doesn't wish to present herself in the most flattering way at all times?"

Quilla crossed her arms, tilting her head to frown at him. "And you don't find the gown I'm wearing flattering?"

He gave her a sly, sideways grin, then a wink that made her press her lips together. "I think you'd be perfectly lovely in a burlap sack. But the dress is not flattering, no. The color does not bring out your eyes, which would benefit greatly from a color like this."

He reached for a bolt of vivid green fabric, not so bright as to be an unreasonable choice, but far more vibrant than she usually wore. The color of emeralds, the weave of it seemed to shimmer slightly, though the cloth itself was of fabric inexpensive enough not to overburden her purse.

"And with your skin tone, against the black silk beauty of your hair, a gown of this material will make you glimmer and shimmer like a goddess herself."

Quilla had been touching the cloth, enjoying the smoothness of it, imagining how it would look sewn into a gown. At his words, she took her hand away and looked up.

"I'm no goddess."

"Woman you begin and woman you shall end," he quoted with a half bow, never taking his eyes from hers. "But do you not also know that every woman has a bit of goddess inside her, my lady?"

His use of one of the Order's principles did nothing to help his case. "I'm not a lady, yours or otherwise. I'll take the dark blue."

The man put his hand over his heart, pouting as though wounded. "At least don't deny yourself the pleasure of that fabric merely to spite me. It really would make a delightful gown for you. And," he pointed out, "'tis less expensive than the blue. You could buy the green and another length, too, for the same expense."

"Know you the contents of my purse, as well?" she demanded, putting her hands on her hips. "You're an arrogant swain, aren't you?"

"I am, indeed. And completely without shame."

Quilla regarded him for a moment, realizing something interesting. She liked this stranger, even with his blatant flirting. Much of the time, attention she garnered from men bordered on lewdness, if not outright rudeness. Or else men seemed afraid to approach her. Very few seemed able to speak to her normally, as a man to a woman, with all the verbal dancing that went along with it.

"And if I buy the green, as you suggest, what other cloth should I buy as well?"

"The crimson," he said without hesitation, "though I can tell you right now, you won't."

That set her back on her heels for a moment. "No? You are so certain? And why not?"

"Because you'd only wear a color like that to entertain a lover," he said simply, without a hint of lasciviousness, though nevertheless her cheeks burned. "And you are not a woman who takes lovers."

Most of the time, Quilla knew what to say or how to stay silent when she did not. Now, silence was a necessity, not an option, for though she opened her mouth to speak, nothing came out.

"I've stunned you into speechlessness. I apologize." The man gave another half bow, hand over his heart. "You asked me a question and I gave you an answer."

"You don't even know me!"

"Does the bee need to know the flower before it sups? A bird know the wind before it takes flight? The sea know the shore before it creeps upon it?" The man smiled. "Does a man need to know a woman before he loves her?"

"Yes!" Quilla cried, angry now, an emotion in which she rarely indulged because too often it served no purpose in her life. "Yes, he does! And you don't know me at all!"

Quilla stalked away from the fabric booth without buying anything, her cheeks flushed and her heart pounding. *Does a man need to know a woman before he loves her? What rubbish! What nonsense! What an arrogant cad!* Fuming, she pushed through the crowd without heeding the people who complained as she forced her way past them.

By the time she reached the other side of the marketplace, she'd returned herself to some semblance of serenity. Deep breaths. Meditation. *True patience is its own reward,* repeated over and over until she began to believe it. It was imperfect, but better than the anger had been.

That he'd been correct did not make her feel better. Of course she was not a woman who took lovers. When she was in the service of a patron, she belonged to that patron. Sometimes, but not always, and far less often than people understood, that service included sex. She did not consider patrons, even those with whom she had sex, to be lovers.

When not in the service of a patron, Quilla did not have time to tumble from bed to bed. And what man would willingly allow his lover or wife to leave him for service to another? Love might be the most powerful of human emotions, but even jealousy could overpower it. No. Though many might consider Handmaidens one more breed of whore, the fact was, Quilla was more often celibate than not.

Her stomach panged, and Quilla put a hand to it. Spotting a small café ahead, she sat at one of the tables and ordered a flagon of warmed, spiced wine to combat the chill in the air and a crock of vegetable stew. It arrived along with a hunk of fresh brown bread, oozing with creamy butter, and she dug in at once.

"Excuse me, mistress?"

Quilla looked up from her meal to see a young lad clutching a paper-wrapped package. "Yes?"

He held out the bundle. "Gentleman in blue said to give you this."

Quilla looked around but saw nobody fitting the description. "What gentleman?"

"The fancy-talking one."

Quilla took the package and dug in her waistpurse for a coin to give the lad, who looked at it shrewdly and said, "He gave me two."

"Then you don't need mine," Quilla said and made as though to grab it, laughing when the lad darted away into the crowd.

She undid the cord holding the paper closed, and let out a gasp when she saw what was inside. The green fabric, along with the same material in deep crimson. Quilla touched the fabric and looked around again for her benefactor, but saw no sign of him.

"Arrogant swain," she murmured, but with a smile.

She tucked the fabric back up in the paper and retied the cord. Then she finished her meal, thinking about the fair-haired man who'd gifted her with such expensive treasures. No sign of him.

She'd received expensive presents before, been decked with jewels and cloth of gold, with live butterflies to adorn her hair. Somehow, the simplicity of this gift moved her more than any she'd had.

Does a man need to know a woman before he loves her?

"Foolish," she murmured, dipping her bread again into the stew.

By the time the sixchime sounded, Quilla was well ready to return to Glad Tidings. She'd spent a fair amount of her coin on winter-weight leggings, new boots, fur-trimmed gloves. Delessan had been generous with his purse this first time, and though she could have spent the money on baubles and trinkets, Quilla thought it was better used to provide herself with practical things. She had little need for cosmetics and perfume. She'd also purchased several books, a sheaf of fine writing paper, several pens and pots of ink, and a leather-bound journal she intended to give to Gabriel for use in his work. The sturdy cover would hold up better than the one that had been ruined. She'd also bought a small peg and block game for Dane, meant not only to entertain but to engage the mind.

"Finally, her ladyship arrives." Florentine stuck her head out through the carriage window, but her usual brusqueness was toned down. Her plump cheeks were pink, and her mouth kept darting in and out of a smile. "Shake your moneymaker, Handmaiden!"

"'Tis impossible to shake my brain," Quilla replied with a chuckle, handing her packages to Billy to stow. "And I'm not late. The sixchime has not yet finished ringing."

"'Tis your arse I was referring to, and I know you can shake that. Get in. Let's go."

Quilla thanked Billy for opening the carriage door, and grabbed hold of the handle to pull herself up and into the carriage. "I thought you were supposed to be picking up Master Jericho, Florentine."

"We did, you daft lass," retorted Florentine, and as Quilla's eyes adjusted to the carriage's dim interior, she saw the man sitting on the seat.

A fair-haired man with eyes she knew to be a deep, twinkling blue. The man from the fabric booth.

"Jericho Delessan, at your service," he said. "A pleasure to make your acquaintance."

If Florentine guessed the pair had already met, she didn't let on. Instead, she made swift introductions between Quilla and Jericho, then settled back in her seat, her kerchief over her face, and began to snore.

Delessan's carriage was large enough to seat four, but with Florentine sprawled across the seat, Jericho soon had to scoot ever closer to the door. After a moment, he smiled at Quilla.

"Would it be all right if I sit next to you for the rest of the ride? This is rather uncomfortable."

She nodded. "Of course."

He switched seats, and she made certain to give him plenty of room. "Thank you for the material," she said after a few moments, deciding there was no point in pretending he hadn't given it to her.

"If I'd known we were going to be sharing an abode, I'd have given it to you in person."

He thinks his smile is charming. "If you knew that, you shouldn't have given it to me at all."

His eyebrows lifted, giving her a clearer view of his vivid blue-sky eyes. "No?"

Quilla shook her head, not smiling in return. "No. I know you know what I am. If you know anything about my place in the household, you would know 'tis inappropriate."

"A Handmaiden is not allowed to have friends?"

She gazed at him for a long moment designed to make him uncomfortable in the silence. It didn't seem to work, because he only continued smiling pleasantly at her, leaning back in his seat, arms crossed over his chest and one leg propped on the other.

"We are not friends. We are strangers, sir."

His smile became a sunny grin, far less studiedly charming and supremely more appealing because of it. "But now we have been introduced. We are not strangers."

"Then we are no more than acquaintances. Certainly not friends."

"All friends begin as strangers."

Quilla bit the inside of her cheek. "Indeed."

"So I ask you again. Handmaidens are not allowed to have friends?"

She studied him. "Is that what you wish? To be my friend?"

"Certainly." He spoke as though she ought to have no doubt as to the purity of his intentions, but his smile and the gleam in his eye told her otherwise.

"'Tis too early in our acquaintance to know if we shall be friends, or not." Quilla's reply was meant to set him back, but Jericho didn't seem at all put off.

"And too early for us to be enemies, as well."

Again, she bit the inside of her cheek to keep from smiling at his irredeemable cockiness. "I concede that to be true."

"Fine," he said, as though that settled everything. Then he turned to look out the window and said nothing more to her for the rest of the trip.

U ncle Jericho!"

"Nephew Dane!" Jericho got on one knee, mindless of his fine trousers and the mud on the cobblestones, to gather the boy into his arms. "Have you been well?"

"He has been abominably behaved." Gabriel's reply made his brother look up, and Jericho stood to offer his hand.

"And I suppose the blame for that lies upon me, does it?"

Gabriel shook Jericho's hand with no more expression than he would have had the other man been a stranger. "He comes home from trips with you far too used to being indulged."

Jericho looked down to Dane, who was hugging his legs. "Is this true? Have you been getting into trouble?"

Dane had the grace to look shamefaced. "Yes, Uncle."

Quilla handed Billy most of her packages as she stepped out of the carriage, keeping only one bag. Gabriel's gaze found and caught her, and the frown creasing his brow eased a bit. She could not help the smile that crossed her lips when she saw him. Jericho looked from her to his brother and back again, and he smiled, too, but as though he were assessing the situation, not out of any great pleasure.

"I was not aware you'd gone to the market, Handmaiden."

She stepped forward. "I plead your mercy, my lord. Were you missing me?"

"Yes, brother. Were you missing her?"

The smile Gabriel had put on for Quilla faded at his brother's remark. "No. I know I told you I did not require your presence today."

"Next time, I will be certain to tell you if I am going away from the house." Quilla watched Dane, who danced around his uncle, trying to dig into his pockets. "Young Master Delessan, I have brought something for you."

Dane's face brightened, and he ran to her. "Have you? Oh, have you, Quilla Caden?"

She held out the small wooden game, which consisted of a block of wood drilled with holes in the form of a triangle. The leather bag of fitted pegs fit on the back of the game, and they clacked as Dane took the present from her. He looked at it, then gave her an unabashed squeeze around the middle that knocked away her breath.

"Thank you!"

He was not really an ill-mannered lad, she thought, returning his hug. "You are most welcome."

"So the sweets in my pockets shall go unclaimed?" Jericho's words made Dane turn and run back to his uncle.

Gabriel frowned. "Jericho, the boy doesn't need—"

"No, maybe not," Quilla murmured. "But what child doesn't want them?"

Gabriel's head swiveled to look at her. "Want and need are not the same thing, Handmaiden."

She couldn't deny the truth of his words. "No. But both hold equal power, don't they?"

"If I had sweets in my pockets, would you dance around me the way he does?"

"If it pleased you." The standard reply, but said with teasing. She put her hand in the bag and closed her fingers upon the leather journal. "I brought something for you, as well."

"Did you?" He cocked his head to look at her. Behind him, Jericho had lifted Dane in the air and the boy was laughing himself into hiccups. Gabriel kept his eyes on hers. "What is it?"

She handed him the journal. "For your work. To replace the one that was ruined."

"I have other notebooks. You needn't have wasted your coin on another."

She raised an eyebrow, her gaze solid on his. "Then perhaps I shall take this one back?"

He did not laugh, as he never did, but the corners of his mouth tilted the barest amount. "Perhaps I can force myself to use it."

She handed it to him, and when he took it, their fingers touched. "I hope it pleases you."

Before he could answer, a feminine shriek shot across the court-yard. "Jericho!"

Gabriel straightened, his gaze leaving Quilla's and growing distant again. He took two measured steps away from her, the sudden formality between them as solid as a wall of brick. "Saradin."

Saradin lifted her skirts to skip across the stones, her golden curls atumble over her shoulders. "Jericho Delessan! You have returned!"

"Ah, sister," said Jericho, turning.

His posture, so easy in the marketplace, in the carriage, and with his nephew, became stiff. He left off holding up the bag of sweets with which he'd been tormenting Dane and handed them to the boy, then put his hand over his heart and executed a perfect bow that stopped Saradin in her tracks.

"Brother," she replied coyly. "It has been too long since your presence graced this house. It has been sore lacking in frivolity."

She threw a glance over her shoulder at Gabriel, whose posture now echoed his brother's. Two men, so alike in stature and form, the only difference in their features the color of their hair and eyes. They faced off, a woman and a child between them, and the air fair crackled with sudden tension that Saradin appeared not to notice.

She held out her hand to Jericho, who seemed to have no choice but to take it or else seem rude. He brought it to his lips with such brief attention that it was clear to Quilla, at least, that he wanted no part of Saradin's flirting. Gabriel's wife, on the other hand, giggled like a schoolgirl and fluttered her hands at him before turning back to her husband with flushed cheeks and bright eyes.

"Your brother has been naughty, has he not, my lord husband? Depriving us of his company these long months?"

"Indeed." Gabriel looked at his wife, not at his brother. "He has been most inconsiderate."

"But he's back now." Saradin nodded as though pleased with herself. "And oh, what gay times we shall have. I've learned a new card game, Jericho, which I must teach you. 'Tis most merry."

Jericho nodded stiffly. Gabriel might not be looking at him, but he had not taken his eyes off his brother until now, when his gaze flickered to Quilla, then back to Saradin. His smile grew bright again, though it didn't seem to meet his eyes.

"I look forward to it."

"Come, wife," said Gabriel. "I'm certain my brother is fair weary from his journey and would like to eat and rest."

"Oh, yes, of course." Saradin turned on tiny, slippered toes and clapped her perfect little hands. "I've told Florentine to make tea in the parlor. Let us see if she's done so!"

She swept past Quilla without a second look, and Quilla's amused glance followed her. The woman was either oblivious or a great actress, or a good mixture of both. It did not bother her to be so ignored. She knew the woman treated the house staff in the same manner—invisible unless needed.

With another look at his brother, Jericho took Dane by the hand and started toward the house. "Let's go find Jorja, shall we?"

Dane skipped alongside his uncle, chattering away, and after a moment, Gabriel looked at her. "You are dismissed, Handmaiden. Seek your entertainment elsewhere until the morrow, when I should have need of you again."

"Yes, my lord." She watched him go, then went inside to her own room.

Chapter 6

Jericho's presence at Glad Tidings helped the house live up to its name. With Gabriel's brother in residence, more laughter rang through the halls, Florentine made better desserts because the other lord Delessan liked sweets, and the young lord Delessan ran rampant through the house, terrorizing the staff with his uncle-approved escapades.

The rest of the house might have been in high spirits, but Gabriel withdrew to his work and his temper, leaving Quilla at a loss as to how, exactly, to soothe him. He snapped more ferociously when she confused amelium with bareelium. He threw vials of half-completed potions against the walls when they did not coagulate correctly, and left her with the mess of broken glass and stinking fluid to clean. He worked at an almost frantic pace, as though by focusing on his work he need not focus on his brother, his son, or his wife.

Quilla tried hard to understand him, but he would not be understood. He did not want to be understood, nor soothed. Placating him was impossible. He wanted cocao when she made tea, scones when she brought simplebread, her aid when she busied herself with other tasks, and her absence when she offered her help.

"This is clearly not crystallized quartz!" he shouted at her one day when she tried to hand him a bottle with a faded label she thought had contained the ingredient he wanted. "Are you an in-bred simpleton that you cannot comprehend what it is I wish of you?"

"Are you an arrogant, crotchety curmudgeon with absolutely no idea of how to treat people?" she shot back, and threw the vial down so hard it bounced on the scarred wooden floor but didn't shatter. "Yes! Yes, you are!"

She turned to stalk out of the room, heart pounding and tears sparking behind her eyes. *True patience*, she reminded herself, but it didn't work. Fury made her hands shake. She hadn't made it half-way to the door when he caught her by the elbow and spun her around to face him.

"How dare you speak to me that way?"

She yanked her arm from his grip. The faint rise of his brows showed surprise, perhaps at her strength. "How dare you continue to abuse me so?"

He made as though to grab her again, and she stepped back, her arms going up to cover herself in a defensive posture. He watched her and did not try to reach for her again.

"I thought Handmaidens were bound to please their patrons."

She did not relax her stance. *Submissive* did not mean *without defense*. There were patrons who did not understand the line, and despite what he'd told her about never giving in to the desire to hit someone, at that moment she did not trust him.

"And patrons are understood to at least attempt to be pleased."

He scowled. "I hired you to assist me with my work. To make my life easier."

"And yet nothing I do makes you happy!" she shot back. "You're incapable of being pleased!"

He took a step toward her, and she raised her hands, her posture clear. She would strike back if he touched her. Gabriel looked at her hands and did not move closer.

"You would allow me to take a strap to your back, but you would not allow me to come closer when I would apologize for my behavior?"

She narrowed her eyes. "One has naught to do with the other. Is that your intent? To plead my mercy for being an insufferable prat? Or maybe you intend to bruise my arm again with your inconsiderate grip."

He blinked at her words, and in an instant had bowed his head, one hand over his heart. "I do plead your mercy, Handmaiden. I was out of turn. I beg your forgiveness. I have been . . ."

"Insufferable," she repeated. "Intolerable. Rude. Shall I go on?"

He kept his head lowered but raised his eyes, hand still over his heart. "I don't believe 'tis necessary, no. I am full aware of how ill I have treated you."

She put her hands down and brushed hair from her face, then put her hands upon her hips. "I have told you already. If I do not please, you need only release me. Say it thrice over. 'I release thee,' and I shall go. You can get another Handmaiden."

"I do not want another Handmaiden." His voice was low.

She lifted her chin. "Then might I suggest you explain to me how I might tell crystallized quartz from its neighbor on your table? So that I might be better able to assist you."

He stood straight and took his hand away from his heart. "You are not leaving?"

"Have you achieved absolute solace?"

"No." A hint of tilt at the corners of his lips. "It would not appear I have."

She swept by him, head held high, back to the table. "Then no. I am not leaving."

For the rest of that day, he did not raise his voice to her, and she felt his eyes upon her when she knew he thought she could not see.

Glad Tidings did indeed have a garden of stone. Quilla knew in the spring the beds would once more bloom with life, but for now all the plants had been cut back to the root, leaving behind little but dry, brown stems. The paths were well kept and of finely crushed white stone, lined with larger red rocks she knew had been imported from another place. Large boulders dotted the garden, too big to have been brought, which meant they'd been there before the garden was planned. Many of them had interesting shapes, carved by weather and wind.

Today, both were unfavorable; the sky gray and overcast, promising snow, and the wind's finger pinched her cheeks until they burned. It would likely be one of the last days she'd be able to walk these paths until the springtime sun warmed them, and she intended to take advantage of it. Quilla bent to pick up a stray stone from the grass around the pond and tossed it into the water, watching the ripples and smiling at the sight of several fat copperfish rising to the surface, slow from cold but still as lovely.

"Care you don't fall in. The edge is soft there."

She turned to see who'd spoken, and ducked her head in acknowledgment. "I will take care, thank you."

Jericho grinned and stepped up beside her, pulling out a small bundle from his pocket. He showed her what it was, a napkin filled with crusts of bread. "I come to feed them sometimes."

"Don't let me disturb you, then." She turned to go.

"Don't." Jericho put a hand on her arm. "I didn't mean to chase you away. Here. I'll even share the crumbs."

Quilla smiled. "You don't have to do that."

Though his hair and eyes were different, his smile was much like his brother's. At least in shape. Jericho's smile was broader. More ready to bloom.

"Of course I don't have to." He held out the bundle. "Here."

She took a crust and tossed it into the water. A great, gaping mouth opened beneath it immediately, swallowing the bread whole, and she yelped in surprise. Jericho laughed.

"Don't worry, Quilla. I don't believe he has a taste for Handmaidens."

She slanted him a glance. "What on earth is it?"

Jericho tossed another crust, which disappeared almost as rapidly as the first, though from a dozen tiny mouths rather than the large one. "This pond is much deeper than it appears. Plenty of room in it for eels."

Quilla took a step farther back from the edge. "That mouth was enormous."

Jericho grinned. "We've never seen his entire length, but eels can grow to twenty arrows long in idyllic conditions."

She looked at the pond, which looked as though it could be rowed from end to end in half a chime. "This hardly looks to be idyllic conditions for an eel that size."

"Well, you never know what environment is going to cause a creature to thrive, and which is going to cause it to suffer."

"No, I suppose not." She broke her crust into small pieces and tossed them into the water one by one.

"And what of you, Tranquilla Caden?"

She frowned, her eyes on the water. "What do you mean?"

"Are you thriving?"

"Are you comparing me to an eel?" She gave him her full gaze, a brow lifted.

Jericho smiled, and again the resemblance to his brother was made more obvious. "I am."

Quilla made a small, unamused face. "I'm not an eel, my lord Delessan."

"You don't have to call me that. You made it pretty clear you're my brother's. Not mine."

Quilla studied him. "Should you need the services of a Handmaiden, I'm certain the Order could provide you with one of your own."

Jericho shook his head. "I don't need a Handmaiden. I'm fairly able to content myself, thanks."

That earned him a small smile. "'Tis well, then, that the world is not filled with men like you, else I'd be out of a job."

"Ah," he countered swiftly. "But if the world were filled with men—and women—like me, you would have no need of a job, because your purpose would be fulfilled."

"True." She nodded in agreement. "But that seems unlikely to happen within my lifetime, at any rate, so I shall be grateful for the chance to work as long as I can."

"Is that really all it is to you? A job?"

Quilla dusted the final crumbs from her hands, and though they were but the tiniest specks, more dust than anything else, the water still rippled with copperfish silent below its surface, feeding upon what she'd dropped.

"I'm not certain what you mean."

He stared at her until she looked up at him, then replied, "Are you happy in my brother's service?"

She gave him what she'd learned was often the best answer to an inappropriate question. "Why do you wish to know?"

"Curiosity."

"Ah." Quilla bent to pick up another stone but hesitated before tossing it, remembering that gaping maw, the glimpse of one elliptical eye. "And are you always so concerned about your brother's affairs?"

Jericho laughed and touched a fingertip to his brow in acknowledgment. "Point taken."

She stared back at the water. "I am as happy here in this service as I have been in any other."

"Really?" Jericho bent to pick up some rocks of his own to plunk into the water. "Why do you sound so underenthused?"

She looked at him. "I'm not!"

"You're happy here. Really." His tone clearly stated he didn't believe her.

Quilla nodded. "As happy—"

"That does nothing to convince me." Jericho turned to face her. "My brother is difficult, to describe him kindly."

"I know this." She smiled. "I've had worse. Few worse, but some."

Jericho rattled the pebbles in his palm. "Don't you have to say that about him?"

Quilla began walking along the path. Jericho followed. The eel made ripples in the water and she caught a flash of silver in the pond's depths. Perhaps her imagination. Or not.

"No, I don't have to say it. 'Tis true enough. I've had patrons who were worse than your brother."

"And you liked them, anyway."

Quilla laughed and looked at him. "No, my lord Delessan. I didn't like them."

"Don't you have to like them?"

Now she stopped walking and put her hands on her hips. "Sinder's Arrow, no. I don't have to like them. I am required to serve. To provide absolute solace. I do not need to like them!"

Jericho frowned as though pondering. "How on earth can you provide absolute solace to someone you don't like?"

"'Tis no easy task," Quilla admitted. "It takes much meditation. An unselfish heart is its own reward."

"Do you like most of them?"

Most people never bothered to ask about her work. On her rare visits home, her family ignored her Calling, preferring to act as though she'd been away on retreat, or to school. Her patrons didn't seem interested in anyone but themselves, and most assumed she liked them, even when she didn't.

"Most I do. Yes."

"And they become your friends?"

"Many of them. Many I grow to have great fondness for. Yes."

"But you have to be their friend." He sounded very sure of himself. "So are they truly your friends, if you must needs make a friendship with them? When you have no choice, is it real admiration, or necessity?"

Quilla frowned. "I always have a choice, my lord Delessan."

He laughed, tipping his head toward the late harvesttime sky. "So you say. Think you that because I have no need for a Handmaiden I know not their purpose?"

He looked at her with one eye squinted against the sun that had decided to break through the clouds. "You have to be their friends, their confidantes, their lovers, their nursemaids. Their caretakers and serving girls and cleaning maids."

She lifted her chin. "And what of it?"

"Do you not know the difference between a friend of choice and one of necessity, Quilla Caden? When's the last time you had one?"

"I have friends."

"Of choice?"

"Yes!"

"Can I count myself among them?"

She gave him a long, level look. "I don't know."

"Fair enough, Quilla, but be warned. I intend to make you know."

He touched his fingertips to the base of his throat, his lips, and his forehead in quick succession—the Traveler's Gesture—and with a smile still on his lips, turned and left her to stare at the water's black surface. The surface of the pond had gone still again, but Quilla knew she would never forget the way the water had frothed, or the secrets it held beneath the calm surface.

The last thing Quilla expected to find when she opened the cupboard lift was a face. She let out a yelp, then put her hand over her heart. "Young lord Delessan! You scared half the life out of me!"

Dane giggled, then looked apologetic. "I plead your mercy. I was playing pirates."

By himself. The lad needed playmates beyond his uncle and the houseboys. Quilla smiled. "And the lift is the place to do it?"

He nodded eagerly, his small face wreathed with a grin. "Aye! For 'tis small, like the hold of a ship! And I am pretending to be captured by pirates."

"And who is playing the pirate?" She set the tray on the hall floor. Her work with Gabriel was done for the day; she'd been dismissed.

Dane looked crestfallen. "Nobody. Sometimes in the summer when Robie Vassermidst comes to stay with his grandma and grandda he comes to visit me here and we play pirates, together. But he went away to school. Father says next year I'm to go away to school, too. Mama says no, I'm to stay here and get a tutor."

Dane swung his legs out of the lift and dangled them, kicking the wall and leaving black marks with his shoes. When he saw her look of disapproval, he stopped. Quilla bent to use the napkin from the tray to wipe away the marks.

"And what of you," she asked him. "What do you wish to do?"

"I'd like to go to school. Robie Vassermidst says there's pudding every night at dinner."

Quilla smiled at the thought. "You must study very hard in school. There's more to it than pudding at dinner."

He nodded. "I know. Father says I must study very hard, too. He says I must learn to do more than read, I must learn figures and sums and all manner of things like that. Uncle Jericho says 'tis important to learn how to count and such, too, because if I want to join him in his business I must needs know how to do that sort of thing in my head, without benefit of parchment."

Quilla nodded, considering what he'd said. "Your uncle and your lord father are both correct."

"Did you go to school, Quilla?"

She shook her head. "I had a tutor, much as your mother proposes for you. But I often wished I'd been able to go away to school, and I've always thought it important to keep learning. To keep teaching myself."

"Even now?" Dane seemed impressed. "That you're old?"

Old? "Even now, that I'm old. Yes."

In his laughter, he looked and sounded like his mother. "Oh, Quilla Caden! You're most merry!"

She had no time to ask him why he found her statement so amusing, for down the hall came Gabriel, his hair slick with wet and a fresh coat and vest upon his body. He paused when he saw them.

"What is this, Dane?"

"Dane was helping me with your tray, my lord." Quilla gestured for Dane to get down from the lift, which he did with alacrity and a shamed face. "Have you need of me?"

Gabriel shook his head. "No. I am seeking my lady wife."

Quilla nodded. "Of course."

"Mama's in her sitting room," Dane offered. "She has a head-ache and sent me away. Allora Walles has put a cool cloth over her eyes and is reading to her."

"I see we have no need of a newsletter. Not with Master Dane in the house." Gabriel's indulgent tone made Quilla smile as she bent to put the tray into the lift.

"I daresay he knows everything that goes on here," she said.

Dane nodded, full of self-importance. "Oh, aye. Jorja Pinsky says 'tis because I am a nebby little brutus and must stick my nose in the world's business, but Florentine told her to shut her fat lips, because I am my mother's son in more than feature."

Quilla kept her gaze on the tray, not wanting to laugh. From the mouths of children come embarrassing truths. She'd have to remember to watch what she said around the boy. Not unless she had no care about hearing it turned around and spat out for the world to hear.

"Is that so?" Gabriel sounded speculative, and she glanced over at him. "What do you suppose she meant by that?"

Dane shrugged, dancing with the innate inability to remain still that all boys seem to have. "I don't know, Father. Can I come with you, Father? To see Mama?"

"If your lady mother has a headache, perhaps 'twould be better for her if you did not attend."

Dane sighed, shoulders lifting. "She was fine when Uncle Jericho visited. But then she shouted at him, and he left, and that's when she made Allora put the cloth on her eyes."

Quilla was still watching Gabriel when his son revealed a bit more truth. Her patron's expression darkened. Dane didn't appear to notice, but kept up his chattering. Gabriel's entire body had gone stiff.

"Dane, go find Jorja."

Dane looked momentarily chastened, but then nodded and skipped away. "Good-bye, Father!"

Gabriel stared after him, then looked at Quilla, who still stood by the lift. His face showed no emotion. She paused, thinking he would speak to her, but he did not. He turned and moved off down the hall toward his wife's rooms.

S he'd prepared a light luncheon for him. Sliced bread, sliced meat. Mustard. A small flask of ale. A nice cloth on the table.

"My lord, do you care to pause in your work?"

Gabriel looked up, eyes magnified once more by his lenses. "Hmm? What?"

"Your mercy for disturbing you." She gestured at the table. "I made luncheon for you."

He took off his headpiece and set it aside, then rubbed his eyes. "Yes. This is a good stopping point."

She helped him off with his white coat, but didn't reach for the other coat. His brief pause made her smile to herself. He'd been expecting her to help him put on the other. When he reached for it, she put her hand on the sleeve of his white shirt.

"Leave it off."

He fixed his gaze upon her. "So you say?"

"I do."

He tilted his head. "And why, pray tell, do you tell me to leave off my coat and wander about in naught but my shirt?"

"Because I think you shall be more comfortable in your shirt and not all constricted in your coat," came her reply.

"You think being without my coat will please me."

"I do." She tugged his sleeve, moving him toward the table.

"And I think luncheon will please you, as well. At least, I hope so. I'm fair starving today."

She set out the plates and served him, then herself while he watched. She took a bite of the bread and meat and looked up, catching his glance while she chewed and swallowed. She wiped her mouth and sipped some ale to wash down the food.

"My lord?"

"You . . . your manners."

Embarrassed, she wiped her mouth again. "I plead your mercy—"

"No. They're not bad. They're just . . ." Gabriel seemed to struggle for words. "You're so carefree. With me."

"You would like me to be more formal."

He toyed with his napkin, frowning. "No."

Quilla took a breath and let it out, slowly. "I understand you are more used to a rather more formal approach from your staff. But if I am to be your Handmaiden, I am more than a serving lass. At least, I should be. I could be. If you allowed it."

This he seemed to expect, because he leaned back in his chair and fixed her with a stern look. "I told you. I do not expect you to warm my bed."

"Is there no way for a woman to care for a man that does not involve his bed?" She asked the question carefully, not trying to be rude but wanting to be clear. "Can you not accept my caretaking of you as friendship?"

Gabriel reached forward and lifted his mug of ale, draining it before answering. "You are my friend because you must be. No other reason."

She frowned. "Your brother said much the same, and I'll give you the same answer I gave him. I choose my friends."

At the mention of his brother, Gabriel's eyes flashed. "And you would have Jericho as a friend?"

"I have no reason to consider him friend, nor foe."

"But you would choose me?"

"I would so choose, my lord. For I find much about you to admire." She spoke the truth, not flattery.

He scowled. "Pretty words."

"With truth behind them."

He scowled further. "I told you in the beginning my reasons for sending for you. 'Twas to avoid all that rubbish."

"Being cared for is rubbish?" She couldn't help the way her voice rose a bit in surprise.

He dove into his sandwich and chewed furiously without answering. Quilla set hers aside. "My lord Delessan. Please tell me why you find it so difficult to believe I might actually enjoy your company for my own reasons and not because I am duty-bound?"

"My brother is the charming one. The golden-haired swain. The one our mother loved. The one everyone loves." His words spoke of loss and longing, but his tone belied any such emotion. Gabriel kept his voice flat, his face without expression. "Jericho is the charmer, the one with friends, the one who can woo anyone to near anything. 'Tis why he took over our fathers' business and not I. He had the demeanor for it. I did not."

"I see."

He looked at her, then back toward the fire. "I don't think you do."

What she saw was two brothers, each who wanted what the other had and neither able to appreciate their own blessings.

"So tell me," she said.

"I am the elder brother. I am the steady one. The responsible one. I have ever had to be such, since he was born. I have always had to watch out for him, my younger halfling brother who looked like my mother when I did not."

"And all of these are reasons I should not wish to befriend you?"

He stared at her. "I'm only telling you the way it is. You make your own judgment."

"Sometimes, we allow ourselves to focus with such intensity upon what we believe others think us to be, we create ourselves in that image."

"You think I'm wrong?"

She shook her head. "There can be no denying you are the elder. And you seem to be the steadier. But he is not handsomer than you, and though his charm is more obvious, I am convinced you could equal him. If you tried."

His brow raised. "You sound as though you are challenging me, Handmaiden."

She smiled and sipped some more ale. "I only speak what I see. 'Tis for you to choose if you would attempt more frivolity."

"And for you to choose my friendship," he added, his tone considering.

"Yes. Of course."

Gabriel bent back to his food. "It does not please me to be frivolous."

Quilla made no reply to that, and when the food was finished, she tidied it up while Gabriel got back to work, but she caught him humming beneath his breath while he did.

You've been avoiding me."

Quilla looked up from the book in her hand. The library at Glad Tidings was not well stocked, perhaps because Gabriel's private collection of volumes was kept in his room and not upon the library shelves. Still, she'd found a few novels of interest, a collection of unused religious texts that made her shake her head, and an odd assortment of personal letters bound into covers made of glue-stiffened paper.

"I have done no such thing." She turned back to the book, but Jericho Delessan was no more used to being ignored than his brother, for he leaned on the bookshelf next to her. She caught the faint scent of herb floating about him and looked again at his face, searching for signs that he'd been indulging. A hint of redness in his eyes was all that showed, but it was enough to prove her nose hadn't been wrong. She couldn't ignore him, so she sighed and moved away.

"You have. You never join us for dinner, nor for cards."

Quilla gave him a rueful shake of her head. "Certainly you can see how such a thing is impossible, my lord Delessan."

"Is it?"

"I'm not a guest in this house, and you well know it."

Jericho followed her as she moved to sit in one of the comfortable chairs in front of the fireplace. "No, but you're no chambermaid or kitchen drab, either. You're something else, entirely, and I'm fascinated by it."

She looked up at him. "Fascinated? How flattering."

Her attention turned to the book in her hand, but though she turned its pages, her eyes scanning the text, she could not concentrate. At last, she looked up with an exasperated sigh, to find him staring at her.

"Staring is ill-mannered, my lord Delessan."

"My other lord Delessan," he put in with an unabashed, smug grin. "I can hear it in the pause you give it. You don't say it, but 'tis there. 'Other.'"

Quilla closed the book on her finger to keep the place. "You seem to believe you know much about me."

"I'd like to know more. I'd like to know all about you. How you came here. Why you do what you do. All of it."

"Am I to be interviewed?" She sat back in her chair and looked at him. "Shall you write an account of our conversation and send it to the newsletters?"

"No. My curiosity is for me, alone."

"I came here by carriage. I do what I do because 'tis my purpose and my place to do it." She opened the book again.

She had not satisfied him. Jericho made a disgusted noise. "Do I threaten you, Mistress Caden?"

She looked up again. "Of course you do not. Do you mean to?"

His grin, meant to soften her like butter before a fire, gleamed. "No. 'Tis unintentional, yet I know I do."

"I just said you do not."

"Well then, you're lying." Jericho crossed one leg over the other and linked his fingers around his knee. "Because the way you avoid me tells me I threaten you. I'd like to know why."

"I do not—you don't—" She cut off her protest, refusing to give him the satisfaction of the sort of reaction she suspected he expected.

He said nothing, just watched her with the same knowing smile on his handsome face. She bent back to her book, determined not to speak and not to flee, either. She read the same page over twice before admitting to herself she could not understand a word of it.

"You do not threaten me," she said at last. "And I do not avoid you. We simply have no need for interaction."

"We're interacting now," he pointed out.

"And I have not run away, so there. You see? I do not avoid you."

"You probably should," he said matter-of-factly. "Else my brother will surely chastise you for encouraging my company."

"I am not!" She bit down again on the protest and glared at him. "My lord Delessan, I have been relieved of my duties for the day. By your brother, my patron, who does not require my company at the moment. He has given me permission to utilize this library as I see fit, and all I've done is take advantage of his generosity. I have done nothing for which any chastisement would be necessary."

"Well, not yet, you haven't." Jericho wiggled his eyebrows and broadened his grin. "I've been told I'm quite the ruiner of reputations."

She'd had enough. Quilla closed the heavy novel and lifted it. She stood, making certain her dress fell in smooth lines to her ankles, then crossed to him, and leaned in close.

"Are you?"

His gaze flickered, grew languid, along with his lazy smile. He reached to curl his fingers in the end of her braid. "I'm not proud of that, by any means."

"No?" She leaned closer, letting him feel her breath on his face. "Something tells me you're the liar, now."

He tilted his head, lips parting, tongue making a slow, sensual sweep across them. "My lady, you wound me."

"I do, indeed," she whispered. "And I am not your lady."

She dropped the heavy book directly in his lap. Jericho's breath shot out of him. His face went pale and he hunched forward as Quilla stepped neatly out of the way.

Then she turned and strode out of the room, at least giving him the courtesy of waiting until she'd closed the door behind her before she burst into laughter.

Full winter had fallen, and along with it, snow. Drifts of white blown by the wind swirled and heaped in the garden and against the house, so high on the eastern side it covered a few of the lowest windows. Bertram kept a path cleared from the kitchen to the stable, but the rest of the household was kept inside, fires lit and tempers short with the seclusion.

"What we need's an entertainment," Florentine grumbled as she pounded down a swelling bowl of dough and began to knead it. "Somewhat to keep us all from tearing out each other's throats. 'Tis too long until the Feast of Sinder. Someone will go mad and take an ax to someone else before much longer."

Quilla had sought the warmth of the kitchen and dubious comfort of Florentine's company rather than face the silence and chill of her lonesome room. "I know the girls have been playing cards at night. A regular tournament, they've started, with the game Master Jericho taught them. The one he learned from Mistress Saradin."

Florentine sniffed, meaty fists pounding the dough into submission before tearing it into three hunks and rolling each into long strands, which she began to braid. "Those simpletons need more to do than play cards."

Quilla got up to stir the bowl of stew bubbling in the pot over the fire. "You're the one who said we need an entertainment."

Florentine finished braiding the hallah loaf and set it aside to rise again near the fire's warmth. "Don't you know what we finds entertainment, Handmaiden?"

"Firstly, tell me who you mean to encompass with your *we*, as I'm fair certain Allora Walles's idea of entertainment is far different from your own." Quilla smiled and leaned against the warmed bricks next to the bread oven.

"Ah, that moronic bitch is finding the same entertainment she always does, of that I've no doubt, only seems she's set her sights a bit higher than a chaff-strewn stable." Florentine, ceaseless, moved to the bowl of sand-covered potatoes and began to brush them off, being careful to catch every falling grain of sand in another bowl.

"Poor Bertram."

"And poor Billy, and poor Pipp and poor Took," said Florentine. "And don't forget the stable lads Luke and Perrin. She's had her way with them, I'm sure of it, and left them with naught but the memory to keep them warm at night. Though I've no doubts they'd not go running to sniff her skirts again should she lift 'em, the sluttish twat."

Quilla bit her lip at Florentine's blunt portrayal of Mistress Delessan's lady's maid. "Are you so certain she is that?"

Florentine grinned, and Quilla marveled how the woman's smile
turned her from gruff and mannish to almost but not quite pretty.
"No, but 'tis wondrous fun to say, ain't it?"

Quilla shook her finger. "Florentine, Allora might not be my
favorite person in this household, but I can't judge her bedtime
habits."

"No, I don't suppose you would." Florentine gave a sly grin.
"Though I haven't any issue with doing it. And besides, I don't guess
it matters much to you whose bed she's warming?"

"You're trying to draw my curiosity into the slop bucket." Quilla
ladled two bowls of savory stew and set one down in front of the
cook. "And it won't work."

"Not even if I tell you I heard the distinctive sound of Allora
Walles's whiny little screams of ecstasy coming from our other lord
Delessan's rooms for three nights running?"

Quilla's hands barely paused in setting down the bowls, and she
kept her face studiedly neutral. "What the other lord Delessan does
with his nights is not of my concern."

"'Tis not what he does with his nights but with his prick that I
should think would interest you."

Quilla looked up. "Florentine, you know that's not true. I am
Gabriel's Handmaiden. My concerns are for him alone."

"And he's not taking you into his bed, either," retorted Florentine, "the daft git. So nobody would blame you for turning your
gaze to one who would."

That made Quilla's mouth open in surprise. "I've told you again
and again, I am not a whore. I'm not here to fuck him, Florentine!
That's not . . . it's not my purpose and my place . . ."

Her hands were trembling, and she fisted them to keep them
still, stunned and discomfited by her display of emotion.

"'Tis your place if 'twould bring him comfort, no?"

"He doesn't ask for that."

"I thought," said Florentine, "you was supposed to just know. To give him what he needs before he knows he needs it. All that rot. Ain't you just supposed to know? Or is it that you're too afraid he'll turn you down and you think you won't be able to stand it?"

Quilla went to the case holding the flatware and slid open the spoon drawer, pulling out two and shoving them both into the bowls. "And I thought your job was to bake bread and roast fowl, not to dissect mine."

"Oooh." Florentine didn't look at all put in her place. "If you're going to insult me, Quilla Caden, you're going to have to do better than that."

Quilla put her hands on her hips. "Well, how about this, you nosy bitch? My purpose is not any of your concern. If my patron wishes me in his bed, to his bed I'll go, and because 'tis my place to be there and no other reason."

"Better, but I'm still not sufficiently wounded, emotionally. A few disparaging remarks about my appearance might do the trick. Or might not."

A smile tilted Quilla's lips against her will. "You have poor taste in dresses and the color green does not suit you."

Florentine put her hand over her heart. "Oh, oh you wound me, you foul-tongued harpy!"

Quilla laughed. "I'm sorry."

Florentine opened her eyes, rolling them. "Mistress, you'd need to say much worse than that to make me weep."

"I know it. We can't all have a talent for insult."

"Nor can we all have a talent for complacency," said Florentine, scooping a mouthful of stew. "But we create a nice balance, do we not?"

The friendly words surprised Quilla, who smiled. "I think so, yes."

"A friend is someone who'll tell you what you need to hear even when you don't want to hear it, no?"

"Among other things, I think so. Yes."

Florentine gestured toward Quilla with the spoon. "Then you'll take this as coming from a friend, Quilla. That ornery son of a bastard up there needs more from you than tea and dusting. And if you wait for him to ask for it, you'll be failing in your duty."

"Why are you all at once so concerned about my duty?" Quilla asked, stung. "When I came here, you called me a whore because you assumed I'd be sharing his bed."

"When you came here, I didn't know you'd be good for him," Florentine shot back.

"You think I'm good for him?"

"I think you could be better for him," said Florentine, typically not blowing any sunshine when smoke would suffice. "He's too stubborn to see it, but you should."

"Are you suggesting I seduce him?" The thought held more appeal than she might have admitted a few months ago. "I've never . . ."

"Never had to? I don't imagine so." Florentine gave Quilla's face and body a long, lingering look tinged with playful lasciviousness. "But then you've never had our lord Delessan for a patron before. They're all different, no?"

"They're all different, yes."

"And you feel different about this one."

Quilla shook her head. "No. He is my patron. That's all."

Florentine let out a snort. "If you say so. And neither does a certain yellow-haired swain catch your eye, either."

"Of course not."

Florentine sighed. "You're not much of a liar."

Quilla dipped her spoon into her stew and sampled it. "And you're an unsubtle harridan."

She looked up to see Florentine's mouth hanging open for a moment. "Sinder's Balls!"

Quilla ate some more stew while Florentine shook her head.

"You've managed to cut me, Handmaiden."

"I'm sorry."

"No," said Florentine with a broad grin. "You ain't."

"You're right."

Florentine regarded her steadily. "Convince our master we needs an entertainment and I'll forgive you."

Quilla laughed. "What sort of entertainment, Florentine? We've gone back to the start of our conversation. You told me card tournaments are not enough."

"Invisible Mother, no." Florentine waved her hands. "Don't you know what staff finds the most entertaining? Parties."

"You want me to suggest to my patron he throw a party for us?"

Florentine scoffed. "By the Quiver, no, you dolt. He would never. A party for us would be absurd. A party for them's what lives in this house abovestairs. A real brannigan. For him and his lady wife, and his beloved halfling brother."

Quilla raised an eyebrow. She wasn't familiar with the local term, *brannigan*, but gathered from Florentine's face that it was some sort of large party. "Forgive me, Florentine, but the thought of Gabriel holding a party for himself is even more absurd a thought than asking him to throw one for the staff."

"Again, you don't know the master as well as you think you do. He enjoys parties, with the right guests. They put him in a grand mood. He can be quite the host when it suits him. You just need to convince him it will suit him."

"A brannigan, as you call it, will create much work for you and for the maids, the stable men . . , for all of you. How can that be entertainment? I should think the girls would far rather finish all their chores during the day and play their cards at night."

Florentine gave a grunt. "Idle hands pall after a while. You have your purpose and your place, and we have ours."

It made sense, put that way. "And why am I made the emissary to convince him to have a party?"

"Ahh, not only a party. A brannigan. An endless, grand affair with much carousing and entertainments, and food and drink and general merriment. With hunts and games and dancing, and illicit sex in the bushes."

"Anyone who wants to have illicit sex in the bushes now would be mad," Quilla said. "And you didn't answer my question."

"You, my dearest popkin, are the emissary because you're the one supposed to give him what he needs before he need it, not me. I feed his body. You feed his soul, remember?"

As if she could forget. "I'll do my best."

"Then I'll start preparing," answered Florentine, "because your best will leave him thinking 'twas all his own idea, of that I have no doubt."

B ring me that vial of crystallized quartz," Gabriel asked, and Quilla left off the minor task she'd been doing to comply. He took it from her and added it to the mixture he'd been working with all morning. A brief, acrid scent filled the air, accompanied by a wisp of smoke. He muttered a curse. "It's not working right."

"Come sit," said Quilla. "Have some tea and think on it for a while. Perhaps the solution will come to you."

He nodded absently, and she noted how much easier it was to serve him when he wasn't paying attention. He allowed her to un-button his coat and lead him to the chaise lounge, where she'd placed the small table set with tea and biscuits. He took a biscuit and dunked it into the tea she poured, then ate it without relish.

The set of his shoulders told her of his tension, and she moved behind him to begin kneading the sore muscles.

He bent his head forward to let her get to the knots at the base of his neck. "'Tis a simple enough formula. I can't think of why I'm not able to re-create it."

Quilla's hand soothed and smoothed. "Perhaps you are discontent."

His head lifted and he turned it to look at her. "What?"

"Discontent. Bored," she repeated carefully. "You've been working with little surcease for weeks. The weather has meant even your walks have been curtailed."

"My work has become somewhat tedious of late," he admitted and let out a soft groan as her fingers found a particularly tense knot.

"Perhaps you would benefit from a change of pace, my lord." She walked her fingers up his neck to rub along his scalp, the thick, dark hair tickling the backs of her hands. "Perhaps the company of like-minded companions would stimulate you intellectually."

"Is that your professional opinion," he said wryly, "or has Florentine put you up to the idea of convincing me to have a brannigan?"

She ought not have been surprised that he'd guess, but she was embarrassed he'd caught her out. She kept up her massage, glad he faced away from her so as not to see her pinked cheeks.

"Well, Handmaiden? Why so silent? 'Twould please me to have an answer from you."

"Florentine did ask me to try and woo you toward having a party, yes. But I do think you might benefit from it, as well."

He put his hand over hers, stilling it, and twisted his body to look at her. "Do you?"

"You know I do. Else I would not have been convinced to try."

His fingers curved over hers. "And what of you? Would it please you to have a party?"

She twisted her wrist to put her hand palm up beneath his. "Aye, because I do think you could use something in your life other than work."

His fingers tangled with hers and he pulled her hand until she came around to stand in front of him. It discomfited her to stand above him; it wasn't her place to look down on him, so she moved to kneel. His grip stopped her. She looked at him, and he tugged her toward him, turning her sideways to sit upon his lap. Without letting go of her hand, he used his other one to anchor her waist.

"But what of you? Do you not have any desires beyond what you think will please me?"

"You know I don't."

"I don't believe you don't."

She smiled, looking down at their clasped hands, then up to his face. "I should think by now I'd have convinced you."

His smile tweaked the corners of his mouth and crinkled small lines at the corners of his eyes. "I don't believe you have no desire beyond what you think will please me."

His fingers had begun to trace a slow, circling pattern on her side.

"If it pleases you to think so, then I'll do nothing to prove otherwise."

"Clever." He shifted her closer to him, took the hand in his, and looped it over his shoulder so she couldn't help but lean close to him.

Gabriel tilted his head back, his eyes following the lines of her face and the curve of her mouth, before returning to hers. "'Twould please me to know you have desires of your own that are not hinged on mine, Handmaiden."

His eyes caressed her. His hand continued its slow, smooth

stroking, sliding inch by inch along the fabric of her gown, up her side until his fingers had almost reached the swell of her breast. Then back down again, just as slowly, to the jut of her hip. Slow. Smooth. Seductive.

She ran her tongue along her bottom lip to moisten it, and his eyes were drawn to the sight like a snake to a mouse in the grass. The expression on his face made her heart beat faster. Heat had kindled between them, an almost palpable flare.

"I have desires," she whispered, throat hoarse. "I am human."

"Are you?" He reached up to stroke his hand down the length of her braid, stopping at the ribbon tying off the bottom. "I thought maybe you were an angel sent from the Land Above to give me absolute solace."

She smiled. "I am here to do that, my lord, but I assure you I am no angel."

"No?" He shifted her yet again closer and tugged her braid to bring her face closer to his. "Can you assure me you are, indeed, made of flesh and blood?"

"I can," replied Quilla with a smile that moved her lips close enough for him to capture with his own.

". . . want my lord husband! You can't keep me out!"

The door to Gabriel's chambers flew open with a bang that caused a precarious pile of books to spill. Quilla was on her feet before she knew it, but whether she had leaped or he had pushed her, she wasn't certain. He was on his feet as well, turning toward the door just as Saradin stumbled through the doorway, yanking her arm free of a very flush-faced Allora Walles.

"Let go of me, you silly bint!" Saradin jerked herself free of Allora's grip. "Else I'll slap you sillier!'

"My lady Saradin, please . . ."

The crack of Saradin's hand on Allora's face was as loud as a teapot shattering on the floor. Allora stifled a cry, but to her credit, did not step back. She tried again to grab her mistress's arm. "My lady, please . . ."

"Let her go, Mistress Walles, 'tis well." Gabriel stepped forward, hand extended. "My lady wife. What brings you to my chambers midday?"

As usual, Saradin's hair was ornately styled and her cosmetics applied with a heavier hand than Quilla would have used, but expertly done for all that. Her gown, too, was a bit fancier for day wear than was usual, the dark blue underdress set off by an overdress of lighter blue shot through with gold threads.

Quilla was accomplished in fading into the background when necessary, to not calling attention to herself, to being unnoticed unless needed. Again, in Saradin's presence she had no need to do so. Saradin's eyes swept past Quilla as though she did not exist, as though the space in which she stood was empty.

"My lord, I tried to stop her."

"Shut up, Allora." Saradin's pretty face didn't even crinkle as she snapped the words. "My lord husband is pleased to see me, is he not?"

"Always, my lady wife." Gabriel took the hand she extended and brought it up to brush his lips along the back of it. "And of course."

Saradin smirked. "I told that bint the same, only she tried to get me to stay in my room. A prisoner in my own room! What stupidity! I've a mind to cast her out into the snow!"

Gabriel's gaze flickered toward Allora, who wrung her hands. "No need for that, Saradin. She was only doing her job."

Saradin sniffed, dancing forward on tiny, perfect feet shod in slippers finer than any Quilla had ever owned. Her dark, sooty lashes stood out like flakes of ash against her creamy pale cheeks. A single curl had fallen from its place atop her head and now hung in gleaming splendor to her shoulder, looking for all the world like a spiral of gold.

Quilla turned and glided away on silent feet to stand by the fire, the flames giving her something upon which to blame the heat in her face. She watched Allora out of the corner of her eye, but the lady's maid was still wringing her hands, most likely awaiting another slap from her mistress.

"You may leave us, Allora." Gabriel's voice was kinder than it had been before, and kinder than Quilla thought she deserved. That thought made her chest constrict.

Saradin's girlish giggle set Quilla's teeth on edge. "Husband, isn't it time for you to take leave of those potions and concoctions and spend some time with me?"

"You know my work is important, Saradin, and can't be left off at a moment's notice."

Saradin flickered a look in Quilla's direction, a mad, sly look that showed her the woman had noticed her, after all. Which made the extent to which she'd ignored her that much more of a slap . . . Quilla admonished herself not to think so. *What is wrong with you!*

As she watched Saradin flirting with Gabriel, she knew. *You're jealous, Tranquilla. Jealous of the man's wife.*

That thought so disturbed her she had to turn and face the flames. Behind her, she heard the low sound of Gabriel's chuckle, the rustle of Saradin's gown, the soft noise of skin on skin. Was he kissing her?

She didn't turn to see, instead busying herself with sweeping up some of the ash that had crept free of the fire's edge onto the white marble fireplace surround.

"You work so hard." Saradin's voice had a pout in it. "Too hard, my darling. You ought to give yourself some leisure time, too."

"Actually, I was thinking of having a brannigan."

The casual way he said it made Quilla drop the dustpan, which clattered and sent up a cloud of dust over her hands and hem.

"Honestly," Saradin said with a sniff. "Your chambermaid is extremely clumsy, Gabriel."

Chambermaid! Chamber—Quilla clamped her tongue between her teeth, biting with such ferocity she tasted a squirt of bitter blood. The woman knew Quilla was no chambermaid, no fetchencarry, no body servant. Quilla knew Saradin knew the truth. Mistress Delessan was deliberately insulting her position, demeaning it.

I am his Handmaiden. I am his comfort. I am what he needs before he knows he needs it, not his bedamned chambermaid!

Yet Gabriel did not correct his wife, though he had to have known what an insult she'd given to Quilla. "Would you like a brannigan, my lady wife?"

Saradin giggled, the sound like fae chimes that nonetheless grated on Quilla's nerves like gravel on a toddler's knees. "A party! A brannigan! Who shall we invite?"

"Whomever you like," replied Gabriel in a genial tone Quilla had never heard from him. It made her turn to look at him. He turned to Allora. "You may go, Allora. I will take care of my lady wife."

Allora bobbed into a curtsy. "Yes, my lord."

She left the room, and Saradin began chattering about guests and food and room arrangements, while Quilla merely stood by the fire with ashes on her hands.

After a moment, Quilla left the room as well, for even though he hadn't said a word, Gabriel had dismissed her as thoroughly as if he'd shouted at her to get out.

Chapter 7

Jericho looked like summer with his bright golden hair and eyes the color of a sky untouched by clouds. His ready smile, too, made brighter any room he graced, but he did not smile now. Jericho stared, pensive, out the window of the third-floor parlor, where Quilla had gone to do some mending while the rest of the house laughed belowstairs.

"Forgive me, my lord Delessan," she murmured. "I did not know you were here."

He looked up. She expected a glib remark. He gave her none, not even a hint of a grin. He gestured toward an empty chair across from him.

"Don't leave on my account."

Quilla took the seat, grateful for the sunshine. More snow had fallen overnight, but the day had dawned with brightness, and the glare off the white reflected through the windows. She lifted a stocking from her basket, then the needle and thread, and began to sew up a hole in the toe.

"The ladies here would throw that away and buy another. Not mend it."

"I am not one of the ladies here, and I have not the luxury of such waste."

He leaned back in his chair. "My brother would buy you another pair of stockings."

She looked up at him. "I'm certain he would, my lord Delessan, however, my intent is not to waste your brother's coin in buying me new stockings when I can easily repair the old."

"You've used the material I gave you, I see."

She touched the skirt of her gown, made from the green fabric. "Yes. Thank you for it."

"But not the red."

"No, my lord Delessan. Not the red."

Jericho's laugh also reminded her of summer. Of carefree days. "I should be but half offended, then, as you've used but half my gift."

"You shouldn't be offended at all." Quilla made a few tiny stitches, closing the hole. "I may use the red someday."

"Will you?" He leaned forward. "I wish you would, Quilla. I wish you'd make a dress of it and wear it."

"Do you?" She looked up at him, her fingers pausing in their stitching. "Why?"

"Do you want me to answer that?"

"I wouldn't have asked the question if I did not seek an answer."

Jericho passed a hand over his face. "If you were mine, I would not hide you away in a garret room. I wouldn't dress you in drab, dull clothes that do nothing to show your beauty. I wouldn't treat you like a—"

"Like a what?" she asked, amused. "Like a Handmaiden?"

This silenced him for a moment, and she realized he was not being charming. He was being sincere. Quilla put down her mending.

"My lord Delessan, there can be no point to this. Stop, now."

"Stop what? Being honest?"

She sighed. "Stop wanting what you can't have. You only cause yourself grief."

"And what about you? Are you not caused grief? I see the way you look at him."

She set her jaw. "You see nothing but your own greed reflected."

He shook his head and leaned forward, close to her. "No, Quilla. I don't. I see you look at him, and I see him not looking at you. Not at all. How can he ignore you that way?"

"'Tis not my—"

"Don't you ever wish for someone's arms about you?" Jericho's voice dipped low. He moved to the edge of his seat, even closer to her, and reached to run a hand down the length of her braid. "Do you never wish for solace of your own?"

"I—" She got up, her basket forgotten, but he was on his feet as fast as she, and blocking her way.

"When was the last time anyone did something nice for you?" Jericho gripped her upper arms, his hands warm and strong, holding her in place. He pulled her step by reluctant step, closer, until the heat of his body aligned with hers. He brought his mouth to her ear, whispering, his breath a caress along her neck. "When, Quilla?"

"My patrons are always—"

"No. I mean someone who did something nice for you, Quilla Caden, not a Handmaiden to whom they have responsibility. I mean something beyond clothes, or food, or shelter. When was the last time someone pleased you?"

She shivered. "Let me go."

He wasn't holding her hard enough she couldn't get away. He wasn't hurting her. But he was not letting her go. Jericho's mouth moved again against her ear, and he almost, not quite, nuzzled her neck.

"Let me go, what?"

"Please."

He chuckled, low, making more hot breath caress her skin. "No, Quilla. Let me go, Jericho. I want to hear you say my name. I want to hear you taste my name on your tongue the way I taste yours whenever I say it."

She opened her mouth to protest. She stiffened her body to yank her arms free of his grip. Yet in the end, she did not. *Women we begin, and women we shall end.* The principle was meant to embody spirituality and humility, but now it held another meaning for her.

"Have you ever had a lover?"

"No."

He sounded truly sorrowful. "That is a shame, Quilla."

"I have never needed one."

"Everyone needs someone to love them." Somehow his grip had loosened, and his hands slid around to her back rather than gripping her arms. His mouth did not move from its place by her ear.

She tensed, ready to flee, but again something held her back. The truth of his words kept her in place. It was wrong, and she cursed herself for it, but she couldn't make herself move away from him.

"Everyone needs someone to hold them, once in a while." His arms went around her, holding her against him. "Everyone needs someone to care about them. You need it, too. Someone who cares if you laugh or if you cry. Someone who knows how you like your tea, and your dreams, and your favorite color. Tell me you do not want these things, Quilla."

Tears burned her eyes, and she closed them. "I cannot, because I would be lying."

He nuzzled her neck again, his whisper filling her mind as his scent filled her nostrils and the heat of him flooded her body with warmth. "You offer so much to others, yet you take none of it for yourself."

This was wrong. It was disloyal. It was not her purpose and her place, and somehow, she found again the strength to say, "Let me go."

"Do as I said, and I will."

She licked her lips, her voice aquiver with emotion and yes, she would admit it, desire. Desire for what he'd offered, indirectly. Desire for the promise of something beyond what she had. It would have been easy for her to give it to him, then, and to let him give her what he wanted, but it would still not have been what she wanted.

"Let me go, Jericho."

He sighed and his hands tightened on her once more, but he stepped away. She wiped her eyes with shaking fingers. He ran a hand down her face; she jerked away.

"I love the sound of my name in your voice."

"If you care for me at all, as you claim," she told him, "you will never behave this way again."

"And if I don't?"

Don't care? Don't behave? Quilla did not ask him what he meant. She pulled herself away from him and left the room, not realizing until much later she'd left her mending basket behind. She didn't even miss it until she found it settled upon her bed with a square of Alyrian silk, enough to make an evening wrap, inside. The colors matched the red fabric perfectly. Quilla took them both and put them in a box at the back of her wardrobe, and did not look at them again.

Preparing for the gathering put the household into a tizzy unlike Quilla had ever seen. Kirie, Rossi, and Lully gossiped and chattered as they cleaned and scrubbed and mopped and dusted—but cleaning, scrubbing, dusting, and mopping were not her place. Florentine bustled and shouted and cooked, and again, those things were not Quilla's place, either.

Her place was with Gabriel, bringing him solace, which had become a near impossible task. She'd thought him difficult to please before, but now . . . now no matter what she did, or how she tried, he would not be soothed.

She'd begun to think convincing him to hold a party was the wrong idea, that Florentine had tricked her into suggesting it to supply the house with amusement. That made Quilla turn over the scene in her mind of him speaking with his lady wife—for she knew that though it had been her idea to put the thought into his head, it was the desire of his lady wife that had made him acquiesce.

She'd thought herself immune to jealousy. It had taken her some time to realize the feeling for what it was, and a bit longer to admit it. She was jealous of the mad lady Saradin. Her golden hair, her eyes of green, her lovely clothes and petite figure. But most of all, Quilla was jealous of the attention Gabriel paid her.

She'd experienced it before. Couples whose marriages were undergoing rough times, who brought in a Handmaiden. She'd never minded if being in a home made an indifferent wife suddenly solicitous of her husband's pleasure. In the end, it was her duty to bring solace. If that was part of it, it was all part of the package.

But this . . . this was different, though she hated admitting it to herself. This was watching her patron's eyes alight when Saradin swept into the room, chattering inanities about party games and foods. This was watching him put aside his work to let her kiss him, allowing her to take him by the hand and draw him into the bedchamber.

This was being invisible to him, her patron, for though he still drank the tea and ate the simplebread she continued to prepare for him every morn, he rarely spoke to her.

Quilla had been told Saradin was mad from taking a dose of

something from Gabriel's workshop, but she saw no sign of insanity in her patron's beautiful wife. Slyness, churlish selfishness, and shallowness, yes, but her eyes gleamed with an intelligence belied by her brainless behavior and silly, little-girl voice. She might seem to ignore or discount Quilla's presence, but she did not. Saradin did not need to speak to Quilla to insult her.

Though she wasn't supposed to serve more than one patron, and she did so out of a sense of resigned obligation and not real pleasure, she fetched and carried at Saradin's indifferent commands for tea and biscuits, for the lights to be dimmed or brightened and the fire kindled higher to combat her seemingly constant chill.

Quilla played the part of fetchencarry because Gabriel did not tell her not to, and because to do otherwise would bring him displeasure. She suffered the glares of Allora, who sometimes attended her mistress to her lord husband's chambers and sometimes did not. She even remained silent in the face of Saradin's sniping about tasks performed incorrectly.

Quilla's eyes were for her patron, for Gabriel, and nothing Saradin requested of her was more than something to be done to please him. It amused her, though she wouldn't show it, to follow Saradin's increasingly churlish commands, because the more calmly she did it, the angrier it seemed to make the lady mistress.

What upset her was the fact Gabriel did not seem to notice what his lady wife was trying to do. He seemed neither to notice nor care the place to which Saradin was trying to put Quilla—to demote her position to that of a servant, and not only a servant, but her servant. Not his.

On the days Saradin did not visit Gabriel's chambers to giggle and gossip about guest lists and dinner menus, Gabriel occupied himself even further with his work, and was even worse tempered as a result of the time he was spending away from it. This, at least, Quilla knew how to combat with tea and simplebread, with scented oils and massages, with a calming voice that did not rise to shrill giggles at the end of every sentence.

She gave him her silence, which he seemed to crave, and she made his job as easy as possible to do so that although he was spending less time working, he could accomplish more.

This assignment was not her most difficult. She'd dealt with wives who'd behaved more cruelly. She hadn't quite counted on the extent of Mistress Saradin's slyness.

"Gabriel, my darling," said Saradin as she swept into the room, eyes asparkle and cheeks prettily pinked. "I simply must speak with you about the arrangements for the brannigan."

He turned from his work, and Quilla caught the glimpse of annoyance in his dark eyes. She busied herself with the leather-bound journal she'd bought him, into which she was carefully copying lists of supplies and receipts. Saradin swept past her, elbow knocking the pot of ink, which spilled.

Quilla grabbed it up, but the damage had been done. Ink had splattered the ledger's thick parchment pages, ruining the morning's work. Worse, it stained the leather cover. The pages could be removed. The cover looked ruined.

Saradin didn't bother with an apology, ignoring Quilla the way she always did. "Gabriel, darling—"

"I'm working, Saradin," he said impatiently. "Make whatever arrangements suit you best."

"But I need you," she said, voice just this edge of a whine.

Quilla wiped her hands, though ink had now stained them, as well. The lady mistress should watch her tone, she thought, attention fixed on the mess in front of her. Gabriel wouldn't suffer a whine for long.

But Saradin knew how to woo her husband, the way many such wives did. She sidled her way into his arms with a coo and a wiggle Quilla caught from the corner of her eye.

"I need you," Saradin repeated, tone gone low and breathy, an entire other meaning in the words this time.

"Sara," said Gabriel, though by his voice Quilla could tell he'd already given in. "Can't this wait until later?"

"No."

Invisible Mother, Quilla thought sourly, doing her best to ignore them the way they obviously had no trouble ignoring her. *The bint is going to get on her knees for him right in front of me.*

The thought so disturbed her, and being disturbed even more so, that Quilla got up and went to the fire to poke the flames higher. From behind her she heard soft, low giggles and the noise of skin on skin. Yet he did not dismiss her, and it was simply not her place to go.

In the next moment she heard the click of the bedchamber door closing, and she looked up. Disquiet settled over her, and she fended it off by getting to work. She kept herself busy dusting the vials and bottles on his worktable, lifting each one a scant inch from the tabletop to dust beneath before replacing it in exactly the same place so he'd be certain not to notice it had been moved at all. It wasn't easy to listen to the squeals of ecstasy coming from Gabriel's bedchamber, but Handmaidens did learn diplomacy and the ability to close their eyes and ears when the situation warranted it. So she closed her ears to the sounds of Saradin screaming Gabriel's name and the distinctive thud-thud-thud of a headboard knocking against a wall. She tried to ignore how hearing it made her feel.

The sound of the door opening made her look up. Saradin, hair not so neatly coiffed and cosmetics definitely smudged, came out of the bedchamber. A cat licking cream from its whiskers had never looked so smug. Quilla turned her attention back to the desk from which she was carefully scrubbing ink.

To her surprise, Saradin approached her, standing so close there was no possible way for Quilla to ignore her. Quilla put down the cloth and brush she'd been using, and looked into the other woman's eyes. Green and tilted like a cat's, and shining with malice.

"He won't need you anymore." Saradin's broad grin nearly split her face in half. She didn't look half so pretty with it on her lips.

"I will wait for my patron to dismiss me," replied Quilla evenly, "or until my term of service is ended for the day."

"Consider it ended. He's sleeping now, anyway, and won't wake until the evening, I'm sure of it. He won't need you anymore."

She repeated the words with just enough inflection to show Quilla she meant for more than the rest of this day.

"I plead your mercy, my lady, but that will be for your lord husband to decide. Not you."

Saradin's smile, if anything, grew broader. "My lord husband has exhausted himself this day, and will not be requiring your services. But if you'd like me to wake him to confirm that fact with you—"

"Of course I would not." Quilla didn't raise her voice.

Saradin lifted a perfectly groomed eyebrow anyway. "Tell me something, slut. Did you like listening to us? Did you stand outside the door and finger your cunny, imagining it was your thighs his face was between? Because, my little fetchencarry, my darling chambermaid, my sweet and so effusively ineffectual and pliant Handmaiden, it was not you in there he was fucking so lustily." She paused to lean forward, so close Quilla could smell the mint she must have chewed after breakfast. "But it was not you. 'Twas me. His wife."

True patience, Quilla thought, willing herself to be calm though Saradin's nasty accusation and sly grin made her jaw clench. "'Tis not my place to listen at doors, my lady."

Saradin let out a snort of disbelief and reached out a hand to stroke along the length of Quilla's braid. Her hand stopped at the

bottom and fisted in it, not yet tugging but with the obvious promise that she could at any moment.

"Don't you tell me about your place. I know what your place is,
and your bedamned purpose, too. And I'm telling you, he won't
need you anymore."

Quilla didn't move. Her gaze was steady in Saradin's. "Then
'twill be my patron's place to tell me so."

Saradin sneered and yanked on Quilla's hair hard enough to
make tears of pain sting her eyes before she let go. "And he will,
never fear that. I'll see to it."

"I regret you feel so threatened by my presence." Quilla's voice
did not shake by benefit of years of training in controlling her emotions and not from any lack of them.

"You don't threaten me!" Saradin didn't seem to have such self-
control, because her voice cracked and broke on the words. "How
dare you suggest my lack of competence as wife is what drove my
husband to acquire you! How dare you suggest he could find better
pleasure in you than in me! How dare you come to my home and
seek to supplant me, you gods-bedamned whore!"

Quilla said nothing.

Saradin narrowed her eyes. "I will put you from this house, you
disease, you harpy! I will put you from this house!"

"And I will go if 'tis my patron's will," said Quilla. "Not yours."

Saradin made a noise that in a dog would have been called a
growl, and stepped back from Quilla. "He seems not to understand
my subtle hints that your services are no longer required. He seems
to think the snow precludes you from going, though I assure you, if
we can arrange for the arrival of guests to our house, I can be certain to arrange for you to be sent away."

"Of that I have no doubt."

"'Tis my name he was moaning," said Saradin at last, triumphant. "Not yours."

Quilla did not want to dignify the madwoman's unsubtle accusation with denial, but the words rose to her lips before she could stop them. "I have not shared his bed. If 'tis your worry that I have begun to steal his affections, you needn't."

Saradin's eyes widened. "Dare you suggest such a thing is even possible?" Again, Quilla said nothing, for sometimes silence is the more powerful retort. Saradin's mouth thinned, and she cast a contemptuous glance up and down Quilla's body before settling on her face.

"You fat, stupid slag," she said at last. "You ugly, cow-faced bint."

Words were only that and could not hurt her.

Saradin glared. "I should slap that smile off your face right now."

Quilla did not move. Saradin raised a hand, but with a glance toward the closed bedchamber door, did not hit. And that, Quilla realized was a more telling action than any of her words had been.

"I will make him put you out," muttered Saradin. "I will make him!"

Quilla turned her back and picked up her scrub brush again. The next thing she heard was the sound of the door slamming. It took quite some time and many repetitions of the Five Principles for her to stop her hands from shaking, but by the time she'd finished removing the ink stain, they were still again.

They came in sleighs drawn by huge and bulky horses blowing steam from their nostrils like dragons breathing smoke. The snow had fallen fast and deep, making travel difficult, but apparently the invitation to a brannigan thrown by the Delessans was enough incentive to bring out even the least hardy of travelers.

From her window in the garret, Quilla watched them arrive.

Sleigh upon sleigh, some filled with guests, others carrying baggage. She watched Bertram and Billy struggling to bring in the trunks and bags, while Gabriel and Saradin greeted the guests, the men dressed with as much care for color and fabric as the women. Gabriel alone stood out among the bright hues and patterns in his sober-cut black coat. Though he greeted the arriving guests with handshakes and kisses to the cheek, the tense set of his shoulders and the way he seemed to pace back and forth told Quilla he was wishing he was at work.

His obvious anxiety created her own, for she was unable to do anything about it. "Doesn't the silly bint see he needs his work?" she murmured to the glass in front of her, which frosted obligingly at the touch of her breath.

Jericho was there, too, in a coat of royal blue that set off the brilliant gold of his hair. The pair of them, Saradin and Jericho, looked as though they belonged together, both blond and dressed in the height of fashion, both laughing and pink-cheeked in the winter sun.

Young Dane, who'd been allowed to greet the arrivals with his parents and uncle, ran back and forth in the snow like an overeager puppy. Next he'd be leaping into the piles of snow that had been shoveled away from the walks, she thought fondly, as the boy did just that. He disappeared up to his chin, and though she couldn't hear the squawking, she could see the tantrum on his face.

Bertram and Billy pulled the boy out and dusted him off while Jericho threw back his head and laughed. Saradin seemed to be more interested in the cloak one of her lady friends was wearing. Gabriel bent low, seemingly to scold the lad, and Jericho broke in to pull the boy away. Quilla couldn't see the look in Gabriel's eyes, but she could imagine it all too well.

With a sharp, well-executed bow to the guest and his wife,

Gabriel turned on his heel and disappeared inside the house. Without waiting another moment, Quilla left her room and went to his. He would need her.

The small sense of smug self-satisfaction disturbed her, and she pushed it aside with the preparation of tea. When he banged through the door a few moments later, she'd already set out the cup and saucer, but she'd added something else. A small glass filled with amber liquid.

He stopped when he saw her, and his eyes fell on the glass. He took it up, sniffed it, then tossed back the whiskey in one gulp and handed her the glass. "Another."

She pulled the bottle out from behind her back, already uncapped, and filled his glass before returning it. She put the lid back on the bottle and set it back on the shelf next to the fireplace, just as the teakettle whistled.

"How do you know I won't want more?" Gabriel drank the other shot and watched her pour the hot water into the teapot.

Quilla looked up at him. "Because you can't work if you're intoxicated. I know you wouldn't risk ruining your work through haphazardness."

He put the glass on the table and crossed his arms over his chest. "I'm not sure I like being so predictable."

"You're not predictable," Quilla said, surprised but being honest. "It's been quite difficult for me to learn you, and I still fear I will misjudge, every day."

He raised a brow. "Really? You don't appear to lack self-confidence."

"And you appeared to be gleefully greeting your guests," Quilla pointed out. "And yet I imagine the foremost thought in your mind was getting back to your experiments."

"You were watching me?" He sounded amused.

She gave a small grin. "It's my duty to be aware of you, my lord."

Gabriel laughed, low and brief, but a laugh just the same. "And it was obvious, was it?"

"Not obvious, no. I daresay your lady wife was fooled. And the guests themselves. Your brother might not have been."

Gabriel's mouth turned down. "My brother revels in such pageantry as much as my lady wife does."

"But how good of a husband you are to treat her to something she so dearly loves."

He cocked his head to look at her. "'Twas you who broached the subject with me, as I recall."

"But it was your lady wife who made you say yes."

Gabriel's intense gaze covered her, piercing her, his eyes locking with her own. "Is that what you think?"

"Am I wrong?"

He shook his head slowly, once, then again. "Tell me, Handmaiden, what do you see when you look at my lady wife and me?"

"It's not my place to make judgments, my lord." Quilla busied herself with pouring the tea and fixing it the way he liked it.

"It would please me to hear your opinion."

"I have no opinion—"

"It would please me for you to make one."

Quilla sighed and looked up at him. "I see that you love her very much. Enough to put aside your work for her. To please her."

He made a soft noise from deep in his throat. "My lady wife is a faithless, scheming madwoman who at the moment is experiencing a period of lucidity."

The observation was true, but surprising for the fact it came from his mouth. "I see a sense of obligation there, as well. And perhaps . . . guilt."

His gaze grew shadowed. "I gave her my name. It's my duty not to abandon her."

Quilla nodded, watching him. "My lord, you have behaved better toward her than many men would."

He half turned, his hand on the back of his chair. "She's like a sickness that will not go away. I know what she is, and yet when she is this way I can almost convince myself she'll always be this way."

Quilla came around and put her hand on his arm, gently pushing him to sit. "Nobody could fault you for her behavior."

"I can fault myself."

"We are often our own harshest critics."

He took the cup of tea she offered, but did not drink it. He looked at her, more naked honesty in his gaze than she had ever seen from him.

"I do not regret sending for you, Handmaiden."

She put her hand over his for one moment, squeezing his fingers briefly before drawing them away. "And nor do I regret being sent for."

Then he finished his tea and got to work, and she assisted him in a silence that was as rich with meaning as a thousand words.

The arrival of the guests had sent the entire household into a state of uproar so riotous it was as though a magicreator had cast a spell over everyone.

The kitchen bustled and jumped with preparations. The unused rooms on the third floor teemed with activity that spilled over into the halls and down the stairs, into the library, the sitting rooms, the gallery, the conservatory, and the music room.

The maids giggled and twittered. Florentine muttered and cursed. Bertram and Billy fetched and carried.

And Quilla . . . Quilla Waited.

Gabriel still had work to do, but now he rose before the dawn to finish it by the midmorning chime, when the guests roused themselves from wine and cocao-sated sleep. Then he left the workroom and Quilla to become the sociable host Florentine had said he could be.

The games began in earnest after luncheon, always a fine spread laid out by Florentine in the main dining room, complete with the finest settings. Snap Me, Quoites, Charades, Piquet, and more. All lovely, genteel games played by men and women in lovely, fashionable clothes with lovely, fashionable faces. The afternoon saw flower arranging in the conservatory, or sleigh rides, or ice-skating on the pond. The gentlemen, led by Jericho, sometimes took themselves into the woods on horseback, ostensibly for hunting, but really, Quilla thought, for the excuse to drink away from the watchful eyes of their female companions.

Saradin had been careful with her guest list, inviting the neighbors in groups of even numbers, providing a companion for each guest. Winston and Carmelia Somerholde brought their son Boone and daughter Genevieve. Donnell and Arbutus Fiene brought daughters Lavender and Marzipan. Persis Adamantane was the single, eligible gentleman and the toast of the local society for his wit, charm, fortune, and lack of interested female relatives who might judge his choice of spouse. And of course, Jericho had been set up as escort for Genevieve or Marzipan, whoever Persis didn't want.

"As though we're responsible for the next generation," Gabriel muttered one day, peering out his window at the group of young men and women gathered in the courtyard below. They were going skating on the pond, an activity he detested and refused to join.

Quilla was busy helping him tidy up the vials on his table. She glanced toward the window.

"Perhaps 'tis in our nature to make pairs."

"It's in my wife's nature to meddle," Gabriel replied. "What business is it of ours if Genevieve Somerholde ever gets married or not? That's her father's business, not mine. And yet I'm footing the bill for her courtship while she stares, moon-eyed, at Persis Adamantane and waits for him to fall madly, passionately in love with her."

"Which is unlikely to happen," Quilla murmured. "As it seems he is more infatuated with her brother."

Gabriel gave her a sharp look. "And yet he may marry the girl anyway, since the brother he cannot have. How did you . . . should I even ask? Do you think somehow, it would please me to know?"

She laughed, putting away the last of the tools and straightening the pile of notes and his pen and ink. "No, my lord. It was simply something I observed. Your guests don't notice me."

"But you notice them."

"They are difficult not to notice."

She turned and caught sight of him looking at her with an expression she didn't recognize. "My lord?"

"How do you occupy your time when you are not with me, Handmaiden?"

"I've been helping Florentine in the kitchen. She can use the extra pair of hands."

At that, he reached out and lifted one of hers, rubbing his thumb over the back of it. "You shouldn't be doing that. You're not here to serve in my kitchen."

"If it doesn't please you—"

He pulled her a step closer, scrutinizing her hands, which were stained with ink from writing his notes. "These hands are not for work such as that."

"My lord, when you don't require me, and Florentine does, 'tis no hardship for me to help. I like the kitchen. It's less . . . quiet." Less lonely, she meant to say, but didn't. "I find no purpose in sitting alone in my room."

He nodded and let go of her hand, but examined her, up and down, until she felt self-conscious enough to pass her hands over the front of her dress. "Is something amiss?"

"No." He shook his head. "I was callous not to think of inviting you to attend the activities."

She raised an eyebrow at him. "I am not a guest in your home."

"Neither are you my servant."

"I am something else, indeed," Quilla said with a small smile. "Something in between."

"And yet you could converse with as much grace and charm as any of the wind-headed ladies I have in my parlor."

The compliment was pretty, but useless. "I am not here to impress anyone with my grace and charm, my lord."

"No, but it would seem they are." Gabriel took off his laboratory jacket and held it out to her to hang, which she did. "And yet I think I would rather speak with you on the philosophy of Sinder, or the history of Gahun, or any number of topics I am certain you would be able to discuss."

She smiled. "You know you may speak with me about anything you wish, and I will do my best to please you with my response."

"And study what you don't know if I desire it, so that we may be able to pontificate." He smiled at her, going to the washbasin she'd already filled and cleaning his hands, then holding them out to her for drying.

"If it pleases you, of course."

"And if it pleased me for you to come and do the same sitting in my parlor rather than here, in my chambers?"

Quilla hesitated, patting the soft towel over his hands. "Of course I would do it, my lord, though I hope you would be . . . more considerate . . . than that."

"Considerate? To whom?" Her answer didn't seem to surprise him. Instead, it was almost as though he were testing her.

"To your lady wife, perhaps. There is no extra male for me to sit with. 'Twould throw off her arrangements."

"Clever girl. Cheeky, but clever." Gabriel was already holding out his arms for her to help him with the coat he'd wear downstairs. "You don't wish to sup at my table? You prefer eating in the kitchen with an ill-tempered cook and vapid, giggling housemaids?"

"Does Allora sit at your table and attend your parties?"

She began buttoning his coat for him, smoothing the lapels as she spoke and dusting off the shoulders.

"Allora Walles is not my concern."

She looked up at him as she finished straightening his tie and smoothing his coat lapels.

"Allora Walles is my wife's maid. She does not sup at our table, but she does, at times, attend our amusements."

"To serve your lady wife," Quilla pointed out. "Not to discuss politics or art."

"Would it make you so uncomfortable to be included?" he asked, putting a hand over hers to still the motion of it.

She looked into his eyes. "My lord, yes. It would, indeed. I would be out of place in your social hall. I would have little in common with your guests, and my presence there would cause your lady wife consternation . . . which would not bring you solace."

"And yet, if I asked you to come, telling you it pleased me, what would you do?"

She smiled. "You did ask, and I am telling you why you should not."

His mouth curved upward. "And if I demanded?"

Quilla looked up at him and gave an exasperated sigh. "My lord, do you insist on constantly testing me?"

"Would you come if I demanded it?"

"You know I would."

He nodded, his smile fading but the expression in his eyes unreadable. "I won't demand it of you, Handmaiden."

She nodded. "Thank you, my lord."

Gabriel sighed. "Though it would be nice to have someone to talk to."

This pleased her more than anything he'd ever said. "You may speak to me at any time about anything, my lord. You know that."

His hand came up to push the heavy weight of her hair off her shoulders. "I know it."

Then he left her, and she could not stop smiling.

Chapter 8

Another week passed in such a manner, with Quilla assisting Gabriel from morning until just after luncheon. She had the rest of her time free. She'd read all the books in the library, and in his. She'd baked enough simplebread to feed a small army. She'd helped with the dusting and the cleaning, but could not do much more of that because she got in the way of the maids.

Although it was not the first time she'd spent much of her day secluded from anyone but her patron, that was the way some households worked, and she accepted that. Here, now, for some reason, it bothered her more than it had before.

She needed no long periods of meditation to figure out why. She enjoyed her time with Gabriel, and did not enjoy as much the time away from him. She liked to watch him work, to see him solve a puzzle and complete a task. She liked to earn a smile from him, or a word of praise.

He would never be a man who charmed with laughter. Not like Jericho, who flitted from female to female and left a path of adoration and sighs behind him. Oh, the ladies fawned over Gabriel,

too, at least as much as etiquette allowed since he was wed. But not
in the way they did for Jericho, who was almost shameless in his
flirtation.

Quilla saw all of this from her hidden places. She might not
participate in the games or the jaunts, but that didn't mean she didn't
see what went on. How Genevieve's cheeks pinked when she looked
at Persis, or how his eyes wandered to her brother's more often.
How Lavender and Marzipan mocked their mother behind her
back, because she insisted upon wearing flannels against the cold.
How Donnell Fiene picked his nose when nobody seemed to be
watching.

No, she was not part of the brannigan, but she could not help
but become involved with it. It affected her patron, and therefore it
affected her. He spoke not of his increasing ennui with the party
and his desire to return to work.

He was trying, she realized, to be more like his brother. Like
cramming an overlarge foot into a too small shoe. Gabriel was attempting frivolity.

And it was making him miserable.

She'd never been in a situation quite like this one, where a patron insisted on putting himself into situations he despised, over
and over. No matter what she did to soothe him during the day, no
matter how hard she worked to make the small amount of time he
spent working as free of stress as she could, the evening invariably
came and with it, his forced participation in the activities.

Worse, each day Saradin begged more from him. Attendance
at breakfast. His presence at luncheon. She wooed and charmed
him with pretty words and smiles, with coos of encouragement and
anything else she could manage to get him away from his workshop . . . and therefore, away from Quilla.

Whatever else Saradin Delessan might be, she was not stupid.
She might play at it as part of her madness or perhaps to make her-

self appear more appealing to those for whom an intelligent woman posed a threat. But she was not stupid.

Quilla knew this, had seen it in the woman's eyes during each confrontation. She knew Saradin was smart and spiteful. She suspected she was cruel. She had not expected her to be vicious.

The evening had fallen, and the conservatory shone with lamplight. Pools of it shone through the heavy glass walls to form golden puddles on the drifts of snow outside. The plants inside, the riot of green growing vines and flowers forced to artificial bloom, looked even more beautiful cast in golden light than they did beneath the winter sun.

Saradin had planned for dinner in the conservatory, an idea greeted with cheers and applause from her guests and muttered cursing from the staff.

"Don't she know how much work 'tis for us to drag all that food there and back again? Not to mention the linen and flatware and china . . ." Florentine grumbled and groused, but was in her element planning the elegant affair. There was to be roast swan, intact, stuffed with an entire duck, and a capon inside of that. A bounty of side dishes would accompany it, using the best the household could offer.

"She's got us stripping the cellar bare for this, she does!"

"Florentine," Quilla chided. "You adore this, and you know it."

The cook grinned. "I do. I do indeed."

But though she did, indeed, adore the preparations, the location had proven to be something of a logistical problem.

The kitchen was located in the far back of the house, down a flight of stairs and dug half into the ground to help combat the ever-present heat from the fireplace. The dining room and ballroom were directly above it, both accessible by the cupboard lift.

The conservatory, on the other hand, was on the house's far side, past the foyer and the sitting room and parlor. It had been added on after the house's initial construction, and its access was therefore gained through a short, elegantly appointed but narrow and curving hallway opening off a little-used morning parlor.

It made bringing dinner there quite difficult. But not impossible, and quite impressive, in the end. Quilla, driven to distraction by Florentine's ceaseless complaints, had offered to help with the transport, as the cook had admitted she didn't quite trust the maids or the houseboys with the more fragile glasses.

So Quilla, though she did not have to, helped load a cart with steaming dishes and pushed it to the conservatory, where the sound of laughter reached her before the scent of flowers and perfume.

Lolly and Rossi had already gone in to serve the wine. Vernon the butler held the door for Quilla to push the cart through, then took over.

"I'll take it from here, mistress," he said. "And thank you kindly for the help."

"'Tis my pleasure, Vernon." Quilla smiled at the older gentleman. "Are you certain you don't need my help?"

He shook his head. "No, mistress. The footmen will help me."

Quilla smiled at the thought of Bertram and Billy playing footmen. "Perhaps our lord Delessan needs to hire more staff."

Vernon chuckled. "Aye, and you know he won't do that, even if he could at the moment. Not when he's got us to provide for him."

Quilla nodded. "I know it. But it does make it harder on you."

Vernon leaned closer to say in a low voice, "And you of all people should understand, mistress, that 'tis our purpose and we enjoy it."

"This I do know," she said with a smile. "I'll be in the kitchen with Florentine, should you need something run out."

"I'll ring for you if I do."

She nodded and watched him push the cart into the main area where the table had been set up. She heard the *oohs* and *ahs* of the guests as he revealed Florentine's masterpiece. And then, foolishly, she thought to take a peek at it herself, because she knew Florentine would want a firsthand account of how the guests had reacted to her creation.

Tall potted trees shielded the conservatory door from the hall entrance, and Quilla moved behind them. Through the break in the leaves she glimpsed the table, glowing with its display of crystal and silver.

The guests were as decorative as the table, glittering with fine fabrics and jewelry, their smiles shining with white teeth, faces gleaming with bright eyes. They all looked with impressed joy at the center of the table where the swan, gloriously browned and smelling delicious, had been revealed.

Florentine will be so pleased.

All of them, except for Mistress Saradin, whose voice suddenly rang out with false good humor: "And what lovely bird is this that lurks within the branches of yonder tree?"

All eyes turned at once to Quilla, who felt the weight of each individual gaze, but none heavier than Gabriel's.

"Come out of there, my dear girl." Saradin's tone was unctuous, and she gave a light trill of laughter to cover it up. "Look, everyone, 'tis my husband's chambermaid."

"Handmaiden," corrected Jericho without making it seem as though he were correcting her—but firmly enough that his words couldn't be ignored.

Jericho had done it, but not Gabriel. Quilla lifted her chin a bit and glided on silent feet from her place behind the tree. She gave a slight curtsy, aware her dress was not of appropriate design or quality and had been smudged with flour, but also aware that a woman's demeanor will always make up for her lack of dress.

"Handmaiden?" This made one of the Fiene daughters, Lavender or Marzipan, Quilla couldn't tell the difference, giggle. "Oh, my lord Delessan, how . . . how . . ."

"How interesting," put in Persis Adamantane, whose eyes gleamed with approval. He turned to Gabriel. "My good man, you didn't tell us you had a Handmaiden."

"I did not think it of import." Gabriel's gaze held Quilla's for the span of a heartbeat. He did not look pleased to see her.

"She has been helping my lord husband in his work," put in Saradin almost too quickly. She nodded and smiled at the other ladies at the table. "With his records."

Madame Somerholde smiled and nodded, looking at Quilla with a smirk. "Ah, yes, my dear Saradin. I see that by the ink stains on her fingers."

Saradin laughed prettily, perhaps encouraged by the snipe of her friend. "Come closer, dear Tranquilla. Let us take a look at you."

"She's not a display," Jericho told Saradin.

And again, it wasn't Gabriel who had come to her defense. Quilla looked at her patron, whose face was implacable and bore no expression she could discern beyond ennui.

"Oh, Jericho." Another pretty trill burbled from Saradin's throat. She tossed her head to make the feathers in her hair dance. "You're such a treat."

"Yes, Handmaiden," Gabriel said at last. "Do come closer. Let us have a look at you."

Quilla looked at him but answered in the way she knew he was expecting. "If it pleases you."

She heard the titters and murmurs as she walked toward the table, but she kept her gaze on her patron's until she reached the end of the table.

"I thought Handmaidens were . . . more . . . exotic," she heard Genevieve Somerholde whisper to her brother.

"I certainly thought they were better dressed," spoke up Madame Somerholde to Saradin. "Sara, dear, you should tell Gabriel to give the poor girl a decent gown."

"She has been working in the kitchen, I believe." Gabriel's gaze did not waver.

"The kitchen?" Madame Fiene's giggle was echoed by her two indistinguishable daughters. "Oh, my."

Quilla would have placed any amount of wager that Madame Fiene had never set foot in a kitchen, much less worked in one. "Indeed, my lord Delessan, I was."

Saradin's laughter was as glittery as the crystal glassware, and as brittle. "Imagine that."

Gabriel cut his eyes to his wife for one moment before looking back at Quilla. "I daresay nobody at this table has ever seen a Hand-maiden before."

"I know I have not," said the elder Somerholde through his bush of a mustache. He stared at Quilla with unequivocal delight. "I daresay I also thought them to be more exotic."

Quilla caught sight of Jericho's expression, which could have been carved from stone. Again, she noted how much the brothers looked alike, though one fair and one dark. Jericho looked angry at the treatment of her. Gabriel, however, only looked . . . intrigued.

"She will be whatever I wish her to be," said Gabriel calmly.

Saradin's pretty face went dark before she lightened it with a practiced smile. The ladies at the table exchanged glances, putting gloved hands to rouged mouths, affecting surprise. The gentlemen's eyes all brightened at his words.

"Anything, my good man?" This from Persis, who sat up straighter in his chair.

"Anything it pleases me for her to do."

Quilla had not spoken, had allowed them to talk around her as though she did not exist as anything more than a garden statue to be gawked at and commented upon. She wore her dignity like a cloak, better dressed in it than any of the more fashionably attired ladies seated in front of her. She watched Gabriel watch her, but could not judge his intent. Once again, he had gone dark to her.

"Turn around, Handmaiden. Let them take a look at you."

Quilla did, one slow rotation, returning to her spot to see every pair of eyes riveted upon her. *No greater pleasure*, she repeated in her mind. Serene. Calm. Whatever he was about, it was nothing she had not been through before.

Some people would not be satisfied until they saw the extent to which she would go.

"And you say she helps you with your records?" asked Boone Somerholde suddenly. "Can't you just get an assistant?"

Gabriel stood, his gaze locked on Quilla's. "I could, young master Somerholde, and I've had them. Chambermaids as well, to clean up after me. Secretaries to keep my records and make my correspondences. But you see," he said, walking around the end of the table and coming close enough to reach out and touch her, if he wanted, "a Handmaiden is so much more than that."

"Really?" Master Fiene sounded doubtful and gleeful at the same time. "How so, old man?"

"I think we've—" began Saradin, as though at last realizing that in her attempt to shame Quilla for her own gain she'd begun to bite her own tail.

"Yes." Gabriel's answer cut off his wife as though he'd put a hand over her mouth. "Much more."

Gabriel looked at his guests, all of whom were staring, eyes wide. Jericho alone refused to look. His gaze was narrowed and stormy, and kept fixed on the table in front of him. Small spots of color had risen on his cheeks. He clutched his napkin in front of him.

"Tell me, Handmaiden, what is it you do for me?"

"I am your solace and your comfort," she replied easily. "I am what you need before you know you need it. I am your Handmaiden."

"And if I tell you to write a letter for me?"

"If it pleases you for me to write it, I shall do so, my lord."

A murmur went around the table.

"And if I tell you serve me something to drink?"

"'Tis unlikely you'd need to tell me of your thirst before I'd guess, but I would serve you."

Her answer made the ladies at the table frown. The gentlemen, on the other hand, looked envious. Saradin's face had gone pale but for twin spots of color high on her cheeks.

Quilla looked down the table at the staring faces, then back into Gabriel's eyes, which had remained implacable, though a smirk teased the edges of his mouth.

"What else does she do?"

Quilla thought the voice belonged to Boone Somerholde, but she didn't take her gaze away from Gabriel's long enough to notice.

"Should I tell her to sing, she would do it for my pleasure. Or dance. Should I tell her to read to me, or recite poetry, or paint a portrait, she would do it." He paused, his smile creeping a bit further into his eyes. "Though there is no guarantee that it would look like me."

"She will do anything you tell her?" She was fair certain it was Persis who'd asked that question.

"Anything I tell her," said Gabriel softly. "And much I don't."

A stunned silence seemed to have pervaded the table, unbroken even by snide whispers. Gabriel seemed amused, but Quilla had learned one thing, at least, about her patron. It was most often when he seemed amused that he was ready to become angry.

"It would please me to have you attend me at dinner, Hand-maiden."

She nodded, though the acquiescence was unnecessary. She followed him as he turned on his heel and went back to his seat.

"So, Somerholde," Gabriel said as though the entire event had not happened, "you were telling us about the expansion you're planning to your estate."

"Well, my good man . . ." Somerholde launched into a long-winded description of his plans.

Quilla took the flagon of wine from its place on the table and filled Gabriel's glass. From her place at the other end of the long table, Saradin lifted hers and beckoned. Quilla took a step toward her, but without breaking the conversation with Somerholde, without saying a word, Gabriel put a hand on her sleeve to stop her. Quilla understood at once. She was not to serve the mistress, and it was to be quite obvious her place was not as serving maid.

But as Handmaiden.

After a moment, in which Saradin's face grew dark and darker, pale eyes becoming the color of an angry sea, Kirie stepped up to take the flagon from Quilla's hand and hurried down to fill Saradin's glass.

Gabriel kept his attention on Somerholde's blustering and his hand on Quilla's sleeve for a moment more before letting go.

He was making a point, but what it was, Quilla had yet to determine. He was angry. And he was punishing someone for it . . . but was it her? Or was it his lady wife?

"It sounds lovely," broke in Saradin, waving the maid away with an impatient hand. "Madame Somerholde, you will have the delight of furnishing your new rooms, will you not?"

Madame Somerholde stuttered an answer, her eyes going back and forth between Saradin and Gabriel, whose expression had become charming and pleasant, his attention on his guests and not on Quilla at all.

"Yes, I have already planned a buying trip," continued Madame Somerholde uneasily, pinned as she was between two such fierce gazes.

Gabriel flicked his eyes toward the platter of swan, which had now been cut into steaming, savory slices glistening with gravy. Quilla took his plate and filled it for him, then set it in front of him again.

"Saradin would love for me to take her on such a trip, I am certain," said Gabriel. He made no move to slice the meat in front of him, and though it was not an act he'd expected or allowed before, Quilla took up his knife and fork and began to cut it for him. "But, alas, my work prevents me from being the conciliatory husband she would like."

Saradin's eyes had fixed on the motion of Quilla's hands cutting the fowl, drawn the way a hound will eye an unattended plate. "Don't be silly, Gabriel. You are . . ." She hesitated briefly, barely, as Quilla finished with Gabriel's plate and again stepped back to his shoulder. "You are the most gracious and considerate of husbands."

"Mama said she's going to take me this time," Genevieve spoke up, apparently immune to the tension circulating the table at the silent battle between husband and wife. "She said she's going to pick out some furniture for my dowry."

The word made all the girls giggle. Saradin's lips thinned in an attempt at a smile.

"What a fortunate girl you are, to have such a mother."

"We will also be taking a trip to Alyria," put in Madame Fiene, as though not wishing to be outdone. "Isn't that so, my darling?"

Her husband, who had been staring with unabashed admiration at Quilla, nodded. "Yes, my dear. Quite right. We shall. Next summer, exactly so."

This caught Saradin's attention, and she looked away from Quilla for a moment to address Madame Fiene. "I've heard there are women there who still choose to wear the veil, though they needn't. Do you suppose that's true?"

"Oh, I do think so, yes." Madame Fiene took a large sip from her goblet, heedless of the way the wine dripped on her powdered décolletage.

Saradin looked back at Quilla. "Why a woman would choose such subservience is beyond my ken. Why choose to kneel at a man's feet when your proper place is at his side?"

Again, the weight of many eyes burdened Quilla's shoulders, but she showed no sign of noticing. She kept her attention upon her patron. A perfect Handmaiden, putting on a show because he wished it. A show that was also her reality, no game. This was her purpose and her place, and though there were those who would seek to shame her for it, she would not be shamed.

"A woman who knows her place is to be greatly valued," said Gabriel to Saradin. "And one who repeatedly oversteps her place shames herself. And her husband."

Ouch.

"Even the great Sinder did not require his Kedalya to serve him on her knees," said Saradin. "Sinder allowed Kedalya was his equal, if not his better, for she had the gift of bearing children, and he did not."

Gabriel looked around the table at the other men, and gave a sharp chuckle. "Well, 'tis a fine thing, then, that I sit at the head of this table, and not the great Sinder."

"I heard Alyrian silk is the finest available," cut in Madame Somerholde, and the tension eased a bit.

Quilla buttered a roll and put it on Gabriel's plate. When he took a bite of it and butter glistened on his lips, she took up the napkin from his lap and wiped them clean. She did nothing she hadn't done before, or wouldn't have done had they been alone in his chambers, but having an audience to her work pricked at her serenity. She was not ashamed of what she was, but neither did she appreciate being made sport of. She didn't care to be used to put another in her place . . . except that in this case, perhaps, she did.

"My brother should be able to tell you that," said Gabriel. "As 'tis his business to know of such matters."

Quilla happened to be glancing up as Jericho answered, and she found him staring at her. His blue eyes had gone dark in the lamplight, liquid pools of blackness surrounded by a thin rim of blue. His gaze lured her, but his words snared her.

"Alyrian silk is the finest, indeed, and should be worn only by those women who have beauty enough to compare to it."

"Then you shall be certain to buy some, Carmelia," Saradin said.

Jericho, still staring at Quilla, said nothing. After a moment, he bent back to his food, making a great show of cutting it and moving it around his plate, but eating very little. The conversation turned to furniture and textiles, and the places one went to find the best quality. Jericho kept silent except when pressed directly by one of the Fiene girls.

"A woman's best asset is not her wardrobe but her spirit," he answered to her question about what sort of fabric was most flattering. Everyone turned to look at him; he kept his eyes fixed on the table.

"Indeed?" replied Saradin. "And what, then, is a man's?"

Jericho looked up at his brother. "His honor."

"Particularly as regards a woman's spirit, I suppose?" Gabriel's reply sounded casual, but was not.

Jericho's stony expression flushed, and his eyes flicked down the table at Saradin, then up to Quilla before meeting his brother's again. "Among other things, yes."

Solid, uncomfortable silence hovered over the table, broken then by Genevieve's light trickle of laughter. "Shall I tell you of the most interesting book I've read?"

Quilla smiled slightly. She had thought the Somerholde girl to

be as dim as winter sky, but she'd been wrong. The girl was apt . . .
for though she made the shift in conversation seem wind-headed, it
worked.

"Oh, do," said one of the Fiene daughters. "And I shall tell you
of the one I've just finished."

Jericho didn't look away from his brother. Gabriel, however,
cocked his head with deliberate spite toward the Somerholde girl.
He raised a finger to Quilla without looking at her.

"Wait," he murmured, and Quilla folded herself into the Waiting on the floor next to his chair.

It was a relief, in a way, not to have to stand and be stared at.
Waiting was peace, and meditation. Waiting was easy.

"You arrogant son of a bitch!" Jericho's voice rang through the
conservatory, and the clatter of his chair falling as he stood startled
even Quilla.

"Brother—"

"Shut up, Gabriel!" Jericho stalked around the table to tower
over Quilla. "She is a person, not a doll!"

"She is a Handmaiden," came Gabriel's calm reply.

"Get up," Jericho said to her. "Quilla, you needn't—"

"Go sit down, Jericho." Gabriel's voice had become a silk-sheathed
blade. "You are making a fool of yourself in front of our guests."

"Get up, Quilla," said Jericho in a low voice. "You don't have to
let him do this to you."

She looked up at Jericho, "My lord Delessan—"

"It would not please me for you to address this issue," said
Gabriel as though he were discussing the weather. "Sit down, brother,
or leave the room."

Jericho looked at Quilla, who said nothing, then around the table. Though she could not see the faces, she could imagine the
expressions upon them. Even while Waiting she could feel the embarrassed fascination of the people at the table, a combination of

polite horror and gleeful expectation at the scene being laid out before them.

"Husband, this is not the place," began Saradin, and in the same mild tone, Gabriel interrupted her.

"It would not please me, wife, for this conversation to continue."

Oh, clever and horrid man, Quilla thought, grateful her eyes were below table level, because she would not have liked to see the look on Saradin's face. At least she knew now for whom his chastisement was meant.

Jericho's head snapped up and he stared down the table, presumably at Saradin. After a long moment made longer by the lack of conversation, Saradin spoke up lightly.

"Tell me, Madame Fiene, if you prefer your settee to be upholstered in Alyrian flaxen or Gahunian weave?"

At the other woman's answer, the guests again moved toward safer topics. Jericho said nothing else, gave not even a bow of leave, but turned on his heel and stalked away. After a few more moments, Gabriel reached down and tapped Quilla on the shoulder.

"Go," he said, and Quilla got gracefully to her feet and did as he'd commanded.

The rest of the chastising came the next morning, and she began to understand him a bit more. Gabriel did not speak to her when he came out of his bedroom and went straight to his worktable. He shrugged into his laboratory coat before she could help him, and he turned his back on her when she reached a hand to do the buttons.

He remained silent as he went about his work as if she was not there. Though she'd been assisting him with the work for weeks, he did not take the vial she offered, but instead plucked another from its case and used that. The implication was as clear as if he'd shouted.

"I have displeased you."

He made no answer, but continued with his work. The deliberate refusal to acknowledge her stung worse than a slap, for a slap could be given out of love and disinterest never could.

She might, in the past, have angered patrons. Sometimes, absolute solace was not without its price, and she paid it for them when they were unwilling to pay it for themselves. She had also, on occasion, failed to please a patron through inaction or by not guessing appropriately what he wanted, but she'd always done her best to remedy the situation.

She had never, through her behavior, displeased a patron so greatly as to make it seem as though she'd failed in her duty.

The situation unnerved her, and she went to prepare his tea and the simplebread, adding a crusting of sugar on the top of it. She brought it to him. He didn't acknowledge her. He continued his work, every subtle movement a study in his carefully artless refusal to pay attention to her.

The day wore on but Quilla stubbornly refused to accept defeat. She busied herself with tasks around the room, and that which she would normally have made unobtrusive she made less so. The meals she brought languished, uneaten, on the table, until at last she took them away. The notes she wrote while watching him work were ignored.

At last, when the afternoon came and he began to unbutton his coat in preparation for joining the rest of the company, she stepped in front of him.

"I plead your mercy, my lord."

He stepped aside to move around her. She matched his move, looking at his face. "Do you wish me to go? You only have to say so."

His eyes looked down into hers, his face expressionless. "You seem to think yourself quite capable of making your own decisions, Handmaiden."

Of all the answers she might have imagined, that was not one of them. "What have I done to displease you?"

"You told me you did not wish to accompany me to dinner. Yet there I found you anyway."

Long practice kept her face from goggling. "My lord, I—"

"Do you know what commotion you caused by showing up there?"

He pushed past her, tossing his white coat onto the back of the chair and moving toward his bedchamber. "You threw the entire house into a tizzy! I honored your request not to take you there, and instead you snuck in to watch us unawares!"

She had never entered his bedchamber before, but the sting of his accusation was enough to get her moving. Her feet hesitated but a moment on the threshold. It was worth it, for he looked surprised as he turned to face her.

"You know I would have been there if you had but requested, and I appreciate that you did not. I was not sneaking in to watch you unawares. I was helping Vernon, as the rest of the staff was otherwise occupied!"

"I have told you that is not your job!"

"My lord . . ." Quilla sought the right words. "You did not forbid me from making use of myself when I am not with you."

He ran his hand through his hair, shoulders slumping. "My lady wife . . . she is . . ."

There were many words Quilla would have used to describe Gabriel's lady wife, but she refrained. "Your lady wife is insecure with her place in your eyes. She wishes to maintain her status in front of her guests. 'Tis easy enough for her to pin blame upon me for her own uneasiness."

"She's jealous. She believes you a threat to her place in my life."

Quilla nodded, moving closer, loosening his tie and pulling it free of his collar. "I know. I cannot blame her for it. 'Tis difficult to understand the relationship between a Handmaiden and her patron."

He allowed her ministrations. "She believes you share my bed, though I assured her that is not the case."

Quilla smiled as she unbuttoned his shirt in preparation for helping him change. "But she understands, as any woman does, that the possibility of my sharing your bed is nearly as distracting as knowing it has already been done."

He stopped her hands and put a hand beneath her chin to lift her face toward his. "She fears you are displacing her in more places than just my bed."

Quilla's hands stilled on his shirtfront, half unbuttoned. She tilted her head to meet his eyes. "And how did you respond to her accusations?"

"You are my comfort. You are my solace. You are what I need before I know I need it." His hand moved along her jaw to cup the back of her head, pulling her closer by one step. Their bodies aligned, fitting together like pieces of a puzzle.

"When I saw you there, in front of all those leering, pompous prats, I was proud—and angry, too. Proud at how you could make them all speechless with your grace and serenity. Proud how even taunting does not make you rise to it."

"And angry?"

"Angry that your place was not at my side. That they viewed you as an absurdity, an oddity to be exclaimed over. Angry that you were not clothed in a gown of gold, with feathers in your hair."

"My lord. . . ."

"Angry at any who would have you."

"I am your Handmaiden, my lord." Quilla put her hands on his shoulders, tilting her head to look up at him. "There is no other who can have me, no matter how they might want me."

"Until you leave me."

His reply made her nod and furrow her brow. "Do you intend to send me away?"

His hands smoothed along the ridge of her spine. "You will leave when your work is finished. When you have brought me complete solace."

"That is the intent of my service to you, my lord."

His face twisted and he tightened his arms around her, burying his face in the side of her neck. His fingers found the end of her braid and he tugged off the ribbon binding the bottom, setting loose her curls to cover his face.

"And if I never reach it?"

"Then I will have failed in my duty. The Order, after a time, will call me back as not being the right Handmaiden for you. You'll choose another, if you like, and I . . ."

"You'll be sent to another patron!"

She put her arms around him, holding him close to her. "Yes, quite possibly."

He groaned, a sound that twisted her heart. She held him tighter, as tightly as she could, standing on her tiptoes to better put her arms around him.

"What is wrong?" she asked. "Please. Tell me what I can do."

His lips moved upon her skin as he spoke. "If you do your job, you will go away from me. If you do not do your duty, they will take you away from me. You are to be my comfort and what I need before I know I need it, but I do know, now. And I am . . . I am . . ."

"You are what?" she asked gently. Tears pricked her eyes, and never before had the thought of leaving a patron made her weep.

"I am not able," Gabriel whispered, hot against her ear. His hands moved in restless circles on her back. He nuzzled his face into her hair, against her cheek, his lips tracing a path on her temple and down the line of her jaw. "I am not able to do this."

He stood abruptly, putting her from him with such sudden force she nearly stumbled. He ran a hand through his hair, pushing it off his forehead, and turned his back to her. "I am not able to allow this, Handmaiden."

Tears escaped her eyes and traced a burning path down her cheeks to burn, salty, on her lips. She licked them away. "If I do not please you . . ."

"You please me overwell," he replied, voice low, gruff. "But I told you before. I do not require your assistance in my bedchamber. I made a vow when I married her. I can do no less than to keep it."

A vow Saradin had not kept, but it was not Quilla's place to mention it. She nodded, though he could not see her, and she left, still in silence.

Chapter 9

orry, but you've got a long face." Florentine set the bowl of stew in front of Quilla with a thump. "What's gone wrong with you?"

"Nothing." Quilla spooned some stew into her mouth. "Why should you assume there's something wrong?"

"Because there's naught that goes on in this house I don't know, and I know you've not been sleeping."

"Nonsense. I go to bed every night."

"Ha!" Florentine shook a spoon at her. "I didn't doubt your going to bed, Quilla Caden. 'Tis the sleep I doubt."

Quilla calmly ate more stew. "I sleep well enough."

Florentine made a rude noise. "You must think me a ruddy fool."

"No. Just overconcerned."

Florentine settled down at the table across from Quilla and dug into her own bowl of stew. She made smacking noises with her lips, groans and moans of small pleasure, and sighs of delight.

Quilla watched her, amused. "You do love your own cooking, do you not?"

Florentine looked up with squinted eyes. "And whose else should I love, if not mine own?"

"True." Quilla took another bite. "For you are fair accomplished with it."

"Ha," said Florentine again. "Think you I don't know you could run this kitchen as well as I? If it pleased him."

"Then let us both be thankful it does not," said Quilla, refusing to rise to Florentine's obvious bait.

Florentine smirked. "They're playing cards tonight. Think you he'll be in fair mood, or foul, on the morrow?"

"Perhaps it shall depend upon the amount of coin that leaves his pockets." Quilla sipped some mulled wine. "They do game each other quite fiercely, do they not?"

"Oh, Somerholde and Fiene do love to play for gold, indeed. Our lord Gabriel is not so enamored of it, but he'll do it, to be a good host."

"And the ladies?"

"Gossiping in the parlor, I should think." Florentine looked to the row of bells along the kitchen wall, each marked with the name of the room to which it connected. "Mostly about you."

Quilla bit her lip on a smile. "You don't really think so, do you?"

A guffaw from Florentine. "Naw. For they're all too bloody polite to talk about you in front of his lady wife. But let her leave the room and their lips will flap so fast they'll blow out the lamps, mark my words."

Quilla laughed. "You have so little faith in human nature, Florentine."

"I have every faith in human nature, Quilla Caden. Faith that we're all more easily led to evil than good. That if there are two choices to be made, we'll take the easier and most beneficial to ourselves. That the right path is almost always the rockier, and though the smooth might lead us to the Void, we'll take it even knowing it, because that, my friend"—Florentine punctuated her speech with a wave of her spoon that dripped gravy on the table—"is the way of human nature."

Quilla frowned, considering. "I don't agree."

"You don't have to," replied Florentine. "I'll still think the same."

Quilla laughed just as the bell for the parlor rang. "They're calling you."

"Not me." Florentine rolled her eyes. "They're calling for a maid. Which one shall I send?"

"Whose turn is it?"

Florentine heaved herself up from the table and went to the door leading to the small room where the maids and houseboys waited when not actively serving. "You act as though 'tis a hardship for them to go. They'll argue over who gets to go to see the ladies' dresses. Catch a whiff of fine perfume. 'Tis their job to do this."

"Then perhaps the question I must ask is which has displeased you the least today?"

The bell on the wall jangled again just as Florentine reached the doorway. "Oh, hold your knickers up with one hand while you diddle with the other. Lolly! You!"

A beaming Lolly scuttled out of the room, her cheeks pink. She smoothed her dress. "And shall I take the tea with me?"

Florentine made a long-suffering sigh. "Of course you should, Miss Feathers-for-Thoughts. They're not ringing because they want to look at your pretty face."

"I'll help." Quilla stood and pulled a tray from its slot in the cupboard. "The water is hot and the scones already baked. You just put a crock of butter and some jam on the tray, there, and I'll get the napkins."

Florentine grumbled. "See? Taking over my duties."

Quilla laughed. "Sit down and relax a moment."

The bell jangled again, longer this time.

"Ah, Invisible Mother," Florentine cried. "Go, girl! Go!"

She helped Lolly load the tray onto the small service lift. With an exasperated sigh, she pulled out a ball of twine and a wooden sword. "The young master's been playing in the lift again I see. I'll make it go, you run up the stairs."

Florentine tugged the pull rope to lift the tray to the second floor, then peered up the shaft. "Looks like she got it," she said, satisfied, and came back to the table. "What do you say we play some cards, ourselves?"

It was infinitely better than sitting in her room alone, even if she did borrow one of Gabriel's books to read. The cozy fire, the hot tea, and the scent of baking bread made the kitchen a much nicer place to be. And the company wasn't terrible, either, Quilla thought with a smile as Florentine got out the deck of cards without waiting for Quilla's answer.

"What's that for?" Florentine dealt the cards. "That grin makes you look like a rat what's escaped the trap with the cheese."

"Thank you," Quilla answered impulsively.

Florentine's look showed she thought Quilla was bent. "For what?"

"For being my friend."

Florentine burst into a guffaw that seemed to rattle the teacups on the table. "I'm not your friend."

Quilla took up her cards, arranging them in order of suit. "Protest if you like, but you are."

"I'd just as soon dump you in yonder fishpond as look at you sideways."

"You see?" answered Quilla serenely, putting down her first trick. "You are my friend."

They played for hours, while the bells sometimes jangled, and the maids and footmen came and went. Florentine had prepared a midnight supper with finger breads and sweets, and by the time the serving of that was done, Quilla was yawning.

"I must seek my bed, Florentine."

"Go, go." Florentine flapped her apron. "My only solace with these late affairs is that I can guarantee they'll not want to be fed until the midmorning."

"Not my lord Gabriel," Quilla said. "He'll be up at dawn's blush, same as always."

"Which means you will be, too. You get to your bed."

Quilla bid the chatelaine good night and climbed the stairs toward her room. She made it to the landing on the second floor, where she needed to leave the stairwell and seek the other set. The stairs leading to the third floor and her garret room were tucked into a small alcove at the far end of the hall, past the point it turned. There were only two doors at the corridor's end, one on each side facing the alcove. One led to a storage room for the maid's cleaning supplies and the other, larger, an unused guest room. Tucked away as it was at the back of the house, it was not the most fashionable place to put guests who would otherwise wish to be closer to their peers and have a better view and nicer amenities.

Just as she passed it, however, the doorknob turned. Startled, for the hour was, indeed, late, she ducked into the alcove and hid herself in the shadows.

A soft, feminine giggle caught her ear, and she looked at the door. Two figures broke the gloom, shadowed forms just a bit darker than the dimness surrounding them.

The smaller was the giggler. "Shh. Don't wake anyone."

It did not take a scholar to figure out what they'd been doing. But who were they? In the dark it was impossible to tell. The shorter figure giggled again. The figures joined, became one, before separating again and slipping off down the hall.

One of the Fiene girls, perhaps? Or Genevieve Somerholde? It could even have been one of the maids, meeting Bertram or Billy for a liaison.

Whoever it was, the concern was not hers. Right now, Quilla's only thought was the softness of her bed. And moments later, eyes already closing, she found it.

M y father says I am to be an alchemist like he is." Dane arranged the biscuits on his plate in solemn formation.

"And why would you wish to do that?" Florentine poured him a cup of milk, her hand hovering over his hair as though she wished to ruffle it but had withheld the urge.

"My father says Alchemy is a noble profession and that it takes a great mind to know it." Dane bit into a biscuit, the crumbs dotting his pink lips. "I should like to think I have a great mind."

"I'm sure you do." Quilla watched the boy with amusement, and something else. He was adorable. What would it be like to have a child? The thought sobered her expression. It was not her place to be a mother; she knew that when she entered the Order. Just as a Handmaiden could not expect to marry or maintain a long-term lover, so was motherhood an unattainable goal.

"My father says I need to put more attention into my studies and less into my games."

"Your father don't know enough about the value of playtime," Florentine grouched and added another cocao biscuit to Dane's plate. "Have another bikky, love."

"Save one or two of those for me, please." Quilla pointed at the tray she was preparing for Gabriel. "I'm about ready to take this upstairs."

"Ooh, let me ride with it! Please!" Dane gave her a cocao-smeared grin.

"There is not enough room on the lift for you and the tray." Quilla shook a gentle finger. "You'll spill the cream."

"I won't! I'll sit ever so still!" Dane clasped small hands together, his blue eyes pleading.

"Absolutely not," said Jorja Pinsky. "You came down to the kitchen for breakfast, not a ride on the service lift."

"And what a fine breakfast he's been provided," said Quilla as she arranged the last of the items on the tray. "Cocao biscuits."

Jorja frowned. "'Tis what he wanted."

"And do you think children should always have what they want?" Quilla paused. "Rather than what they need?"

"I need cocao biscuits," replied Dane smartly, licking the white milk mustache on his upper lip. "Because Florentine makes them the best!"

Quilla had to smile at him, but she shrugged toward Jorja. "His lord father wouldn't care to know he's been eating cocao for breakfast."

"Why not?" Jorja pointed at Quilla's tray. "He does it himself."

Quilla laughed. "Ah, but he is a grown man and able to make those decisions for himself. And besides, 'tis not his whole meal."

Jorja frowned further, looking at Dane. "The lady mistress did tell me I should give the young master what he likes."

Florentine gave a loud sniff, though she'd been as instrumental in loading the child with cocao as the nursemaid. "The lady mistress has little concept of controlling one's urges."

That was harsh criticism from the cook, especially in front of the child, though Dane seemed not to notice. He looked happy to chomp away on the treat, cramming more biscuits in his mouth as though afraid they'd now be taken away.

"Besides," said Jorja defensively, "when he wakes so early, he's ready for a proper breakfast by the time 'tis served, anyway."

"I'm the boy who eats two breakfasts," Dane said promptly, as though reciting a lesson. He grinned, showing cocao-smeared teeth. "Don't be cross, Quilla."

"I'm not cross. But you'll have your lord father to answer to, should he discover what you've been about."

"Will you tell him?" Dane looked dismayed.

"No. 'Tis not for me to tell him of your actions."

"Unless it pleases him to be told," put in Florentine under her breath.

Quilla ignored that comment and lifted the tray.

"Do you want to marry my father, Quilla Caden?"

The question, posed in Dane's childish voice but with Florentine's inflection, stopped her. She settled the tray onto the lift and turned.

"No, young master Delessan. Why do you ask?"

He shrugged. "Because Robie Vassermidst says his mother prepares his father's breakfast every day, even though they have a cook to do it. Robie Vassermidst says his mother takes care of his father's clothes, too, instead of a valet. Robie Vassermidst says—"

"Robie Vassermidst has a tongue that wags at both ends," said Florentine.

Dane looked stunned. "He doesn't! I've seen his tongue! It's hooked inside his mouth, just like mine is!"

He turned to Quilla. "And you do those things for my father, Quilla Caden. So I wondered if you wanted to marry him. Because if you did, then you would be my mother. Wouldn't you like that? To be my mama?"

His simple question made her throat close suddenly with emotion. "You already have a mother who loves you very much, Dane."

Dane nodded, his attention turning back to the last cocao biscuit on his plate. "Robie Vassermidst said his mother makes him eat porridge for breakfast."

Quilla shared a laugh with Florentine while Jorja smiled uncertainly. "Porridge is not so awful."

"No." Dane shrugged with a child's steady acceptance. "But not as nice as cocao biscuits."

"Very little is." Quilla closed the door to the lift and headed for the stairs. "I don't suppose I could convince you to have this waiting for me when I get up there, could I?"

Florentine acted as though Quilla had asked her to cut off both her hands and poke out her eyes. "As though 'twould kill you to pull the rope yourself?"

"Thank you, you're a dear," replied Quilla with a smile.

"I'm not!" came Florentine's shout up the stairs after her. "Quit trying to slander me!"

"It's not slander if it's true!" Quilla called back.

Since the day after the dinner party, her patron had done little more than give her brusque and sometimes biting orders. Aside from brief, one-word answers, he barely spoke to her. More telling, he did not look at her. At least, not when he believed she could see him.

It made for very frustrating days. Though he did not tell her not to, when she Waited he often ignored her. It had become something of a battle of wills. Quilla, who'd had long practice in Waiting, always won, because no matter how long she Waited, he always ended up being the one to speak first.

He did not tell her not to be with him but he did not encourage it. He asked nothing of her and though her training meant she should have been able to anticipate his needs before he asked, she found herself unable to do even that.

The man didn't appear to need anything.

He entered the room each morning, drank his tea, and ate whatever she had put before him. He stood still while she brushed the crumbs from his jacket front, his eyes locked at a point above her head, moving away without even a nod to acknowledge her efforts—not that she needed praise, she reminded herself sternly, turning down another of the neatly kept paths toward the pond, where the houseguests were ice-skating.

She did not need praise, but she would have liked him to speak to her. To look at her. To smile. And yes, she admitted to herself, to notice her.

It wasn't a Handmaiden's purpose or place to crave attention. Indeed, the ultimate goal was to provide such seamless service that the patron could not notice it, to become such an invisible but necessary part of the patron's life that only the Handmaiden's absence could be noted.

This had never bothered her; in fact, it was a point of pride, a goal to strive for and one she had upon occasion reached. But this was different. Gabriel Delessan was not simply not noticing her.

He was ignoring her.

The sound of laughter met Quilla's ears as she rounded the path. The guests were having a sledding party. She could see them gathered on the small, sloping hill just beyond the pond. The pond itself had been swept free of snow, to allow for ice-skating. The plank dock leading to the gazebo in the pond's center had been sprinkled with salt, and a nice fire burned in a barrel to provide warmth for hands gone numb with cold.

Though the hill on this side was gentle, it sloped off steeply on the other side, and there the gentlemen rode. Bertram and Billy had dragged the long, smooth-bottomed sleds from the stable and set them up at the top of the hill. The housemaids, clad in identical woolen cloaks, stood around a table laden with snacks, while another fire burned and a crock of mulled cider hung over top to keep warm.

"Quite the lovely party."

Quilla turned to see Jericho. "Yes. Lovely."

He gestured with his chin toward the group. "They all of them could be doing this at their own homes, but they wouldn't. They only do it in packs. And on my brother's coin."

"You speak as though that bothers you."

He shrugged and pulled the collar of his coat closer around his neck. A breeze kicked up and tossed his blond hair back from his forehead. "'Tis not really my place. And you'd know all about that. Wouldn't you?"

Quilla turned to look at him. "Why have you such an issue with my place?"

He gave her a long look but said nothing at first. Then he turned back to stare up the hill at the laughing guests. "You know why."

"Jericho . . ."

His head swiveled so he could stare at her again, lips thinning. "So it's *Jericho*, is it, now? We've graduated to that?"

"Would you prefer me to not address you by your name?"

"Don't you want to know if it would please me for you to address me by my name?"

Quilla looked out across the pond, where Dane was skating, arms pinwheeling as he turned in circles. "I am not required to please you."

"And because you're not required to, you don't care to, is that the way it is for you?"

Anger wanted to sharpen her voice, but she softened it so as not to give him the satisfaction. "I care, Jericho. Just not in the way you'd wish me to."

"No?" His voice dipped low, and he turned to shield her from the sight of the party guests. "And how do I wish you to? Can you answer me that?"

"I would rather not."

He stared at her until she looked up at him, then asked her another question. "Are you happy in my brother's service?"

Again, she replied as she always did when faced with a question she found inappropriate. "Why do you wish to know?"

"Curiosity."

"Ah. And are you always so concerned about your brother's affairs?"

Jericho touched a fingertip to his brow in acknowledgment. "Point taken. However, in this instance, I think 'tis not my brother I'm concerned about."

"Would you have me believe it's me?"

"Aye." Jericho had not turned his gaze from hers, and though Quilla now kept hers focused on the lake, she could feel his eyes burning into her.

"It would be my suggestion, then, that you find something else to occupy your thoughts."

"How long will it take, do you think?"

She glanced at him, finding his eyes on her face as she'd suspected. "For what?"

"To soothe him."

"As long as it takes," was her reply.

"That answer is insufficient and also cowardly."

Quilla's small smile disappeared entirely, and she turned on him. "What are you about, my lesser lord Delessan? What purpose do you seek in trying to dissuade me from my job? I am here to perform a function, hired by your brother, which for the purpose of my job means I belong to your brother. I am his and no other's. It's not your concern my feelings on the matter, nor my thoughts. If I love it or hate it should not be any of your concern!"

His feathers seemed unruffled. A breeze had kicked up, making Quilla pull her cloak tighter around her throat, but Jericho didn't seem to mind the chill. The breeze lifted the tips of his blond hair and tumbled it over his forehead in an untidy mess that nevertheless did not distract from the vivid blue of his eyes.

"Do you?" he asked simply. "Love it? Or hate it?"

The question, stated with such simple boldness, made her start to scowl, but she forced her face to smooth. "Neither."

"I've made you angry. At least there's that."

Again, training and conscious effort kept her from goggling in surprise. "Were you trying to?"

"I'm trying to make you feel something, Quilla, and anger seemed the easiest way to breach the door."

"Why?" She kept her voice pitched low, aware that the breeze could take her words and send them to ears not meant to hear them.

"Because if you won't let me love you, the least you can do is allow me to be your friend."

This set her back a literal step. For a moment, she couldn't breathe. "What? You—"

"Don't you remember what I told you the first day we met?" He stared out over the pond, shielding his eyes to watch his nephew being chased by his chubby nursemaid.

Does the bee need to know the flower before it sups? A bird know the wind before it takes flight? The sea know the shore before it creeps upon it? Does a man need to know a woman before he loves her?

"I do. I didn't believe it then, either."

Jericho pulled his cloak tighter around his throat. "Then all the more reason you should believe me now that I've had the chance to know you."

"Oh, Jericho." She didn't know what to say.

"Don't. Please, Quilla. I know you are my brother's. I know it's your purpose and your place to cater to him, and not to me. And I know that even if it weren't that I am not the sort of man you'd choose. He's smart, and I'm but merry." He turned and looked at her with such sincerity it made her want to take his hand. "But please, think on this. If you should fail—"

"Do you believe I will?"

"If you should fail," he continued, "will you know this of me? That I would not take his place. That I would not have you as sent from the Order, but as yourself."

Quilla had to look away from him. "Your friendship would mean more to me than I can say, Jericho."

"And the rest?"

"The rest is not for me to comment upon. Please understand." She kept her eyes upon the pond, and the young boy skating there. "But know you this of me. I do consider you a friend, and one of choice, not necessity."

"Go, Jorja! Go!" Dane's voice rang out over the pond.

The nursemaid, huffing and puffing, skidded to a stop at the pond's edge. "He's wearing me out, that one."

Quilla laughed, watching the boy fall on his bottom "For shame, Jorja. You should be able to keep up with him."

Jorja lifted both wobbling chins. "You try!"

The boy tried to get up and fell again, skidding across the ice. "My father says you must attend me, Jorja!"

"His father can come out and freeze his arse," Jorja muttered. "I'm not paid enough for this business."

"Jorja!" Dane called imperiously. "Jorja! Get over here!"

The boy struggled to his feet, slipping on the ice, but at last managing to stand upright. "Look at me!"

"I sees you, I sees you," Jorja muttered, not even bothering to look over her shoulder at the lad. She let out a huff and stretched fat hands toward the sputtering fire in the barrel. "Who could miss him with all the caterwauling."

Quilla watched Dane, whose arms whirled as he skated, his

childish laughter high-pitched in the thin winter air. "I'll be glad to help you watch him, Jorja, so long as I'm here."

Jorja grunted and reached for the cauldron set to warm over the blaze. She dipped some hot cider into a mug and slugged it back with a smack of her lips. Then she settled her bulk onto the wooden log bench next to the fire.

"Watch me!"

Quilla shaded her eyes to do it, the late setting sun a glare of red and yellow against her eyelids. She blinked, watching the boy gliding and twirling. It looked most merry. Perhaps she would try.

"'Tis not as easy as it looks."

She turned to give a raised-brow glance at Jericho. "No? I thought I saw you out there the other day."

He grinned. "And you are trying to insult me by insinuating that if it's not easy I should not be able to do it?"

Quilla shrugged, looking back out at the ice. "Perhaps you inferred that meaning."

"Well said."

Jorja snorted from her place on the bench, but said nothing. Jericho made a leg at her, and gave a half bow.

"Have you something to say, good lady? Pray tell, do speak."

Jorja might be lazy, Quilla thought, but she wasn't stupid. She didn't seem about to sass the young master any more than she'd have done the elder.

"Uncle Jericho! Watch me!"

"Gladly, nephew Dane," called Jericho. He strode to the edge of the pond, hands in his pockets, his rakish red scarf fluttering. "Go like the wind!"

"I am!" cried Dane, small legs pushing.

"Mind he don't work himself to a frenzy," cautioned Jorja, even as she could not be bothered to lift herself from the bench. "'Tisn't good for children to be so active."

Jericho gave Quilla a look that made her bite her lip to keep from laughing. In an aside, he said, "No, it's better for children to be fed sweets until they burst and keep them docile in front of the fire."

Quilla laughed softly, watching Dane. "It's not so far from their treatment of him."

"Not if I have any say. Of which I understandably have little. But I do my best to see the lad has sport in his life."

"You gave him the skates?" She didn't really need to ask the question, as the answer had been evident in his eyes.

Jorja made a strangled mutter. "Quilla, I gots need of the necessary. Would you?"

Quilla nodded, thinking too much cider was not a wise thing in which to partake, so far from the house. "Of course."

Jorja hauled herself off the bench and headed back toward the house, while Quilla and Jericho stayed in a silence that had become comfortable.

"Uncle Jericho! Watch me!" Dane slid along the ice, falling again and getting up again with a disgruntled cry.

"I'm watching you, Dane!"

And Quilla, watching Jericho watch the boy, made a connection that, upon the realization of it, seemed so obvious she could not believe nobody had noticed it before.

"He's yours, isn't he." A quiet statement, not a question.

Jericho, to give him credit, did not try to dissemble. "I like to think so, yes."

Quilla turned to watch the lad, who was no longer skating. He'd found a large stick on the ice and was poking it downward, over and over again, and yammering something Quilla could not understand.

"I was barely grown when she came to Glad Tidings." Jericho's gaze had gone far away. "Saradin, shining like a golden star, fallen

from the heavens. Of course I was half in lust with her the first
moment I saw her. She wanted naught to do with me. She'd come
to be our chatelaine, but her eyes were on a greater prize."

"Gabriel."

He nodded, smiling faintly. "Yes. Lord of the manor. She wanted
only the best, our Sara. The second son wouldn't do. Well, not at
first."

"Oh, Jericho." Quilla pitched her voice low.

He shook his head, watching the boy on the ice. "When she decided my brother's infrequent attentions were not enough for her,
she came to me. And I tell you, Quilla, not as excuse but as truth.
She never left me alone. She thought of every excuse to get me
alone. To touch me. To woo me, and yes, I know how that sounds
but you should know I was young and she, very beautiful."

"Many men use their gender as excuse, but in fact, that's all
it is."

"You're saying I could have resisted her, and you're right. I could
have. And should have. But I didn't." He looked at her. "And I'd
have regretted it ever since, if not for that one thing. That boy,
skating there on the ice. I'd not change a thing I did, ever. Because
of him."

"And now?"

"And now, she would have me pay court to her as I did when I
was younger, and it makes her angry that I won't. But that pleasure
has palled, Quilla Caden." He slanted her a sideways glance. "You
think less of me for making love to my brother's wife? I take the
blame for it, and more, for I've never been man enough even to
admit to him the truth."

"You think he hasn't guessed?"

"There can be nobody in this household who hasn't guessed,
though none will speak of it."

"And you've always known?"

He nodded slightly, then turned to look at her. "She's never said as much. I'm not even certain she'd admit it."

"And you've never said anything about it?"

He shook his head, slight smile still upon his lips. "Of course not."

"Because you love her?"

A flash in his gaze told her she'd guessed wrong. "No. Because I love him."

The boy, obviously. But also, someone else. "Your brother."

"Does it surprise you, Quilla Caden? That I might actually find affection for the beast who is so constantly growling? I wouldn't think it to be such a surprise. After all, you also have affection for him."

As he had not, she did not dissemble. "I do, indeed."

"It's your duty to have affection for him." Did he tease? She could not be certain.

"It's your duty to also have affection for him, as he is your brother."

Jericho laughed, turning to face her. "You have ever a way with words."

She smiled, helpless not to, for though he had angered her in the past, she could not deny his charm. "As do you."

"So you have forgiven me?"

"I am unaware there is anything for which I needed to forgive you."

"Dishonest flattery does not become you."

"You bad thing! You dirty thing!"

Dane's taunting voice made them both turn. He hacked at the ice with his long stick, his blond hair tousled by wind and exertion, cheeks pinked from cold. Again, he raised the stick and brought it down, hard, upon the ice.

"Dirty thing! Don't make that face at me!"

"What's he going on about, I wonder?" Jericho murmured fondly.

"Dirty, nasty beastie!"

"The eel," Quilla said only a half beat before the same words came from Jericho's lips. "Dane, no!"

The boy looked up only briefly, looking more like his mother then with twisted, gleeful lips and blue eyes burning with naughty glee. He bent back to his task, poking the stick down and down, faster as though he wanted to get in as much as he could before someone came to stop him.

"Dane! Stop!" Jericho put his foot to the ice, slipping. "Stop, lad!"

Quilla followed, stepping carefully. They made their way toward the pond's center. Seeing them approach, Dane began whacking harder, his small face bright with effort.

They were nearly there when the ice exploded all around them.

Chapter 10

A long, black column of smoke shot from the center of the pond. Smoke without fire beneath. Chunks of ice and snow flew forward, and Quilla threw up her hand to cover her face. Her forehead stung and she let out a small cry as she slipped and went to her hands and knees. She put her fingers to her face, and they came away speckled with blood.

The ice beneath her knees cracked with an ominous sound. It shifted under her, and she spread out her weight so as not to crack it further. Ahead of her, chunks of ice as thick as her fist rolled toward her, spraying water and grit.

She heard Jericho yelling. Dane screaming. And another voice, that of a creature teased to rage, a beast not meant for the air.

She lifted her head to see Jericho clutching a screaming Dane and pulling the boy away from the column of black smoke, which, she realized, wasn't a column at all but the body of the eel itself. It had risen from the water and now slammed its head across the ice, snapping its jaws and spraying more water and chunks of ice.

Its body was the thickness of hers, though all sinewy sleekness and boneless fluidity. Its jaw seemed to open out directly from its neck, wide as it now gaped and snapped while the beast writhed its way across the ice toward the man and boy.

The water churned where its tail thrashed. The water tossed up onto the ice made everything even slicker, though thank Sinder it didn't seem to be breaking further.

The eel heaved itself one measure farther out of the water, humping its way along the ice as a snake moves along the ground. The great jaws snapped again, needle-sharp teeth coming down on the ice hard enough to send chips of it skittering toward her.

Jericho could not seem to get Dane off the ice. He pulled the screaming, flailing child by the back of his coat, but as Quilla watched, they both slipped and fell.

The eel lunged forward, its small dull eyes seeming to focus on the boy. Quilla, on its other side, scrabbled on her hands and knees toward it. She grabbed up the stick Dane had been using to tease the eel. First, she used it to get herself standing. Next, she whacked the eel with it as hard as she could.

The beast's body writhed, the blunt, triangular head swerving in its pursuit to face her. Quilla lifted the stick again, bringing it down so hard upon the eel's body the wood splintered and broke in half.

From the corner of her eye, she saw Jericho pull Dane upright and fling him toward the shore, out of the eel's reach. The boy's wail reached her ears but Quilla could do naught but wield the broken-off end of her weapon as the eel began sliding back into the water.

The movement was a retreat, and yet it brought the creature closer to her and shook the ice around the hole it had made hard enough to send her to her knees again, her hands splayed on the frigid surface, praying to the Invisible Mother that the cracks appearing would hold together long enough for her to get off the pond.

"Quilla!"

Jericho ran and slid toward her, reaching for her hand. The eel snapped but couldn't reach him as it continued its smooth slide back below the pond's surface. It seemed to struggle for an instant upon the ice, but the momentum of its retreat must have been greater than its desire for attack, because in another moment even the great jaws had slipped below the surface.

Jericho's hands gripped her shoulders. The next moment found her in his arms. Without thinking, she returned the embrace, her heart still hammering and breath coming in gasps.

"Are you all right?"

She nodded.

"You're bleeding."

She'd forgotten the scrapes on her forehead. "I'm fine."

Concern filled his eyes and he drew a hand along her face, showing her it had come away streaked with blood. "We should get you inside."

"Dane?" Quilla looked for him. The boy had made it to the edge of the pond, where Jorja had gathered him to her while she screamed and wept.

"He'll be fine."

Quilla shivered, a combination of cold and shock setting in. She looked at Jericho's face. The warmth of his breath, redolent of mint, caressed her cheek. He still had an arm around her shoulders.

"Are you all right?" she asked him.

Before he could answer, the ice beneath them moved. The cracking sounded like festival flameballoons exploding. Less than a breath later, icy water soaked her skirt and stung her legs beneath.

"Move!"

Quilla didn't hesitate. She moved. She pushed with her knees and got to her feet, slipping and falling at first but then managing to stay upright as Jericho yanked the shoulder of her cloak.

No more time for speaking. No time for thinking. Only time for running as fast as they could across the slick and breaking surface of the ice.

Behind them she heard the moist *thwap* of the eel throwing itself once more out of the pond. Ice and water sprayed her back. Quilla didn't dare look back, though a gust of breeze and the clash of teeth on teeth told her the beast was snapping, literally, at their heels.

They were only a few arrows from the shore when the ice broke out from beneath them. She sank in water up to her thighs, her cloak and dress soaked and weighing her down. Jericho fell in beside her with a bigger splash. Something moved around her legs, the swirl of her hem or perhaps a smaller eel. The larger one still writhed behind them, the ice cracking and disintegrating under its weight as it moved.

Quilla flailed her arms with Jorja's screams echoing in her ears. She had no voice to scream. The water had stolen her breath. All she could think of was getting out.

And then, his hand in hers, pulling. Jericho curled his fingers around hers, his strength moving her through the water faster than she could have made it on her own. She pushed, he pulled. Soft mud sucked at her boots, but she could not kick them off. He pulled harder. A wave of water, pushed forward by the eel's attempts to reach them, aided them at last and the water reached her knees, then only her ankles, and finally after an eternity, Quilla stumbled onto ground.

Jericho lay beside her, panting, his fine clothes covered with muck. His blond hair looked darker with wet. He looked more like Gabriel than ever.

She turned her head toward the pond. Chunks of ice bobbed in the churning water, but of the eel there was no sign.

"Thank the Invisible Mother," she murmured, spent. "I thought it might leap out onto the shore after us."

Jericho sat up. "I told you it did not care to eat Handmaidens."

How could she find a smile, after that? Somehow, she did. "No. It would seem its meal of choice is little lads who poke at it with sticks."

Jorja was still screaming. Dane appeared to have been stunned into silence. Quilla's feet and legs had gone numb, and the weight of her sodden clothes almost kept her on the ground, but she knew she would need to get inside and out of her wet things if she hoped to avoid freezing to death.

"Shut your hole," she snapped at Jorja, who had tried Quilla's not-quite-infinite patience to its very limit. "Get the boy inside. Check him for injuries. Get him into a hot bath. For the love of your mother, Jorja Pinsky, stop your blubbering and tend your charge as 'tis your duty to do!"

Jorja stopped screaming like Quilla had bound her mouth. She grabbed Dane into her arms and began going as fast as she could with him toward the house.

"We must needs get us both inside, too." Jericho put his arm around her. "Come, Quilla Caden, before we both become as iced solid as that pond once was."

She wasn't sure she could make it into the house, but once again Jericho's strength aided her. Walking kept her warm enough, at least, though by the time they reached the doors to the house she was breathing hard and her teeth chattering so fiercely she had bitten her tongue.

The household was in an uproar. Lolly and Kirie accosted her as soon as she entered, grabbing off her cloak and stripping her down right there in the back kitchen hall. Quilla made no protest; nudity did not concern her, and false modesty had no place in this situation. She helped them as best she could with numb and shaking hands, buttons flying from the throat of her dress as Lolly tugged it off her. She stood for only a moment naked before Kirie wrapped a blanket around her but in that moment Quilla looked up and saw Jericho's eyes upon her. His own clothes had been stripped from him, though he still wore his underdrawers. He looked quickly away, and in the next moment Rossi led her toward the small garden parlor usually used as a place for the ladies to sit and arrange flowers. The fire had been stoked to blaze, and Billy was already pouring pitchers of steaming water into a basin in front of it.

Quilla was pushed into the chair in front of the fire and her feet plunked into the steaming water. Lolly brought a towel to dry her hair. Rossi was doing the same for Jericho.

"Where did they take the lad?" Quilla found the voice to ask.

"To the nursery. He's already in the tub," said Rossi. "Playing with his boats and singing songs. Jorja fainted and needed to be revived."

"Who did that, I wonder?" Quilla's chattering teeth slowly stilled under Lolly's ministrations.

"Florentine slapped her so hard it left a mark," said Kirie from her place by the fire, where she was warming towels. "And Jorja said not a word. Can you imagine?"

"I can imagine very well," replied Quilla. "If she does not lose her place here, I will be greatly surprised."

"Or us ours," said Jericho. "As we were the ones watching him."

Billy reappeared with a robe which he helped Jericho put on, while Kirie brought a warm gown for Quilla. She slipped it over Quilla's head, and though she would still need a bath to rid herself of the dirt and muck, at least the ice had begun to disappear from her veins.

"Has anyone told my brother and his wife the fate that nearly befell their son?"

"Yes, my lord. Florentine herself has gone to fetch the master from the gentlemen's games," said Lolly.

"And the lady mistress?" Quilla accepted the hot rum Rossi had handed her. She sipped. "She will want to know, too."

"She's not been found, as yet," said Lolly with a quick glance at Kirie. "Though our lord Delessan has begun tearing up the house in search for her."

Quilla met Jericho's gaze, which had shuttered itself but was not unreadable. His mouth thinned, and he waved Rossi away impatiently. From the hall came the sound of shouts and running feet, though no one entered the garden parlor.

"They will find her soon, I am certain," said Jericho. "And Sinder's Mercy when they do."

"She will need more than Sinder's Mercy," murmured Quilla.

"You're right," agreed Jericho. They shared another look of understanding. "She will need my brother's."

There had been more shouting from abovestairs. More slamming of doors. By the time Quilla could convince Lolly to let her get up and leave the garden parlor, however, silence hung over the entire household. It was the hush of every ear being turned toward something waiting to happen, and Quilla was fair certain she could guess what it was.

She went to Gabriel's chamber, passing doors cracked open to provide listening ears with easier access. The door to his workroom was closed, and the moment she lifted the latch, shouting broke the silence in the house.

"Damn you to the Void!" Saradin's shrill voice echoed in the hall, providing, Quilla thought, ample interest to the held-breath residents. "Damn you, Gabriel Delessan!"

The sound of shattering glass came next. The thud of some heavy object being thrown. The crack of flesh on flesh.

Quilla threw open the door and stopped at the sight in front of her. His table had been overturned. Beakers and vials on the floor. Books and paper scattered everywhere, with a pot of ink spilled in a spreading puddle on the desk. Saradin stood in the midst of the destruction, hand upraised.

Quilla watched as Saradin slapped Gabriel's face hard enough to turn his head. The sound of it hurt Quilla's ears. The sight of it hurt her heart.

"Don't you dare judge me!" Saradin screamed. "Don't you dare! Not when you have your own whore to serve you night and day, your dripping-cunt slut to warm your bed!"

She used the back of her hand this time, sending him staggering one step in the opposite direction. "The whore you parade around in front of our guests to humiliate me! The whore who eats and drinks and shits and fucks in my house! My house! My. House!" She punctuated the last words with two more slaps that looked hard enough to break her fingers.

She had raised her hand again to strike him when his hand came up and caught hers. His fingers closed down over hers, forcing them to curl into a ball. Saradin made a pained yelp and tried to get away, but Gabriel held her fast.

"She is not my whore," Gabriel said in a voice so thick with contempt and loathing it made Saradin recoil as though he'd been the one to slap her. "She is my solace and my comfort, two things you, my lady wife, have never been."

Saradin's scream rose from her throat like smoke into the sky. "You bastard! You cock-sucking son of a whore! How dare you! I am your wife! I am the mistress of this house!"

"And you are a whore who was fucking a man not her husband while our son nearly died, Saradin!" Gabriel's voice shook. "Dane could have been dead an hour gone and you'd not have known it because you were so busy putting Boone Somerholde's cock down the back of your throat!"

She slapped him with her other hand, and he grabbed that one, too, yanking both her hands down between them to hold her still.

"You are the whore, lady," Gabriel said, his voice colder than the ice on the pond. "You are unfit to be a mother, unfit to be a wife. You should go to your lover, if that's what you please, and leave me and my son without the benefit of your poison presence in our lives."

Saradin struggled in his grip without success at gaining release. Her pretty face twisted. "Your son? He's not—"

"Shut your fucking mouth!" Gabriel roared, though Saradin kept speaking.

"—your son!" she cried, triumphant, eyes flashing with mad brilliance. She kicked out at him, yanking her hands in his grip. "He's not even—"

"I said for you to shut your mouth!" Gabriel hit her hard enough to make blood appear at the corner of her lips, though probably not hard enough to send her to the ground. She crumpled anyway, hands shielding a face Quilla could still see bore a smile, though the words coming from her mouth belied any humor.

"Monster!" Saradin screamed. "Faithless brute! Stupid, gulli-ble—"

He bent and grabbed her up by the hair, his fist raised to strike her again. Quilla crossed the floor in five strides to grab his arm and keep it from coming down.

"My lord! No!"

Saradin laughed, eyes flashing back and forth from Gabriel to Quilla. "Ah, so the bitch comes to save her lord and master."

Gabriel let go of her, adding a push that knocked her again to the ground. She sprawled for real this time, skirts spreading out around her. Saradin let out a cry of rage tempered with surprise—as though, despite all that had already happened, she could not believe he would actually throw her away.

Gabriel shook off Quilla's hand and strode to the ruins of his worktable. He stooped and grabbed up a small bottle, which he tossed at Saradin. It landed neatly in the lap of her skirt. She lifted it, then looked up at him with wide eyes, the screams for a moment forgotten.

"Do us both a favor," Gabriel said in a voice like stone. "Next time, make sure you finish the job."

Then he turned his back on her, and Saradin got to her feet. She staggered as she rose but there was no hand to steady her. She gripped the small bottle but did not take it with her. Instead, she tossed it to the floor at Quilla's feet, where the glass broke and released a stream of silver liquid that broke apart into a hundred tiny beads that within moments had rejoined to form a whole. Without another word, Saradin left the room, slamming the door behind her.

For one eternal moment, Quilla was not certain what to do. She had never faltered in this way before. She had perhaps at times questioned which course of action would be best for her to take. She had, upon occasion, done the wrong thing. But she had never, in all her time of service, not been able to make a choice at all.

The moment ended when he turned to face her. His eyes held no expression. Naught she could read or interpret. Yet, somehow, that made it easier for her to understand what it was he needed.

"Get you gone from my sight, Handmaiden."

She might have touched him, had she not sensed that to do so would be to invite his anger. Instead, she Waited. At least, the physical position of the Waiting—the mental place remained out of her grasp. On her knees before him, head bowed, hands placed one palm against the other's back in her lap, Quilla Waited for her patron to speak.

When another long moment passed without a word from him, nor a gesture, nor a movement, she lifted her face to look at him. His face had gone the color of expensive parchment. His lips, pale, too, had compressed into a thin line, neither smile nor frown but something horrid in between.

"I could have lost him."

Five words that spoke more than a thousand ever could. Quilla got to her feet and put her arm around his waist. She thought he might faint, and if he did, she would be able to do little to support him. If she could get him to sit, she might fend off his tumble.

Gabriel fought her attempt at assistance and refused to take the seat into which she was gently trying to force him. "Walk with me, my lord," Quilla said, instead. "Let me draw you a bath."

He allowed her that, following without protest as she led him through his bedroom and into the privy chamber, where she urged him to sit and at last he did, on the wooden bench along the wall. She wet a cloth with cool water and placed it on the back of his neck as he put his face into his hands.

"I could have lost him, Handmaiden."

"But you did not, my lord. And he will be fine."

She turned the spigot to fill the large bathtub, making certain to light the brazier underneath to keep the water hot. She turned back to Gabriel and knelt at his feet, removing his boots and stockings and setting them aside. She unbuttoned his shirt and opened it, pulling it off his arms to leave him bare-chested. The tub had filled quickly while she worked and the water steamed.

"Prithee allow me to help you stand," she said, and he did. She loosed the buttons of his trousers and slid them down over lean hips and strong thighs. He wore thin linen underdrawers beneath and she removed them as well before taking his hand and urging him toward the tub. He got into it with the stiff-legged vulnerability of an old man, or one who has been wounded. Gabriel settled into the water with a sigh, and Quilla turned off the spigot.

The narrow, polished wooden planks making up the floor had darkened with wet when he got into the tub. It soaked the hem of her gown. She reached for a pitcher and a handful of soft soap.

"Will you allow me to wash your hair?"

He nodded, eyes closed, head tipped back against the tub, his fingers gripping the curved wooden rim so tight the knuckles had gone white. Quilla lathered his thick, dark hair, keeping the soap from his eyes and rinsing again and again with a clean pitcher of water until she'd finished.

By that time, his grip had relaxed and the rise and fall of his chest slowed. Taking the soap and a fresh pitcher of water, Quilla set them on the floor near the drain set into the center of the floor. Then she stripped out of her gown and scrubbed away all signs of pond dirt. She washed her hair, too, until the length of it squeaked clean and it fell in rippling lengths down her back. Then she got into the tub with him. Water splashed over the sides.

His eyes flew open, startled. "What are you doing?"

Quilla didn't answer with words. Instead, she put herself into his arms, the front of her against the front of him, their legs tangled in the water. She tucked her head into the hollow of his neck and shoulder.

"Handmaiden . . ."

"Shh," she hushed him. "Quiet, Gabriel."

It was the first time she'd addressed him by his name. He did nothing after that, not for a long time. The water cooled. Then he put a hand beneath her chin and lifted her face to his. His mouth aligned with hers, and he kissed her.

He took her from the tub and to his bed, both of them still drip-
ping, and he dried her with linen sheets and warmed her with the
weight of his body and heat of his kisses as he covered her with
them. He made love to her, and she to him, both taking and giving
in equal amounts.

It had begun as Service but ended up as something more. She
hesitated when his mouth trailed from her breast, over the slope of
her belly, to find the curls between her legs and the small, burning
nub there. But when he pushed her gently back as she tried to sit,
she did as he'd requested without words and let him part her thighs
to make love to her with his tongue and hands.

She gave him her pleasure, the sound and scent and taste of it,
and she shattered on his tongue, calling out his name as her climax
broke her apart and put her back together. When he kissed her
again she tasted herself on him and it sent another surge of pleasure
through her, that he could have been so intimate with her. That his
solace and his need had become part and parcel her own, the two
entwined, that giving her pleasure meant his was made greater.

He closed his eyes when he slid inside her, his breath leaving
him in a gasping sigh. He gathered her to him, buried his face in
her neck, and suckled there as he began to move. Slow, even strokes
that hit her core each time and made her gasp aloud and run her
nails down the seam of his spine.

He bit her skin and she arched beneath him at the pleasure pain
it caused. Gabriel moved inside Quilla, but more than that, he
was with her. Not only bodies joined, but minds aligned, because
when he opened his eyes to meet her gaze, she saw herself reflected
there.

"You are what I need," he murmured, dipping to breath in her
ear as his pace quickened. "You are solace. You are my Handmaiden."

"I am yours," Quilla replied, lifting her hips to meet his thrusts. Another ball of tension had begun to tangle in her belly, radiating spokes of pleasure to every limb. "I am yours."

"You are mine." He shook, his thrust becoming uneven, his breath a rasping gasp. "Tranquilla Caden . . ."

Hearing it was enough to send her over the edge again, and though she was no stranger to the pleasures her body could sustain, this was all at once more and greater than she had ever felt before.

"It would well please me if you would stay," he murmured into her hair before rolling off to lie beside her on the pillows.

"Then of course I shall."

He sighed, eyes already closing. In moments his steady breathing told her he slept. And soon, she did, too.

Quilla woke before Gabriel in the darkness of predawn and got out of bed to bathe and dress, to prepare the fire and the water for his tea. She went to the kitchen to gather some breakfast, for her own stomach grumbled with emptiness and she knew his would do the same.

The way to the kitchen wasn't long, and she had a good memory for the twists and turns of the corridor. Even so, she was grateful for the light of the candle as she made her way to the kitchen. The fire had been left to embers, and the red glow cast the room in an odd half light that did nothing to help the ache in her head.

Quilla set her candle down on the table and blew out the flame, not wanting to waste the wax when the light from the fire was adequate for her needs. She found the loaf of bread, covered with a white cloth, on the counter, and sliced a piece.

So intent on slicing the bread and pulling out the crock of butter, Quilla didn't notice the figure in the corner until it spoke, startling her into dropping the knife she was using. It clattered and spun along the floor, coming to a rest at the feet of the figure, which bent to retrieve it. The person, male or female, she couldn't be certain which, tilted the blade so it caught the firelight.

"Pretty, pretty."

The voice, husky and low, was nevertheless of indeterminate gender, until bending into the firelight again, the fall of hair showed Quilla to whom it belonged. Saradin, profiled in shadows and flickering red and gold, must have smiled because Quilla saw the flash of teeth. Smiled, or perhaps sneered. At any rate, the expression seemed fierce enough to keep Quilla from moving closer.

"Mistress Saradin."

"Mistress is how you may address me, as your mistress I am." Her laugh was like broken glass grating over stone. "Yes. And you're the whore my husband hired to soothe him."

"Respectfully, my lady Delessan. I am a Handmaiden. Not a whore."

Saradin turned her head and spat into the fire, making it sizzle and hiss. "Shut your mouth! You're a whore!"

The unfairness of it never ceased to irritate Quilla, no matter how many times she faced the same accusations. It was not, however, her place and, therefore, not her pleasure, to argue. Instead, she held out her hand for the bread knife.

"Would you like some tea and toast, my lady? I was going to make some for myself. I'd be pleased to provide some for you, too."

The woman gave another low laugh. "You think to woo me the way you do my husband?"

"No, my lady. Only to offer you some of what I was going to prepare for myself. That's all."

"I would take nothing from your hand!" The laugh became a snarl. "Nothing, do you hear me?"

With a strangled, snarling cry, the woman launched herself at Quilla, the blade raised high. Her ferocity made up for the lack of any real skill with which she wielded it. The down slash would have caught Quilla in the shoulder, had she not been turning as the woman struck. Instead of burying itself hilt deep in her body, the knife skimmed down the length of Quilla's arm and hit the wooden table just beside her with enough force to snap the blade from the handle.

Her sudden lack of weapon did not deter Saradin, who screamed and sprang at Quilla's face, her fingers hooked into claws as deadly as any from a beast. Quilla, on instinct, had raised her arm to shield her face after the knife missed her, and when the woman slapped at her, Quilla reached out and grabbed the offending hand, squeezing the fingers to prevent her from using it.

"Whore! Whore! Whore!" Saradin slapped at Quilla. The heat of the woman's breath laced with spittle stung like drops of acid on Quilla's cheeks and forehead. Saradin reached around with her free hand and grabbed Quilla's unbound hair, pulling so hard it bent Quilla forward.

"Let me go!"

"Whooooooore!"

The drawn-out scream hurt Quilla's ears as she struggled with Gabriel's wife, trying not to hurt the madwoman while desperately fighting not to get hurt herself.

Fury and insanity had given Saradin a strength her petite size denied. She whaled away at Quilla, slapping and kicking, and Quilla stumbled back against the table, the mistress on top of her, fetid breath in her face like that of a rabid dog. Curds of spittle had gathered in the corners of the other woman's mouth as she screamed and spat.

Quilla turned her head to avoid being splattered with more of the woman's spittle, and Saradin yanked her hair forward to slam her head down on the table hard enough that Quilla saw stars.

Scrabbling up her body like a crawpappy in a creek bed, the screaming woman kicked and scratched and even tried to bite.

"Get off me!" Quilla's voice rang through Florentine's tidy
kitchen.

The table beneath them moved beneath the force of the woman's
attack. It scraped the stone floor. Quilla couldn't get purchase with
her feet, no leverage to move herself against the woman who snapped
her jaws.

"Whore! Slut! Ruiner of households!"

The insults were easier to take than the hitting, and Quilla focused on getting out from under the woman. The table moved
again, pushed along by Saradin's desperate attempts to climb on
top of Quilla and what . . . beat her into submission? Harm her?
Kill her?

Because that was, she saw with sudden horror, exactly what
Saradin seemed intent on doing. The table had moved so far across
the floor the mistress could now reach a hand into the block of
slotted wood that held the knives Florentine used for cutting and
slicing vegetables. As fast as a striking snake, she yanked a blade
from the block. A long one, and sharp, not serrated like the bread
knife but its edge gleaming deadly sharp.

Thanking the Invisible Mother that Saradin's aim was no better
than it had been the first time, Quilla rolled as the blade came
down, missing her face by a scant handbreadth.

"Whore!"

Quilla didn't bother replying, merely used the power in her
shoulder to knock the woman back a bit. This time, the blade came
down harder . . . and closer.

"See how well you like the kiss of my knife," panted the mistress. "See how you like it up your cunny, fucking you! See how it
feels to have a blade fuck you instead of my husband!"

Quilla had nowhere to go, no room to roll, and the mistress had effectively pinned her. The woman raised her knife again, all screaming done as she pointed it at Quilla's face.

"Get off her!"

In the next instant, unseen hands yanked Saradin back, and Quilla rolled off the table, ending up on the floor. She looked up, her hands in front of her to protect herself. Saradin spit and squalled in Jericho's grasp like a cat in a sack, her eyes focused with venom on Quilla, but the knife was now on the table and no longer in her hands.

"Calm down or I'll turn you on your arse!"

Quilla stood, watching Saradin struggle in Jericho's unforgiving grasp. Quilla smoothed her rumpled dress with shaking hands, feeling for injuries and finding the slice in her sleeve. Her fingers came away wet with blood. The metallic tang of it filled her nostrils and made her light-headed.

Jericho shook Saradin until her golden hair flew. "Enough, you crazy bitch! Enough! Else I mean it, I'll put you down!"

Light filled the kitchen as Florentine came through the doorway and raised the flames on the oil lamps, something that Quilla ought to have done. If she'd been able to see the woman's face and the madness in her eyes, she might have been better prepared. Or not, she amended herself, watching the mistress calm herself so quickly and completely it was as though she'd never held a knife in her hand at all.

"What by Sinder's Bloody Balls is going on in here?" Florentine shouted, tying her robe around her, hair askew, some sort of thick cream covering her face. "Quilla, what by the Void are you doing? And you?"

Florentine pointed at Jericho, who still gripped the mistress's arms so tight his fingers left red marks on her pale skin.

"Keeping this one from killing the other."

"Manhandling your brother's wife is a certain way to get him to kick your arse out to the street, Jericho. No matter what she's done." Florentine smoothed her hair back from her face, eyes taking in the disrupted kitchen and displaced table, the knife on the floor. Her gaze came up to meet Quilla's, and the chatelaine crossed the kitchen to take Quilla's arm.

"You, sit." She pushed Quilla into a chair, then pointed at Jericho. "You. Take her out of here. Billy!"

Hanging the kettle on the fire, Florentine ordered Billy to run and get the master. To Bertram who'd appeared after Billy, she gave the command to find Mistress Walles.

Jericho held Saradin, who was no longer struggling. He looked at Quilla. "She needs taking care of, Flora."

Any other time, Quilla would have been surprised at Jericho's casual nickname for the cook. As it was, her head had begun to spin. The sight of the blood or perhaps the loss of it, or more likely, simply her body's already wobbly defenses. Quilla promptly put her head between her knees, but the world still went first gray, edged with red and then black.

A hand on her face made her flutter her eyes. That, and the raised masculine timbre of voices, shouting. She smelled something sharp and her eyes opened wide. She gasped and choked at the stench of something chemical.

"Are you all right?" This from Jericho, whose concerned face hovered a handbreadth from hers.

Quilla meant to speak, to at least nod, but couldn't seem to manage.

"Get her out of here!" Another masculine voice, deeper. Gabriel.

"My lord," Quilla struggled to say. She was not supposed to be the one in need of care.

"Shh." Jericho smoothed her hair from her face as she struggled to sit. "Don't fret."

She looked to see Gabriel force a spoonful of something between his wife's lips, then hold her jaws shut. Pinkish liquid trickled from the corners of her mouth, but when he let go of her face a moment later, she didn't spit anything out. A moment or two after that the fire in her eyes, directed over her husband's shoulder at Quilla, began to fade. And yet another passed before the mistress Delessan sagged in her husband's arms, face going blank.

Quilla pushed Jericho's hand from her hair and sat, wincing at the way her dress, stuck to her with dried blood, pulled and stung the wound. "I'm fine."

"Just sit for a moment more."

"I'm—"

The entrance of Allora Walles, who pushed Bertram out of the way when she stumbled into the kitchen, interrupted Quilla's protest. At the sight of her mistress in her master's arms, Allora's face went the color of snow. She gathered her cloak around her—a cloak, not a robe, Quilla noticed shrewdly, also seeing how the maid's hair was rumpled and strewn with bits of chaff.

"My lady!" Allora cried, rushing to her.

"Your lady has behaved most grievously," said Gabriel. "Wandering about when she should be safe in bed, sleeping."

Allora ducked her head, bobbing a curtsy. "She was asleep, my lord, I swear."

"I want none of your oaths. She was not sleeping. She was out of bed and well enough, strong enough, to attack my—to attack her." He barely glanced at Quilla, who had begun unbuttoning her dress in order to slip out of the sleeve and assess the damage left behind from Saradin's knife.

"I gave her the draught, my lord, I swear to you I did." Allora had the good grace to blush and smooth her tangled curls back from her forehead. "Perhaps she didn't drink it."

Gabriel looked at the woman sagging in his arms and passed

her off to Florentine, who walked her to Allora. "Perhaps she did not. But 'tis your duty to make sure she drinks it at night, Allora Walles, to prevent this sort of thing from happening. If I had anyone else she trusted enough to care for her, I'd turn you out right now."

Gabriel in a normal mood was intimidating enough. Gabriel Delessan angry, truly angry, was enough to make Allora Walles burst into terrified tears. Not because he was screaming, no. A raised voice might be a tool for lesser men. All Delessan needed to do was turn his gaze upon his wife's maid, to speak in a voice as cold as the depths of Loch Eltourna. It was more impressive and frightening than if he'd railed and yelled, and Quilla had no doubt that Gabriel knew the exact impact of not only each word, but each syllable he spoke.

"My lord, I plead your mercy!" Allora got on her knees—actually got on her knees in front of him, which made Quilla grit her teeth before she noticed and forced her jaw to relax. "I put her to bed and went—"

Gabriel reached down and plucked a piece of straw from her hair. "I don't pay you to fuck. I pay you to tend my lady wife. Get off your knees and take her to her room, and do the job you're paid to do."

Allora got up, nodding, and put her arm around Saradin's waist. "Come, my lady. Let's get you to bed."

Whatever Gabriel had given her had made Saradin pliant and docile, and she smiled, eyes closed. "Yes, Allora, yes, yes."

Quilla watched as Allora led Saradin out of the room. When she looked up again, she saw her patron staring at her with a look she couldn't determine. In the next moment, she no longer had to guess, because his gaze grew stormy and he crossed the kitchen to snatch her now empty sleeve.

"What are you doing?"

"My lord, I—" She'd meant to say she'd been trying to take a look at the wound. The flash of his eyes stopped her. She pulled up her sleeve.

"Leave her alone, Gabriel. She's been hurt." Jericho pushed his brother aside to stand in front of Quilla, who put her hand on his arm.

"No, it's all right."

"Get out of the way, Jericho."

Jericho looked at his brother, and stepped out of the way, inclining his head. "She's yours, after all, though I do think you should take better care of her."

Quilla got to her feet between them, a hand on each of their chests. If she hadn't still been so woozy, she might have found the situation amusing and surreal. She'd never had two men posturing over her before. And that was a ridiculous thing to have happen, because there could be no contest between them.

She turned to face Gabriel. He was her patron. She belonged to him. Jericho's kindness could not replace the simple fact of who she was. Gabriel's Handmaiden.

"My lord, I apologize. I was not thinking." She tried to put her arm back in the sleeve, but the wound and dried blood made it too difficult. She hissed in pain. Gabriel's eyes flashed again.

"Stop," he said. "Florentine, get a wet cloth for her, are you out of your mind? She's bleeding all over the place."

Florentine gave a sniff, but did as she was told, pushing Jericho out of the way. "Move, you great git."

Jericho stepped away. Quilla could see him from the corner of her eye. He was watching her.

"Do we need a medicus?" Gabriel's voice was gentle and pulled her attention back to him.

The fact he even needed to draw her attention embarrassed her. Her mind ought to be on him. She shook her head, looking at her arm. The wound had bled freely but didn't appear to be deep enough to need stitches. "I don't think so."

Gabriel took the wet cloth from Florentine and wiped away the smears with gentle hands. Quilla winced, but the pain was numbing. She'd bear a scar.

"I'll be all right." The words came out more a reassurance than she'd intended, and she wasn't certain whom she was reassuring: herself, or him. "Really."

She put her hand over his. He looked down at it for a moment, then back to her eyes. His gaze snared her for a moment and she could not speak.

"Forgive me, brother, for overstepping my bounds." Jericho gave a terse, well-executed bow, turned on his heel, and left the kitchen.

Florentine handed Gabriel a length of towel, stripped to make a bandage, which he tied round the wound. A crimson rose bloomed on the white sackcloth at first, but a small one, and after a moment spread no farther.

"If that's all the excitement for now, I'm off to bed. The sun rises early," Florentine said pointedly.

"Go. I'll be fine," replied Quilla.

Gabriel waited until the cook left the kitchen. "Can you stand?"

She nodded, getting to her feet. The floor swayed beneath her, and she put out a hand to steady herself. He caught her by the good arm.

In the next instant, he'd bent and put an arm beneath her knees to scoop her into his arms.

"My lord—"

He made an impatient noise. "I don't want you falling down the stairs."

"Nor do I want you to fall down them," she murmured, letting her cheek fall against his chest. "I am no feather pillow."

The deep rumble of a chuckle took her by surprise. "Indeed,

you are not. But I'm not so weak that I can't carry you at least part of the way."

As he put his foot to the first step, he shifted her weight more firmly in his arms. His fingers tightened on her. She kept her body relaxed, though a vision of the two of them tumbling down the stairs like broken dolls made her want to tense.

"You don't need to carry me to help me," she told him quietly.

He made it up to the first landing before pausing. His breath was heavier. Against her cheek the pounding of his heart grew fiercer.

"You can put—"

"Hush, Handmaiden."

"If it pleases you."

He shifted her again, and Quilla curled her arms around his neck to do what she could to ease the burden of her weight. She took her own deep breaths, using the meditations of the Order to keep her mind clear.

Gabriel took a deep breath and started up the next flight of stairs, which were steeper and less decorative than the first had been. By the time they reached the second landing, his arms trembled and sweat dotted his brow. He stopped again to rest.

"I'm feeling better, my lord."

He hitched her higher up, resettling her in his arms. "Only a bit farther."

She murmured a soft noise of assent and kept up her meditations.

"What's that you're mumbling?" Gabriel's voice came in breathy puffs, but they'd reached the top of the stairs. He leaned against the wall, but didn't put her down.

"And help me have the strength to deal with stubborn men," she replied, sharing the last part of her meditation. "'Tis a prayer to the Invisible Mother."

He seemed too winded to have much ire. "I am not *men*, Handmaiden, must I tell you a hundred times?"

Quilla wiggled until he allowed her to slide out of his arms. Her feet rested on the floor, but he still supported her. She allowed him, though she felt well enough to stand on her own.

"No, my lord."

He grumbled. "I thought Handmaidens were supposed to be told only once."

She smiled, something he wouldn't be able to see very well in the hall's dim light. "I am not *Handmaidens*."

Gabriel wiped his face with the hand not around her waist. This hall, if taken to the right, led to the stairs to his workshop and studio. To the left, those to her garret.

"I believe I can manage the rest of the way on my own, my lord."

"And I believe it necessary for me to be certain you get to your bed without further incident."

Quilla smiled again. "If it pleases you."

"Yes, it bloody pleases me."

He made to pick her up again, not quite as easily as he'd done in the kitchen. Quilla laid her head against his chest, aiding him with quiet and pliant nonresistance, though she felt his struggle. When they got to the end of the hall and the narrow doorway leading upstairs, it was very clear there would not be room for him to take her up in his arms.

He set her down on the first step, his arm about her waist and her arm still behind his neck. She lowered it but kept close to him. He smelled good, and his effort to help her touched her more than it amused her.

"You can follow me up," she whispered, the dark and quiet seeming to invite silence. "To be sure I make it there all right."

"Yes."

She slipped her arm from his neck and started up the stairs, his presence at her back an unexpected comfort. Dizziness assailed her again by the time they reached the top, and she was grateful for his hand upon her. A tiny corridor led the way to her room, and she used both hands on the walls to help her get through it.

She paused in the doorway to turn the oil lantern up, to give the room a brighter glow, then moved toward the bed.

"This is your room?"

She paused in turning down the covers, turning to look at him. He walked around the room, looking at everything. It didn't take him long to catalog the contents with his eyes, for there wasn't very much in it.

"This is the room in your house to which I've been assigned."

He grunted, going to the door to the washroom and opening it, looking around inside, rattling the washbasin on its stand. Then he came out and peered into the wardrobe.

He turned to face her, looking around the room with a frown. "This room is . . ."

Quilla bent her head to hide a smile. "This is the room you provided for me."

"It's very unwelcoming."

Quilla sat on the bed, her arm aching. "I've had worse."

He crossed to stand over her. "I plead your mercy. I didn't realize. I had Florentine make the arrangements."

Quilla shook her head. "All you are required to provide is a place for me to sleep and bathe, clothes sufficient for the climate and my duties, and nourishment. You've done all that."

Gabriel crossed his arms over his chest, his frown deepening. "And yet you've taken it upon yourself to clean my rooms, provide me with a new teakettle, organize my books . . . polish and scrub and turn what used to be a cold and uncomfortable place into something warm and welcoming."

She nodded. "All part of what I do."

"And yet you don't wish for the same? This room doesn't even have a carpet!"

She lay back against the pillows and pulled the covers up around her with a sigh. "Of course I would like a carpet. The floor is cold. But if you do not see fit to provide me—"

"Think you I am so ungenerous as to deny you a carpet to protect your feet from the cold stones?" He seemed outraged, but something else, too. He seemed . . . hurt.

Quilla settled against the pillows, her former weariness coming back, exacerbated by the attack in the kitchen. She stifled a yawn. "It's not my place to ask of you, remember?"

His eyes narrowed. "How can you be so complacent?"

She sighed. "It's what I am. That's part of being a Handmaiden, but more importantly, it's part of being me. If you wish to provide me with a carpet, I shall be glad to have one."

"Of course I want you to have a carpet! I am not a monster!"

"I would not think so."

He made a noise that was almost a growl. "And anything else you need, you shall have. I'm not a miser."

"I would not think that, either."

He glowered, arms crossed, and sat down in the small wooden chair next to the bed. "Are you afraid of me?"

She shook her head, turning on her side a bit to look at him. "No."

That seemed to mollify him. "And yet you truly would not ask me for something so simple as a rug to keep your feet from the cold?"

"I have stockings which can do the same, and which you have already provided," she pointed out.

"You should rest now. I don't expect you to be there when I wake tomorrow, do you understand?"

She nodded with a small smile. "But you understand I will be, anyway?"

He sighed as though her answer pained him. "If I told you it would please me for you to stay abed tomorrow, to not wait on me at all, would that keep you here?"

"I suppose it would." Quilla snuggled down farther into the blankets. "But I would find my day overwhelmingly dull if I had nothing to do but stay here."

He nodded, as though thinking. "And yet I would not have you risk your health by using that arm for at least a day."

"My lord, you are kind." The compliment was sincere, and for a moment something flashed in his eyes. Pleasure, perhaps. Or surprise. It faded into a scowl.

"I don't want to have to explain to the Order how I damaged one of their Handmaidens."

He got up and moved toward the door, saying over his shoulder, "I'll send some things to you tomorrow to make this less of a cell."

"You did not damage me, Gabriel," Quilla said quietly to his back.

He paused in the doorway. "You are my Handmaiden. You are my responsibility. If it's your duty to care for me, then it's as much my duty to care for you in return. To provide you with what you need to be able to give me what you do. Allowing my lady wife to attack you . . . was unthinkable."

"You did not allow it. It happened beyond your control."

He glanced over his shoulder at her. "There is nothing in this house which is beyond my control, Handmaiden. I make certain of that."

He closed the door with a click behind him.

Chapter 11

The next day, Quilla was grateful Gabriel had told her to stay abed, for when she opened her eyes it was to a rap on the door and the sun streaming through the window. She'd slept, actually slept, and much better than she'd expected to. She sat up to the sound of the gentle knocking.

"Come in."

Bertram peeked his head around the door, a grin on his freckled face. "Delivery for you, mistress."

Quilla sat up, expecting her arm to be stiff but finding it more pliable than she'd thought. It twinged when she bent it, but the bandages weren't any further stained and she had a good range of motion. She wouldn't need to stay in bed the entire day, after all.

"Hello, Bertram. What did you bring me?"

"Bring it in," he said to someone behind him.

The door opened and Bertram entered, followed by the stable hands Luke and Perrin, carrying a rolled up carpet. Behind them were Pipp and Took, all carrying crates and boxes. And yet behind them were Lolly, Kirie, and Rossi, also loaded with packages and boxes.

"What's all this?"

"My lord Delessan sent it. Says he wants this room to look like a palace and not a prison!" Bertram motioned to the men to put the rug down.

They unrolled it, and Quilla gasped, sitting up higher in bed. The colors were gorgeous: purples, greens, reds, and golds, with threads of deep blue around the border. She'd been in enough fine homes to know the quality of this rug meant it was expensive. Far too costly to be shoved into a garret room like this.

"There must be some mistake."

Bertram tugged at his cap. "No mistake, miss. Lord Delessan had it tooken out of his own chambers, he did. The one he doesn't use no more."

For a moment, Bertram shared a glance with the clearly disapproving housemaids, and his freckled cheeks blushed pink. "Not that I'm in any place to be saying, you understand. He just told us to bring it up here, and so we did."

Lolly held up a basket full of what looked to be wall hangings. "Should we go to put thesen up, mistress?"

Quilla looked at the fabrics, then at the bare stone walls. The hangings matched the rug. "Did these also come from his chamber?"

"Ahyuh." Lolly nodded.

"Did he order you to strip the place bare?"

Lolly giggled. "Ahyuh. If the furniture'd fit up here, he'd have had us bring that, too."

Quilla felt a little overwhelmed with his generosity. She'd been given many gifts, but no patron had stripped his own quarters, even ones he no longer used, to provide her with comfort. She swung her legs out over the edge of the bed, but Rossi waved her back.

The tall girl was imposing enough to keep Quilla in her place.

"You sit back, mistress. The master, him gave orders, us. You weren't to help us a lick."

"I need to use the necessary," Quilla said with a smile. "Am I allowed to do that, at least?"

For one moment, she was certain Rossi, intent on keeping the master's order intact, would deny her the privilege. That could have been awkward, indeed. But the housemaid nodded and stepped out of the way so Quilla could get out of bed.

In the tiny washroom, Quilla stripped out of the nightgown and ran some water in the basin, splashing her face and rinsing her body. She took off the crusted bandage, and though it pulled a bit at the wound, the few drops of blood that leaked out were negligible. She looked at the cut. It would leave a scar. She redressed it, tying a fresh cloth around it and tying it tight to prevent the ends from unraveling. Then she brushed and braided her hair, tucking the end close to the nape of her neck to keep it from getting in the way. Pulling a gown from the back of the door, she slipped it and some fresh undergarments on, then went back out into her bedroom.

It had been transformed. The floor, now covered by the exquisite rug. The walls, draped with fabric. Baskets had been stacked in the corners to create shelves, upon which more cloths had been draped. Even a few plants had been hung from the ceiling, pretty green things with trailing vines that created a lovely pattern in shadow against the wall hangings.

"Invisible Mother," Quilla breathed, taken aback by the change in the room.

She hadn't minded the way it was before. It was better than some and not so nice as others she'd had. But now . . . now the room was, indeed, a palace.

She loved it. She looked around, moved by another sight. Books. He'd given her books, an entire bookshelf, floor to ceiling.

She moved toward them, but the housemaids took her and forced her with gentle scolding back into bed to rest while they worked. By the time they finished, Quilla would not have known this room from any other in Glad Tidings.

He had done more than give her his hand-me-downs. He had given her as much consideration as he would have any of his guests. He had made her room into a haven.

"You'll be all right, then, mistress?"

"Yes, Kirie, I shall be fine." Quilla held up the book she'd had Bertram pluck from its place and bring her. "With this to keep me occupied, I shall be well."

Kirie nodded and pointed. "Fresh water to drink there. No bell for you to ring, so if you needs anywhat—"

"I'm sure I won't." Quilla smiled, propped up against the pillows like a grand lady and feeling more tired than she'd have admitted but an hour before.

Bertram and the stable lads vanished, leaving the housemaids to smooth her covers and fuss over her until she waved them away, laughing. "Go! Go, else Florentine will have your skins! Have you not the other guests to attend?"

The three girls exchanged looks. Quilla closed her novel and looked at each of them in turn. Rossi's face remained impassive, but Kirie and Lolly, sisters, couldn't hide their expressions of mixed consternation and glee.

"He's sending them all away," said Kirie after a moment. "Says he don't care that they must travel through snow and ice, they're to get gone from his house—"

"—and that Boone Somerholde is lucky our lord Delessan doesn't call him out, as well," finished Lolly. "And Persis Adamantane started the drink when he found out Lord Somerholde the younger was the one found with the lady Delessan, and he's not stopped since!"

"Oh, my." Quilla could think of nothing more to say on that matter. "And what of the Fienes? They had no part in any of it."

"Madame Fiene told our lord Delessan he ought to be ashamed of himself for treating his lady wife so, and our lord Delessan did tell her she ought to mind her own business, as not everyone could be expected to turn a blind eye to the fact their wife was a harlot, though Lord Fiene had certainly years of practice at it, even if no man in his right mind would plow Madame Fiene's furrow any longer since she contracted the oozing pox."

Quilla's jaw dropped. "Gabriel said all that to his guests?"

Rossi, who had busied herself straightening Quilla's blankets while Lolly and Kirie told the story, broke into the conversation. "None of them's his friends, mistress. They his lady wife's friends, not his. He don't care what they think, him."

"No, I don't suppose he does. And what of the other lord Delessan?"

"Master Jericho has been in his chambers since last night and nobody's seen hide nor hair of him." This came from Kirie, with a nod from Lolly to prove it true.

"Oh, my." Quilla studied the leather cover of her book. "It sounds as though Glad Tidings has undergone a rough few hours this morning."

"And the lady mistress—" Kirie stopped herself, as though speech would be disloyal.

Rossi had no such reservations. "His lady wife has been ranting against you since sunrise. Our lord Delessan has threatened to dose her with sleeping draught, but has not, yet. She's screamed so loud she's near lost her voice."

"Oh, by the Arrow," Quilla murmured. "And what of the lad? Who has been shielding Dane from all this?"

The three exchanged another look. "He's with Jorja Pinsky."

"But can he hear the shouting and what's going on?"

This time, the look said they didn't know. Quilla put her book aside. "No matter what the woman has done, she is the lad's mother. And no matter what the rest of the household is doing, that little boy should be sheltered from such goings-on. Doesn't anyone in this house have the sense in their heads to behave in front of children?"

Disgust colored her voice and made the maids look shamefaced. Quilla shook her head at them. "His father?"

"Busy in his workshop, him."

"And Uncle Jericho locked away." Quilla sighed, but there could be no getting up with the housemaids staring at her. Her heart panged for Dane, who might be spoiled and ill-behaved, but was still just a lad for all that.

They fussed over her a bit more until Bertram rapped on the door and said in an apologetic voice, "Begging your pardon, mistress, but Florentine is requiring the use of these three."

So at last, they left her, and Quilla got out of bed and moved around the room, touching each object in wonder and shaking her head at some of the choices. A lamp in the shape of a lady's shoe? A stone bust of some unidentified man wearing a hunting cap?

When she got to the polished wooden bookshelf, she stopped, her throat closed with an uncommon rush of emotion. He'd given her books. Volume upon volume, some bound in cheap paper with letters that smudged, and she'd have expected nothing of better quality. But some were hide-bound, pages printed with better ink and illustrations.

It wasn't the expense of the gift, which, really, was nothing since he'd given her items he already owned. But the thought behind the gift . . . that was something else entirely.

There was no way she could sit in her room all day now, though he'd provided for her entertainment. She had to go thank him. Quilla put on her stockings and slippers and left the room, walking with care to make certain she suffered no ill effects, but making no hesitation in her route.

The door swung open on oiled hinges and she entered. He stood at his table, lifting a beaker of some amber-colored liquid up to the shaft of early morning sunlight streaming in the window. The ray caught the liquid and suffused it with a warm glow that oozed over his face, casting it with honeyed shadows.

She entered the room on soft feet, but without turning to look at her he said, "You're supposed to be in bed."

Quilla went to him and stood in front of him, waiting until he'd put down the beaker. "Thank you."

"It pleases you?"

She nodded, looking into his dark gray blue eyes. "It pleases me very much."

A smile tugged the corners of his lips. "Would you like to tell me what pleased you the best?"

"I can put my vote to no one thing, my lord."

He settled the beaker onto the table and moved a step closer to her. "But if it pleased me for you to choose?"

Whatever he'd been working with had given the room a scent like fruit gone overripe, but this close to him she could also smell his own scent. Something a bit spicier.

"The books," she answered without hesitation. "I would choose the books."

His smile widened. "I thought as much. The care you took with mine showed me you value them."

"I came to thank you."

"Even though you knew it was my wish for you to remain abed today?" He tilted his head to look at her, but didn't seem angry. Instead, his gaze wandered over her face before returning to her eyes.

"I wanted to thank you for the gifts." *And I didn't think I could stand to go a day without seeing you.*

The realization surprised her with its sudden implications. Sudden, dangerous implications. Even so, her gaze didn't drop from his.

"It was very kind of you," she said.

His hand came up to stroke the length of her braid from the nape of her neck to where it fell over her shoulder, and when his fingers reached the curve of her jaw, they lingered to caress her cheek. "I'm not kind."

She nodded, her gesture at odds with her words. "No."

His hand moved back to cup the nape of her neck beneath the thickness of her braid. His fingers curled around her, warm on her skin. He pulled, and she followed, stepping forward until she had to tilt her head back to continue looking into his face.

"How fares your arm today?"

His fingers moved, gently caressing the sensitive skin at her nape.

"It will heal."

"You must take care not to open the wound."

He pulled her closer. Now her body brushed his. The hand at her nape slid slower, to the spot between her shoulder blades while his other went to her waist. Quilla put her hands on his chest, against the white front of his jacket, the material scratchy on her fingertips.

"I would be sorely discomposed if I should find myself without your services for yet another day."

"And I sadly disappointed should I find myself unable to provide them."

His arm tightened around her, and he tilted his head, leaning closer, his gaze on hers, dipping briefly lower to caress her mouth before returning to her eyes.

"That would not please me at all, Handmaiden."

"And I am here to please you, my lord."

But he did not kiss her. Instead, the hand at her hip came up to smooth the hair off her forehead and with a gentle but firm touch, he stepped away from her. "It would also please me to have some tea, if you feel capable of making it."

She blinked and had to swallow hard before she could answer. "Of course, my lord."

He turned back to his beakers and tubes, and Quilla made his tea, which he drank with perfunctory speed as though he had not, perhaps, truly wanted it at all.

It was her least favorite part of the day, late afternoon. The light began to fail and the lamps were lit, bringing with them the smell of fuel that sometimes made her head ache. But more than that, late afternoon, when the light began to fail, was the time when Gabriel dismissed her.

Sometimes, he did it with words. "You can go," and on those days she went and unbuttoned and helped him out of his stained lab coat, brushed off his clothes, served him tea and cake or simplebread.

Other times he shrugged out of his coat and tossed it on the back of the chair, leaving the room without giving her so much as a glance. The problem was, she could never tell which sort of day it would be, not from one to the other, and she could not seem to tie her actions to his reactions, only that the days he did not speak to her were rapidly beginning to outnumber the days he did.

The house seemed quite empty without the bustle and chatter of guests, and though Quilla did not miss any of them, she found she missed the air of activity their presence had provided.

Gabriel had not touched her since the day she'd thanked him for the gifts. If their hands brushed while she passed him a vial, or while she passed him tea, he made obvious care to move away from her. He did not ask for aid in buttoning his coat, nor in unbuttoning, nor in any action for which he had previously allowed her assistance.

The dismissal stung more than it ought. He had needed solace. She had given it. It had meant no more than that. And yet . . . it had. And she could not look at him without remembering the touch of his hands upon her, or the sweetness of his breath in her face.

It distracted her. Made her numb-fingered and clumsy, caused her to drop things.

"Go," he told her, frustrated, one day when she had spilled a beaker of solution for the second time in a row. "Get you gone! You are more trouble than you are worth, today!"

And, fighting unaccustomed tears, she had gone. She avoided the kitchen, where Florentine would surely sniff out her distress with the same alacrity she discovered soured milk amongst the pitchers. Quilla was in no mood to listen to the cook's mocking commentary. Instead, Quilla made her way to the third floor, to the long, bright gallery that stretched all the way across the top of the house.

The windows brought in light, but also cold, for the glass was not much insulation against the winter outside. The bare wooden floors might have been well improved by carpets, but Quilla could only guess that, as the room was not often used, Gabriel had ordered them put elsewhere. The same for the furnishings, which were rather more threadbare than any in the rest of the house. Slightly mismatched as well, as though nobody expected this space to impress.

Which was a shame, she thought, walking the length of the room. It was an impressive room. Floor-to-ceiling windows dominated the outside wall, while portraits of every size and artistic skill decorated the one opposite. Fireplaces trisected the space, and each of the three sections boasted its own sofa and grouping of chairs. A pianoforte at one end of the gallery would have provided music, should any care to play it, but when she touched it with one fingertip the note which sounded was discordant and sour.

The room was, at least, clean and without dust, though the dangling pendants on the hanging lamps could have used a wash. The gallery had been meant to show off family portraits and provide a place for large gatherings, but Quilla found the long room good for something else, too. Walking.

She walked from one end to the other, moving fast to fend off the chill hanging in the air. The activity took her mind off the melancholy. It gave her something to do so she didn't dwell on her patron.

She had reached the end of the gallery when the sound of shuffling reached her ears from the door set into the wall at the other end of the room. Without thinking much of it, she ducked into an alcove that had perhaps been meant to showcase a statue or potted plant. The door opened, and Dane tumbled through the doorway, giggling.

The boy bore no sign of the incident with the eel. His plump cheeks were pink and blond hair tousled as he turned to face his companion.

"Come, Uncle!" he cried. "I can't wait!"

"Patience, Nephew." Jericho entered the room after Dane, something metal and shiny glinting in his hand.

Dane danced, holding up his arms to grab at whatever Jericho held. "Give them to me! Give them to me!"

"Give them to me . . ." Jericho paused, clearly expecting Dane to finish his sentence.

"Please!"

Jericho lowered his hand, and Quilla saw a pair of roller skates. Dane grabbed them up with a squeal of delight and sat in one of the chairs to put them on.

In moments, he was up and off, sturdy legs pumping as he sped along the polished wood. Arms flailing, he swerved as he reached the end of the room and grabbed hold of a pedestal to keep from falling. The bust of a stern-looking man atop the pedestal teetered. A vision of it falling to the floor and smashing to bits made Quilla step out of her hiding place to grab it up with one hand while she hooked her fingers into the back of Dane's jacket with the other.

"Keep your feet, laddie," she said with a laugh, steadying him before settling the bust back in its place.

"Quilla Caden!" Dane's obvious joy at seeing her made Quilla's throat close with emotion. The boy threw his arms around her, squeezing, before setting off on another sprint down the length of the gallery.

"Tranquilla Caden," greeted Jericho as he walked toward her. "You are looking well."

"Jericho Delessan," Quilla replied with a small curtsy and slight incline of her head. "Good day to you."

"Made better by your presence."

She raised a brow at the flattery, but did not otherwise respond to it. Instead, she tilted her chin toward the boy, who'd reached the gallery's far end and had turned to make his flailing, rumbling way back. "We'd best get out of the way, lest we find ourselves victim to those wheels."

Jericho laughed and stepped back, closer to the grouping of chairs and settee in front of the windows. He reached for her elbow as he did, to guide her, and she followed him forward. Just in time, because a moment later Dane flew past them, arms akimbo and face lit with laughter.

The boy made a high-pitched "Wheee!" and kept going, turning at the end to do it all over again.

"Those skates might scuff the floor."

"It can be waxed," Jericho said. "And he's making most merry."

"He is, indeed." Quilla turned to watch Dane, now attempting to spin. "He'll make himself sick if he keeps that up."

Jericho laughed and sat on the settee. "He'll be fine."

Quilla looked down at him. "You're very kind to him."

"How could I be anything less?"

She nodded. "I'll leave you to it, then."

Before she had even half turned, his quiet voice, much unlike his usual boasting tone, stopped her. "You needn't. Unless he wants you."

She turned her head to look at him. "As a matter of fact, I don't believe he does."

"My brother is an arrogant fool."

That prompted a thin smile from her. "And you merely arrogant?"

Jericho shook his head, laughing. "Nay, I think I am both arrogant and a fool, as well. But at least I admit my failings, while my brother continues to believe himself perfection."

Dane rolled by again, this time belting out a song with somewhat racy lyrics that made her raise a brow again. "Your doing, I suppose? The song?"

"Bertram and Billy, I believe," replied Jericho with a hurt look upon his face. "How could you suggest I would ever teach my nephew such a tune?"

She laughed, arms crossed. "Because I believe you'd do it, if for no other reason than to ruffle your brother's feathers."

"His feathers need a good ruffling now and again. He's entirely too complacent and smug in his perfection."

Quilla sat in the chair across from him, shaking the hem of her gown to allow it to puddle around her ankles. "He is not perfect. Nor do I believe he thinks himself so. In fact, I think your brother chastises himself overharshly for sins that are not his to claim."

Jericho's eyes met hers. "We arrogant fools tend to do that."

"You and your brother are more alike than either of you will dare to admit."

"I'll admit it," Jericho said, sitting back against the settee. "Even if he won't. My brother despises me for the circumstance of my birth. That, and my wit and charm and good looks, which far surpass his."

She returned his grin. "I fear he outdoes you in modesty, however."

"He might," Jericho agreed. "He might, indeed."

"Watch me, Uncle!"

"Watching, Nephew." Jericho turned to see Dane roll by on one skate, the other leg held out behind him. "Brilliant!"

"Watch me, Quilla!"

"Watching, Dane."

When she turned back, it was to see Jericho staring at her with a look so naked and honest it froze her in place.

"He is a fool," Jericho said. "For not seeing what you are."

Quilla blinked, unable at first to say anything. "He knows what I am, well enough."

Jericho shook his head. "No. My brother has a gift he refuses to open. He won't ever see it."

"I am his Handmaiden. I can be no more than what I am."

Jericho sat up, moved forward, closed in on her so subtly she could not have pulled away without making it seem as though he'd frightened her. "Is he soothed, yet?"

"I'm still here," she replied. "The answer would seem to be no."

From the end of the gallery she heard the noise of Dane's whooping and hollering, the rumble of his skates upon the bare wooden floor, the thud as he fell. She looked into Jericho's eyes, the shape so much like Gabriel's but the color of a sun-kissed ocean rather than the depths of an unplumbed loch.

"If it means keeping you here longer," Jericho told her, "then I hope you never soothe him."

His hand upon her cheek left a trail of warmth that made her flush. His fingers twisted along the length of her braid before falling away. His palm left an unseen trail of heat along the fabric of her sleeve, ending with her hand, around which he curled.

"If you were mine, I would never leave you so forlorn you need seek the emptiness of a gallery to gather your thoughts."

Quilla pulled her hand from his grip. "But I am not yours. If you find yourself in need of a Handmaiden, my lord, might I suggest you send for one."

Jericho didn't seem taken aback by the sudden coolness she'd forced into her voice. "The one I'd have already appears to be conscripted."

"Stop this. You have to stop this."

"Why?" He leaned back again, one leg crossed over the other, arm behind his head, in seemingly casual repose.

Quilla stood. "Because it does not become you. You want all that your brother has simply for the fact he has it instead of you." Her gazed flicked toward Dane, who'd collapsed on the floor in a fit of giggles. "And I would say you'd taken enough of what is his, already. Stop being such a greedy bastard."

This made him blink and sit up, and she thought she might have offended him. "You call me such?"

"I do," she said. "For one who claims to love him as you do, you certainly don't prove it by your actions."

He frowned, beginning to speak, but she cut him off.

"And as regarding me, my other lord Delessan, you might taunt and tease me as you wish, though 'tis an even more unbecoming behavior than greed."

"I'm not teasing you." His voice had gone low and solemn. "I mean all I say."

"I belong to your brother," Quilla replied.

"You belong to yourself first."

"I belong to the Service of the Holy Family, to the Order, to my patron, and lastly, to myself."

Jericho stood, close enough to her she could smell the scent of the lemonwood in which his clothes had been stored. Their bodies aligned. He put his head next to hers.

"You are so beautiful," he whispered in her ear, not touching her with anything other than his breath. "And you are not only a Handmaiden in my eyes, Tranquilla. You are a woman."

The simplicity and sincerity of those words struck her like a spear, as though they stabbed her, deep in the gut, made her gasp from the impact but not, as yet, feel the pain from the wound.

"I would know you," Jericho told her, still whispering. Still not touching. "I would know your dreams. Your joys and sorrows. I would know what makes you laugh and weep."

A shudder of longing ran through her, for all the things denied her because of her purpose and her place. All that he now offered. Her eyes closed against the sight of his chest in front of her.

She perhaps imagined the brush of his lips upon her temple, the pressure of his hand upon her hip, drawing her infinitesimally closer. Or perhaps she did not. In the end, it didn't matter, because the crash of the poor, belabored bust startled her and Jericho apart.

She saw a dazed-looking Dane sprawled on the floor amongst the remains of the porcelain piece. She pushed away from Jericho and went to the boy, checking him for injuries. She saw none.

"My father will be angry with me," said Dane solemnly.

Jericho shook his head. "I don't think so, lad. It was a figure of my father. He won't mourn the loss."

Dane smiled the Delessan smile shared by his father and his uncle. "I'm sorry I broke it, Uncle."

"Sometimes," Jericho said, his careful refusal to look at Quilla more telling than if he'd stared into her face, "things get broken. All you can do is sweep up the pieces and start over again."

Quilla stood. "Your uncle is absolutely right, Dane."

She ruffled the boy's hair, then turned on her heel and left the gallery without a second look back.

Chapter 12

Sweep up the pieces and start again.

Simple advice, and words she knew he had not meant for the benefit of his brother. Nonetheless, Quilla intended to use them for such. She was Gabriel's Handmaiden. Nothing that had passed between them, no action, no emotion, should change that.

Determined, she let herself into his chambers to discover him seated in front of the fireplace, a glass of liquor in his hand. He looked up, startled, when she came in, but Quilla did not hesitate. She went to him and Waited.

"I told you to go."

She Waited in silence.

"Handmaiden, I told you to leave me!"

Again, she said nothing.

Gabriel made an angry noise. "It pleases me for you to leave me alone."

Then she looked up at him and met his scowl with a calm gaze of her own. "No."

"No?" He seemed flabbergasted. "You say *no*, to me?"

"You say it pleases you to have me leave, but it does not."

His eyes narrowed. "Think you to know my mind better than I?"

Quilla nodded, slowly, eyes never leaving his. "I am what you need before you know you need it."

He sneered, cruelty etched into his face. "And you think I need you."

Another slow nod. "I do."

"To do what?" Contempt coated his voice. "To serve me tea and simplebread? To hand me vials and take notes for me? To sing or dance or make pretty poems? In case 'tis not clear to you, I am working on nothing but intoxication."

"Then I will pour your drinks."

"I don't need you to pour them!" His shout had, perhaps, been meant to make her flinch, but she did not. "I do not need you, Handmaiden!"

"Then send me away." The words were calm only because she had some small skill in controlling her voice; inside, anxiety clutched its skeletal fingers around her heart.

"I sent you away."

She shook her head. "No, my lord. You told me to go away. You did not release me from your service. Should you wish to do that, you must needs say 'I release thee,' thrice in succession. Only then will I be gone from your service."

He stared at her for what felt like a very long time before answering, and when he did, it was not with words. He held out his empty glass to her. Quilla took it as she got to her feet. She filled it from the bottle of worm, wine mixed with opiate, the fumes of which were so strong they made her eyes sting. She gave him the glass, and he sipped it, all while watching her.

Quilla sank again into Waiting. Gabriel drained another glass.

Held it out. She filled and returned it. He sipped again, his eyes now a bit less focused.

"Come here," he said after a time, voice thick.

She did as he'd asked. He reached out a rough hand to grab her wrist and pull her to his lap. The glass spilled, wetting her gown and sending the stinging smell of liquor all around them.

"If I asked you to suck my cock, or to let me fuck you," Gabriel said, "you would do it."

She answered him in the way she always did, voice still calm, though his words had made her stomach jump. "If it pleases you."

He licked his lips, eyes traveling over her face and down her body. His hand ran down her side to the curve of her hip. "And what of pleasing yourself?"

"Do you wish me to suck your cock, my lord? Do you wish me to allow you to fuck me?" She lowered her face to his, their foreheads touching. Voice no longer so calm, but instead slightly shaking. "Would that please you?"

"I want," said Gabriel hoarsely, "for it to please you."

She put her hands to his face. "I would be so pleased, Gabriel."

He groaned and both hands went around her, one fisting in her braid to bring her closer for his kiss. Her mouth opened beneath his, accepting the dive and thrust of his tongue. He did not nibble or tease her lips, did not gently kiss her, did not request with his body that she respond.

His kiss demanded she respond, that she open for him, give in. Submit. Please.

And it did please her to do so. Desire so fierce it made her weak swept through her, making her shake. Her hands threaded through his hair. His pulled up the skirt of her gown to find without hesitation the heat of her center. He slipped inside her in a moment, his thumb finding the pulse of her pleasure, and Quilla gasped into his mouth.

"You want me," he said, mouth trailing along her jaw to fasten on the soft skin at the base of her throat. "Tell me you want me."

"I want you." She moaned as his hand moved inside and against her.

He bit her but the pain at her neck only made the pleasure between her legs that much sweeter. His thumb pressed, on and off, then circled her nub. Her hips moved.

"By the Arrow, I can feel your desire." His voice shook and broke. "I want to taste you. Tell me you want that."

"I want you to put your mouth on me," she whispered, unable to speak any louder. "Please, Gabriel."

His hand left her, and she made a noise of protest, but in the next moment he had pushed upward, off the chair, and laid her down on the rug in front of the fireplace, all in one smooth motion. His body covered hers, the heat of his erection against her thigh, prominent even through two layers of clothes.

He kissed her again, rocking against her, his hard cock pressing between her legs in a way that made her squirm. He sat up, hand going to his tie and tugging it free. Quilla started to sit, to assist him, but he shook his head.

"You will not move."

She lay back and watched him pull off his tie, unbutton and shrug out of his shirt, strip out of his trousers. When he stood naked before her, cast in shadows of gold and black and red from the fire, her breath caught.

Then he knelt beside her and his fingers went to the row of buttons on the front of her gown. They began at the banded collar and went to the hem, and Gabriel began with the topmost one.

He unhooked each button from its hole and spread the fabric as far as he was able, kissing every section as he exposed it. The neckline of the simple white shift she wore beneath began just above the curve of her breasts, and by the time he got there, she was already struggling to remember to breathe.

Gabriel laid open the cloth of her gown over her chest and nuzzled her breasts through the shift, sucking first one nipple and then the other through the material until it was wet through and both nipples stood erect. His fingers continued with the buttons as he kissed and sucked her nipples.

By the time his hands reached her waist, shivers of desire ran through her. His mouth continued to follow the path left by the open buttons, his kisses undulled by the layer of flaxen between his lips and her skin. Farther still, to her thighs, and the heat of his mouth found her heat. He kissed her there, nuzzling through the shift, and she cried out. His fingers moved faster on the buttons, pulling up the hem to finish and lay the gown completely open.

For an interminable moment he stared down at her, doing nothing. Until she spoke.

"Please."

He put his hands to the front of her shift and tore it open, right down the front. The air hit her skin and she gasped and arched her back. His hands smoothed over her breasts, rolling her nipples, then over the slope of her belly, to the tender skin of her inner thighs. He parted her legs, laid himself between them, and kissed her curls. His tongue found her clit.

Quilla stopped thinking.

There was nothing to think of but the way his mouth felt on her, the scratch of his unshaven chin on her skin, the wet heat of his tongue stroking her over and over until the flow of her blood seemed to no longer go toward her heart, but to the secret place between her legs. Her pulse pounded there, every beat of it sending her closer and closer to the edge.

She tightened her fingers in his hair, not holding him to her, holding on to him to save herself from the feeling she was going to let loose from the earth and fly upward to the stars. Fire filled her, and the surge of the sea. The pulse and pound of creation suffused her, weighed her down and lifted her up all at the same time.

The dance of his tongue stopped as she hovered on the brink. His breath puffed against her, a touch as light as stardust drifting through a nighttime sky, or the flutter of a lady beetle's wings against a flower from which it supped.

Then he kissed her again, his mouth infinitely gentle against her skin, and it was, at last, enough.

Fire and water. Earth and air. All combined in elemental force to tip her toward climax. It surely was the gift of the Invisible Mother, this capacity for ecstasy, and Quilla cried out a blessing in Kedalya's name first, then Gabriel's name after that.

For some moments she was unable to move or to speak. Quilla blinked and looked at him, surprised to see his eyes glimmered as though with tears.

"Gabriel," she said quietly. "My heart."

He groaned and covered her again with his body, and slid inside her but did not move at first. Quilla wrapped her arms and legs around him, holding him to her. When he at last began moving, the sensation made her gasp aloud, pleasure filling her again though she'd already been so well completed.

He kissed her, hard, nothing gentle about these biting kisses. His mouth traveled down her throat and to the curve of her shoulder, where he bit the collarbone hard enough to make her cry out; but she did not protest beyond that because in the next moment he soothed the hurt with his tongue and lips and murmured into her ear. Not words of love. No, she did not expect that from him.

His thrusts became more ragged, until he cried out her name again and thrust once more before collapsing on top of her.

His weight made breathing difficult, but Quilla made no complaints. She stroked his back over and over again, and after a bit he slid most of his weight off her but kept his face buried in her shoulder.

Quilla said nothing, for nothing seemed to be needed, and after a while he got up and took her to his bed, where he slipped under the covers with her and held her against him while he slept.

It took her a bit longer to find the oblivion of dreams. Quilla lay in the darkness with Gabriel's hand on her breast, her buttocks nestled against his groin. She heard the creak of the door, and held her breath, shifting naught but her gaze toward it.

In the dark, a pale hand gleamed, a flash of what might have been a golden curl. Then nothing, no sound, no word, not even the hissing sob or cry that meant someone watched them.

Yet Quilla knew they had been watched, and who had stood there.

He did not, overnight, become a considerate and solicitous lover. He did not wake her with kisses and love poetry, nor did Gabriel seem to have more patience for her in the workroom.

Yet Quilla noticed the differences in him. A glance he allowed to linger a bit longer than before. The way he thanked her when she passed him a vial, or prepared his tea. The simple but telling manner in which he allowed her to button his white work coat for him.

To others it might have seemed like nothing, but to Quilla it was as though he'd shouted his affection for her from the roof. Affection; she dared not allow herself to think of it as more than that. Nor did she allow herself to dwell on the turn her feelings had taken for him.

For now, it was enough to serve him as best she could. To make certain the simple pleasures she could provide were constant and consistent. To continue giving him what he needed before he needed it.

To keep filling Sinder's Quiver.

He did not make love to her in front of the fireplace again, but then, he didn't drink heavily, either. But in the afternoon, when he sent her away, he always added, "I would have you here tonight."

She knew what he did in the hours between the time she left him and the time she came back. He spent them with Saradin, or with his son, and Quilla did not begrudge him the time spent with either.

His lady wife had not improved, despite the daily time Gabriel spent with her. Saradin seemed to alternate between ranting rages and sullen silence, at least according to Florentine, who presumably got her information from Allora Walles.

The medicus had come, but could do nothing for her.

"She's mad as May," said Florentine as she rolled out yet another day's worth of bread. "And not from the mercury, mind you. 'Tis her own jealous nature."

Quilla paused in icing the cinnamon-flavored muffins on the plate in front of her. "You would blame me?"

Florentine looked up, face surprised. "No, Quilla Caden. I don't blame you."

"Because it sounded as though you did."

Florentine wiped her hands upon her apron. "Do you feel guilty?"

"Of her jealous nature?" Quilla shook her head. "Of her madness? No."

Florentine knew too much, was too shrewd. "Of taking her place in her husband's bed, perhaps?"

"No."

"What about her place in his heart, then?" the chatelaine asked slyly, punching down the dough again.

Quilla said nothing as she continued icing.

Florentine barked out a laugh. "I thought you'd say 'tis but part of your job."

Quilla shook her head. Florentine laughed again. "No? Not to make him love you?"

Quilla's hands paused. "I don't know that he loves me."

"And what of you?" Florentine pursed her lips and made a rude noise.

Quilla gave her a steady look. "It's not my place to love him."

"Haven't you ever loved a man before?" Florentine shaped the dough into a loaf and set it aside to rise, then dove into the bowl again and did the same with another handful. "Or a woman?"

Quilla shook her head. "No."

Florentine shook her head. "Yet surely you've had 'em love you."

"I do my best to be what they need," Quilla replied. "Not what they love."

Florentine looked upward. "And if what he needs is to love you?"

Quilla looked down at the table, then replied in a low voice, "He is not free to love me, Florentine."

"Think you a marriage contract can stop what's in the heart? People do it all the time, Quilla Caden. Fall in and out of love. Words on a paper can't change it." Florentine paused. "He's taken you to his bed. That should tell you something of what he feels for you."

"Lovemaking is not love." Quilla finished the rolls and set them aside.

"What are you so afraid of?" Florentine's voice sounded surprisingly soft. Almost gentle. It made sudden tears spring to Quilla's eyes, which she forced away by blinking fast.

"I am afraid of failing my purpose," she whispered.

"Because you can't love him?"

Quilla looked up and shook her head, no longer able to keep a tear from escaping and sliding down her cheek. "No. Because I do."

Florentine covered Quilla's hand with hers. "'Tis not a failure, Quilla. I would say that to be the greatest success."

Quilla turned her palm up to squeeze Florentine's hand, and smiled through her tears. "You are a sentimental biddy."

Florentine squeezed back and grinned. "Something I'll deny to my grave."

And then the cook went back to her work, and Quilla went to hers, the words Florentine had spoken echoing over and over in her mind.

There came the day when Gabriel surprised her.

"It would please me if you would join me for dinner this evening."

He made the invitation as though it were of no consequence, but it made Quilla turn from the bookcase, dustcloth still in her hand.

"My lord?"

"Dinner, Handmaiden," he repeated irritably. "This evening. Unless you have a prior engagement?"

"Of course I don't." She smiled.

He frowned. "I've had something delivered to your room. Wear it tonight instead of that rag you've got on now."

Quilla looked down at her dark blue gown, which couldn't be considered a rag even by the most fashionably snide. She pressed her lips together on another smile. "If it pleases you, my lord."

"It does," he snapped, turning back to the notebook on his desk. He scribbled a few more lines, and added, "And wear your hair down."

"Yes, my lord. Anything else?"

He looked up, frowning again. "And be on time."

"Of course."

She went back to dusting the bookcase, glad for something to occupy her hands that did not require thought. Dinner. A gown. And his belligerence, which was perhaps meant to be off-putting but instead only made her smile.

"Must you be so noisy?" he complained.

"I plead your mercy."

Gabriel scowled, rubbing his forehead. "I'm trying to work and you continue to make that infernal noise. Why don't you go, Handmaiden. Use the extra time to prepare yourself for tonight."

She put the cloth down. "If it pleases you."

"It pleases me!" he cried, staring at his notebook.

Quilla went over to him and leaned down to kiss his cheek. "Then I shall go."

Before she could pull away, he'd taken her hand to hold her in place. Then he let her go, as though his own action had startled him. "Good," he said gruffly. "Because your presence is naught but distraction to me."

Which was meant to be an insult but was instead a compliment, she thought as she did as he'd asked and left him.

Quilla had taken extra care with her ablutions in preparation for dinner. She took a long, scented bath and washed her hair, drying it in front of the fire and combing it into long curls over her shoulders and down her back.

The gown he'd sent was simple in design but luxurious in fabric. Beads dangled from the short puffed sleeves and at the hem. With its bodice and overskirt of claret-colored velvet and underskirt of silk in bronze, the gown made Quilla feel like a princess.

She was not quite certain what to expect from the meal itself. She arrived at the dining room, on time of course, to discover the table had been set for three. Fully lit lamps and candelabras brightened the room, and pretty but not exquisite china and flatware adorned the place settings. She saw a basket of braided rolls, a crock of butter, a platter of sliced fowl. Simple food, though certain to be delicious despite its lack of ornament.

Gabriel stood when she entered the room. "Good evening, Tranquilla Caden."

"Good evening, Gabriel Delessan."

"Good evening, Quilla!" piped up Dane from his place at his father's right. "Father says you are to join us for dinner tonight, and Florentine made treacle pudding for dessert!"

"It sounds lovely," replied Quilla with a smile. She moved toward the third place, at Gabriel's left, and he pulled the chair out for her.

Every inch the gentleman, he helped her sit and pushed the chair in for her, too, before taking his own place.

"Father says I am to behave myself." Dane tapped his fork against his plate until a look from Gabriel silenced him. "Father says we are to make good dinner conv . . . conv . . ."

"Conversation," Gabriel prompted, then looked at Quilla. "It's time he learned to eat with adults. He's been indulged at the nursery table long enough."

"I'm happy to eat with you, young Master Dane," Quilla told the boy. "And have conversation."

"Father says the lady is not expected to guide the conversation, only to respond, and that 'tis the gentleman's job to make sure she feels included."

Quilla raised an eyebrow and looked at Gabriel. "Is that so?"

Dane nodded. "Oh, yes. Father says women like to talk, but usually about silly things like dresses and poetry. Would you like to talk about dresses, Quilla?"

Quilla shook her head. "No, Master Dane. I don't believe so."

She kept her eyes from Gabriel to prevent herself from laughing at the lad.

"Oh, good," said the boy in obvious relief. "Because dresses are quite dull. Though yours is very nice," he added as an afterthought. "You look very pretty. Doesn't Quilla look pretty, Father?"

"She does, indeed." Gabriel's tone was bemused and more casual than she'd heard in a long time.

Quilla looked at him. "Any woman would look lovely in such a gown."

"Florentine wouldn't," put in Dane, which earned a muffled laugh from Vernon as he ladled soup into Dane's bowl. "And I don't think Allora Walles would, either. Her arms are too plump for a dress like that."

"Dane, 'tis not nice to comment on such things."

"Allora Walles thinks she is lovely," said Dane, spooning broth. "But she's not as lovely as you are."

"No, I daresay she isn't." Gabriel spooned some of his own broth, eyes on Quilla.

"And Allora Walles pinches! Quilla never pinches!"

"I certainly do not," Quilla said as Vernon filled her bowl.

"Jorja doesn't pinch, either. She does pull my ears, though." Dane scowled, stirring the soup in his bowl and then dunking a bit of roll in it. "She says I'm naughty."

"And I'm sure she has reason to say it," Gabriel said sternly. "If your manners at this table are any indication of the way you behave elsewhere."

Dane looked chastened, but only for a moment. "Quilla, have you told my father about my skates from Uncle Jericho?"

Gabriel looked up from his soup to stare at her. Dane continued on, not noticing his father's interest.

"Father, Uncle Jericho gave me skates and Quilla and Uncle helped me use them in the gallery! And I skated all the way back and forth, and I learned to spin . . ."—Dane paused, biting his lip— "and I broke a bust, but Uncle said you wouldn't care, as it was of his father."

"Is that so?" The easy tone had vanished.

Dane nodded, slurping soup so it splattered on the tablecloth. "Father, if Uncle Jericho is your brother, why haven't you the same father? And, Father, will I ever have a brother or a sister? Will I, Father?"

Gabriel had pushed away his bowl, and Vernon removed it. Quilla spooned the last mouthful of broth into her mouth, refusing to allow his sudden change of mood to upset her.

"Because I should like a brother or sister, Father." Dane handed his bowl to the butler, who then began serving from the platter of fowl. "But one who has the same father as me, I guess. Because you're the best father, ever."

This made Gabriel turn to his son, mouth slightly open. "So you say?"

Dane nodded firmly. "Uncle Jericho does buy me merrier toys, Father, but I still think you're the best father."

"He buys you merry toys because he has no other responsibilities to you," Gabriel said.

Dane grinned, his smile a near exact copy of Jericho's. "I did have the most merry time with the skates. Didn't I, Quilla?"

"You did."

"And Quilla and Jericho took you to the gallery to use them." Gabriel looked at her, tone belying his next words. "How nice."

"She was already there when we got there," Dane said. He struggled mightily with cutting his sliced meat, until Vernon leaned over to do it for him. "But then I skated and she talked with Uncle."

"And I wonder what they talked about," said Gabriel, face turning stony.

Quilla cut her own meat and sliced her potato before looking up at him, keeping her expression calm. If this dinner was going to disintegrate into ugliness, it would not be of her doing.

"We discussed many topics, my lord."

"Did you?" His food remained untouched.

"They always talk," Danc said. "Mostly about boring things, Father."

"Not about gowns and poetry?" Gabriel asked.

Dane laughed and shook his head, replying with his mouth full. "Sometimes he makes her mad and she cries. But other times he makes her laugh, so I guess that's all right. Isn't it, Quilla?"

Gabriel's expression now changed again, eyes narrowing. "Yes. Isn't it?"

"Your uncle Jericho and I speak on many subjects, Dane," said Quilla, though her answer was really for Gabriel. "Your uncle and I are friends."

"A friend who makes you laugh and cry?" Gabriel's question pitched low, but she heard it. "What sort of friend does that?"

Quilla lifted her chin. "An honest one."

Dane kept up the chatter, eating his dinner without seeming to notice the sudden tension from his father. *Likely because he's used to the man's mood swings.* She had no reason to regret her conversations with Jericho Delessan. She had done nothing wrong. Whatever problems the brothers had were between them and ran far deeper than her presence in their lives.

Quilla finished her food, though she had little appetite for it. Gabriel might think he needed to fight with her, but Quilla was supposed to know what he really needed. And it wasn't to battle with her about his brother in front of his son, who loved his uncle but worshipped his father.

When the pudding had been scraped clean from its bowl and Dane told firmly several times there was no more to be had, Jorja arrived to take her young charge away.

"Thank you for having dinner with me, Father," Dane said formally, holding out his hand for Gabriel to shake.

"I am pleased with your behavior," replied Gabriel with equal formality.

Dane came around the table to say good night to her, as well. "Good night, Quilla Caden."

"Good night, Dane Delessan," Quilla replied, but when he held out his hand for hers to shake, she pulled him into her arms for a hug, instead.

He smelled of sweet little boy, like active play and too much dessert. His hair ruffled against her cheek, and when his arms came around her neck to hug her in return, she closed her eyes at the sudden rush of emotion that filled her.

"Good night," Dane whispered, and she felt the press of his lips against her cheek. "Sleep right, Quilla."

"Sleep right, Dane." She hugged him again, then let him go.

Jorja took him by the hand to lead him from the dining hall, but at the last second, Dane tugged free his hand and ran back to his father. Gabriel looked surprised at the way Dane threw his arms around him and hugged him, too, but after only a moment his arms went around his son and he hugged him back.

"Sleep right, Father."

When the boy had gone, Quilla pushed away her plate, dessert untouched. Gabriel made no play at games. He dismissed Vernon and settled back into his chair after filling his glass with wine again.

"Have I ever made you cry?"

She held out her glass to be filled, and sipped before answering. "Do you measure my esteem by the amount of tears I've shed? Is that what you wish to know?"

He said nothing, just sipped, watching her. Quilla matched his gaze. The wine was good. Strong. The color of rubies in her glass.

The color of the gown he'd bought her. If he had questions, she could only wait for him to ask.

"Have I made you cry, Handmaiden?"

"You have not, my lord."

"And yet neither have I made you laugh."

Quilla sipped again, letting the sweet, rich flavor fill her mouth before swallowing. "What are you asking me?"

"How did my brother become your friend, yet I have not?"

The question, posed in a voice so honest, so vulnerable, made her put down her glass and go to him. She settled herself onto his lap, arm around his shoulder, fingers whispering through his hair.

"You are more than a friend to me, Gabriel."

He put his face to the comfort of her bosom, his cheek hot on her bared flesh. "I am your patron. I know."

"You are. And I am your Handmaiden."

His arms tightened around her. "And 'tis your purpose to give me solace."

"And my pleasure, too. This you know."

He held her tighter against him. "And when you have brought me absolute solace, you will leave me."

Grief in his voice matched the fullness in her own chest and the burning of tears in her eyes. "That is the way it's done. Yes."

"Then though it is wrong, I do not wish to be so soothed." Incredibly, he shook a little, his arms holding her close to his body. His voice, muffled against her chest, broke. "I won't be."

"Then I will have failed in my duty, my lord," Quilla whispered, eyes overbrimming at last. She put her face into the springy, dark warmth of his hair and held on to him as tightly as she could. "Then I would have failed you."

He looked up at her, face bleak, dark eyes gone hollow. "You could never fail me, Tranquilla. You are—"

"Oh, you gods-bedamned bitch!" The slurred voice from behind them made Quilla look up.

Saradin looked rather less pulled together than she had during the brannigan, and only slightly less wild than she had the night she'd attacked Quilla in the kitchen. Her blonde hair looked weighted and lank, the tangled strands pulled into some semblance of style made sadder because of its lack of finesse. Allora Walles had been falling behind in her duties. Saradin's gown, finely cut and adorned, nonetheless hung upon her like sackcloth. One belled sleeve had torn, and through the gash Quilla could see a long, angry scratch.

"You smelly, oozing cunt," Saradin continued, the ugly words falling from her lips like toads. "You bold and heartless prick!"

"Saradin," Gabriel said, as Quilla got up from his lap.

"You. Shut. Your. Mouth." Saradin sneered and advanced upon them. "I know what she is. She's a whore. And you are a whore-monger."

Gabriel's voice was cold. "Where is your nursemaid?"

"I don't need a nursemaid!" Saradin swiped a hand over her face, pulling it into a grim mask. She smiled, and Quilla saw with some disturbance that her teeth were yellowed. "I am not a child! I am your wife! Your lady wife!"

"Then behave as a lady," said Gabriel. "Though why I should expect you to start now, I don't know."

This cold reply seemed to affect Saradin more harshly than his shout. Her face fell. She crumpled. She sank to the floor, skirts bunched around her knees. Her forehead hit the floor with a smack loud enough to make Quilla jump.

"You don't love me," said Saradin in a voice made of jagged angles and pointed corners. "You. Don't."

Quilla thought for sure Gabriel would soften at the sight of his wife's despair, but he remained where he was. Saradin shook and a silver runner of drool strung from her lip. Several drops of blood beaded her forehead, and the white skin had already begun to purple with bruise. Her fingers twitched into claws and a low, guttural moan escaped her throat.

It hurt Quilla to look at the woman, who, if not in physical pain, surely was experiencing mental anguish. She went to Saradin, who rightly should have been her enemy, and put her arms around her shoulders to help her sit.

"Ring for someone," she told Gabriel, who at first did not move. She looked up at him. "Ring for aid for your lady wife, my lord!"

Only then did he move to the line of ribbons along the wall, each connecting to a different bell. He yanked one, hard, and Quilla heard the faint jangle from far away.

"Sit, my lady," she soothed. She dabbed at the cut on Saradin's forehead.

Saradin shook harder. Beneath Quilla's hands, Saradin's flesh seemed to harden and soften, in rhythmic waves almost like contractions. But what she meant to birth was illness, not a babe, and Quilla could do nothing but wipe away the spittle clinging to her chin and look into the woman's glazed green eyes.

"Don't. Touch."

"I want to help you," said Quilla.

Saradin shook harder, her jaw clenching tight. Her body went rigid. Her eyes rolled back in her head.

"My lord, help her!"

"'Twould be better if she simply left this place," Gabriel said, though he knelt next to his wife and his Handmaiden, and took Saradin's hand. "For all of us, but mostly, for her."

Saradin's eyes, pupils so dilated they looked entirely black, rolled toward him. Her hand clenched down on his. She spoke through her clenched jaw.

"Hate . . ."

"Yes, I know you do," said Gabriel. "For all you've ever shown me was contempt."

Saradin shook her head, but seemed unable to speak again. Her gaze went to Quilla's face. She reached for Quilla's hand, bore down on it, hard enough to hurt, but Quilla didn't think she meant to.

Saradin blinked. Her body stiffened once more. Her eyes closed, and she went limp in Quilla's arms.

"My lord, will she be all right?"

Gabriel sighed. "'Tis the poison she took. It brought her to madness and eventually, it will kill her. But not quickly, and in much pain."

Quilla looked down at the limp figure in front of them. "It's a terrible thing, to have loved so much."

He looked up, face hard. "She did not do this out of love, but out of spite. Because she knew by hurting herself it would hurt me. Do not pity her, Handmaiden. My wife brought this upon herself because she has ever been a selfish and self-absorbed woman who thinks of nothing beyond her own needs."

Quilla again wiped Saradin's now slack mouth free of drool. "But to see her this way . . . do you not pity her at all?"

"She took my love," Gabriel said, "and she burnt it to ash and tossed it in my face to blind me with it."

Bertram entered the room, his step quickening when he saw Saradin lying on the floor. "My lord—"

"Take lady Saradin to her quarters," Gabriel said as he got to his feet. "And if you see Allora Walles there, send her to me."

"Yes, my lord." Bertram bent and scooped Saradin into his arms, where she dangled like a child's cast-off doll. He cradled her close to him as he left the room.

Quilla got up from the floor. "Gabriel."

He did not look at her face. "I think . . . it would please me if you would leave me, Handmaiden."

"What will you do to her?"

His eyes now moved to her face, but he was not looking at her. "Allora Walles has shirked her duties here for the last time. She will get her due punishment and be sent away."

"Send her away, my lord, if you must," Quilla told him. "But waste not your time in retribution."

"Do not tell me how to run my household," Gabriel said coldly.

Quilla backed up a step at the ire in his gaze. "No, my lord."

He gave her his back. "Go away."

She did, leaving the dining room as a clearly shaking Allora Walles entered. She had little sympathy for Allora, who had shirked her duties time after time. She stepped aside to let the maid pass, and Allora still had the presence of mind to sneer at her, so whatever punishment she was to be meted was deserved.

Still, her feet slowed as she walked farther down the hall. Her duty was to Gabriel. To bring him the solace he denied desiring. It was her place, even if he didn't want it to be, and she could do no less. She could not stand by and do nothing while she thought he might be doing something he would regret.

Her steps slowed, and she turned. She did not quite run; for though she knew she couldn't let Gabriel do this, that it would stay with him far too long and leave him with guilt, for all she knew it was her duty to prevent him from continuing the punishment he did out of anger . . . for all that, she did not hurry, because no small part of her would be glad to see Allora crying.

She entered the room at a half run. "My lord! Stop!"

His hand raised, the end of his leather belt swinging. Allora wept and wailed, and again Quilla could not help the contempt that threatened to spill out in a sneer. So far, he hadn't even touched her.

"Gabriel, that is enough." Quilla put her hand on his arm. "She is not worth this effort."

His arm shook under her fingers. "Let go of me."

It pained her to admit it, but she did not understand him right then. His anger. His punishment of Allora Walles seemed overharsh to Quilla. He hadn't beaten Jorja Pinsky, and her neglect had almost cost his son his life.

"I said," he spoke through gritted jaws, "let me go."

She ran soothing fingers down his arm. "Gabriel. Let her go and come with—"

He turned on her, swift as a fox snags a rabbit, and shoved her hard enough to make her stumble back two steps. She did not cry out, though her mouth opened. "Would you take what was meant for her?"

Allora looked at Quilla from red and weeping eyes. Quilla looked back at him. "There is no love lost between Allora and me, very true. But you told me once you did not wish to become your father. Don't do it for something as worthless as this."

"'Tis not the question I asked you." He wrapped the end of the belt around his fist and stared at her. "Would you take the punishment she deserves?"

Allora let out another strangled sob. Quilla looked at Gabriel from the corner of her eye.

"If your intent is to strap me in her place, then I can only answer you one way."

His laugh had no humor to it. "If it pleases me."

"If it pleases you to beat me in her place, then I can do naught but bend to it. But if you ask whether I am willing to take her punishment? I would rather not."

"Get out of the way, Handmaiden."

She stepped in front of Allora. "I have no love in my heart for this one, but I can't let you do this."

"I'm warning you, Handmaiden." His voice went low, hard. His eyes, hard, too. "If you do not get out of the way, then you will get twice what she would have."

Without another word, Quilla unbuttoned the front of her dress, shrugging out of it without hesitation. She still wore a small bandage over the wound on her arm. She turned her back to him, put her hands on the table.

Allora looked over at her with wide eyes. Quilla glanced back before turning her attention back to the table, and her hands upon it. She'd spread her fingers wide, the sign for being all right. Not that he'd know it, or know that the closer together her fingers the less comfortable she was with what was happening.

"Handmaiden," Gabriel said from behind them. "You don't want me to do this."

"Should you wish to do it, my lord, then your wish is my action."

He made a low noise. She heard the sound of the belt being drawn through his hands. The slight whistle of it as he raised it. Her ears, long attuned to such noise, created a picture in her head, and Quilla let herself relax, not tensing against the pain she expected to come any minute.

"Get out," she heard Gabriel say, and the sound of shoes on the floor told her Allora had scuttled away like a beetle whose rock had been overturned.

She Waited. She imagined his arm held high, belt dangling. Ready to strike . . .

"What are you doing? Stop!"

The sound of Jericho's voice made Quilla turn. He crossed the room to her in moments. His arm went around her shoulders, and she winced at his touch on her wound.

"Jericho, no," she murmured.

"Stop it, Gabriel!" Jericho's voice shook with anger. "What the hell are you doing?"

Now Quilla turned, expecting anger on her patron's face. What she saw was worse, somehow, as his eyes moved from his brother, to her, to his brother's arm around her shoulders. What she saw was nothing.

He turned away from her, the tension in his shoulders evident and visible. Then he left the room without saying anything else.

Quilla shrugged off Jericho's arm and rearranged her gown. "Let me go. You are a troublemaker."

"Troublemaker?" His voice sounded angry. "Because I stopped him from beating you bloody?"

"He would not," Quilla said sternly, "have beaten me bloody."

Jericho scowled. "He had a strap raised above your back. He was going to hit you with it."

"He would not have!"

"How do you know this!" Jericho shouted, grabbing her by the arms. "What would you have done had he raised that strap to you, and hit you with it?"

"I would have let him!"

He let go of her and stepped back, dismay twisting his face. "But, why, Quilla? Why? Because he is your patron, you would allow him to so abuse you?"

"Not because he is my patron, no."

His shoulders sagged. "Then what reason, Tranquilla Caden?"

"You know my reason, Jericho."

He nodded, looking down. "I suppose I do."

"You love an ideal. Not a woman."

He looked up at her, eyes narrowed. "Don't you tell me who, or what, I love. Don't you dismiss me that way because it makes it easier for you!"

His reaction made her step back. "I'm sorry. I never lied to you. I never made you believe—"

"No. You didn't." He pushed past her and out of the room.

She stared after him for what felt like a very long time, and then she went to find Gabriel.

He was not in his room, and though she waited for him to come back, the light of day had begun to stretch pink across the sky before he did.

"Gabriel," she said from the doorway to his bedroom as he entered the workroom. "Come to bed, for I am fair certain you are weary."

Without a word, he did, pushing past her and toward the bed, where he lay down. She took off his shoes and did what she could to make him comfortable before she slipped into the bed next to him and put her arms around him.

"I don't love him," she whispered against Gabriel's shoulder.

He turned to face her, his arms going around her and gathering her close. She felt wetness against her cheek as he pressed his face to hers, the covers a cocoon around them, a cave. A shield.

And they needed to say nothing more after that.

Chapter 13

It was the first time she had known him not to work. Gabriel stayed in bed all day, the rise and fall of his breathing like a metronome in the blinds-dimmed room.

Quilla stayed with him until she was certain he would not wake anytime soon, and then she slipped from bed and washed and dressed, and she went to a part of the house in which she'd never been.

Saradin Delessan's rooms were luxurious, spacious, and well appointed, with tall windows letting in the sunlight. A fire crackled in the grate, but the room still kept a chill.

The mistress sat in a chair near the window. Her hair unkempt, her clothes in disarray, she looked up when Quilla came in. Her eyes blazed. Her mouth twisted, and she laughed.

Quilla sat down in the chair across from her patron's wife, looking at the other woman calmly. Saradin laughed harder, her chest hitching. Silver drool strung itself from her mouth. The laugh became a cackle and a shriek. Saradin leaned forward, mouth stretched with the screaming giggles, pausing every so often to take in a deep, gasping breath before starting to laugh again.

Quilla watched her without expression for a few moments. Then she slapped Saradin's face hard enough to almost knock the other woman off her seat. Saradin's laughter cut off sharply, leaving behind silence.

Her hand went to her cheek, where the white imprint of Quilla's fingers was filling in with red. The blow had knocked her sideways, and now she turned upright, slowly. A low, grinding growl came from her throat. She used the heel of her hand to wipe the spittle from her chin.

"You dare."

"I dare," replied Quilla. "Sit up straight and listen to me, Saradin Delessan."

Saradin did, the sly light of madness still in her eyes but underlaid now with comprehension. She spat to one side and touched her lips as though to check for blood, but there was none. Quilla had been careful not to cut her, though Saradin had not shown her the same consideration.

"You will listen to me," Quilla told her without inflection, neither kindness nor cruelty.

Saradin nodded.

Quilla leaned forward to look into Saradin's eyes. "You will stop your torture of him, do you understand? You will cease this badgering. You will cease these histrionics, these hysterics, you will keep yourself under control."

One short burst of laughter escaped Saradin's lips but she clamped her mouth shut on it immediately. "I am mad, unless you hadn't heard."

"We are all of us mad," replied Quilla, an edge of ice creeping into her tone. "We are all of us damaged in some way."

Saradin's body quivered and her eyes fluttered. More drool puddled at the corners of her mouth, and she wiped it away. "You think 'tis so simple?"

"No. I do not think 'tis simple at all. But I do believe it is necessary." Quilla sat back in her chair, watching the other woman. "You are a spiteful, selfish, and shameless bint, but you are his wife and the mother of his child. Gabriel feels he has a duty to you. And you are making him sick from it."

A flash of something— grief, perhaps, if the woman could feel it—shaded Saradin's green eyes momentarily gray. "I only want to love him."

"No. You only want him to love you. 'Tis not the same thing at all." Quilla looked her over, this woman who had everything any woman could have wanted, and who had thrown it all away.

Saradin didn't flinch. A grin stretched her mouth, baring teeth. "And what threat do you promise, should I discover my madness unchanged, my mind unhinged? What threat do you promise, if my mind is unhinged? What threat? What threat do you promise?" Her repeated words were not rambling mutters, but purposeful spears of language, thrown with skill.

"There is no help for your madness," said Quilla. "I merely tell you to cease being such an unbearable bitch."

Saradin turned her face so her mouth whispered against Quilla's ear, almost a kiss. "You ask me to do this for him?"

"No, my lady," replied Quilla, in her own whisper. "For yourself, for I daresay that is the one person for whom you have ever done anything."

"And if I do not? Do not? And if. I. Do. Not?"

Quilla leaned in even closer, keeping her voice pitched low. "Then I will take him away from you entirely, you stupid bitch, and you will have nothing."

Saradin's hand flashed out and tangled in Quilla's hair, yanking her head back. It hurt, but Quilla made no sign of it. The woman was fast, and yes, she was mad—but she was not entirely unpredictable.

"I would like to kill you."

"I don't doubt that, my lady. But you won't."

"No?" Saradin sneered, yanking Quilla's head back farther and shaking her. She was strong, for being so small. "It would not be the first time."

"Say you true?" Quilla put her hand over Saradin's and used the leverage to stand. Though the other woman still had a handful of her hair, Quilla's height allowed her to shove Saradin into her chair again.

Saradin let go of Quilla. "The eel enjoyed her. As he'd enjoy you, too."

Quilla looked at her. "You killed the other maid. The one who carried his child?"

Saradin pulled her feet up onto the chair and wrapped her arms around her knees, her body shuddering and quaking again. Her teeth chattered. "Bitch thought to give him a son, a real son, his son. Bitch thought to take my place. Little cunt thought to replace me . . ." Her voice trailed off and she laughed again. "I don't think he ever fucked her, mind. I don't think he did. She wanted him, though, I knew it, I smelled it on her, saw it in her eyes, smelled it and tasted it on her. . . ."

"You killed her and she was not even his lover?" Quilla's voice dipped low with disgust.

Saradin's strangled laugh edged out from clenched jaws. She shook harder, eyes fluttering. Her fingers linked so tight her knuckles turned white as she held her knees close to her body.

"He is mine, he is mine, he is mine, Handmaiden, and you can fuck him but he is mine!"

Quilla stood. "Remember what I said, Saradin."

Saradin sneered and spat again on the floor, turning her face away, but she did not argue. "Get out of my room."

"If you truly love him, you would not hurt him so."

"I said get out!"

Quilla looked again at the woman, but said nothing else, and left her to her madness.

D on't know what he thinks we'll do without Allora Walles." Florentine's muttered grumble caught Quilla's ear.

"He has dismissed Allora because she did not do her duty, Florentine."

The chatelaine sniffed and added spice to the stew before turning from the fireplace, hands on her ample hips. "And left us the burden of caring for her, instead!"

"She doesn't leave her room," said Quilla implacably, arranging her tray of tea and biscuits.

Since Quilla's talk with her, Gabriel's wife had not made a peep. She'd stayed in her room, not speaking, barely moving from the window long enough to eat or sleep. It had been almost a week.

Rossi had been promoted to the position of lady's maid, which seemed to thrill her and cause Florentine what seemed to be an unwarranted amount of consternation. Now, the cook frowned and looked Quilla up and down.

"Rossi isn't made for that job, being run ragged by a mad-woman."

Something in the way Florentine said the girl's name made Quilla look up from the plate of biscuits. "Her charge has been most subdued, Florentine. I should think Rossi would enjoy the respite."

Florentine frowned. "I like Rossi here. She's the best of the three."

"Most likely why Gabriel chose her." Quilla studied her friend, realization dawning along with a slow smile. "Florentine. You and Rossi?"

Florentine looked startled, then scowled, bustling around the kitchen and not looking at Quilla.

Quilla laughed lightly. "That's . . ."

" 'Tis what?" cried Florentine, turning, eyes ablaze. " 'Tis what?"

"Lovely," said Quilla. "Lovely for the pair of you to have found one another."

Some of the fire went out of Florentine's gaze, but she didn't soften entirely. "She's too young."

"Florentine, you're far from too old."

The cook bent back to her work, using sharp movements that betrayed her agitation. "I was a lad a long, long time ago."

Quilla put down her tray and went to the other woman, touched her shoulder. Florentine looked up, her face softer than Quilla had ever seen it. She blinked back tears, and the sight of them moved Quilla near to tears herself.

They sat at the same time, Florentine as though her legs had given out, and Quilla following.

" 'Tis been more than twenty years since I ran from Alyria in the aftermath of the revolution. I'd lived my whole life as a lad, Quilla Caden, and lived in fear of being found out by those who'd have killed me for it."

Quilla took Florentine's hand. She knew little about Alyria and the way of life there, just that there had been a war, and that women had once been forced into servitude there.

"They didn't let us love women," continued Florentine in a voice unlike her normal bluster. "But I did. Born female, living male, loving women . . . I was a freak of the worst sort. And then, the war, and the women rose up and the prince became our king upon the birth of her son. . . ." Florentine's voice shuddered. "And they were allowed to take off their veils. I could have become a woman, but I was afraid, Quilla. Because what was I? A man? Or a woman? Living as one and loving the same? So I ran, over the mountains, and then I met Master Gabriel, and he brought me here."

"And now you've found someone to love," Quilla said gently. "Where is the shame in that? You are as you were made, Florentine. You can be nothing else."

"If she fails, as Allora did," Florentine said in a low voice, "he will send her away, as well."

"Rossi won't fail. She is smarter than Allora Walles ever was. And Saradin is quiet, now. Rossi will be able to care for her appropriately."

Florentine took her hand from Quilla's and wiped her face, voice gruff. "Saradin has been quiet before. I don't trust her."

"Nor I," admitted Quilla. "But I believe Rossi will be fine."

Florentine sighed. "He never should have married that bint."

"But he did," said Quilla with a small smile.

"And now we are all stuck with her."

"Yes."

Florentine looked at Quilla. "Would that he'd met you sooner."

"If he had not married her, he might never have needed me."

Florentine rolled her eyes. "When will you stop being so bloody complacent?"

"Oh, perhaps when I die," Quilla teased as she got up to finish with her tray.

"Huh," huffed Florentine. "Maybe sooner than that."

"You never know," answered Quilla. "You never know."

The wind rustled the leaves in the trees and made Gabriel cough. And heat—welcome at first after the many dreary months of winter. Hot wind and the sound of coughing woke Quilla from her sleep.

The instant she opened her eyes, they stung and watered. Gabriel still coughed beside her in the bed, not beneath the trees in the meadow, not under a hot summer sky. She sat upright into the cloud of smoke hovering over the bed and fell back at once, choking.

Quilla covered her mouth and nose with her hand and shook Gabriel, who had ceased coughing. She cried out his name, but he did not respond. She shook him harder, and he stirred feebly.

From someplace far away, she heard the sound of shouting, mostly drowned out by the roaring that she knew now was not made by the summer breeze in the trees.

"Fire!" Quilla shook Gabriel harder. "Fire! Wake up!"

He didn't respond. Quilla, still naked, rolled out of bed and hit the floor with a thud hard enough to clack her teeth together. The air was clearer down here, but not by much, and she gasped in a deep breath. She crawled to the privy chamber and reached for the taps on the bathtub. Water splashed, ringing, against the tub's metal sides. She threw in every towel and washcloth she could find, soaking them before dragging them out. She wrapped one around her body, her head, her hands, then flung the others over her shoulder and crawled back beneath the ever-lowering layer of smoke to the bed.

"Gabriel!"

She slopped the sopping cloths over his face and he startled, eyes opening. She realized she could see him, that the light from outside was highlighting his face, not white moonlight but the shifting red gold of fire.

"Fire!"

He blinked and started to sit. Quilla put her hand on his chest, pointing to the smoke now hovering mere arrows above them. She tugged him until he rolled off the bed and onto the floor.

The fall and the soaked towels seemed to revive him, because he shook himself and reached for her. She could not hear his words, though his lips moved. The noise of the fire, the sound of the rushing wind overwhelmed all other sound.

She helped him wrap himself in the cloths, already drying in the heat. "We have to crawl! Stay low!"

He could not have heard her, but he nodded in understanding. They crawled. The floor under her bare knees was hot. Smoke made her cough and blinded her; her head connected solidly with the door frame because she misjudged the distance. The tears of pain helped wash the smoke from her eyes. Gabriel's hand closed upon her ankle.

Invisible Mother, Quilla prayed as she crawled. *If ever I have offended thee with thought or action, I beg forgiveness. Save your servant, Holy Mother, I beseech thee. Or if not me, please, by the Land Above, save the one I love.*

The fire's roar grew louder in the hall. Quilla could see nothing. Gabriel moved up alongside her, his face so black with smoke the whites of his eyes appeared startling.

"Dane!"

She saw his lips form the name of his son and fear again thudded her heart. She nodded. Dane's room was on the second floor along with the other bedrooms. To get there, they would have to get down the stairs.

How they made it she would never know, for the smoke curtained the stairs and made watching their path impossible. Backward they went, knees and hands, bumping with every step until, at last, she tumbled backward into the second-floor hall and Gabriel caught her.

"Window!"

Gabriel pointed toward the end of the hall. Quilla nodded.

Again, they crawled. Her knees began to bleed. A bit farther down the hall, the prostrate form of a man blocked them.

Bertram, red hair blackened with soot, face smeared with ash, lay unconscious. Quilla unwrapped one of her hands and put the now barely damp towel over his face. He did not wake. She could not feel the beat of his heart or see the rise and fall of his chest, but she did not think he was dead. She did not want to believe it.

Gabriel stood, the upper half of his body disappearing into the smoke. His hands came down to lift Bertram, and Quilla followed as Gabriel dragged the houseboy down the hall.

Glass broke, the pieces like diamonds scattered on the hall carpet. Before she could stop herself, Quilla had crawled atop some of them, and the cuts on her knees bled afresh. She used a towel to brush the floor clear, but glass still stuck in her flesh, and she had no time to pick it out. A sudden influx of wind made the smoke roil. The fire's roar grew louder, the sound of a beast approaching from behind.

In another moment Gabriel knelt in front of her. Blood streamed down his arms from dozens of cuts on his now bare hands. He put his arm around her waist and hauled her upright. She found the wall with her hand, and then the window frame, still bristling with glass. The air rushing in tasted so sweet she thought she might intoxicate herself with it.

Gabriel yanked the towel from around her head and used it to smash out the rest of the glass from the window frame. He pushed her to the window. He meant to push her out.

"No!" Quilla shook her head, resisting. "Dane!"

Flames licked out of the windows on the second floor. *Oh, sweet Invisible Mother! Those are Saradin's rooms!*

In the courtyard below, she saw figures. Billy. Florentine. Some of the stable hands, passing bucket after bucket of water to each other and splashing them at the house. The cobblestones glistened.

The snow around the house had melted, leaving bare earth, ringed with white, behind.

"Go, Quilla!"

"No! I won't leave you!"

Just below them was the roof to the small portico. The snow had melted off it and was running in rivulets down the gutter. Bertram lay on the ground just below it, one of the housemaids bent over him.

"Go, Quilla!"

She shook her head, resisting. Gabriel gave her no other chance at protest. He grabbed her arms, the pain of her unhealed wound making her cry out. He lifted her over the sill. Her hands grabbed for purchase. He pushed harder. A piece of glass he'd missed tore the flesh of her palm. Blood made her grasp slip. She dangled, falling, and only his grip upon her arm kept her from tumbling to the ground.

Gabriel lowered her as far as he could. Her toes brushed the roof of the portico. He let her go. Quilla stumbled, slipped, and went down hard enough to crack the clay tiles. She tried to scream but had no breath. She slid toward the edge of the roof until her feet hooked into the gutter and stopped her from going all the way over. She slipped more, scraping her side along the gutter as she rolled over the side, but managing to catch herself at the last minute yet again.

Strong hands grabbed her calves, then her waist, and she let go, falling into Jericho's arms. He, too, had been blackened by smoke, his blond hair gone gray with it. He wore a shirt and trousers, the shirt undone to his waist, sleeves unlaced and flapping. His bare feet slipped on the half icy cobblestones. He set her down, taking her by the arm to get her away from the house.

She slipped and almost fell but he held her up. "Gabriel went to get Dane!"

He could have heard no more than one word out of her sentence, so hoarse and choked had been her voice, but whatever he heard made him turn back to the house.

"Dane is still inside?"

He did not wait for an answer, but pulled his shirt off over his head and thrust it into her hands. It took her an eternity of instants to understand why—she was still naked and had not noticed.

Quilla turned toward the sound of shouting and saw the stable hands Luke and Perrin rolling what appeared to be a cartwheel wrapped in tubing into the courtyard. Jutting from its top was a handle. A pump handle. She turned from it to shout after Jericho, but he had already run back toward the house and disappeared into the door as she watched.

She pulled his shirt over her head, the sleeves too long and the hem hitting her midthigh. Her feet were cold. Luke and Perrin had unrolled some of the tubing, and Billy had grabbed the end, pointing it toward the house. Luke jumped on top of the wheel. She saw now that the tubing trailed off toward the garden. He pushed the pump handle. Water jetted from the end of the house. Perrin and Billy ran toward the house with it.

Of course. A hose. Her mind, dulled by shock and smoke, had not recognized it. Quilla stumbled on the uneven cobbles, but before she could fall, another strong hand caught her.

"Up, girl," grunted Florentine. "Let's get you tended to."

Quilla did not move at first, her eyes locked on the sight of Glad Tidings. Flames now flickered in some of the third-story windows. The entire second floor appeared to be covered in red and orange and black. Smoke poured from the windows, which began to break one after another.

"Come, Quilla!"

She followed Florentine on numb and bleeding feet. The blood from her hand had slowed, gone thick, but painted Jericho's shirt with crimson calligraphy. Florentine sat her on a bale of hay covered by a horse blanket, and grabbed up another from the ground to wrap around Quilla's shoulders. It smelled of beast, of warmth and comfort, and as Quilla pulled it close, she shook so hard her teeth clattered.

"Sinder save them," Florentine said as another window scattered glass onto the courtyard below.

"Invisible Mother save them!"

Quilla turned to the sound of the voice, and her face felt suddenly frozen into stone. "Jorja!"

The nursemaid's cheeks had streaks of white left behind in the soot by her tears. Her grief did not impress Quilla, who stood and slapped the woman across the face as hard as she could.

"What are you doing out here when they are still inside!"

"Quilla—"

Quilla ignored Florentine and slapped Jorja again. The nursemaid went to her knees screaming pleas of mercy, but Quilla ignored those, too. She slapped Jorja's face a third time, knocking her over. Quilla slipped in the mud left by the snow, but struck again.

"What are you doing out here when they are still in there?" Her fingers doubled up and she punched Jorja, missing her nose but catching her jaw and knocking the woman to the ground.

"Quilla! Stop it, Handmaiden! Stop!"

Again, Quilla ignored Florentine, fury making her strong enough to shake off the chatelaine's grasp. Quilla grabbed the neck of Jorja's night rail and hauled her upright, shaking her like a weasel shakes a chicken to break its neck.

"Quilla, 'tis not her fault! She took him! Saradin took Dane!"

Quilla let go of Jorja, who fell back to the ground, wailing. Quilla turned. "What do you mean?"

Florentine put her hands on Quilla's shoulders. "She took him, Quilla. Saradin took Dane and set fire to her rooms. 'Tis not Jorja's fault."

"Oh, by the Arrow." Quilla spat the taste of smoke from her mouth. "Oh, that cursed mad bitch!"

"Yes." Tears had also streaked Florentine's cheeks. "Yes, she is that."

Quilla reached for Florentine's hand. Their fingers linked, and they stood side by side, watching the house burn in front of them.

Time had slowed, had stopped, and yet had begun to go twice as fast. The roof of Quilla's gable room collapsed. Her vision doubled, tripled, blurred with tears. Florentine's fingers tightened in her own, the wound on Quilla's palm covering their hands with her blood.

And then, she saw her. Saradin, atop the roof. The wind picked up her long blonde hair and spread it out behind her like a wedding veil scattered with fireflies. She wore a dress of flame, the black lace of smoke at her hem and sleeves, the ripple of yellow and gold at her throat.

"Sweet Invisible Mother," said Florentine.

Quilla took a step toward the house, her hand outstretched, but Florentine held her back from going farther. "Dane?"

Saradin screamed, the sound horrid and high, the screech of a teakettle left too long on the flame.

"She's going to jump," said Florentine.

But though Saradin might have planned to take a final flight from the burning roof, another figure appeared beside her, out of the smoke. They struggled, wraiths dancing in the smoke.

"Gabriel?" Florentine cried.

"No. Jericho."

Saradin screamed again. A jet of flame burst from the roof, obscuring the struggle for a moment before revealing it again.

Both of them were cloaked in flame. Saradin hovered on the

edge of the roof, arms outstretched as though she were trying to fly. The wind buffeted her hair and the flaming shreds of her night rail, and for one last instant, she did, indeed, seem about to soar. Before she could leap, Jericho pulled her back from the edge.

Saradin disappeared, tumbled onto the roof. Jericho teetered on the roof's edge, against the flame-licked balustrade. And then he fell. It took but a moment to turn the man who'd danced and laughed with such inherent grace into a broken, lolling puppet whose strings had been shorn.

Quilla heard a sound like growling and realized it came from her own throat as she ran toward the body sprawled in the muck made by the fire-melted snow. Jericho's blood mixed with the mud and spread on the cobblestones. Quilla slipped and went to her knees, reaching for him.

He was not dead. Jericho smiled at her. Crimson lined the edges of his teeth and left his lips looking kissed. His blue-sky eyes no longer matched; in one the pupil had dilated into a void, while the other had shrunk to a pinpoint.

Blood from his ear painted his blond hair. Quilla pushed the hair from his forehead as she knelt next to him and then took his hand.

"It would seem," he told her as more red burbled up to paint his lips, "I cannot fly."

She hushed him. "You'll be fine, Jericho."

Even now he tried to charm her. "Fine as silk, Quilla Caden."

She smiled for him. "Jericho, we will get a medicus—"

His slow blink and the fading of his smile stopped her. Tears fell onto his face, mixing with the blood on his mouth. His tongue slipped out, as though to taste, and he focused on her.

"I would make you feel," he whispered, each move of his lips spreading crimson. Now it oozed down his chin and over the line of his jaw, down his throat.

Quilla hushed him again, stroking his cheek. "You have made me feel, Jericho."

He smiled, gaze dimming. "You did not belong to me, Quilla."

"No." She bent to kiss him, tasting blood and tears, the taste of a metallic ocean. She touched his cheek. "Friend by choice, Jericho. Not of necessity."

From behind her she heard shouts, but she did not turn. She kissed him again, hearing the whistle of his breath from something broken inside him. Again, she stroked his hair back from his face. He'd begun to shiver. The ground beneath him had gone red. So much blood. He took in another gasping breath, and when he let it out, he was gone.

A low keen slipped from her lips and she bent in grief over his body. The shouts behind her grew louder, while the sound of rushing wind filled the air. She turned her face on Jericho's chest. The water sprayed from the hose was putting out the fire, though as she watched the third floor caved inward. The flames disappeared while more black smoke billowed out.

Another familiar figure staggered out the back door, a smaller form draped over its arms. Gabriel, carrying Dane, face pale and eyes closed.

Quilla could not move. Jericho's bare chest—for he'd given up his shirt for her, hadn't he? He'd done that for her—was already chilling beneath her cheek. No *thump-thump* sounded in her ear. He was dead. Gabriel was alive. Dane, it seemed, was alive, for as she watched, his father lay him on the ground and the boy began to twitch and shake with cough.

Gabriel was alive, and still, she could not move. Both of them bent over figures on the ground. Both of them looked up. Her gaze met his from across the courtyard. She saw him look at her. At his fallen brother. She saw this, saw the grief in his eyes, and still, she could not move.

She could not move, even when he shouted for someone to help him with his son. She could not get up, not even when he turned from her. She could do nothing but crouch on the cold, wet ground with her arms around a corpse and weep for a man who had loved her not for what she was, but for whom.

Chapter 14

Fever had struck her, and for three days Quilla knew nothing but a strange bed in a room she did not recognize, and the face of a stranger who poked and prodded and sewed her wounds with practice but not compassion.

"You will not bleed her," she heard Gabriel say, and when she looked up, saw his pale face, expression as though carved from marble. "She's been bled enough, already."

"As you wish," replied the stranger. Obsequious, and yet when Gabriel was not looking, the man leered at her and passed a hand over her body in a way that made her want to scream, but she had no voice.

She had escaped the fire, but now it raged within her. Faces floated in front of her. Florentine. Kirie. Bertram. Gabriel . . . and Saradin, whose green eyes had become smoking black holes and behind whose teeth flames licked when she smiled.

She woke to the sound of humming and turned her head. Every part of her ached. Her hand wore a thick white bandage. She sat up, head swimming a little, to see Lolly sitting by the fire, sewing on a quilt square.

"Water?"

Lolly looked up, her mouth parted in surprise, and put aside her sewing to bring the water. She held the cup to Quilla's lips but would allow nothing but the smallest sips.

"Where are we?" Quilla asked, her thirst assuaged for the moment.

"The little manor," Lolly said, then explained further. "Master Gabriel's father built it for his lady wife as a retreat. A summer home. 'Tis much smaller than Glad Tidings, though still comfortable. We've all moved here."

Not all of them.

"Dane? How is he?"

Lolly smiled and sat on the edge of the bed. "The young master is fine. His father saved him from the fire with no ill effects."

Quilla sat up. "And Gabriel?"

"Our lord Delessan is well," Lolly assured her, putting a hand on Quilla's shoulder to keep her from rising. "He is well, Quilla Caden."

Tears pricked Quilla's eyes. "Jericho is dead."

"Aye."

"And the lady Saradin?"

"She perished in the fire. I'm sorry."

Quilla was not sorry. "She set the fire."

Lolly hesitated, but then nodded. "Yes."

Quilla's mouth thinned. "She ought to have ended her own life, if 'tis what she wished. Not taken others with her. She'll find the Void."

Lolly nodded again, slowly. "You shouldn't stress yourself, Quilla. You've been ill."

"How long?"

"Three days."

Three days she had lain abed. Three days she'd neglected her purpose. "I have to get up."

"You can't. Master Gabriel said—"

Quilla pushed the other girl aside. "He'll need me."

Lolly stepped back as Quilla got out of bed, but didn't argue further. "We're worried about him."

Quilla looked up at her as she unlaced the front of her gown with stiff fingers. Moving was difficult, for she could not raise her injured arm more than halfway and her back, as well, protested with every move. The bandage on her hand made unlacing almost impossible, and she fumbled with the ties.

With sure fingers, Lolly helped Quilla undo the front of her gown and step out of it. Quilla looked down at her naked body, marked by cuts and bruises, but no burns. Along her arm, where Gabriel had gripped her to push her out the window, a pattern of bruises left behind by his fingers had begun to go from purple and black to the first shadings of green.

Lolly handed her a dress, not one of her own. It smelled of smoke. Quilla stepped into it, forcing her hands through the long sleeves, and was at a loss when she realized that, unlike hers, this gown buttoned up the back. Lolly did it up for her, then smoothed the fabric over Quilla's shoulders and held on to her for a moment.

The housemaid looked at Quilla. "He is in bad shape."

Quilla nodded, the motion making the world begin to swim before her eyes. "I will go to him."

"Invisible Mother go with you," replied Lolly. "I think you'll need her guidance."

"She has often given it before. Tell me where he is."

The little manor was not so large she could lose her way. She found his room moments after leaving her own, though she had to pause before opening the door to catch her breath and stop her head from swimming. She meditated for a moment to clear her thoughts, to ready herself for Waiting. Then she pushed open the door.

Quilla had seen Gabriel upset, but she had never seen him so despairing. She had seen him intoxicated before, both joyous and melancholy; she had never seen him look as he did now, as though the Void had taken him and spit him back out, half chewed.

The rooms he'd assigned himself were even more austere than his former chambers, emphasized by the lack of even a worktable or desk. A bed, the covers rumbled and pillows scattered as though by restless sleep, took up most of one corner. An armoire another. The fireplace with its ornate carvings marked this room as a master suite, even if the furnishings did not.

Gabriel sat in a chair facing the fire, which had been allowed to burn down to coals though plenty of wood filled the scuttle. An almost empty bottle of worm rested on the table next to the arm of his chair, his glass tumbler glowing amber from its contents. More surprising to her than the opiate-laced wine, which she knew he used, was the more unfamiliar tang of herb in the air. She had never known Gabriel to indulge in any intoxicant other than alcohol. Herb was his brother's indulgence, not his.

"Go away." Herb had slurred his voice a bit but could not account for the flatness of his tone.

Quilla stepped through the doorway and out of the shadows. "How did you know it was me?"

"I've had almost every part of you against my face at some time or another, Handmaiden. I think I know the scent of you well enough. That, and nobody else would be foolish enough to risk my anger."

She came forward still farther. "Lolly told me how to find you."

"Remind me to get rid of Lolly when I am able."

His voice was slow, lazy, unamused but with that same lax quality sometimes caused by frivolity. It was the voice of a man imagining some merry joke to which nobody else was privy—or of a man laid so low by grief that nothing seemed real any longer, and all had become an amusing dream in order to be borne. A man for whom there could be no humor in anything but who must find humor in everything in order to bear it.

"I did not think to see you so soon," Gabriel continued.

"I came as soon as I was able, my lord."

His glanced over her, looking but not really seeing. "Go away."

"You know I will not."

He stood, the movement sudden and unexpected enough to almost make her take a step back. "I said for you to go away, and I meant it. There is no place for you here any longer, Handmaiden."

She did not falter. "Are you telling me you no longer need me?"

"I no longer want you. That is more important." His gaze was dark and terrible, eyes burning bright.

"You would truly send me away?"

He did not drop his gaze from hers. "Everything that has happened is because of you."

The accusation was so unfair, so hurtful, Quilla could only stare. No longer his Handmaiden, bound to provide solace, but a woman whose heart was on the verge of being broken by the man she loved.

"Nothing to say to that?"

"You would blame me?"

Something shifted in his gaze for a moment, almost revealing something within before dropping down a shield of implacability.

"Everything that has happened is because of you," he repeated and turned his back to her.

She went to him, reached for him, put her hand upon his shoulder. "Gabriel. Please. Do not shut me out."

"To shut you out would imply I have, somehow, let you in."

She did not take away her hand, and the register of her voice dropped. Became pleading. "Gabriel. Please. I—"

"I know." She heard the sneer tug his voice, though she could not see it tug his face. "'Tis your purpose and your place to soothe me. And I tell you again, Handmaiden. Get you gone from me. I don't want you anymore."

"But if you need—"

"Fuck my need!" he shouted, pulling away from her and turning at last to give her the full force of his fury. "You are done here! Your damned duty is done! You have failed!"

She lifted her chin, allowing herself anger. "If I have failed you, it's because you've thwarted me at every turn. It's because you find more comfort in your misery than you do from anything else!"

She did not see the back of his hand, but even if she had, she wouldn't have ducked it. His slap caught her full on the face and sent her staggering, then to her knees in front of him, holding her stinging cheek. Tears blurred her vision.

"That is your place," Gabriel said. "On your knees."

She tried to Wait, and could not do it. True patience failed her. Her heart remained selfish. The thorns had become too sharp for her to appreciate the beauty of the flower.

"I am your Handmaiden. I am your solace and"—her voice faltered, but she kept on—"your comfort. I am what you need before you know you need it."

Gabriel put his hand to his crotch and rubbed himself without evident pleasure. "And if I need your mouth upon me?"

She rose higher on her knees and reached without hesitation toward him, but her fingers stopped a breath from touching him. She looked up at him, unsure if she would find her voice until she actually spoke.

"No."

"No?" His hand snaked out and grabbed a fistful of her hair, pulling her upright. He shook her as a mother dog shakes its naughty pups. "You tell me *no*?"

She put her hand over his to lessen the pain of his grasp, but did not otherwise try to get away. "I say no!"

Gabriel pushed her down and took several steps back, away from her. "Get back on your knees."

She looked at him, her equilibrium shattered, self-confidence gone, her world tilted on its axis and spinning too fast. Years of training no longer mattered.

"I will not."

"What's the matter, Handmaiden? Have you forgotten your purpose and your place? You've been on your knees for me before."

She had, but not for this reason. Not for her humiliation.

"You need not do this."

"And do you not understand, it has nothing to do with need, and everything to do with want! Are you not here to fulfill my every desire? Now, I tell you again, get on your knees."

She looked up at him and shook her head. "No, Gabriel."

This time, she brought up her own hand when his came down, and hers blocked the blow. The force of it reverberated down her arm, but she kept steady.

"Submissive does not mean without defense," Quilla said.

Something indefinable glittered in his gaze. "Have you found your limits, Quilla Caden?"

She did not answer, and after a moment he took his hand away. "I am not asking you to do anything you have not done before, and eagerly."

Still, she said nothing, and Gabriel stared at her. His gaze raked her from head to foot. "What sort of Handmaiden does not do her master's bidding?"

Quilla put her hand over her heart, which had physically begun to hurt. Now her silence was from inability to form words, rather than pointed refusal. She could not speak. She could not breathe. His words, the name he'd called her, hurt worse than his slap.

He laughed without joy, his smile cruel and unflattering. He was again the man she had first met surrounded by gloom and the acrid stink of chemicals. Tears fell faster for what had been lost.

"What sort?" He paused, contempt on his face making her cringe but not step away. "One who has failed."

Failed.

Before she could say anything, had she words to speak, Gabriel leaned in close. Like a lover stealing a kiss he put his mouth to her ear. His breath caressed the side of her face; the brief, hot moistness of his lips brushed her earlobe.

"If you will not get on your knees to suck my cock, then you will surely get on your knees to crawl for me."

She did not immediately obey. His hand on her shoulder pushed her toward the floor, and she ended up on her hands and knees. The bare wooden floor scraped her palms. A splinter gouged her, bringing blood to the wound not healed. He walked back, away from her.

"Crawl for me," Gabriel said. "You told me once you had never tested your limits. I would test them, now."

Trembling, Quilla put her forehead to the floor, hands by the side of her head, palms up. He had seen her Wait in Readiness, and in Remorse, and in Submission. Now she Waited in the fourth position, one she had never used. Abasement.

"I plead your mercy, my lord—"

"I said *crawl*!"

The fury in his voice spurred her forward. Her gown tangled around her legs, making her lurch forward. Somehow that lack of grace made it worse, as though humiliation could be made worse by clumsiness.

"Let me see those lovely legs. Lift your skirt."

She did, hiking up the length of material around her waist with one hand while she moved forward on the other. Now her knees scraped the floor, and that small sting was made tenfold worse by Gabriel's laughter. She moved forward again at his demand, her stomach twisting in her gut. But she did it, perhaps helpless to not do it, and not because she was his Handmaiden.

Because she loved him.

"That's it," she heard him say. "Crawl for me."

She shook so fiercely she bit her tongue and tasted blood. That metallic ocean again—it made her stop. She turned her head to look at him.

And then she got to her feet. Her dress fell back to her feet, the hem sweeping the dirty floor. She looked at her scraped and filthy palms, then up at him.

"Get back on your knees," Gabriel said. "For one task or another."

She shook her head. Her heart seemed to turn inside her chest, the pain of it sharp, like a knife. "No."

"No?" His voice had gone soft. Dangerous. His fingers tugged his belt from the loops, and he wrapped the buckle end of it around his palm. "You still tell me *no*?"

She stared at him unflinching, though every inch of her felt as though she was shaking out of control. "I will not do this."

Gabriel slid the end of the belt through his hands, drawing it between them. "What of your purpose and your place? What of your duty, Handmaiden?"

He sneered. This was not the man she loved. This was a monster. She sought any sign of the man she loved, but found none. Only a grief-twisted monster, and though she knew she ought to find pity for him, create excuses, there were none to be had.

"You have failed in them."

She lifted her chin, facing him without tears. "'Tis my purpose and my place to bring you solace. To make you happy. What you are asking is not to do either, but instead to bring me misery."

A terrible smile turned his mouth ugly. "Perhaps 'tis your misery that will bring me solace."

She swallowed against a parched throat. "I am your Hand-maiden. Not your whore, or your whipping boy. If I have failed—"

"You have brought me nothing but misery!" he yelled. The belt snapped taut again between his hands. "And I would appease mine own through watching yours, but you refuse me even that!"

He had broken her. She heard her own voice, coming as though from another throat, something far away and without emotion.

"If I no longer please you, then release me."

"You will not do what I ask?" A hint of incredulity had found its way into his voice at last, and the belt slackened in his grip. "You will still refuse me? You will choose failure over pleasing me?"

"If I no longer please you," Quilla repeated, "then you may release me. You know how it must be done."

"And if I do not wish to release you?"

She stared at him steadily, though her mind had gone as far away as her voice and she did not really see him. "If I no longer—"

"Shut up!" The whistle of the belt striking the back of the chair emphasized his cry. "You're not some bloody key-wound doll!"

She said nothing, her spine straight, though everything inside her felt twisted. The landscape of her emotion had become a barren wasteland with storm-stripped trees and drought-cracked earth.

The belt cracked down again, this time onto the table next to her, coming close enough for her to feel the breeze of its passing. She did not flinch. Her eyes stayed wide and fixed upon his face. She had broken, but she would not bend.

A third time, he raised the belt and she steeled herself for its sting on her shoulders. Gabriel did not strike her. His hand hesitated at the top of its arc. She saw the leather shake as his hand shook.

"I release thee," he said the first time. He lowered the belt, tossed it aside with a low, disgusted cry. He looked at her, face naked with anguish, and the sight should have moved her but no longer could. His eyes, red-rimmed, welled with tears, he stepped toward her as though it hurt him to do it. "I release thee."

Quilla did not move. She did not soften. She could not. She'd gone dead inside. She felt his hands on her upper arms as Gabriel came close and gathered her against him. She felt his breath in her hair as he pressed his face there. She felt the thump of his heart against her chest. She heard him whisper, heard his voice catch and break, felt his tears against the side of her neck as he wept against her.

"I . . ." He shuddered, but said nothing further.

"I release thee." Black ice coated the words, and she heard him moan as he spoke them.

He fell at her feet, gathering her hem in his hands and covering his face with it, but Quilla stepped away from him without waiting for him to move out of the way. She left the room without looking back, not even when he called out her name.

Chapter 15

The world's beauty is such that not even death is forever. Flowers die and leave their seeds to bloom again in spring. Bare trees grow green. Everything cycles toward the new, everything has a place, all that dies becomes reborn in its own time and for its own purpose.

One full spring had gone, one full summer, one season of harvest, and one of snow. Quilla was a year older, her face thinner, her hair longer, her hands one year unheld, her lips one year unkissed.

One year, and she was no longer dead. She had, like the flowers and the leaves, bloomed again. Now she sat on her front porch, a glass of chilled tea at her side and the scent of spring breeze on her face.

She wore red, a color she'd once been told she would not choose. She wore it in memory of a man who had loved her when he should not have, and in thought of a man who had not when he had needed to. She wore no shoes and the loose fabric of her skirt exposed her calves to the fragrant air.

She sipped her drink and watched the path leading through the meadow to her front door. In the summer the grass would be high and dust would announce a visitor. Now, springtime rain had dampened the dirt, and the grass had not yet sprouted; she saw the man on the other side of the meadow with no trouble at all. She watched him walk toward her, but she did not rise to greet him.

She had finished her drink by the time he reached her porch. The honey she'd used to sweeten it clung to the bottom of the glass, and she tipped it up to drink the last bit, swiping her tongue over her lips to rid them of the stickiness.

He wore not the fashionable coat of a lord now, nor the white coat of an alchemist. He wore a white shirt, loose at the throat, and dark, travel-worn trousers gone ragged at the cuffs. He'd tied his dark hair at the nape of his neck with a leather cord. Beard scruffed his cheeks.

"They told me in the Order you had gone." He looked up at her. "They would not tell me how to find you."

"And how did you?"

He looked up at her. "What worth is wealth if it cannot bring you what you most need?"

She had been wrong to think she had found her way back to life; to existence, yes, but not to life.

She stood and stepped away, turning her face. Seeing him was nearly too much; like staring into the sun, it might leave her blind. He followed her inside her bright and comfortable cottage, far less grand than Glad Tidings but imbued with far more warmth. She settled him at her scrubbed, worn table and put the kettle on to heat.

"You remember, still. How I like it." He meant the tea, which she put before him in a heavy porcelain cup painted with gilly-flowers.

The words "I do" of course hovered on her tongue's tip, but she swallowed them. She poured another cup and busied herself with sweetening it to her taste. She stirred it, then set down the spoon and watched amber liquid make a small puddle on the tabletop.

"Where is Dane?" she said finally. "Where is your son?"

"He is with Florentine and Jorja. With those who love him well when I am unable to care for him. He is safe, Quilla. I swear to you."

She looked up then, her gaze calculating. "He is safe. But is he well?"

"He weeps at night for his mother, and for his uncle who loved him as I should have." Gabriel paused, his gaze meeting hers. "And he weeps for you. As we all do."

She got up from the table and went to the sink to pump herself some cold water. She looked out the window to the small garden in her backyard that would someday grow onions and tomatoes.

"I can scarcely imagine Florentine weeping over anything," she said at last. "Much less over me."

Untruth did not lie with ease upon her tongue, for she had, in fact, seen Florentine weep and could imagine those tears without difficulty. She filled her glass with sweet, cool water and drained it.

"We all miss you sorely."

She allowed a faint smile to pass over her lips as she turned to face him. "You came all this distance to tell me of a household weeping for the memory of me?"

He nodded, looking at his tea. "I did so, yes."

"I see." She crossed her arms in front of her, a gesture of protection, though he had done naught to threaten. "And what of you, Gabriel Delessan?"

"I have missed you more than any of the others," came the reply, pitched low but still audible. His gaze rose to meet hers, and in the light from the window she saw the red reflection of her gown in his eyes. "I have been nearly torn asunder from missing you."

Quilla did not yield. She had left the Order, a Handmaiden no longer. She did not need to please him.

He sighed and put his head in his hands for a moment, and she saw the elbows of his shirt were worn. He needed taking care of. She stayed where she was, her gaze lingering on him while he did not look at her.

"How long will you be staying here?"

He looked up at that, disbelief and gratitude mixing in his expression. "You aren't sending me away?"

She turned her back and pretended to busy herself with a pan of bread rising on the counter. "I know the length of your journey, Gabriel. I would not send you on your way with an empty stomach and travel-sore limbs. You may take such rest as you need."

She glanced over her shoulder at him, wanting to make her meaning clear. "'Tis only me, here. I am beholden to myself alone. I choose who stays or goes."

The chair scraped along the floor as he stood. She saw him from the corner of her eye, his shape a familiar shadow, his proximity creating a tingle of awareness along her skin—but wisely, he did not touch her.

"I would be glad of your hospitality, Tranquilla Caden. I would be honored by it."

She kept her back straight as she punched and kneaded the dough. "I do not live a life of idleness here, Gabriel. And I have little need for an alchemist. If you would stay, then you'll need to work for your board."

"If it pleases you."

Her own words thrown at her that way, from him, stilled her hands inside the soft, warm dough. "I will not know if it pleases me or not until it is done."

Then he moved away from her, and she felt the loss of his

almost-touch keenly, but she said nothing, and they stayed together in silence for the rest of that day.

She woke before the dawn to a crackling fire and tea set out for her; to bread sliced and toasted and glistening with butter and jam. The way she liked it. She had not been the only one to watch and learn, to remember.

Quilla sat at the table across from him. He'd shaved and bathed. He smelled good, like soap and work, like fire smoke and also fresh air. A cut across the back of one hand had her reaching for it.

"What happened?"

"I am still more skilled with a mortar and pestle than an ax. 'Tis naught. A scratch."

It was more than that, and she stood to retrieve a small basin of water and some rolled bandages from the cupboard. "If you don't dress this, it could get infected."

In silence he allowed her to tend his wound, capturing her fingers with his before she could pull away her hand. He held it until she looked up at him. His thumb traced the curve of her palm and the scar there.

Quilla tugged gently, and he released her. "You would do well to change that dressing daily."

He nodded, not arguing. Watching her. She stared back at him, but she was the first to look away.

It didn't seem to matter that he was better suited to brannigans and academic pursuits than physical labor. Gabriel took over the chores of chopping wood, of clearing the garden of stones, of lining the path with rock crushed by his hammer. He greeted her every morning with tea and breakfast, and a fire, and he sent her to bed every night with the same words.

"May the Invisible Mother keep you."

At last, one night, she relented. Her foot upon the stairs, she glanced back at him, lying on his pallet by the fire. "Until the morning comes," she finished the traditional blessing.

That night, she did not sleep so well.

A cry woke her in the night and she was out of her bed and down the stairs before she knew quite what she was doing. The fire had gone low and dim, but she saw him with no trouble. He'd thrown off the light blankets and curled on his side in a ball.

Another cry escaped him, and she went to him. Touched his shoulder. "Gabriel."

His eyes opened and he sat, covered in sweat. He reached for her and she allowed him to hold on to her, her arms going around him and his face tight against her breast.

"The fire," was all he said.

She stroked her hand down his back, feeling the muscles and the knobs of his spine where he'd grown thinner. Then she extricated herself from his grasp and went to the sink to fill the kettle. When she turned round he'd wiped his face and straightened his clothes.

"Something to eat?" she asked, slicing bread and putting it on the table, then hanging the kettle over the fire.

"No."

She gave him a glance from the corner of her eye as he took a chair. She pushed some stray hairs off her face and tucked them into the braid she wore for sleeping. Gabriel watched her.

"Will you ever forgive me?" he asked.

She didn't answer him. After a moment in which silence stretched between them, the kettle whistled. She removed it. Made tea. Sat across from him at the table.

"How long do you plan to stay?" she asked.

"If you don't want me here—"

"That wasn't the question I asked, Gabriel."

He sighed and scrubbed his face. "I intend to stay until you forgive me."

"And if I never do?"

"Why won't you!" His shout did not make her flinch. She sipped her tea and regarded him with a raised brow. "Why will you not forgive me, Quilla!"

"Perhaps because you've not said you were sorry."

He got up from the table so fast his chair fell over. "I am sorry! I am sorry I treated you so! Don't you understand that? Can you not see it? I plead your mercy!"

She slammed down her cup, and it broke. Tea spilled across the table. She stood, too.

"You're an arrogant son of a bastard!" she shouted. "Asking for forgiveness when you deserve none! I did nothing to deserve your anger and your ire! Nothing! All I ever did was care for you!"

"Because of your purpose and your place?"

She made a disgusted noise at his shout. "Of course! I was a Handmaiden, Gabriel! 'Twas the reason you called me to Glad Tidings, wasn't it? To care for you?"

"And later?"

"Later was different!"

They squared off, the table between them, else she wasn't certain she wouldn't have slapped his face. Anger made her careless and had brought color to her cheeks. She tried to catch her breath and couldn't quite manage.

"And Jericho?"

"I didn't love your brother!" she cried. "Not the way I loved you! And you were a fool to think otherwise. As he was a fool to try and take what was yours, so you were a fool to think that's all he ever wanted!"

"Loved," was what Gabriel said, as if the rest of her words had been silence. "Then. But not now."

She gave him her back. "You know what it's like to have your love burnt to ash and thrown in your eyes to blind you, for you told me so yourself."

"I plead your mercy," Gabriel said. "It's all I can do."

Another man might have wept, or gone to his knees. Another man, a different man, might have begged her. But she did not love another man, she loved this one.

"You do not need to sleep on the floor," she told him at last. "There is an extra room abovestairs. You can have that."

She left him and did not wait to see if he would follow.

And here I will plant gillyflowers." Quilla paused in the bright spring sunshine to wipe her forehead. The day had warmed considerably. She had black, rich earth all over her. They'd been digging all morning.

Gabriel rested on his shovel to look at the patch she'd pointed out. "Gillyflowers are little more than weeds. Why cultivate them?"

"Because I like them," was the first and easy answer. "Because they are lovely to look upon. And because the lady beetles like them."

Gabriel nodded, looking along the neat rows they'd worked together to furrow. "They are different, plain but beautiful at the same time. Unassuming until you stop to notice their beauty." He looked up at her, a small grin on a face beginning to be browned by the sun. "Like you."

She'd been turning as he said it, and the smile and the simple, easy sincerity of his words caught her off guard. She watched the path of his hand as it rose to wipe the sweat from his brow, and she remembered how that hand had felt against her skin. Her heart *thump-thumped*, making her dizzy.

He was there at once, his hand under her elbow and one at the small of her back. "Quilla? Do you need something?"

She nodded and turned in the circle of his embrace to face him. "Yes, Gabriel. I do."

He put his arms around her, holding her steady when she feared she might stumble. The wind came and pushed the hair off his forehead, and her hand followed the wind's kiss, coming to rest against his cheek.

"I love you," Gabriel said. "I know I don't deserve to. But I love you, and I beg your forgiveness for the wrong I did you. I have found I do not wish to live without you. I want you and I need you; there is no difference between them."

She let her eyes travel over every inch of his face. The face she loved. "You wish me to be your Handmaiden again?"

He shook his head. "No, Tranquilla. Not that. I want you by my side, not at my feet."

She took a deep, shuddering breath. "Gabriel. I love you. But I'm not certain—"

"All I ask is that you give me the chance to prove myself." He put his hand over the one on his cheek and again let his mouth brush her palm. "I would be what you need before you need it. I would be your solace and your comfort."

Tears welled in her vision and she wiped them away. "You would do such, for me?"

He nodded slowly, then put his arms around her waist, urging her closer to him. His lips met hers briefly. "If it pleases you."

And Quilla laughed, the sound like lady beetles dancing amongst their flowers, and Gabriel joined her. They laughed and kissed and laughed some more, until breathless, she pulled away to look into his eyes.

"I would spend the rest of my life pleasing you, if you allow me," Gabriel said.

"The rest of my life is a very long time."

He smiled, a man transformed, and even the memory of how he'd been fell away beneath it. "Then I should think we must start now."

Quilla nodded, a smile of her own on her lips, and kissed him again. "If it pleases you."

And what she discovered, when she took him by the hand and lay with him on a bed of sun-warmed grass, was that it pleased both of them very much, indeed.